ANNI MOON

& THE ELEMENTAL ARTIFACT

BY

MELANIE ABED

ILLUSTRATIONS BY HISHAM ABED

Oculus Print

ANNI MOON AND THE ELEMENTAL ARTIFACT
By Melanie Abed

Publisher's Cataloging-In-Publication Data
(Prepared by The Donohue Group, Inc.)

Names: Abed, Melanie. | Abed, Hisham, illustrator.
Title: Anni Moon & the Elemental artifact / by Melanie Abed ; illustrations by Hisham Abed.
Other Titles: Anni Moon and the Elemental artifact | Elemental artifact
Description: [New] international edition. | [Pasadena, California] : Oculus Print, [2016] | The Anni Moon fantasy adventure series ; book 1 | Interest age level: 011-018. | Summary: Anni Moon is thrown into the world of Elementals when her best friend, Lexi, is kidnapped and it's a race against time to save their lives.
Identifiers: ISBN 978-0-9907062-4-3 (print) | ISBN 978-0-9907062-0-5 (Kindle mobi) | ISBN 978-0-9907062-2-9 (ePub) | ISBN 978-0-9907062-3-6 (Apple ibook)
Subjects: LCSH: Friendship--Juvenile fiction. | Orphans--Juvenile fiction. | Kidnapping--Juvenile fiction. | Magic--Juvenile fiction. | Fantasy fiction. CYAC: Friendship--Fiction. | Orphans--Fiction. | Kidnapping--Fiction. | Magic--Fiction.
Classification: LCC PZ7.A243 An 2016 (print) | LCC PZ7.A243 (ebook) | DDC [Fic]--dc23

For Grandma, who read to me first,
For Raffy, a great friend,
And for Sham, who helped Anni grow.

CONTENTS

CHAPTER 1

MESSENGER OF MESSAGES

Already dressed in her hand-me-down Waterstone Academy uniform, Anni Moon took advantage of the last few quiet moments before she had to rush into the chaos of the school's kitchen for her morning chores. Any minute, the clock tower would chime and she would have to go. With her back against the tower's high windows, she sat in her usual spot on the lumpy window seat cushions. She was reviewing notes for her afternoon prep exam on the Periodic Table of Elements when something outside darted past the window.

The strange flying creature gave her such a jolt that she sprang off the cushions and, in the process, dropped her science book on her left foot. She hopped around in pain on her good foot, then tripped over a moth-eaten afghan, and finally knocked over a dustpan that was filled with ashes. The tower's paisley and mahogany common room was engulfed in a cloud of soot, and for a moment, she couldn't see what was outside.

"Anni Moon! Anni Moon! I need to speak with you, Anni Moon!" said a small yet firm voice.

The creature flapped against the glass panes as it called her name. Anni stood stock still until the soot cleared and she finally saw it. It looked like a bat. No. A rat. No. It had bat-shaped wings but the body of a rat: whiskers, tail, and all. Whatever this creature was, its brown leathery wings were beating against the glass. It was wearing a little outfit, too, but strangest of all, it was talking to her.

"Go away," she said and jumped behind the curtains. She pulled the drapes closed with one hard tug, and the tower's common room was cloaked in darkness. Panting, she leaned against the wall. She wanted to look outside, but she was afraid that the creature would see her.

"Lexi? Lexi?" Anni called out.

She fumbled in the dark over empty packing boxes that littered the floor, careful not to trip over the food tray she had left for Lexi before she opened the small, oval door.

"You'll never…"

The room was empty and Lexi's bed was made, which was strange. Lexi always overslept, and every morning, Anni woke her up. Not only were they best friends, they had been roommates for the last three years at Waterstone Academy for Girls.

Before Anni stepped inside, she saw it, lying on the floor, still perfectly folded with crisp edges. The letter—that awful, dreadful, hateful letter—that came three days ago, demanding that they pack up and move out of the tower common room. This room had been Lexi's home for as long as she could remember. It had been Anni's since she moved in three years ago.

Anni caught sight of Lexi's bedside clock. "Eggs! Is that the time?"

She was late for kitchen duty! How had she missed the clock tower's chime? She picked up Lexi's untouched tray, backed out of the room, and closed the door.

She raced over to the common room's double doors with the tray balanced against her hip, but before her hand touched the knob, the doors burst open. She lost her grip and the tray went flying. Cold hot chocolate and a gelatinous mass of marshmallows soared into the air and collided with a gooey peanut-butter-and-banana-honey sandwich, which landed on the door, floor, and Anni.

2

"What is this?" asked Rufous Finnegan, Waterstone Academy's security and all-purpose assistant. He was a young male dressed in a regulation gray uniform, and a proud germophobe who always wore a pair of sterile gloves. "Food violation!" His fistful of keys jangled as he took note of this infraction on his Waterstone Academy clipboard.

Anni sat on the floor, peeling pieces of bread and banana off her skirt. There was no hope for her favorite black-and-white-striped socks, a gift from Lexi; they were soaked in wet cocoa and she since didn't have another pair, she took them off to dry.

Finnegan glared at Anni. "Why's it so dark in here?"

"*No!*" Anni yelled.

He flung the drapes open, but there was nothing outside except gray clouds. Whatever Anni thought she saw was gone.

Finnegan scanned the room. "These boxes are empty. What's wrong with you? Can't you read?" His lips curled into a smile as he pulled an official Waterstone Academy embossed letter from his clipboard, waved it in her face, and read: "'Miss Alexa Waterstone and Miss Anni Moon: Please have all your belongings packed and ready for removal this Saturday afternoon. The new school owners will be moving in the following Monday.' You must be ready to vacate the room by Saturday morning." He folded the letter and sneered at her. "It's about time you two charity cases were pushed out. This is a Headmaster's tower, not a hideout for worthless little orphan girls. Speaking of which, you're late for kitchen duty, but I'm not here for you. Where's Lexi?"

"Sleeping," Anni said. "Why do you care?"

"None of your business." Finnegan leaned in. "You think you have the right to know everything, don't you? News flash: you don't. Things are changing around here, and with any luck, you'll get chucked out. Now, get downstairs before I make you." He grabbed her arm and yanked her toward the door.

"Hands off, Minion!"

"*What did you call me?*"

Whoops! She had never called him Minion to his face before. This was a first, and boy, did Finnegan's face flare red. She slipped out of his grasp and headed for the hall, but stopped short when a perfectly dressed woman blocked the doorway. Shock turned to relief, and the corners of Anni's mouth lifted but quickly died back when she saw the woman's warning look.

3

"At last you've found her. I'm so relieved," said Vivian Sugar, a Waterstone Academy counselor. She wore an impeccably tailored suit that made her look older than she probably was, but she was easy to talk to, not stiff or reserved. Vivian Sugar exuded a casual, yet calm grace, and her voice was just as sweet as her name. "Thank you, Rufous dear. I've been looking for her. Could you please tell Cook that Anni has an appointment and cannot attend kitchen duty this morning?"

"I'm sorry, Miss Sugar, but I can't." Finnegan poked at his clipboard as if it was a law book. "Have you seen this room? The girls have not packed. There's food and drink everywhere." He waved his clipboard around, creating a gust of air that ruffled both Anni and Vivian's hair. "And it needs to be cleaned before the Murdrocks move in!"

"Then you haven't heard," said Vivian, flashing a winning smile as she patted her blonde, bobbed hair back in place. "I completely understand your duties, Rufous, and I wouldn't dream of upsetting things." She gently rested her hand on Finnegan's clipboard and he flinched. "However, the Headmistress is extending the girls leniency through the weekend—"

"I haven't heard this." Rufous Finnegan looked taken aback. He shook his head. "No. I was told that the new owners would be here by—"

"I'm sure all of this will be explained later. However, Anni has an appointment with Headmistress Turnkey at this very moment, and she really mustn't be late, Rufous."

"I do?" asked Anni, confused. She would remember something like that, mostly because it usually meant she was in trouble.

"Yes, you do," said Miss Sugar with a half-smile and a wink.

Anni steered past them both and headed for the hall, taking her time and eavesdropping.

"Now, Rufous…"

"Yes, Miss Sugar?" said Finnegan, more tersely than before.

"Call me Vivian, Rufous. And please, if you would be so kind as to clean up this mess and take it back to the kitchen. We really mustn't keep Cook waiting." Vivian tittered, "We both know how she gets."

Anni didn't dare wait to hear Finnegan's reply. She took the stairs two at a time, deciding it was best to stay clear of him for the rest of the day—or forever—if she could.

As she made her way down the stairs, she decided that there was no such thing as talking flying creatures like the one she imagined in the window. She was being silly. At the bottom of the stairs, the main corridor was deserted. Everyone was tucking into breakfast in the dining room, which made her stomach grumble. It's where she would be collecting dirty plates and cups, if Vivian Sugar hadn't rescued her.

She walked up to the Headmistress's office door, ready to knock.

"And where exactly do you think you're going?" asked Ms. Downsnout, the Headmistress's secretary. She rolled her tea trolley up to the door, blocking Anni's way.

"In there," said Anni. "Isn't she expecting me?"

"No. She most certainly is not."

"Are you sure? Because—"

"The Headmistress is getting ready for a barrage of meetings all morning and afternoon long. As you can see, I am equally busy. Therefore, I'll give you to the count of three to get back to whatever it is that you should be doing." Ms. Downsnout pushed the cart inside the office and closed the door behind her.

Did Miss Sugar make up her meeting with the Headmistress in front of Finnegan so that Anni got out of her kitchen duties? Miss Sugar did wink, after all, and it was the kind of thing she'd do. Either way, since she wasn't expected for kitchen duty, she wasn't going to waste a rare kitchen-duty-free morning. The first order of business was to find Lexi, and she knew exactly where to look. She headed right back down the hall until…

"I don't understand," said Egbert Frode Moon indifferently. "If Lexi is not in her room, then perhaps you know where she is?" Egbert was a lanky man with large ears who paid little attention to his wardrobe: from his coffee-stained button-down shirt, to his cardigan with moth holes, and his pants, which were always several inches too short for his long, dark legs. He also had a slight hunch in his shoulders, which Anni supposed was due to Egbert's never-ending obsession with the oversized wristwatch he was constantly leaning over. Even now, standing in the middle of the foyer and blocking Anni's only way outside, Egbert didn't even bother to look up from his wristwatch when he said to Finnegan, "And where's Anni?"

Anni plastered herself against the wall. If there was anyone she avoided more than Finnegan, it was Egbert, and now they both stood a mere ten feet away from her hiding place.

Even though Egbert was now Anni's guardian, he was no replacement for Anni's previous legal guardian, Mabel Moon, the kindest woman anyone could ever hope to know, and the previous Headmistress of Waterstone Academy. Ever since Anni was a baby, Mabel Moon was Anni's everything, and the closest and only thing she had to a parent. In those happier days, Anni couldn't have imagined a better life than the one she had, but all of it changed three years back, when Mabel mysteriously disappeared and was later declared dead. Anni never even got to properly say goodbye. Upon Mabel's death, all her assets were frozen, which left her brother-in-law Teddy Waterstone, and their beloved Waterstone Academy, bankrupt and in need of funding. Egbert had been forced to step in and take over, and not only had he inherited Mabel's troublesome legal affairs at Waterstone, he inherited Anni as well. Far too busy to console a heartbroken girl, Anni assumed she was just another task on Egbert's schedule, and when he hired Finnegan to handle odd jobs, she had become one of them.

"Miss Sugar told me Anni had a meeting with the Headmistress," said Finnegan.

"Nonsense. The both of us will be in meetings all day," said Egbert.

Anni panicked. They were walking toward her. She dashed into the sunroom across the hall and hid behind the closed drapes of the double glass French doors. She jiggled the handle, but it was locked!

She peeked through the drapes as she gripped the handle tighter.

"Finnegan, you deal with this. The Headmistress is expecting me," said Egbert. "Locate Lexi first and then find Anni."

Finnegan left in a huff. Egbert stood in the hallway, still adjusting his watch as Ms. Downsnout exited the Headmistress's office. "She's waiting. The paperwork is laid out with a tea service. Is there anything else?"

"No," said Egbert. "And no calls. Let us know when Murdrock arrives."

Anni ground her teeth. Whether it was due to her grip or sheer luck, the garden door clicked open. Carefully and quietly, she slipped outside.

With the intention of finding Lexi, Anni raced across the open lawn toward the clock tower, their secret hideout, on the opposite side of the grounds. It was drizzling and the grass was very muddy. Chicago's spring started late, and all the buds on the trees refused to open, making them bare like skeletons.

"No, no! Ugh, double eggs!"

A large, shiny copper lock closed the loop of a heavy chain through the door's latch. The clock tower had been locked up from the outside. Anni slumped down onto the wet grass. Lexi couldn't be inside, but where was she? Why was the clock tower locked up? And was it the reason the clock tower hadn't chimed that morning?

Getting back inside the school without getting caught was risky. She had just stood up when something dark darted across the sky. It swooped down at her.

"Arrgggghhhh!"

She stumbled and ducked. The flying creature, the same one that tried to get in the common room window, was circling above her.

"Anni Moon. Anni Moon. Stop. Stop. I have a message for you."

The small, hairy, vest-wearing creature closed its leathery brown wings and plopped down on the grass beside her. He clutched his chest, one paw covering a small, golden emblem stitched onto his little red vest, as he panted and wheezed.

"Message?" Anni mumbled. "What! This is weird...you're a rat...no, a bat. And you're *talking* to me?"

"For snozdoddles' sake, Anni, of course I can speak."

"Uh..." Feeling extremely dumb, not to mention a little bit crazy, Anni said, "Okay so what's your message?"

"It's not *my* message," said the creature, half-standing with his palms pressed on his small kneecaps. He pulled himself upright and said, "It's *your* message. I'm Brat, First Order Elservice Fleet. We are messengers of messages—no questions required. Only a reply will suffice. I'm starting your message now." He pulled out a tiny whistle from inside his tiny vest and gave it a squeak. "Your message is, 'Dear Anni Moon. You are not to leave Waterstone Academy for Girls under any circumstances. No matter what happens, you are not to leave the school.'"

"What?"

Brat pulled out the tiny whistle again and gave it another squeak. "Again, your message is, 'Dear Anni Moon. You are not to leave Waterstone Academy for Girls under any circumstances. No matter what happens, you are not to leave the school.'"

"Huh?"

Brat shook his little head and raised his whistle once more.

"No, no." Anni raised her hands. "Don't say it again. I heard you the first time...none of this makes sense. Where would I go?"

Brat's eyebrows furrowed. He paced and mumbled to himself, "I knew I should have listened to Avis Crumplehorn and taken that course on *human interaction*."

"Human?"

Brat looked up. "Yes. Yes, you are a human and I'm an Elemental. Glad we got that straight. As I was saying, I've delivered your message. Now, what's your reply?"

"Er, I know I'm human. What's an Elemental? And who's this message from?"

"Moppins! That's classified information! And I couldn't tell you even if I wanted to." Brat's eyes widened with a look of shock. "Besides, answering questions is not a part of my job title. I'm no common scandaroon! Only your reply will suffice. You are Anni Moon, twelve years old, at Waterstone Academy for Girls—correct?"

"Thirteen…in a week. Why should I listen to some random anonymous person I don't even know, or you, a bat-rat thing that calls itself an Elemental? Why is that classified, anyway?"

"Oh, moppins, not again," Brat swayed. "I'm feeling mopple-toppined." He put his hand to his head and shook it. He mumbled, "Must be down to all the Funk."

"Funk? What's Funk?"

"Oh, no, never you mind. Back to business. Can you, Anni Moon, please confirm that you successfully received your message and that you'll stay put?"

"Yeah, I got your message. What are you exactly?"

The creature stood proudly on its little feet. "Don't you listen? I told you. It's *your* message, not mine. And I'm Brat, First Order Elservice Fleet, messengers of messages."

"What does that even mean?"

"Confirmation of delivery. Check. I'll be on my way now."

It seemed like a stupid question, but she had to ask, "You haven't seen or delivered a message thingy to someone named Lexi, have you?"

Brat circled overhead and said, "Of course I've seen Lexi. I delivered her message two days ago." And he was off.

CHAPTER 2

LEXI WATERSTONE

Lexi Waterstone opened her eyes, but everything was dark. She panicked as muffled voices echoed around her. Flat on her back, she flung her hands against the surrounding walls; it felt like she was in a coffin.

It took Lexi a minute before she realized she had fallen asleep inside a cupboard within the Headmistress's office. This knowledge didn't quell her anxiety. How did she get there? With a deep breath, she wiped away her tears and the cold sweat from her brow. Clueless of the time or how long she had slept, Lexi forced her brain to remember.

It was just before midnight when she had been locked out of her room. She went downstairs, and when someone—she didn't know who—crept down the main hall, she dashed into the only unlocked room she could find, which unfortunately happened to be the Headmistress's office. Once inside, Lexi froze at the sight of the spiral staircase in the far corner; the door at the top of the stairs was the Headmistress's personal quarters and the faint beam of light casting a glow from beneath it meant the Headmistress was still awake. At any minute, she could open her door and see Lexi standing below in the middle of the room.

Terrified of being caught, Lexi ran to the tall bookcases and hid inside the nearest empty cupboard. It was the only safe place she could think of; back when Anni's Aunt Mabel was Headmistress of Waterstone Academy, they used it to play hide and seek. Lexi was lucky that it was empty. Otherwise, she never would have fit inside.

She planned to wait in there until the Headmistress's light went out and sneak away when the coast was clear. She didn't plan to fall asleep.

"Close the door," said Headmistress Turnkey.

Lexi jumped as the Headmistress's voice brought her back to the present. There was nothing she could do now; it was too late to leave, and she was stuck. Her fingers fiddled with a small pearl pendant that hung from her necklace. It was worse than she imagined; someone else was inside the office with the Headmistress. It wasn't like she could just pop out of the cupboard right then and explain to the woman why she was hidden in there. She wasn't sure if she could even trust Charity Turnkey, Headmistress or not.

Things were not as carefree as they once had been back when Teddy Waterstone and Mabel Moon ran Waterstone Academy for Girls; back then, the halls seemed brighter, more full of life and fun. Teddy was Lexi's legal guardian, just as Mabel had been Anni's. Neither of the girls knew anything about their real parents, but to them, Teddy and Mabel were all the family they needed. But even then, Lexi had a secret, one she couldn't tell anyone, including Anni. Teddy assured Lexi that it was for an important reason and he would explain everything to her on her thirteenth birthday.

Lexi preferred to remember Waterstone Academy when it was a happy place, but after Mabel left, all the life seemed to slowly drain away from the school. The strain was physically visible on Teddy, too. A once jovial, stalwart man had turned serious, worried, and gaunt. However, when Teddy vanished nine months ago, just as Mabel had three years earlier, Lexi tried to pretend everything was all right, that he would come back, but the Murdrock takeover changed her mind. These last couple days, she kept replaying the last time she saw him. Teddy's weary eyes had peered deeply into hers as he said, "If I do not come back, no matter what happens, you must keep your secret. Don't forget what I taught you, and know that I love you. You will hear from me one more time." That was the same day Teddy gave Lexi the pearl pendant necklace she now had twisted so tight around her index finger, it was cutting off the blood supply.

It made Lexi sick to think about Teddy, and her hands always started to tremble when she did. She focused instead on the cupboard doors. If memory served, there was a small hole in the knotted wood that was just big enough to peep an eye through and see into the room. Her fingers fumbled over the door until she found a piece of masking tape covering what she hoped was the hole. As she peeled it off, a blinding blast of blue light pierced through. Her head snapped backward and thumped against the cabinet wall. The room went quiet. Terrified, she held her breath, but the silence seemed endless.

When the Headmistress spoke again, Lexi raised her eye toward the hole.

"Have you heard any news? And don't make it glossy for my sake."

"Nothing official," said a man's voice. Lexi knew at once it was Egbert Frode Moon. Not only was he Anni's guardian, but in Teddy's absence, he had been named Lexi's temporary guardian as well. "I assume you saw the latest. It doesn't look good—"

Before Egbert could finish, another blinding flash of blue light engulfed the room. Once Lexi's eye settled, she saw a projected news article floating against the back wall, but it was too far to read the print.

"Clearly, the speculation has started. You know me, Egbert. I don't care for idle chitter chatter. I want to know what you think. Have you heard from Teddy? Or is it true that his Opus stone has been found *cracked*?"

Lexi gasped.

"It's true." Egbert paused. "It's Mabel all over again. I warned Teddy. Charity, you were there when I told him not to go. Join S.E.C. and you end up dead, but he wouldn't listen to reason. Teddy said he was the only S.E.C. member that could go and finish Mabel's work. Teddy's not coming back. He's gone for good, and I'm left to clean up another mess."

Lexi's heart pinched and a small whimper escaped her lips. Fortunately, they didn't hear her. Even though her heart tried to tell her she was wrong, deep down she knew that what Egbert said was true. If she needed further proof, she had it when Brat delivered a message two days ago: "My dearest Lexi, if you are hearing this message, it means that I have gone. You must prepare yourself for changes ahead and guard your secret with vigor. Do not fear what is to come.

Embrace it. Your life has its own destiny, and as such, I have made provisions for you. Above all else, know that I love you. Follow the signs." Lexi knew it was from Teddy, even though Brat didn't say who it was from and the message didn't include his name.

"Ah, I see," Charity said in a shaky voice. "I suppose in my heart, I was hoping for a different answer. Egbert, I wouldn't discredit the S.E.C. After so many Elementals were lost, the Council was the one thing that helped them move on. I'm surprised you never joined—"

"Finnegan has found more pockets of Funk lingering around the school. He can't find the source of how it's getting in," said Egbert. "Have you felt it?"

"Yes, it's been making me ill. By the look of me, I'm sure you've noticed, but I haven't had time to deal with it, given the Murdrock acquisition. I still can't believe that this school is passing into another family's hands. The Waterstones have been around for as long as I can remember. Egbert, what about the girls? What do you plan to do?"

Lexi's pulse pounded so loudly that she nearly missed what Egbert said next.

"Nothing's set in stone. Zelda is trying to convince Krizia to let them stay with her. I'm working on getting E-passes."

"I hope you have a better plan than that. Or are you expecting a miracle? Human transport's a six-month DeFunkification process, and that's if Krizia says yes! What are you going to say to the girls? As far as I know, they don't know anything about our world. And I certainly hope you do a better job than you did last time. Anni hasn't been the same since Mabel—"

Something crashed upstairs inside the Headmistress's room. The noise stopped their conversation cold. The Headmistress turned to Egbert. "What was that?"

Charity and Egbert rushed up the spiral stairs into her personal residence.

For a second Lexi couldn't move, as their words ran laps in her head. It sounded like Egbert planned on taking her and Anni into the Elemental Realm. The problem was that Anni didn't know anything about that world. Lexi knew she couldn't worry about that; she needed to get out of the Headmistress's office fast, before Charity and Egbert returned.

With trembling anxiety, Lexi forced her way out of the cupboard. She darted out of the office and down the corridor. Her feet moved faster than she ever let them go—until she plowed right into something that felt like a brick wall.

A shower of letters scattered across the foyer's floor. The mailman, a grumpy fellow, judging by his scowl, yelled at Lexi for being a whipper-something, how she had ruined his day because he had a bad back, and that he most certainly had no intention of picking up the letters that fell under the furniture.

Mortified that she nearly flattened the elderly mailman, Lexi's emotions caught up with her. She frantically collected the strewn mail between huge, heaping sobs.

The mailman looked very uncomfortable when he said, "Don't cry," in a softer tone than he used before. "I know. How would you like to sign for a package? Would that cheer you up?"

"Sign?" hiccupped Lexi as she handed back the last handful of the letters.

"Yes. I've got a package here. Came all the way from Brazil!" He opened his shoulder bag and quickly pulled out an orange card. "I'll need you to sign here." He pointed. "You don't happen to know a…let me see here…a Lexi Waterstone, do you?"

Lexi swallowed. "That's me," she said, half-smiling.

"Oh, well, there you go. Lucky, isn't it?"

Lexi signed for the package as the mailman eagerly released it into her care. He tipped his hat before he left. "Hope it's a good one."

Lexi stared at the tight scroll on the package. The handwriting looked messy and rushed, but she was positive she knew who it was from. All packages were supposed to go through the office first, but she just couldn't do that, not if it was from Teddy. Instead, she tore up the stairs, taking them two at a time, but her nerves got the better of her when she saw a teacher heading down the stairs one flight above her.

Lexi looked at the package with desperation. She couldn't risk it. She ran back down the stairs to the foyer. Thankfully, it was deserted. She shoved her package behind the floor-length tapestry, double-checking that no one could see it, and just as she made her way back to the stairs, there was Vivian Sugar.

"Lexi dear! There you are. I've tried your room twice now. I've been very concerned about you with…Have you been crying?"

"I…" said Lexi, flushed and praying that Miss Sugar hadn't seen her hide the package. Vivian was nice enough, but Lexi felt unnerved by her intense stare, which was why she said, "I got locked out of my room last night."

"Oh, no!" Vivian patted her on the shoulder. "That sounds dreadful. Have you not eaten? Wait, I know. Let's go to my office. You can tell me about it, and I can put you at ease. I just had a tray sent up with all kinds of goodies."

It pained Lexi to say yes. She didn't want to leave her package behind, nor did she want to talk about her feelings with Vivian. She knew that dodging Waterstone's school counselor was wrong, but she also knew she couldn't put it off much longer, what with the letter she got telling her she had to move out of the tower, or the glaring, ubiquitous news that the Murdrocks were officially taking over Waterstone. Besides, Anni adored Vivian, so Lexi agreed. It couldn't be that bad.

A small but sunny little room with walls in warm buttery shades greeted them. Miss Sugar relaxed her perfect posture into one of two salmon-colored armchairs next to a round coffee table that was brimming with a beautiful tea service, including cookies, scones, and tiny saucers loaded with different jams.

Miss Sugar ushered Lexi to sit and handed her a plate with two chocolate chip cookies. "Here you go. This will make you feel a million times better."

Lexi sat precariously, trying to relax but finding it difficult. She took the plate of cookies but didn't touch them. "Miss Sugar—"

"It's Vivian, dear. Go on, take a nibble."

Lexi took a bite. The flaky, buttery goodness with an added dash of melting chocolate hit the spot. She finally understood why Anni had been raving about her visits with Vivian—food being one of her favorite pastimes. With cookies and tea and no Brunhild, the school cook, looming about, it made sense why Anni enjoyed this.

"Forgive me if this sounds indelicate, but the news about the Murdrock acquisition must have upset you a great deal. I'll admit, even Anni has been tight-lipped about the issue."

Lexi steeled herself as best she could.

"Yes," Lexi said quietly. "I don't know. Guess I'm like Anni; I don't talk about it much…Mabel was like a mother to her and an auntie to me."

"Yes, that's very true. When we first spoke, Anni had a hard time saying Mabel's name," said Vivian gently. "I don't expect you to do that, either. It's just that, with everything going on, I want you to know that I'm here if you ever want to talk. After all, Mabel and Teddy's families have run this school for generations. I would be surprised if you weren't bothered by everything."

Lexi nodded, feeling faint. She wasn't ready to discuss Teddy, even though that was a leading comment. Not yet. They sat in silence for a few more seconds. Suddenly, Lexi became unexpectedly angry with Vivian. At the same time, she was startled by some kind of gray mist, almost invisible, creeping up from the corner floorboards. Lexi's skin prickled as if a dead, clammy hand grasped the back of her neck while an unbearable weight fell onto her shoulders. A cauldron of guilt bubbled in her stomach as her secrets flooded her mind and emotions. Vivian appeared oblivious as the yellow walls turned a sallow green.

She knew she wasn't really mad at Vivian. This was Funk; Teddy had told her about it years ago. He said that Funk was a nefarious force, an invisible shadow to most humans, that was capable of creating all kinds of mayhem, making people feel angry, sad or afraid, but he never told Lexi that she would be able see it. Poor Vivian raised a hand to her forehead, without a clue as to what was going on. Or did she? Lexi always wondered about the teachers at Waterstone, trying to guess who was an Elemental or a human. It didn't matter, because she had made Teddy a promise that she would never talk about it.

"Lexi? Oh, my. Are you unwell?" asked Vivian.

"Um, tired, I think. I didn't sleep well."

"You should go upstairs and lay down. I'll send a nurse to your room. We can talk another time. I think you should rest now. Will you promise to go straight upstairs?"

Lexi nodded as Vivian walked her to the door.

When her foot hit the slate floor, Lexi felt fine. She turned back to glance at Vivian's room, and it, too, returned to its previous cheery state. All the strange visions and unpleasant sensations of the Funk disappeared. Everything went back to normal—everything was fine except Lexi couldn't shake one thought.

The realization came fast and quick. What had she been thinking? How was she going to explain all the secrets she had been keeping without destroying her friendship with Anni?

CHAPTER 3

CUCLOCKEYBEE

nni stood rooted to the spot. The talking bat…rat…thing shot into the air and was gone without a trace. Did that just happen? She shook her head. Surely Lexi would have told her if a talking rat/bat thing left her a message, wouldn't she? No, this was crazy. Just a figment of her imagination, that's all. However, the raindrops hitting the top of her head were not.

She dashed across the school grounds and took shelter under the awning of Waterstone Academy's front door. She wondered whether she should tell Lexi about Brat. But if she burst out and said it, Lexi might think she had lost her mind. Did she really want to start a conversation about a talking rat/bat? She didn't. She had to find Lexi.

She peered into a window next to the school's front doors and saw Ms. Downsnout placing the mail into the proper slots for the staff and students. Anni paced by the door, wishing the woman would hurry it up.

Her plan was simple: she had an hour before lunch duty to slip inside, run upstairs, and find Lexi. Finnegan was skulking across the lawn toward the kitchen. He didn't seem to see her, but he was far too close for comfort. Finally,

Ms. Downsnout finished sorting the mail and walked around the corner to her desk.

Stealthily, Anni entered the empty foyer. Then she headed for the stairs.

"Looking for someone?" asked the self-proclaimed queen bee, Miranda Firestone, her square jaw jutting forward, looking like it worked too hard to get the words out. Anni wasn't sure what flounced down the stairs harder: Miranda's red hair or her two cronies.

"Eggs," Anni muttered.

"Do you even *know* what you're saying?" Miranda sneered at her. "We missed your terrible breakfast service this morning. Did you get fired? When the Murdrocks take over, they won't keep silly little hum—orphans like you around."

Anni ignored her and headed toward the stairs.

"What about your little weirdo friend? Will she take your job in the kitchen, or will they kick her to the curb, too?"

Anni spun around, turned to Miranda, pointed her finger, and said, "Don't you dare talk about Lexi! Get your facts straight; next time you lie about me to Finnegan—"

"Did I hear my name?"

Anni wheeled around. Finnegan was standing in the hall next to Brunhild, the school's cook, whose greasy face rippled with fury.

"Here she is," said Finnegan, grinning wickedly. "Sneaking off from her chores."

"Who do you think you are, Cinderella?" said Brunhild, spittle flying out of her mouth with each word. She dragged Anni by the arm down the hall. "Just you wait; you'll be the first to go. If I had the staff, I'd fire you myself. Dishes undone, trays upstairs, broken."

Enraged and unable to contain her temper, Brunhild yelled in incoherent German, none of which Anni could comprehend. That, coupled with Finnegan's malicious smirk and Miranda's fits of laughter, made Anni wish she could disappear. Once they got to the kitchen, she shoved earplugs into her ears and tried to tune out the world.

The one o'clock school bell rang. Anni collected her things, ready to leave.

"Oh, no you don't." Brunhild smiled.

"I have a science test review."

Finnegan came into the kitchen, his arms folded, blocking the door. "Today, you'll be skipping that test review. Get notes from someone, if you have any friends. As punishment for lying about this morning—"

"I didn't lie. Ask Viv—Miss Sugar. She'll tell you."

"Don't interrupt! I also don't care. You will finish those piles of dishes *by hand*, and shine the copper pots until they gleam. When you are finished, wash that excuse of a uniform by hand, and you're banned from Friday night privileges. One peep out of you, and Brunhild will find plenty of other things for you to do."

Anni fumed at the injustice of it all, but she remained quiet.

Finnegan left. Brunhild watched Anni clean the rest of the dishes and pots from a comfortable chair as she read a book, *The Seven Secrets of Highly Successful People*.

It took two hours to do all the dishes by hand and shine the pots, plus another hour to wash her uniform to Brunhild's satisfaction. Anni had an extra pair of shorts and a shirt upstairs, but Brunhild wouldn't let her get them and made her put on something from the lost and found bin. The choices were horrible: all she could find was a pair of neon red spandex pants and a bedazzled crop top in shocking pink. Anni despised pink.

When Anni left the kitchen, she didn't take out her earplugs, just in case Brunhild started yelling again. She had to pass through the dining hall to get to the service stairs, which she wanted to use while dressed in the ridiculous red and pink outfit. But when she opened the door, she was hit first by the sounds of the movie she'd been forbidden to watch. Right after that came the guffaws, washing over her like a tidal wave. It didn't help that Miranda was in the front row.

Anni felt her cheeks burn. She casually strolled through the dining hall, walked up the main staircase until she was sure no one was around, and ran the rest of the way. By the time she reached the tower's common door, she was ready to lock herself inside and never come out again. She abandoned her selfish thoughts at the sight of Lexi slumped on the old, lumpy sea green sofa that Anni used as a bed. Lexi lifted her head from her hands when Anni shut the door. Something was very wrong because Anni had never seen her friend look this unraveled before, except maybe the last time she saw Teddy.

"Hi," Lexi mumbled. "I was locked out last night..." An unwrapped package rested on her lap, and she held a small card in her hand. "It came for me in the mail." On the brink of tears, she said, "I'll be in huge trouble for this if I get caught. The mailman just gave it to me. No one else was there. It's from Teddy, I'm sure."

Anni rushed over. She pushed aside the parcel's paper and saw an old patchwork doll with braided hair and dark skin like Lexi's. She checked the postmark. "It's addressed to you. You're not in trouble if it's yours."

"But Anni," said Lexi. "I'm supposed to report it straight to the Headmistress. She asked me months ago to do that if anything came from Teddy. She said any communication had to go through the office first. Even Egbert said—"

"Ugh, forget that! Especially *him*. He'd take it in a second. You'd never see it again. Don't show anyone that doll."

"I know, I know, but I'm too old for dolls. This has to be a message." Lexi bit her lip. "I think it's a clue, but I don't understand the note."

"Just say you had it from before. Throw it on your bed. Where's the card?"

"It came tied to the doll's necklace." Lexi handed Anni a small piece of paper.

No signature, no "Love, Uncle Teddy," only a word—and an unusual one at that. Anni repeated it. "CUCLOCKEYBEE. Is that all?"

"Yes! I'm never going to figure it out."

Anni paused, thought about it, and said, "Are you sure Teddy sent it?"

"It's his handwriting, but messy and rushed…" Lexi's hand trembled as she pulled out an old postcard from Teddy and showed it as a comparison to the package's inscription. "It's exactly the same, right?"

"Hmm, I'm not sure. It looks similar, but it doesn't make sense. If he wanted you to have it, why can't he come back and deliver it in person and stop the Murdrock takeover?"

"He's not coming back," said Lexi pointedly as she looked away.

"What?" A tinge of hurt rippled in her voice. Anni knew that averted glance all too well. She employed it herself whenever anyone asked her questions about Mabel. "But we don't know anything yet. Not for sure anyway," she said, desperately thinking that if what Lexi just said was true, both of their lives would change forever. She didn't want to think about that reality, especially if it meant moving in with Egbert. So she forced herself to swallow her alarm and focus on Lexi. "Well, the clue is simple enough to figure out."

"Really?" Lexi's eyes bulged behind her giant, round glasses.

Even though she didn't like to say her aunt's name aloud, she needed to tell Lexi why she understood the clue. Like a rusted hinge on a door, the name passed through her lips with a squeak. "Mabel."

"Oh," said Lexi.

Anni was relieved she didn't have to repeat herself. "She set up scavenger hunts around Waterstone and Edgewater. Those two weeks every summer when you and Teddy went away, she made clues for me with a bunch of words mashed together. Anyway, *CUCLOCKEYBEE* has four words: cu, clock, key, and bee."

Lexi stared intently at the letters, too, until she said, "But what's CU?"

"No thanks to Finnegan the Minion for trying to make me fail my test, but I know my Elements."

"*What?*" Lexi gasped as her mouth fell open.

Anni wanted to give Lexi a little hope, but even she was beginning to doubt if this was possible. In a softer tone, she said, "Science class. The Periodic Table of Elements."

"Oh, right," said Lexi between short breaths.

"Cu means copper. And if I'm right, the first part of the clue is copper clock. That's where we would start. Can you think of any copper clocks around here?"

Lexi straightened up. "I think there's one next to the Headmistress's office."

"Behind the secretary's desk. Let's go check it out!"

"Anni, what if someone sees us?"

Anni grinned. "No one will, at midnight."

CHAPTER 4

MABEL'S KEY

After midnight, the girls made their way down one flight of stairs, but stopped halfway down the second. Rufous Finnegan was heading their way. They ducked behind a pillar on the third-floor corridor. Finnegan passed them on the way to their common room door.

"We're busted," said Lexi, trembling.

Finnegan stood on the landing with his head cocked to the side, listening. Slowly, he pulled out his keys and locked their door. Anni put a finger to her lips until they heard his keys clang farther and farther away.

Lexi wrung her hands, her eyes brimming, "We have to go back."

"We can't," said Anni. "He locked our door."

Lexi chewed her lip, and then nodded. "What are we going to do? I think he did the same thing last night, and I almost got caught in the halls."

"Eggs!" said Anni. "Why'd he do that? Who told him to?"

"I don't know. Do you think he found out about the doll?"

"If he knew, he'd take it. Anyway, stay here. I'll go check the clock. You don't have to come. It's okay. I'll meet you when I'm done."

"Um, no, no. I should go, too. We should go together."

Perhaps it was the hour, but an ominous presence surrounded them. Lexi flinched a dozen times as they made their way down the stairs. She acted as if the shadows were alive and ready to pounce. Anni shivered. The stone hall felt damp from the storm. She remembered a very different feeling back when Mabel was around, when everything seemed warmer, even at nighttime.

"Look." Lexi pointed at Headmistress Turnkey's door. "Her light's out."

Anni took Lexi's hand and led the way. They inched past the secretary's desk into the formal waiting room, decked out in golden beige hues, with upholstered chaises that matched the wallpaper. Shoved into the corner stood an antique copper clock, hidden behind the long fronds of a potted palm tree.

Anni inched the pot aside. Lexi climbed onto a chaise and teetered on its armrest, inspecting the clock's face. Anni searched the clock's base with no luck, but when she stood, she caught sight of Lexi pushing a small decorative finial.

Gears whirred, ending with a pop that echoed in the halls. A tiny compartment rolled open just under the number six, revealing something wrapped inside a cloth. Lexi took it, closed the lever, and jumped down to show Anni.

Together, they unwrapped the item in the dim light. It seemed to be another clue. Lexi rolled her eyes. "Great," she said. "Now where does this go?"

Anni took the small object, turned it over and grinned. "I think I know exactly where this goes. This morning, I went to the clock tower to find you, but it was locked."

"Really? But it's never locked."

"I know." Anni spoke softly. "This *key* is the second clue of CUCLOCKEYBEE. So far we've found the copper clock, and this is a copper *key*. The word LOCK must be hidden in the word CLOCK, which has to be a third clue. The only place I saw a shiny new lock was on the door of the old clock tower."

Anni didn't understand why Lexi didn't look more excited.

"Aside from today," said Lexi with a furrowed brow. "when was the last time you went to the clock tower?"

"A week ago." Anni shrugged. "Could have been longer. Why?"

"It's weird, don't you think?"

"What's weird?" asked Anni in a whisper.

"What if someone is trying to trick us? Get us to go outside to…this might sound silly, but what if Finnegan's actually protecting us?"

"Finnegan!" Anni snorted. "The Minion's *no* protector! Besides, who'd trick us? It's okay if you don't want to go to the clock tower. I'll go. You can keep watch."

"No, no. I'm being silly, and I'm not letting you go alone."

Waterstone's front doors were locked tight. So were the sunroom's French windows. There was only one door left. The girls tiptoed through the corridors without incident. They reached the kitchen, when the sound of a bullhorn made them freeze.

It was Brunhild; she was snoring. Unfortunately, that wasn't all. The kitchen's outside door butted right up against the Cook's room, and both girls knew that it creaked every time it was opened. Anni had an idea and pointed to a jar of lard on the counter. Lexi grabbed it and together, they greased the door hinges.

With slimy fingers, Anni took a deep breath and turned the door's knob. The kitchen door opened without a squeak. Relieved, the girls carefully shut the door behind them. Across the grounds, Finnegan's gatehouse light was still on. They decided to run around the back of the school in case he might be looking out his window.

The wet grounds made it hard to run. By the time they reached the tower, they were thoroughly splattered with mud.

"You were right," said Lexi, surprised when she saw the copper lock binding the clock tower's door.

Anni took out the key from her shirt pocket. She tried to fit it into the lock, but it fell out of her wet hands onto the grass.

"Eggs!"

Lexi gasped. "Oo, Finnegan's light went out. I sure hope he's sleeping. If Egbert knew we were out here, he would be so mad at us."

"Why would you say *his* name now?"

"I don't know, but whenever you say *Eggs,* it's like you're cursing him," said Lexi. "Never mind; did you find the key?"

With a steady hand, Anni inserted the key into the copper lock and turned it. CLANG! THUMP!

The lock and chains fell on a stone paver and the sound echoed across the grounds. The girls froze. They stared at the gatehouse, and waited for a light to flip on inside. It remained dark, and when they thought it was safe, they looked down.

"Oh, no! It's broken." Lexi's voice wobbled.

The shiny new copper lock was broken into four separate pieces.

"Wait," said Lexi. "Is that…what I think it is?"

Anni peered closer. Without thinking, she reached down to pick up the object Lexi pointed at.

A long golden chain sat cold and wet in the palm of her hand. Dangling off the end of the chain was a dainty silver key that glittered like a diamond when lightning bursts illuminated the sky. The remarkable thing was that both Anni and Lexi had seen the chain before; it wasn't just any old chain, or any old key, for that matter. However, there was one item missing—a small golden locket—that Anni had seen hundreds of times hang around her Aunt Mabel's neck.

In the dim light she raised the chain until the dangling key was hanging at eye level. Anni's fingertip skimmed the key's silvery edge, and she was zapped by a jolt of electricity. Then a low, crackling voice boomed across the sky. "*My gratitude and acknowledgments, human! Notwithstanding, your lack of urgency is akin to that of a gastropod.*"

CHAPTER 5

THE INVISIBLE SPEAKER

A ll it took was one touch of the key, and he knew he had found her.

At long last, hope had arrived; with the help of this girl he would be able to repay his blood debts. Despite the centuries waiting for this moment it had been a long time since he was expected to make a formal introduction, which previously cost him dearly. He was not in any mood to make another fatal mistake of offering his name to anyone, much less a human.

Ancient creatures of his ilk knew better than to share the gift of their names. The mere offering of a name was tantamount to delivering your soul up on a platter, and thus granting another great power over your being. He had made the grave mistake of sharing his true name once before, and had been suffering for it ever since. His last hope was tethered irrevocably to that small iridescent key and the contract bonded within its metal.

This unique key had been forged and bound with Elemental intent, and fashioned from his igneous scale, a potent configuration of iridium and crystalline-pure carbon. For centuries, Elemental Keepers guarded it, passing it down with every generation in hopes that one day a summoner would appear, though none arrived. The very last keeper of this key, Mabel Moon, revealed that a summoner would be born during her lifetime.

He waited, and grew patient with each passing century, no matter his personal suffering. Yet, never in all that while had he imagined the summoner would be a mere child, much less a human girl. Nevertheless, Anni Moon was the one who summoned him, and she alone was capable of ending his eternal imprisonment, eventually, but first there was other work to be done.

The key itself was merely a tool, an invitation, if you will. It was crucial to his plans that the girl kept the key on her, since it allowed him access to her memories, thoughts, and mind. Once he had that, he would find a way to bind himself to her, and thus offer her a formal contract, one she couldn't turn down. He knew very well that *bindings* were against Elemental Law, which strictly forbade the division of essence from one living being to be transferred to another, but being a creature of such primordial lineage, these insignificant Elemental Laws meant little to him, and, if anyone disagreed, he could always breathe fire on them.

All he needed now was for the Child to seal the contract.

There was plenty of time for plotting, manipulation, and the orchestrating of events—but for the moment, he'd decided to take a little nap, for there was much scheming to be done.

CHAPTER 6

M FOR MURDROCK

Lexi had a strange feeling about Mabel's key; it's why she didn't touch it.

"Anni?" she asked, wondering why her friend looked so puzzled, and kept searching the sky. "What is it? Do you think someone saw us?"

The clock tower's door creaked open. Lexi jumped. She didn't think she could take another surprise. It was bad enough that she was able to see the Funk in Miss Sugar's office but, when they sneaked downstairs, the Funk was lurking in every dark corner of the school. What made it even worse was that she couldn't come right out and tell Anni it was Funk, especially when she had so much more to say.

"We better get inside," said Anni.

Lexi's stomach was full of knots. Part of her wanted to go back inside the school, pretend these events weren't happening, forget everything—the doll, the note—but another part of her needed answers. She was frozen with indecision.

BOOM.

Thunder rolled ominously through the low clouds like a bowling ball down a never-ending alley. Goose bumps raced over her arms when a white fiery vein of lightning hit a Franklin rod on the school's roof.

"We can't stand here," said Anni. "That probably woke half the school."

Lexi knew Anni was right. They couldn't stand outside. Together, they picked up the broken lock and used the chain to brace the door shut from the inside. Anni found two flashlights stashed by the door.

Lexi felt safer inside, and her breath steadied once they closed the door. She'd been in the tower hundreds of times and knew it like the back of her hand, but when she flipped on her flashlight, they both got a shock.

Crates stacked upon crates filled the clock tower's interior. Lexi could only assume that someone must have filled the tower sometime at night, when no one was looking. Only a narrow path led to a spiral stairwell that wound around the perimeter. Their flashlights barely lit the way.

"Anni, who did this?"

"No idea...Let's go up a floor. Maybe we can see better from there."

They climbed three flights until they were above the majority of boxes, but even then, there were still more crates stacked on the upper platforms. The girls sat on the wooden floorboards and pointed their flashlights around. No discernible marks explained the ownership of the crates other than a single stamp of the letter M.

"Murdrock," said Anni, but Lexi wondered privately if it could also stand for Moon.

"Moving in before they even sign. Before the school is even theirs—"

"Anni..." Lexi didn't want to talk about the Murdrocks buying and taking over Teddy's school. "When you picked up Mabel's key, what happened?"

"You didn't hear it? It sounded like a mix of thunder, and a low...I don't know, but I'm starting to think you're right. Someone wanted us to find this. I almost wonder..."

Lexi didn't realize it until now, but Anni was right when she said *us* because she never would have gotten this far without her friend. The *CUCLOCKEYBEE* clue was made in such a way that only Anni would know how to find it. Was this Teddy's way of telling her that she could trust Anni with her secret? Or was this something worse, like a trap?

Anni turned the key over in her hands. "I don't get it. How could Teddy set this up? Egbert wouldn't do it. He doesn't care enough."

"Someone else had to do it. It could be Egbert. He's not that bad."

Anni rolled her eyes. "That's because you're too nice." She unfastened the chain and put it around her neck. "This key used to clip on the back of Mabel's locket. She used to tell me it could unlock all kinds of doors and even secrets."

"Really?" Lexi squirmed. "She said that?"

"Yeah, she did…"

Lexi's thoughts drifted back to something Teddy had said: "There are secrets, hidden from both you and me, that only Mabel knows. One day, you will know everything; even death can't stop that."

"Umm, hello…Earth to Lexi?"

"Oh, sorry." Lexi wondered if all of this was related to what Teddy had said nine months ago right before he left. He had warned her things would change—something she tried to forget about. Denial had been her best defense up until now.

Anni opened her mouth but was cut short by the grinding of the metal door chain below. She grabbed Lexi's flashlight and switched it off. Lexi felt her heart start racing again. This time, she thought, they were going to get caught.

Voices drifted up from the clock tower's door. Lexi froze, grabbing Anni's shirt.

Slowly, without making a sound, Anni stood up. She tugged Lexi's arm and they mounted the stairs. Quietly, they climbed another two flights until they were on the topmost platform.

Lights flashed below in broken arches as the mumbled voices faded outside. Sounds of the chain scraped the floor again as the door swung open and closed.

Lexi wanted to turn on her flashlight. She knew there was a door that led to the clock tower's gear room, but they needed light to find it. Anni must have known it was there, too, because she took Lexi's hand and, together, they ran their hands over the wall.

Lexi found the door latch first, and they squeezed inside. A blast of warmth hit her face. Anni shut the door behind her and locked it. The gear room was still warm, even though the clock had stopped working.

"Let's wait here until the storm stops," said Anni, unfolding a furniture pad on the floor.

"That could take all night," mumbled Lexi as she scanned the tidy room.

The gear room was filled with massive cogs and pendulums nearly two stories high. Something unexpected caught Lexi's eye. A small metal disk was laid into the floor beneath the largest pendulum. Almost involuntarily, she moved toward it. "I've seen this before…" It wasn't the disk that drew her, but the engraved symbol on its surface.

Anni joined her. "What is that?"

"I think it's the last clue. It looks like a bee."

"Hmmm," said Anni. "It doesn't look like a bee to me."

Lexi lifted the disk from the floor. It came away easily in her hand, but beneath it was a small burlap bundle nestled inside the floorboard. Anni pulled out the small package and untied the twine. Within the burlap was a folded patch of velvet fabric.

Lexi recognized it instantly. "Can I see that?"

Anni handed her a delicate, aubergine cloth. Gold and copper threads poked out of a duplicate embroidered image of the bee that was on the metal disk.

Lexi's fingers traced the metallic stitching. "I know where I've seen this before…" She paused. It was strange, but for some reason it all led back to Mabel. But maybe that was the point! If she explained that this belonged to Mabel, then perhaps Anni might begin to understand why she had to keep her secret. Lexi wasn't sure, but excitement filled her.

"Okay, so…I've seen this before…I'm not saying it's *hers*, exactly but…"

"Eggs! *Lexi, just say it already.*"

"I saw this in Mabel's room once," Lexi blurted. "I think it's a piece of a tapestry she had in her trunk." Thoughts swirled in Lexi's head. This was it. This would explain so many things. No! Wait! She couldn't just tell her. She had to show Anni. That would be better. "I think I know what we're supposed to do! See, this bee…it *means* something. You're not going to believe me if I tell you, but…but if you come with me, I can show you."

"Okay. Where are we going?"

"Edgewater. Mabel's apartment." Elated at the idea of finally being able to tell Anni everything, Lexi said, "It's *hard* to explain, but if we leave school now, I can show you."

"Leave school? I love that idea, but you're forgetting Egbert lives there. Oh, yeah," Anni laughed. "And I kind of promised a flying rat that I wouldn't leave the school."

"Wait…" It felt as if all her relief and happiness was draining away. "You what?"

"Yeah, it's possible I'm going crazy." Anni laughed. "When I was looking for you this morning, I imagined a flying rat told me not to leave school, oh, yeah, and he said he delivered a message to you. I forgot to tell you because of the doll and everything."

"A rat told you to not leave school, and he delivered a message to me?"

Anni smiled and nodded mischievously. "I know...cuckoo, right?"

Lexi shot her a nervous smile. This wasn't where she wanted to start, with a description about Brat—about what he was. How could she explain that without telling Anni everything else? The fact that she was avoiding talking about it made her feel like a liar.

"Anyhoo...when should we leave? We'll need to be careful and not get caught. Can you imagine the trouble we'd be in?" Anni laughed. "It sounds like the kind of thing I'd do anyway, so I'll take the blame if we do."

Lexi only half-heard what Anni said, but she caught the last bit. There was no hesitation in her voice when she said, "No." Enough was enough. They were going to Mabel's tonight. Egbert or not, Lexi decided this was her chance to be brave like Anni and show her the things she knew were hidden inside Mabel's apartment. At least that would help her start the conversation. The rain outside stopped, and the room fell eerily silent as she continued, "Anni. Promise me. If we get in trouble, you have to say it was my idea."

"What? I get in trouble every day. I'm used to it. What's another—"

"No. If you don't agree, then we aren't going."

Someone didn't want Anni to leave the school, but who? Running down the street to Mabel's didn't really count; it was only five buildings away. Even if Egbert was there, his room was at the other end of the hallway, and he had left everything in Mabel's room exactly the way she left it three years ago. Lexi knew this because she saw it herself.

"Lexi, come on."

"No." Lexi was firm. "I'm serious. Swear on Mabel's key that you'll let me take it."

"Ugh, fine." Anni pulled out the key, held it up, and said, "I swear, on this key, that, even though I don't like it, I'll let you take the blame. Happy? Can we go now?"

"I don't have pockets." Lexi handed Anni the velvet cloth. "Hold on to this. Keep it safe," she said, buying herself a second because talk was a lot easier than action. "Let's go."

Anni beamed. "Awesome!" She stashed the cloth in her pocket.

Together they slipped out of the gear room and headed down the corkscrew stairs. They carefully opened the tower's main door and stared across the school grounds.

BONG! The clock tower rang and echoed across the night sky.

Both girls jumped.

Then they screamed.

CHAPTER 7

A PROMISE MADE

Don't move a muscle," said Rufous Finnegan. "You're not getting away with this." He walked around one side of the clock tower and into view.

"Eggs," Anni muttered as she folded her arms. Lexi trembled beside her.

"It's my fault," said Lexi. "I wanted to come out here, not Anni."

Anni shifted her weight. She knew Finnegan wouldn't believe her.

"Sure it was," said Finnegan. "And flying unicorns exist, too."

"It was," said Lexi. "I wanted to see why the tower was locked. Anni begged me not to come out in the rain."

"Whatever," said Finnegan. He pushed the clock tower door back in place and picked up the broken chain. "This'll need a new lock. There's important stuff in there."

"Yeah," said Anni. "Whose boxes—"

"None of your beeswax," Finnegan barked. "You two follow me."

Anni tried to lag behind so she could speak with Lexi privately, but Lexi kept pace with Finnegan, who kept cursing under his breath about having to fix the lock that night.

"What *are* you doing?" whispered Anni.

"Shush," Lexi whispered back and sped up.

Rain slapped Anni's face. Her mind was awash with conflict; she knew what she had promised, but that was before they got caught. Lexi looked a bit annoyed, but also like she might burst into tears. Surely she couldn't think that anyone would believe her. It was silly, stupid even, considering Anni's own track record. But still, Anni regretted her promise even more because she was about to disappoint Lexi by breaking it.

"Hurry up, you two!"

BOOM.

Thunder rolled through the gray sky as lightning highlighted the clouds in the distance. The rain fell harder once they reached Waterstone Academy's front door.

The foyer was dark and, if it was possible, the halls were colder inside than out. Finnegan made them take off their mud-caked shoes before he escorted them to two separate seats by the Headmistress's office. Cold seeped up through the stone floors into Anni's socks and chilled her all over.

Anni was ushered to a frigid metal bench next to the Headmistress's door and across from a huge statue of the school's founder, H. S. Waterstone. Finnegan deliberately made Lexi sit in the hall on a tufted chair, facing away from her best friend. Anni shivered, mulling over the events. The way she saw it, she was the instigator, and for once in Finnegan the Minion's life, he was right: she had convinced Lexi to follow the clues.

Even if anyone else believed Lexi, there was no way Egbert would. Relief started to take root in her mind. Anni folded her arms and assuredly reclined against the metal bench.

BOOM!

"Goodness, listen to that," said Vivian Sugar, exiting the Headmistress's office and rubbing her folded arms for warmth. "It's getting worse out there." She looked between Anni and Lexi. "I'm relieved you are both safe. The Headmistress was beside herself when she discovered you were out there in that thunderstorm."

Quickened footsteps clattered down the hall accompanied by huffing, puffing, and the smallest tinkling of bells. "Hallo, hallo. Running late, but I'm here, I'm here at last. Bertie couldn't make it—out of town, you know, that sort of thing. No matter."

Within seconds, a short, plump woman stopped before Vivian and smiled at her as if they were long lost friends. She stared at Vivian. Vivian stared back with a polite smile. "Oh bother, so sorry. I'm Zelda, Zelda Scurryfunge, Bertie's—I mean Egbert's—relation. Charity called me in Bertie's stead—I mean, Egbert wasn't available on such short notice."

"Hello, Zelda. How nice to meet you. I'm Miss Sugar, Waterstone's school counselor." She extended her hand to the frazzled-looking Zelda. "Funny," she continued after a second's pause, "has anyone ever told you that you look an awful lot like that mystic on the Internet? What's her name? Dahlia, something... Dahlia Sunshine, yes that's it! You could pass as her twin sister. They do say we all have twins out there in the world."

"Ah, uh. Well, ah, I'm afraid I don't know her. Nope, nope, no relation, I'm afraid. It's just me, Zelda...Zelda Scurryfunge. You know, I help Egbert with the girls from time to time. Helping them with things, girl things." Zelda laughed and looked anxiously at Anni. "Anni? Is that you? Goodness, what did you do to all your long, curly hair?"

"I cut it." Anni didn't want to say she had tried to copy Vivian's hairstyle out loud.

"Hallo, Lexi." Zelda smiled. "So, is Charity here yet?"

Another cold wave of blue light coursed through the black halls.

BOOM. CRACK.

"She's waiting for you. Inside," said Finnegan.

Zelda jumped as if Finnegan had surprised her. Then she stared at him as if part of her brain had short-circuited.

"Egbert's not coming?" asked Anni.

"No such luck," said Finnegan. "He wants to talk to *you* first thing in the morning."

"It was my idea," said Lexi.

Finnegan sneered. "I'm sure it was."

"Oh Finnegan, let the girl tell her side! Anyway, why are you here? Shouldn't you be guarding a gate or something?" asked Zelda.

"No. I'll be in the meeting, too."

Anni's mouth went dry. No Egbert. This wasn't possible.

"Nice to meet you, Vivian," said Zelda. "I'll just nip inside, then."

Finnegan opened the door for Zelda, closed it behind her, and leaned against it, staring at Anni the entire time.

Vivian traded glances between Anni and Lexi and finally said, "All right, you two. Who's willing to tell me what is really going on? Should I be concerned?"

"Let me explain," said Finnegan. "They were caught running across the grounds in an electric storm past midnight and vandalizing school property. I think that about sums it up. Isn't that right, Lexi?"

Anni hated how he was taunting her, like it was unimaginable for Lexi to come up with an original idea.

"Rufous," said Vivian with a deep exhale. "I think I've got this. Why don't you join the Headmistress and Ms. Scurryfunge? I'd really appreciate a moment alone with the girls."

And this was exactly why Anni liked Vivian, unlike the rest of Waterstone's staff.

Finnegan glared at Vivian before he went back inside the Headmistress's office, but the door didn't close all the way. When Vivian went to speak with Lexi, Anni peered through the crack in the door. She heard Zelda say, "Charity, you really don't look well." The Headmistress took a bottle from her desk drawer, put two drops of a mint-green liquid into a glass of water, and swallowed it. Her face went from a near-white pallor to an instantly flushed and healthy hue.

It almost looked exactly like the same medicine Lexi took because of the way it glowed phosphorescent within the water, like it was alive. It probably wouldn't have caught Anni's attention, but years ago, she got very sick when she tried Lexi's medicine. Mabel made her promise she would never do it again because it was specially made for Lexi's asthma, even though she never saw Lexi have trouble breathing.

"Anni?"

BOOM! CRACKLE! BOOM!

Anni flinched as an electric flash of blue light filled the halls and lit the grounds.

Vivian sat beside her. "I didn't mean to scare you. I'm especially glad you're not out there right now, but can I ask what was so urgent that you couldn't wait until morning?"

Just then, Finnegan opened the door. "Lexi, the Headmistress would like a word."

As Lexi passed them on her way into the office, she shot Anni a concerned look.

Anni desperately wished she could read Lexi's mind at that moment, because then she would know what to do. Aside from Lexi, Vivian was the only other person Anni confided in. She was the only adult at school who was nice to her and listened without judgment. Now that they were finally alone, this was her chance to tell the truth, this was the moment to do it, before things got out of hand, before Lexi got into more trouble.

"Anni," said Vivian gently, "you must be freezing." She tucked a warm blanket around Anni's shoulders. "I don't want to get between you girls, but if there's something you want to say..."

Whether it was the blanket or Vivian's reassuring arm wrapped around her cold shoulders, warmth radiated into the marrow of Anni's bones; she felt like a puddle of melted butter. The truth was, Vivian's tenderness reminded Anni of Mabel, and right at that moment she was missing Mabel so acutely that her chest physically hurt.

Without any regard to the cost of the truth, she was ready to tell all. Relaxed and smiling, Anni gazed up at Vivian's kind face. "Well, I sort of promised—"

"*Be warned, Miss Moon.*" It was the same mysterious, rolling voice Anni heard outside. "*An oath made by the key is binding. You shall not break the terms of your accord.*"

Anni looked down the hall, but no one was there. All the cozy warm sensations drained from her body. She turned around to Vivian and said, "Did you—" when suddenly her right hand clapped over her lips, completely against her will.

Her stomach coiled; she had no power to remove her hand from her mouth.

"Anni?" asked Vivian, with a mixed look of amusement and confusion.

"*Doubt my veracity if you will, Child. The woman heard nothing. You alone can hear me. Resistance is futile.*"

CHAPTER 8

THE BAD NEWS

Anni tugged at her hand. It was tightly clamped around her mouth just as Lexi opened the Headmistress's door. Lexi's brows were arched suspiciously as she stared between Anni and Vivian. But for Anni, it was Vivian's changed expression: a combined look of confusion and disappointment that made her feel worse.

Then suddenly, just like that, as if it had never happened, her hand relaxed. Anni tried to make it look like she was wiping her mouth, but she knew she couldn't pull it off. She was too embarrassed to even attempt to explain that she couldn't explain why her hand involuntarily tightened around her mouth, like a toddler refusing to speak right when she was about to tell Vivian everything.

"Anni," said Lexi slowly. "The Headmistress wants to talk to you."

Anni frowned at her. "You mean she believes—?"

"Yes." Lexi shrugged. "It's the truth. She wants us all to come in."

"Lexi, may I have a private word with you before we go inside?" asked Vivian.

Annoyed, Anni rose from her chair and made for the door. She overheard Zelda say, "I assure you, Egbert will disagree entirely—"

"Anni Moon!" called the Headmistress. "Nothing good comes from lurking in doorways. Come in."

She did. Her pulse quickened as she took one of two empty seats before the huge desk. Lexi followed Vivian and took the other. Headmistress Turnkey had never looked as exhausted or as angry as she did now.

"As it stands, Lexi would have me believe that she and she alone devised this dangerous plot to sneak outside in the middle of the night. Of course, I find this admission surprising, given the fact that Lexi, a model student, who's never once been in trouble, decided to risk both your lives in an electrical storm, where I might add that either of you could have been gravely injured....Anni, I will only ask you once. Is this true?"

Vivian touched Anni's shoulder. "It's okay. The truth won't hurt you."

Anni glimpsed Lexi twisting her pearl pendant; she was nervous. Anni felt trapped between speaking against her best friend, the promise she made, and the truth. Could she let Lexi take the blame? The steely glint in Headmistress Turnkey's eyes made up Anni's mind.

Anni tried to stand, but couldn't. She opened her mouth; it snapped shut. By no act or will of her own, her head moved involuntarily, nodding up and down, but that was nothing compared to an even bigger betrayal, when her own lips uttered the word "Yes!"

Dumbfounded, Anni couldn't move or speak to retract her statement. All she could do was watch as Lexi sighed and relaxed into her chair. What was happening?

Headmistress Turnkey's gaze shifted between the girls. She finally said, "I will speak with Egbert personally first thing in the morning, but as of tomorrow, the both of you are officially expelled. This is for the best."

A collective gasp filled the room. Anni was too stunned to move. Lexi, too, sat there in shock. Silence reigned. How could this possibly be for the best? Headmistress Turnkey's word was final and the discussion was over.

Vivian and Finnegan silently escorted the girls to their fourth floor common room. Anni didn't understand why the Minion had to be a part of the escort, but when they entered he took out his keys and waited next to the small oval door to Lexi's bedroom.

"What are you doing?" asked Vivian.

Finnegan stared at Lexi and said, "Headmistress's orders."

"But, Rufous dear," pleaded Vivian. "Can't you allow them to stay together? After all, surely…"

"Anni's lucky I'm not making her sleep in the kitchen. Lexi, say good night."

Anni couldn't believe it. Lexi hugged her, said "Good night," and ran into her bedroom without another word. Finnegan locked her door and retreated to the hall.

Vivian took Anni's hand. "I'm sorry. I would like to speak to you, but," she glanced over her shoulder, "perhaps in the morning. I think it's best if you rest. In the meantime, I will speak to the Headmistress…"

Finnegan jangled his keys. Anni glared at him, loathing every fiber of his being, as he closed and locked their common room door for the night.

Anni ran to Lexi's door. "Lexi? Lexi? I'm sorry. If you let me take the blame you can stay here at school. This is all my fault. I'll tell the Headmistress the truth…"

"Stop." Lexi hiccupped between sobs. "It's okay, but please stop. It's not your fault. I don't blame you. I'm just…tired. I need to sleep."

There was nothing she could do. It pained Anni to say, "Okay."

Her legs moved like jelly over to the window seat cushions and she looked out. Chilled air whistled through the leaded panes. Acid burned in the pit of her stomach. Outside, the rain had stopped and the moon tugged itself away from the blanket of clouds, revealing the clock tower. There it stood, as it always had, with little importance or meaning until now.

Conflicted emotions fought for her attention. The injustice of what just happened played over in her head, but what she couldn't figure out was why she didn't speak out. And what was the deal with that weird voice? After a considerable amount of time feeling guilty, she took a careful breath; it was time for practical measures. Anni reached under the cushion and pulled out her tattered journal; she needed to make sense of things. It was late, but too much had happened in the space of one day for her mind to sort it out. Mabel had encouraged her to do this whenever life got to be too much, or whenever things needed to be expressed that she couldn't say out loud. She treasured her journal, a last gift from Mabel.

She flipped through her filled journal to the last twenty empty pages and wrote down everything, starting with Brat. Whether he was real or not, she put it down, but strangely her mind went blank when it came to that voice she heard outside. Nor could she describe what happened in the hall or inside the Headmistress's office, so she wrote only about hers and Lexi's expulsion. Anni reached into her pocket and pulled out the velvet cloth, and traced the gold stitching with her finger. She sketched the image and added a question mark as a note. Lexi had asked her to keep it safe. Whatever its value, she decided she couldn't leave it in her pocket. She closed her journal, stuffed it under the cushion, got out a needle and thread, and sewed the patch on the inside of her black tank top. She then put the tank top on with the velvet side against her stomach, just to check that no one could see the stitches The metal thread was cold and scratched against her skin, reminding her it was there, and safe, like Lexi requested.

CHAPTER 9

WHIFFLE & EGBERT

C*hild, arise from your slumber. We have a contract to discuss.*"

Anni awoke. She jolted upright and alert, but it was dark and it took a few seconds for her eyes to adjust to the empty common room. She pressed her warm cheeks against the cool windowpane, and a soft chill rippled through the glass. All remaining spells of sleep lifted, as the previous night's events burned vivid in her mind. One glance at the clock tower brought tears to her eyes.

"*Pray, let us forgo the emotional theatricalities and commence with the introductions and basic particulars,*" said a snide yet bored drawl that Anni recognized immediately as that invisible voice from last night. She jerked and spun around, but the room was still empty. "*Asinine though it is, it would appear that you summoned me the moment your feeble fingers absconded with my key. Were you aware that this would happen?*"

Anni frowned, looking up and turning her head. "I didn't summon or abscond anything! This is my Aunt Mabel's." She pressed her hand against the key to make sure it was still there. It was. "Who are you? Why can't I see you? If it's you, Brat, this isn't funny!"

"*Child,*" the voice chuckled. "*I am no mere jester or messenger of messages. And while we are on the subject, I am not particularly inclined to grant you with the confidence of my true name, not yet anyway. Nevertheless, I am prepared to relinquish a title that you may use once you answer my questions.*"

"Hey, did you stop me from speaking last night?"

"*At last, a proper query. However, I have a superior one in return. I've been pondering how a mere child of twelve, a human no less, has the summoning touch! Is this folly?*"

"Thirteen! I'll be thirteen in a week. What you are talking about?"

"*I must say that I find your-general countenance lacking in the skills required for the job.*"

"Job? What job? Look, if you're too chicken to show yourself—"

"*Child, I'm quite certain my appearance would terrify you,*" the voice growled.

"My name is Anni, not Child. Either show yourself or go away!"

"*So be it, but we shall meet again; however, I pray the situation is a favorable one for you. Should the occasion arise and you are ready to converse, you may summon me by simply saying the name Whiffle.*"

"Whiffle? What kind of name is that? You sound like a toy."

He was gone, and the little hairs on the back of her neck rose. It was official: she might be going crazy. Not only did she dislike Whiffle's tone, she had no intention of having another chat with him anytime in the future.

Her mind returned to the previous night's events. Zelda had said that Egbert would disagree with the Headmistress, but counting on Egbert was a high-hanging hope. Even though Anni wasn't sure what he would do, it was all she had to cling to.

She cracked open the window; the air smelled sweet and clean. Since her Waterstone uniform was still drying in Brunhild's storeroom, and her red and pink disco outfit from the lost and found bin was covered in mud, she changed out of her pajamas and put on the only other set of clothes she owned: a white button-down shirt, the black tank top that she sewed the bee patch onto the night before, cargo shorts, and her favorite black-and-white-striped socks, which still had cocoa stains. She wasn't dressed to school code, but after last night, she hardly thought it mattered.

Thinking about Brat, she went to close the window but stopped. A stranger stood in the middle of the peony beds, four floors below, staring directly up at her. Wearing a red and white rose-patterned car coat, a floppy beige sunhat, and oversized white sunglasses, the stranger's face was disguised until a gust of wind revealed short, dark hair. Anni squinted, thinking that the stranger looked a lot like Finnegan, but she had to be wrong; Finnegan had a super weird phobia about dirt and gave out detentions like candy to every kid who tracked mud into the school. Whoever it was stood there lopsided, with one foot stuck inside a muddy gopher hole.

Keys jiggled in the common room door's lock. It startled her into slamming the window shut, but when she turned to look down again, the stranger had disappeared.

"Good. You're awake," said Vivian Sugar as she entered. "I wanted to give you and Lexi some time to talk before you had to be downstairs for the parents' brunch."

"Wait, we don't have to go to the parents' brunch, do we?"

Vivian sighed. "Egbert is expecting both you and Lexi to be there, regardless of what occurred last night. He and the Headmistress are going to make an official announcement about the Murdrock takeover during the brunch. Apparently he has some news to share with the both of you, which is a mystery to me, and afterwards he's taking you and Lexi to Edgewater. Why he doesn't meet you up here instead is beyond me."

"He's never been up here," said Anni. "I always meet him in the sunroom."

"Really? I'll never understand why he's so…never mind." Vivian picked through Finnegan's key ring. "Egbert is meeting with the Headmistress as we speak. Zelda, too. I'm hoping that together they can talk some sense into her."

"Do you think the Headmistress will change her mind?"

Vivian's face fell. "Oh, Anni, I'm not sure…I shouldn't say this, but… expulsion? I think Charity's decision was very wrong and incredibly unfair. I only hope that one of them can sway her to reconsider…" Vivian found the key to Lexi's door. She unlocked it and rested her hand on the wood but didn't open it. "I think it's best if you wake her. I'll give you two some privacy." She paused before leaving. "Anni, if there is anything you want to tell me, anything at all about last night that will help me help you, I promise I will try to do whatever I can to fix this."

Anni bit her lip. There was stuff she wanted to say, but she wasn't sure. First, she needed to talk to Lexi.

"Okay. Thanks she said," and watched Vivian leave.

Anni waited until Vivian left before opening Lexi's door. Hues of golden light flooded in through the eastern windows. Lexi was awake, sitting on the corner of her made bed, twisting her finger around the small pearl pendant hanging from her neck as she stared out the window. She was dressed in her school uniform—an oversized sweater, plaid skirt, and penny loafers—and her hair was piled into a huge, messy bun atop her head. Anni was struck by an overwhelming sadness; Waterstone Academy had been the only home Lexi had ever known. What would she call home now?

"I'm going to miss this," said Lexi, resigned, gazing at Lake Michigan. She dropped her pendant and picked up the patchwork doll by her pillow. Her dark brown fingers laced through the doll's hair. Anni glared at it, wishing it had never arrived.

Lexi stood and offered it to Anni. "Will you keep the doll safe for me?"

"No!" The words flew from Anni's mouth before she could stop herself. "Not if you're going to give up. All *this* trouble started the second you got that stupid thing." Anni thought Lexi gave her a weak smile, but continued. "Anyway, Egbert's downstairs. I'm going to tell him it was me. I'm not letting you get expelled if I can help it."

"Hm. I'm not sure Egbert will believe you." Lexi placed the doll on the edge of her bed and walked to the door. "I doubt he can change the Headmistress's mind."

Mabel's key suddenly felt hot against Anni's chest. At the same time, the golden threads from the velvet patch grew cold against her stomach. Helpless anger swelled up inside her and she yelled, "Why are you acting so weird? Like you knew this would happen, or like something bad was going to. It's like you are trying to leave me! Just like Mabel did! Just like Teddy left you!"

Lexi stared at Anni in silence.

Anni regretted her words. "Oh, Lexi, sorry. I'm sorry I...I didn't mean that..."

"Yes, you did." Lexi's voice cracked. "If you're my friend, you'll keep that doll safe for me." Lexi left the room.

"Wait." Furious with herself and her temper, Anni went after Lexi but turned back, grabbed the doll, stuffed it inside Lexi's old backpack, and flung it over her shoulder. A small piece of paper fluttered to the floor, but she ignored it and dashed out of the room.

Muddled emotions and thoughts carried her down several flights of stairs. A proper, heartfelt apology was necessary, but she worried about Egbert's plans. What if he didn't stop Lexi's expulsion? Anni pushed the thought away as she rounded the last flight of stairs.

"Is it true?" Miranda stood alone in the foyer, with her hand on her hip. Anni ignored her. Miranda blocked Anni's way into the main hall. "I said, is it true?"

"What?" Anni narrowed her eyes. "I don't have time for your games."

"That's not what I heard. I wonder, wherever will you both go?"

Anni felt the blood rush into her eyeballs. She wanted to launch herself at Miranda, but she swallowed her anger. "What do you—?"

"Stop lingering, Miranda, your aunt is in the sunroom," said Ms. Downsnout, who looked extremely harried because she was juggling several items, including Finnegan's clipboard and keys. "Anni," she snapped, "Egbert's waiting. You know the way."

Anni waited until Miranda left first. She knew she needed to steel herself before she entered the parents' brunch. Miranda would've already spread the gossip about her and Lexi by now. All she could focus on was Lexi, alone, with all those eyes on her. She hurried down the corridor looking for Egbert, and found two people arguing in the alcove next to the Headmistress's office.

Anni froze. Egbert, standing there with his annoyingly rigid stance, had cornered Vivian Sugar in front of the statue of Waterstone's school founder, and to make matters worse, he was pointing his finger at her and shaking it. Anni couldn't quite make out everything he said, but she heard Vivian say, "...I have a right to know—"

"You have *no* rights." Egbert didn't waste a beat. "I don't know how you twisted your way in here, but I want you—"

Horrified, Anni cleared her throat. They turned in her direction. Neither registered surprise, but Vivian, with all her grace and poise, walked away without saying a word.

"Where's Lexi?" Egbert barked, frowning at her. "On second thought, I'm glad we're alone. I have grave news, and I'm counting on your assistance today.

It is absolutely crucial that you follow my instructions. Zelda is here to help, because I haven't the foggiest idea where Finnegan is. Regardless…"

Egbert leaned down to face Anni square on. She grimaced and pulled her head back, uncomfortable with such close proximity. She couldn't help but feel that in that brief moment Egbert looked almost human, like he actually felt bad about something rather than locked into his usual robotic ways, but she changed her mind the second he started to speak in his slow measured tone, as if he was talking to an idiot. "After brunch, I need you to promise me that you will stay with Lexi all day. I'll repeat myself again, *after* brunch I need you to promise me not to leave Lexi's side. Do you understand? I do not want you to leave her alone, not for a second. Can you do that?"

It was his tone that always did it. Whenever he spoke to her, like he just did, like she was a moron, she couldn't help but to automatically feel less inclined to listen to the rest of what he had to say. And yet, perhaps for the first time in her life, they both shared a common goal: Lexi. Without fail, his eyes grew flat and his chin jutted out—he never had any patience with her. "Do you have cotton in your ears?"

She hated the idea of agreeing with him. She would never understand how she was related to this man or why Mabel put him, of all people, in charge of her welfare. It was these moments when she questioned why someone like Vivian Sugar couldn't adopt her. Still, she needed something from Egbert.

"Only," said Anni, taking her time, "if you convince the Headmistress to let Lexi stay at school."

Egbert looked affronted; however, his voice remained calm. "*That* issue is not up for discussion, and we will discuss your future later. Will you agree to stay with Lexi or not?"

Her fists balled up as she crossed her arms. She hated how he made her feel like a little girl every single time, like she was useless. She tried to sound like him and used his measured tones to respond. "I'll do it…for Lexi. Not you."

Egbert smiled. She clenched her fists harder, whipped herself around, and stalked off toward the sunroom. She didn't think things could get worse.

"Oh no, you don't," said Brunhild, looking sweaty and irritable.

CHAPTER 10

MUDDY SOCKS

"Not so fast, you. Where's your uniform? Never mind, take this." Brunhild thrust into Anni's arms a huge silver platter, laden heavily with plates of cakes that oozed warm, fruity juices and moist, glistening *canelés*. "When you're done with these, there's the rest." She pointed to a trolley loaded with more silver trays, brimming with more sweets. "Put the plates on every table where the parents are sitting."

Expelled and she still had to work? Anni glared at Brunhild, but Egbert walked right past them. Clearly, he didn't object, nor would he intervene. He was too busy fiddling with his idiot-sized watch like it was the most important thing in the world.

"Are you waiting for Christmas?" snapped Brunhild. "Go on! They won't walk in on their own!"

Seething, Anni entered the sunroom, weaving her way through the jolly gathering of conversing teachers, parents, and students. She placed dozens of different plates of baked goodies around the room without making eye contact with a single person. As she deposited two plates onto the last coffee table, she glanced up.

On a tufted sofa in the middle of the sunroom, the Headmistress sipped her tea, looking paler than the night before. Beside her sat a handsome man, old Hollywood handsome with bright, sparkling eyes, perfect teeth and complexion, and not a single hair out of place.

Anni didn't know who he was, but she didn't like the way he grinned at her, which made her knees buckle. Done with the tea trays, she joined Lexi, Zelda, and Egbert.

Lexi was sitting next to Zelda on the small settee with her eyes trained on the floor. Anni felt terrible; she'd already upset Lexi, and she was sure that Egbert's news would do the same. Of their small group, Zelda was the only person enjoying herself as she attacked the pastries with gusto.

Egbert cleared his voice and sharply said, "Now that *we're* all here…I'd like to say this before *he* speaks." He paused, fixing his eyes on the handsome man next to the Headmistress, and motioned for Zelda to put down her plate, as if it wasn't quite the time for snacking frivolity. "You see…I have some news about Teddy. Please don't interrupt or ask me questions; there is a lot that I do not know and there is no time to waste."

The way he said "news," Anni knew what was coming, but for Lexi's sake, she was glad they were seated in a tucked-away corner of the sunroom, away from prying eyes and ears. Nevertheless, whatever small privacy they were afforded, for Anni, it felt as if time turned backward, to three years ago when Egbert delivered the news about Mabel. This time, she knew better than to look at his face, which only made her angry once his clipped voice started, like he was ticking off a checklist.

Anxious for her friend's feelings, Anni watched as Lexi continued to stare at the floor. She fought her usual impulse to ignore Egbert, just in case he said something that might actually help Lexi. He didn't. In fact, what he said was, "…received reports…Teddy's been missing…feared dead…He's gone, for good."

"Lexi, you know what this means. Things have changed," said Egbert. Anni thought that was a weird comment, because of course things would change! However, when Lexi raised her eyes, Anni was surprised by the brief look Lexi gave Egbert; a strange kind of exchange passed between them that Anni didn't quite understand. "Until I get things sorted," he paused, "I want you packed up today. You'll be staying at Mabel's. Anni, too."

When Egbert finished saying all he had to say, Lexi lowered her head. Just as Anni moved toward her, Zelda enveloped Lexi with her arms.

Anni dared to glance at Egbert. His dull, emotionless eyes made her stomach turn, and the very sight of Egbert's exposed shins, because he always wore pants that were too short for his long, dark legs, gave her the overwhelming desire to kick him. Teddy was his friend and here he sat, almost nonchalant, as if he was dictating his itinerary. Anni couldn't fathom how a man like him could live in the world.

"He was your friend," said Anni without restraint. "What's wrong with you? You're heartless." She turned back to face her friend, but Zelda still had Lexi in a tight embrace.

CRASH.

On the other side of the room, a banquet tray clattered to the floor, accompanied by gasps. Someone yelled, "Help, she's collapsed!" And then another person said, "It's the Headmistress!" And, "She's having trouble breathing!"

People crowded where the Headmistress had fallen.

"You three stay here." Even though Egbert was looking directly at Anni.

The handsome man, who had been previously sitting next to the Headmistress, stood and clapped his hands at the gathering crowd. "Everyone, everyone, please calm down. I am Mr. Murdrock, soon to be the new owner of Waterstone Academy. Let's work together. Please give the Headmistress some space." Several people moved aside as if on command. "That's better. She is breathing, but we must take precautions. Can someone get a cool towel?"

Anni turned to Lexi and Zelda. Both of them watched the commotion with wide eyes, except Lexi's brows were furrowed with concern. Anni was surprised to see no tears on her friend's face; it was as if she had been prepared for the news about Teddy.

Lexi stood, peering over the crowds. "This doesn't look good," she said.

"She'll be fine. She's a tough old bird," said Zelda. "But come to think of it, she has been looking a bit peaky lately."

"Lexi," Anni whispered. "The Headmistress has medicine like yours." Anni gave her a knowing look, and she could have sworn that Lexi's cheeks reddened.

"I saw her take it in her office last night before, you know, and her skin went from pale to normal in a flash."

Lexi looked as if all was forgiven as she whispered back, "You have to find it. She's going to need it. Go look in her office. I'll go upstairs to get mine just in case."

"But Egbert told me to stay with you," said Anni. "I can come with."

"There's no time." Lexi nodded toward Zelda. "I can't explain everything… but I sort of knew about Teddy. I'm okay, sort of. Anyway, the Headmistress needs our help. Egbert won't even know I left. It'll take me a second. Meet you back here. Okay?"

"Okay," said Anni.

The sunroom was a tangled mess of people hovering in concern while others were working their smartphones. No one was watching them, and as soon as Zelda went back to the pastries, both girls sprang into action and darted out of the room.

Anni ran straight for Charity Turnkey's office. She caught one last glimpse of Lexi as she rounded the corner and headed for the stairs. For a second Anni wondered, if she and Lexi saved the Headmistress's life, perhaps she'd let them stay at school after all.

The Headmistress's office door was already slightly ajar when Anni pushed it open. She slipped inside and shut it, hoping no one saw her. When she turned around, she was stunned to see the room entirely upended. Books and paper littered the floor, cabinets were ajar, chairs overturned. Anni made her way to the desk. All the drawers were yanked out—except one. It was near the bottom, and a light glowed within.

Anni pulled it back and a blast of blue light engulfed the room. It took a second for her eyes to adjust as a projection of a news article covered the wall.

THE VOICE - ELEMENTAL NEWS, WORLD NEWS & OPINION

Editor-in-Chief:
Verbum Smith

THE V.O.I.C.E.

Thursday, May 24
County Fleet

THE VIRTUAL OMNINAVIGATIONAL INCLUSIVE CONNECTING ELEMENTALS

NEWS   OPINION   E2   BUSINESS   ARTS

TEDDY WATERSTONE DEAD?

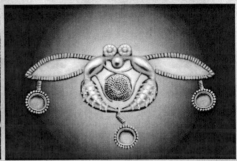

Early Death Detection and Elemental Artifact Missing. Are the Two Connected?

OpEd By: PENELOPE W.
POTBOILER

Dear readers, the scuttlebutt is true. Elofficials have officially announced, and The Opus Stone Network has confirmed, a beloved and well-recognized Elemental, Theodore Ezra Waterstone, has died 245 years before his Death Date. No bodily remains were found, only his *cracked* Opus Stone. That's correct, *cracked*. Elofficium investigators stated that his Opus Stone was discovered outside Brazil's National Museum. Moments after Elofficials verified this most egregious report, the museum discovered that a priceless golden pendant dating back to the Minoan Age, which had been mysteriously donated for the International exhibit, had been stolen that evening. This particular stolen relic, believed to be the original Golden Bee Artifact, and considered the most famous Elemental symbol, was thought to be under Elofficium lock and key, since all Bee icons and imagery have been banned from public display (Section #255 of Elofficium Rulings and Regulations).

At this point, it is unclear if the theft and the early Death Date are in fact related. Given that this most Ancient Elemental Artifact was on display in the human world for all to see begs the question: was this a measure to undermine / humiliate Elofficium authority? The Elofficium have officially declined to comment.

If these events sound eerily familiar, that's because they are. The infamous Mabel Moon, Teddy Waterstone's sister-in-law, disappeared in a near-identical manner three years ago. Rest easy, dear readers, I will continue to follow this story and provide details as they surface. In the meantime, Elofficials have disrupted all TreeTransport facilities within a ten-mile radius of Brazil. All LimBough Operators and Tree Transport employees have asked all E-pass travelers to be patient in finding other connecting branches for embarking and debarking points of travel within the country.

Elementals…Opus Stones…Death Dates…Golden Bee Artifacts? What was this gibberish? Was this true about Teddy and Mabel? The memory of Brat flitted in her head; he said he was an Elemental, and she was a human. Of course she was! But what *were* Elementals?

Anni swayed as she read and reread the lines *disappeared…Teddy…dead… Mabel…dead.* She never admitted this to anyone, even Lexi, but she secretly pretended Mabel was gone on a very long journey that she would, someday, come back from. Seeing these words in print made it harder to keep up this wishful thinking. It felt real now, because of Teddy…

She had to find Lexi.

Voices filled the adjacent file room. Anni panicked. There was nowhere to hide but beneath the Headmistress's desk. She crouched down, but the drawer with the blue light was still open. The projection was coming from a kind of wristwatch, almost exactly like the one Egbert wore, but there was no on or off switch. She shut the drawer and slipped back under the desk as two people entered.

A pair of muddied socks walked toward the desk a few feet away from her nose.

"I told you to find their school files," said a gravelly voice, the kind you get from smoking too many cigarettes. "Not ransack the office, you idiot!" The voice grew in volume as a small pair of black shoes waddled toward the muddy-socked feet. "Just as I thought. This one's of age. She'll have her Opus Stone by now. What are you doing? Give me those school pictures! You already know what both of them look like, you idiot. Let's go. And hide your list; we have to do it now…"

Anni's heart pounded.

A piece of paper fluttered to the floor next to the Headmistress's desk. It landed close enough that Anni could read it. She froze when a skinny, pale hand picked it up.

WHAP!

"Imbecile! Pay attention!" said the gravelly voice. "If you lose that list, it will draw attention to you!"

WHAP! WHAP!

"I swear I'll addle your brains further if you screw up again! I promise it *will* be worse! You find this one. I'll get the other. And put on your blasted shoes."

Silence filled the room as the person with muddied socks stumbled from one foot to the other, attempting to put on a pair of Converse hightops covered in dried mud.

"*Let's go!*"

Her heart hammered as the two sets of feet exited the Headmistress's office door. At first she couldn't move, but her legs yearned to run and track Lexi down; there was no time to wait. She had to move! The paper had the names of two Waterstone students printed in bold ink: Anni Moon and Lexi Waterstone.

CHAPTER II

GOLDEN FINGERNAILS

Anni's pulse thudded so hard she thought her eardrums might explode. Lexi was in danger. Time was of the essence. She waited under the table, counted to twenty, scrambled out, and froze.

Red-faced, Egbert stood immobile in Headmistress Turnkey's doorway. His left temple throbbed and, if it was possible, his face turned a deeper shade of puce; only his voice was controlled and measured. "Tell me you are not responsible for this."

Clearly, Egbert didn't understand. He looked madder than she'd ever seen him. How could she explain? Where to start? Anni exhaled and squared her shoulders. "I came here…"

"No. Stop. Go. Find. Lexi. Stay with her until I find you."

Anni whipped past him and out of the room. There was no time to explain what she saw, especially with Lexi's safety in danger.

She raced into the sunroom. It was crowded. Lexi hadn't returned yet, which meant she had to be upstairs.

Several groups of students and parents poured out of the sunroom and into the halls. It was difficult, but Anni wove her way around them. She dodged people left and right up the main stairs, racing up them two at a time.

Anni was so focused on finding Lexi, she smashed headlong into someone on the second floor. The collision caused her to fly back and hit the ground.

Like a pillar, Zelda remained unmoved. "Anni? There you are. Are you all right?"

"Sorry." Stunned, Anni peered around her. "Have you seen Lexi?"

"I thought she was with you," said Zelda, wringing her hands. "After you two took off, I started fretting. Poor thing. Thought I'd go look for her. She was very upset. I don't think she should be alone right now."

"Yeah, you're right," Anni muttered. There was no time to chat. She ducked under Zelda's arm and raced up the stairs.

In the third-floor corridor, Anni skidded to a halt. Finnegan, looking extremely dazed, wrestled a mop on his way out of the utility closet. What *was* he doing? Finnegan was uncharacteristically dressed in the same outfit she saw outside her window earlier that morning: the same white and red rose-patterned car coat, the same floppy beige sunhat, but no shoes, only socks that were caked with mud!

Confused and terrified, Anni didn't wait around to ask him questions. She tore up the last set of stairs and noticed that the common room door was ajar. She dashed inside. The room was a mess: the sofa was flipped, cushions strewn and curtains ripped. She ran to Lexi's room as a lump formed in the back of her throat. It was the same here, too.

Her eyes fell to the floor next to Lexi's bed. A small piece of paper stuck out from under a crumpled sheet. It was the same paper that had fluttered to the floor when Lexi placed the doll on the bed earlier.

A-
I'm going to the *place* to find the tapestry. Meet me there?
-L

Anni pressed the note to her chest. Lexi was safe; she went to Mabel's. Anni dashed out into the common room and grabbed her journal from under the window cushions; she stuffed it into her backpack with Lexi's doll inside and secured the pack on both her shoulders. Before she made it to the door, her foot crushed something large.

Anni bent down. Lexi's glasses, they were broken. It didn't mean anything, she told herself. It couldn't. Lexi was at Mabel's; she was sure. Anni pocketed the broken glasses and raced out into the empty hall.

She wasn't taking any chances. Sick with worry, Anni ran full-pelt down the creepy, less traveled, red-lit service stairs that led into the school's basement. It was the fastest way to get outside unseen. When she reached the cellar door, she scanned the grounds through the door's small window.

The gardens were vast, open expanses, easily visible to anyone inside the sunroom and many other parts of the Waterstone Academy. However, it was the quickest way off the school property without being stopped. She had to take that risk, even if Egbert happened to glance out one of the school's windows and see her.

The heavy iron cellar door slammed as she raced up an incline. She sprang past the tall shrubs with enough distance, just in case someone jumped from behind them or thrust an angling arm to seize her. No time for even a backward glance, she zipped past the sunroom windows.

A twenty-five-foot-high security fence covered in green plastic encircled the school grounds. Trees and shrubbery covered every inch of the fence's perimeter. Anni hurtled over flowerbeds; her gaze darted left and right, scrutinizing each bush.

Then she saw it.

Like a baseball player sliding into home base, she dove into a tiny gap between a pair of unkempt boxwood hedges. She shimmied under the green plastic and the broken bit of fence, scraping her skin as she squeezed herself into a shallow burrow.

A hollow of overgrown wisteria sheltered and shaded a small nook on the other side of the fence. It was littered with fast-food wrappers and empty bottles and smelled like urine. Anni held her breath as she surveyed the park, looking for suspicious people, like Finnegan and his muddied socks, but the path was clear.

The tiptop of Mabel's apartment building, the only pink building on the block, came into view. The corners of Anni's mouth tilted up. She burst out from the thicket and something dive-bombed her head.

"Go back! Go back! Anni Moon, you're breaking your oath! You promised!"

No. This was impossible, she told herself. The flying rat/bat thing wasn't real, but there he was. Brat kept on dive-bombing her head and wouldn't let up.

"You don't understand. Stop it. Go away," she said, swatting at him. "Stop it!"

"No, Anni Moon. I can't let you break your oath."

Standing still was a mistake. Anni ran up the park's path, trying to outrun him. A few people dotted the park. This was hard, keeping track of suspicious people and now Brat, too. Anni spotted three joggers, a biker, a boy standing next to a tree, a lady pushing a baby carriage, and a little old man sitting on a bench feeding the pigeons. They all looked normal, but she didn't slow down long enough to make sure.

Five buildings stood between her and the Edgewater Apartments. Anni counted them down and picked up her pace.

"You'll get me in trouble. You'll be in trouble. You must go back," said Brat. "I've never in all my years left an assignment incomplete. Please go back."

"Can't," she panted. "Lexi's in trouble. I need to find her!"

Four buildings.

"Lexi?" Brat's voice faltered. "Moppins, is she safe? She always follows the directions. This isn't good. Two mistakes, very bad, very, very bad. She has to be safe. There's the Funk to think of, not to mention the *squatters*, and…"

Three buildings.

"I don't know what you're talking about, but I'm going to find her. She left me a message and that's where I'm going! So you go away. You're not helping!"

Two buildings.

Brat darted less at Anni's head, which she appreciated, but he still flew alongside her, which she didn't. To her left, she saw another boy next to a tree. He stared at her. Or, did he glare? It was hard to tell. His soured face looked almost identical to the boy she saw earlier—he had the same tart expression. It unnerved her.

One building.

"Moppins, moppins, this is a kerfuffled mess…Oh, what to do? I suppose I will have to help you find Lexi. Yes, yes, and when we do, then you can go back!"

Anni ignored his last comment. Edgewater's garden fence came into view, and it couldn't come soon enough. Her plan didn't involve entering the apartment building through the front entrance; the doorman would detain her in the lobby until Egbert got back—Edgewater's residence rules. No. She would travel underground through the garage without being detected by the cameras. It was all about timing.

Anni nearly stumbled over her own feet. Next to a different tree by the driveway stood that boy, the same sour-faced boy she had already seen twice before in the park! Was he following her? How did he get there so fast? Was he working for Finnegan? She didn't waste a second to find out. Plan averted, she tore past him, risking being seen by the cameras over the garage entrance.

Brat flew next to Anni as she sprinted down the driveway. On the way to the elevators, she noticed the parking attendant's cubical was empty. Tempted to peek at the monitors inside, to see if the sour-faced boy followed her, she ran toward the booth.

Bad move. Two Herculean hands lunged at her. She dodged and the hirsute parking attendant got handfuls of air. Even though he was big, she knew better than to underestimate him. All the past games of cat and mouse had taught her that much—not to mention his distaste for children and the fact that he looked remarkably like Brunhild's twin brother. He reached for his wireless and called the lobby.

Anni took off overhearing every other word, "Kid…running…nuisance."

"That's not good," said Brat as he landed on her shoulders.

"Shush!"

Not choosing the elevators, which seemed like the easiest way to get trapped, she opted for the stairs and climbed several sets before hopping on a freight elevator. Brat twitched repeatedly once the doors closed and ran in circles on the elevator's floor.

"What's wrong with you?" asked Anni.

"Elevators," he said. "They're not normal. Unnatural things."

Anni rolled her eyes. "You followed me, remember? I didn't ask you to come."

Ping.

The service elevator opened on the seventeenth floor. Brat flew into the steel hued vestibule. Anni moved toward the water pipes that lined the wall. A spare key should have been hidden behind them, but she only found soot. If the key was not there, then maybe Lexi was already inside.

The service door to Mabel's apartment was unlocked and it opened with ease. Blinding light poured in from the kitchen. Everything looked the same, which surprised her. Egbert had been living there for the last three years, but Mabel's fruit-shaped earthenware sat in the same orderly line on the kitchen table, as did her favorite orange tea set behind the glass cupboards, and all of Mabel's other knickknacks; they were exactly in the same place as if she had never left, as if she was still there.

Dizzy, Anni steadied herself against the wall as memories of a past life haunted her. She didn't realize how much she missed Mabel until she was standing in the middle of their old kitchen. Her hand clung to her chest, holding Mabel's key as if that might ease her pain and confusion. Where did she fit in? What was home? Not here, not anymore. And not at Waterstone, so where would she call home?

"Are you okay?" asked Brat, eyeing her. "Let's go…"

"*Anni*," rippled a soft whisper.

"Lexi?" called out Anni. "Is that you?"

No response.

Anni pushed the kitchen door open and moved forward on wobbly legs, uncertain if the voice was real or imagined. Again, everything in every room was the same, exactly the same. Why did Egbert keep everything in its place, just as Mabel had left it?

"*Anni*," said the whisper again.

She paused. "Did you hear that?"

"No," said Brat, circling the living room. "What?"

"Lexi? Are you here?" Anni heard the strain in her own voice.

No response.

They moved to the hall and inched down the corridor. "Check those," said Anni, pointing to the other two bedrooms. "I'll take this one."

"*Anni*," called a voice. It was coming from behind Mabel's door.

Her hand shook as she turned the knob.

The room was empty. Lexi wasn't there. It didn't make sense. Anni slumped to the floor next to Mabel's bed.

Brat flew in and landed near her. "Why did you think she would be here?"

She ignored him and remembered what Lexi had told her. She whirled around. There it stood at the foot of Mabel's bed: the massive, ancient oak trunk.

"*Find it*," said the whisper, even softer now.

"What was that?" said Brat, staring at the trunk.

She looked at him. "Wait. You heard that?"

"Of course I did, but it's not Lexi's voice. I'm sure of that." Brat's voice quavered. "And listening to disembodied voices isn't a good idea. Don't open—"

Before he could stop her, Anni lifted the trunk's lid.

"Eggs! Empty...Wait..." Her fingertip traced over a small latch on the bottom.

"Don't—" said Brat, flapping overhead.

"Shush! Lexi told me something was in here."

Lexi had mentioned a tapestry; maybe it was inside. Anni placed her finger in the penny-sized latch, slid it to the right, revealing a secret compartment.

The secret compartment wasn't some small little drawer underneath the trunk. Fully opened, it was a small hatch that was connected to a diagonal staircase that led into a separate room below. Maybe Lexi was down there.

Brat gasped. "Mopple-me-toppined. That's not a human contraption."

It was too dark to see the size of the room below, and she could have sworn that something like candlelight flickered below. Was it Lexi? Curiosity warmed her. She had to move fast. The anticipation improved her vision, because on the very top step, she made out shapes that looked like a book, some cloth, and a round, shiny object: Mabel's locket.

Something rattled the staircase below, and an overpowering smell of freshly chopped wood filled the air. Anni climbed into the chest to better reach the top rung. She pulled back her shirtsleeve and stretched out her arm. Her hand passed through the open space, a few inches away from touching the ladder's railing when...

"AAAAHHHHHHHH!"

Out of nowhere, another hand shot up from below. Anni leaped backward. Before she could react, the hand snatched the items sitting on the top step, Mabel's locket included. Anni blinked and the secret compartment slammed shut. She scrambled and searched the trunk's bottom for the latch. It vanished into wood and the compartment disappeared. Mabel's locket was gone. Even more disturbing was that hand, impossible to forget, because the fingernails were made of solid gold.

CHAPTER 12

OLIVER MONDAY

"D id you hear that?" asked Brat as he coned his wing to his ear.

Images of golden fingernails replayed in her head. "No," she said and looked down as Brat frantically wiggled behind her. "What are you doing, Br—"

"Ahem."

Anni jumped.

The smug-faced boy from the park was leaning against Mabel's door! His arms were crossed over his white T-shirt and open black jacket.

"How'd..." Anni sputtered. "Who are you?"

The smug-faced boy didn't answer, but he might have smirked. Who was he? And how did he get inside Mabel's apartment? He remained silent, but his face was pinched, as if something smelled like rotten eggs.

Anni ran toward Mabel's desk, grabbed a small wooden box, and pulled her arm back. "Don't come any closer. You'll regret it."

The boy smirked and said, "You humans sure love your violence." Unthreatened, he sauntered back down the hall.

Infuriated, Anni let her arm fall.

"Who are you?" she yelled. "What do you want?"

"Frazzlezappend-crumpledbottoms-mopple-me-toppined, that was close," said Brat. He flew onto her shoulder. "You can't let them see me. Quick, let me hide in your shirt pocket. I'd be ever so grateful, and I'll be in your debt."

"No way." She pointed to the hall. "I need to deal with…with *him!*"

"I beg you, Anni. I've never failed a mission before. Please, I can't be seen or found out." Brat's tiny eyes were glossy, and there was a touch of hysteria to his voice. "I promise I won't mutter a peep. You have my word."

"Okay, fine." Anni opened her shirt pocket.

Her cheeks burned when she entered the living room and found the smug boy reclining cross-legged on Mabel's mint green lounger, but he wasn't alone.

Standing by the dining table, Egbert spoke into his oversized wristwatch. "I see…keep me informed. I want an update every five minutes." He strode toward Anni and peered behind her. "I thought we agreed that you would stay with Lexi. Where is she?"

Anni was relieved that a band of kidnappers wasn't waiting for her, but Egbert was the last person she wanted to talk to. "I don't know. I have to go find her. Lexi left me a note. It said she was coming here. I'm going downstairs." Before she reached the door, the boy, whose manners were as prickly as his spiked hair, got up and blocked her way.

"Excuse me. Who are you?" Anni demanded.

"This is Oliver Monday," dictated Egbert, looking at his watch again. "He's assisting me today. Finnegan didn't check in this morning—"

"Finnegan was at school! I saw him. He was trying to kidnap Lexi and me!"

"What!" Egbert said. He shot a shifty glance at Oliver but covered it up with a dismissive wave of his hand. "I suppose you're going to tell me he destroyed Charity's office and Lexi's room as well? Absolute nonsense. Finnegan wouldn't. Don't be foolish."

"Whatever, he was there. I gotta go. There's a secret stairwell in Mabel's room that leads directly into the apartment downstairs." She turned to Oliver. "Out of the way." Oliver didn't budge. "Seriously? You're not going to move?"

"Enough with your stories. There is *no* secret staircase in Mabel's *room.* This time, you're staying put." Egbert glanced up from his watch for a brief moment. "But I'd move away from that wall if I were you."

A massive painting, by the artist Boudin, covered the wall. It depicted a dreary seaside village. Oliver nudged Anni aside as a gray dot sped across the Impressionistic hillsides toward the edge of the canvas. Faster than a blink, the dot multiplied in size until it wiggled out one, two, three, four appendages and, lastly, a head.

Anni stared wildly, but Egbert didn't even look up at the person who exited the painting when he said, "We do have a door, Zelda."

"What—" said Anni.

"Phew! Absolutely dreadful," said Zelda, patting down her arms and legs, which made the tiny bells on the pant legs jingle. "That canvas is positively reeking of Funk. It'll take me days to get that smell out. Bertie, you really need to change that painting out."

There was that word *Funk* again!

"Um, what just happened?" asked Anni, but they ignored her. Brat had said something about Funk, too, when he told her not to leave school, but what was it?

Zelda continued to brush her clothes off, as if trying to get rid of something invisible. Finally, she said, "I looked *everywhere*. What would you have me do? I haven't acquired the E-passes yet. I've had a bit of trouble with Krizia—"

"We've got part of that covered," said Oliver.

Anni stared at him. What was covered? What exactly did he know that she didn't?

"We do," said Egbert. "Zelda, where's your Omninav?"

Zelda looked at her wrist and dithered. "Oh, bother. Must have left it behind. Let me see…where did I put it?" She tapped her finger to her chin.

"Never mind," said Egbert as he pulled out another oversized wristwatch like his own. "Take this one. It's secure. Go back and retrace your steps. I'll join you soon."

Zelda raised her eyebrow but took it all the same. She moved toward the massive painting and raised her leg to walk through it again.

"Zelda," said Egbert. "Are you sure I shouldn't send Oliver instead?"

Zelda stopped. "Oh, ho, ho. Not to worry, Bertie. Just seeing if you are paying attention. No, on second thought, I think I'd fancy the elevator instead. There're some lovely watercolor murals with chubby little cherubs, and best of all, they're *Funk*-free." Zelda tapped the side of her nose and smiled at Egbert, Anni, and Oliver. She muttered, "Piece of cake bread," as she left through the apartment's front door.

"I'm following her," said Anni, eyeing the painting with apprehension. "I don't know what's going on, but I'm going to find Lexi!"

"Anni," said Egbert, blocking the door. "There's no secret stairwell that leads into the apartment downstairs. And you are not going anywhere. Not this time."

"Brat! Come out. Tell them." She opened her shirt pocket. Inside, Brat was curled into a tight leathery ball, so small and so round that he looked like a tiny Hacky Sack. "Come on, really?" She turned to Egbert. "Before Oliver found me, these stairs—"

"*Enough!*" It was the loudest tone she'd ever heard Egbert speak in her life, and it shocked her into silence. "I asked you to do one small thing, one small thing! You agreed to stay with Lexi. Did you do that? No." He took a breath and served her with his most intense stare. "Every second I waste, I'm that much further behind on finding Lexi. She's probably distraught. I need to find her, immediately. Can you understand that?"

Anni nodded, although she couldn't help but think that there was something else Egbert wasn't telling her. She started to wonder if it had to do with the way he glanced at Oliver when she had mentioned Finnegan trying to kidnap them.

"Good, because you will not leave my side until I say so. You will not utter a single word of complaint. When you speak, you will answer only with a simple yes or no. When I tell you to jump, you will jump. When I tell you to go, you will go. Do you understand?"

A crashing wave of fury, guilt, and pain washed over her. Egbert was proving to be the worst kind of guardian she always thought he was, but she also knew, even in the deepest recesses of her soul, that if something happened to Lexi because of her own stubbornness, she could never, ever forgive herself. It took all of Anni's strength and love for Lexi to look into Egbert's eyes, nod, and say, "Yes," and actually mean it.

Egbert barely acknowledged her nod before he turned to Oliver. "Get the carrier. We have about ten minutes before departure."

Egbert turned to Anni, his arm outstretched. "Take my hand and close your eyes." Anni's left hand met Egbert's right. She closed her eyes and he pulled her into a fast walk. "Now jump!"

Anni jumped, which felt stupid with her eyes closed. A surprising gust of wind hit her face. The silence of Mabel's apartment shifted and was replaced by echoes of a hundred murmurs. Anni squinted a quick peek.

The three of them walked briskly down a long hall. A bustling number of other people hurried alongside them, pulling suitcases. When they passed a huge glass window, Anni's jaw dropped. She blinked a dozen times, but it was clear. They were in an airport.

CHAPTER 13

EGBERT'S PLAN

Anni looked back at a huge mural under a sign that said *Terminal Five*. "Walk faster. We are late," Egbert said. His swift stride forced her to jog in order to keep up with him. Oliver was already in line at gate number fifty-five.

"Wait," said Anni, trailing behind.

Egbert didn't wait; he pushed forward. He reached Oliver. "You know what to do?"

"Yes," said Oliver. He handed Egbert the rectangular bag and gave him a wry smile. "It'll be fine. We'll cross as soon as we hit the fifth ring."

Egbert shook his hand and Oliver boarded.

"Wait. How did we...never mind," Anni said. "Why are we in an airport? We're wasting time. We need to find Lexi, not drop people off!"

Egbert handed her the rectangular black bag. "I need you to take this with you."

Anni looked inside the bag. "Why are you giving me a cat?"

"You're in charge of taking him home. I need you to board that plane."

"What? No!" Anni shoved the cat carrier back at Egbert. "I'm helping you find Lexi."

Egbert didn't take the bag. His stern expression should have been enough to convince her he meant business. "I realize this will be hard for you, but I need you to get on that plane."

"*Last boarding call for Virgin Atlantic flight 005 to New York,*" called an attendant on the overhead speaker.

"No way. I need to find Lexi. She's my only family left—"

Egbert pulled out two tickets and a small blue book. "You were right. Someone, I don't know who, is after Lexi. I don't know why." His eyes shifted away for a second. "But Zelda has found her."

"Really?" Anni beamed.

"There isn't time. I'm personally escorting her to meet you tomorrow. Here are the tickets for you and the cat. You'll be staying with Zelda's brother, Van, and his wife—somewhere very safe." Egbert averted his eyes as he shuttled her closer to the gate. "They live on the outskirts of a large city. Oliver will help you get there." He pulled something like a candy bar from his pocket. "Oh, you should eat this when you get seated. It's important that you do."

Anni took the bar. The flight attendant was about to close the gate's door. "Hold on," called Egbert, waving his hand. "She's boarding."

Anni felt immobile and didn't know what she should do. Egbert leaned down to face her. His eyes harbored a rare hint of emotion. "Please, for Lexi's sake, I need you to get on that plane. I can't help her unless you're safe."

He waited. The attendant took the cat's bag in one hand and reached out for Anni's hand with the other. The moment stretched into an eternity, and she left him at the precipice of not knowing if she would agree.

"Fine." Anni gave him her steeliest stare. "But if Lexi's not there tomorrow, I'm leaving." She followed the attendant to the double doors of the jet bridge.

CHAPTER 14

LEO'S IN CHARGE

Ushered to the back of the plane by the flight attendant, Anni was glad to have a window seat and the entire last row to herself. Even with the cat carrier, she had plenty of room to stretch out. She couldn't help but wonder why there were so many empty rows at the back of the plane. Oliver sat alone five rows ahead of her, thankfully on the opposite side.

Satisfaction warmed her as she realized she didn't have to endure any of his smug expressions during the flight and only had to gaze on his spiky hair. All the same, she didn't need a babysitter. She'd be thirteen years old in six days on the twenty-first of June. How old could Oliver be? Fourteen? Maybe fifteen?

Although her track record for following Egbert's precise instructions wasn't great, she wondered what would have happened if she followed Brat's advice. Who wanted to kidnap Lexi? Finnegan was awful, but was he really a kidnapper? Maybe working for Egbert made Finnegan crack up; Egbert had that effect on people. And what was the deal with the painting in Mabel's apartment?

Something about that picture tickled her memory. Had she seen Mabel passing through it once before, when she was a child?

Who would answer her questions? She glanced at Oliver. Nope. She carefully opened her shirt pocket, making sure no one was watching. Brat was still tucked into a round leathery ball as she whispered, "Psst, Brat, wake up." He didn't respond. "Of course you're asleep. Listen, when you wake up, I've got questions for you."

She fidgeted in her seat when a handsome young man walked down the aisle. His blazing smile arrested all of Anni's thoughts. Dressed in crisp linen, he looked like he came from a long, sun-soaked weekend on a Caribbean island instead of the gray, drenched skies of Chicago. His brownish mop of hair fell in tight, finger-length curls that hung above his puka shell necklace and his iPod cords.

"Hello," he said to her as he stuffed a bag into the overhead compartment.

Dumbstruck, Anni didn't say a word as he took his seat three rows behind Oliver. She was mesmerized by his caramel toned features and his infectious grin; whatever bothered her seconds ago inexplicably escaped her mind.

When the plane was in the air, the captain made an announcement: "For those of you making connecting flights, we should be arriving on time in New York around five-thirty p.m. Eastern Standard Time. For those of you continuing on to London, we will ask..."

"*London!*" Anni gasped. She pulled out her ticket, which was tucked into a small blue booklet labeled *Passport*. In bold black ink, the boarding pass read: CONNECTION FROM NEW YORK TO LONDON.

"No. No. No. He didn't..." Although Egbert's methods were suspect, she knew he didn't just forget to mention that she was going to another country altogether. Anni was so mad she stuffed the ticket and passport in the seat pocket. When she saw the candy bar Egbert had given her, she threw it, but it fell on the black carrier, waking the cat up.

"He tricked me. Did you know?" Anni said to the cat as she reached for the candy bar. "Sorry, didn't mean to wake you." She opened the wrapper and took a bite. "Gross!" She gagged, searching for something to spit in, but she was out of luck and resorted to swallowing what tasted like a combination of chalk and tar.

The cat pawed the carrier's mesh panels. His tiny nose sniffed the area around the zippered opening, and he finally started to claw on the black mesh door.

"I can't let you out. We'll get in trouble."

The cat resorted to meowing. Anni wondered if he needed to stretch; the rectangular bag looked dark and cramped. She unzipped the top about an inch and put her finger inside the opening. The cat licked her and purred.

"I bet you hate being trapped," she said. "I'm trapped, too, you know. A plane's not a box, but it sure feels like one."

Anni checked to see if the coast was clear. No stewardess in sight, she unzipped the carrier's door flap. "Don't run off, okay?"

The beautiful red tabby sprang out and onto her lap. She scratched his ear and found a nametag hanging from a collar.

"Leo…Hi. Nice to meet you."

Leo purred as he walked around in circles on the seat beside her, until he found the perfect spot to comfortably curl up.

"It's bad enough you're stuck on this plane. It's your seat—you should enjoy it." Anni suppressed a giggle as Leo's tongue stuck out, even though his mouth was closed.

Leo was a brief diversion, but her mind raced back to Lexi. Where was she? Was Egbert really going to put Lexi on a plane? How could she trust him?

"Want to hear a secret?" Anni whispered to Leo. "I'm not going to London. I'm going back to Chicago. But first, I need to escape from Mr. Squinty Eyes Oliver."

She began to form a plan. Grace, an old friend who used to attend Waterstone, lived in New York. If Anni slipped off the plane when it landed, she could call Grace and get help from her and her family.

Leo nuzzled her hand with his wet nose. His green eyes twinkled like glowing green orbs as he stood up and walked in circles on her lap.

"Hyper, much?"

Leo jumped and landed silently in the aisle. He sat there, licking his paw, then started to clean his face. He was cute, for sure, but Anni knew he shouldn't be there. The aisle wasn't empty; a steward, about ten rows ahead, had his back to them as he passed out pretzels.

Leo sauntered toward the galley, pausing at the threshold between the last row of seats and the back of the plane, where the drink carts and bathrooms were. Anni sprang into the aisle when the steward turned around, pretending to tie her shoe until he turned back.

Anni sneaked a peek at the rows ahead of her. The smiling guy was asleep against a shaded window, but Oliver turned and nearly looked right at her. She ducked. This wasn't good. She would have to put Leo back into his carrier for sure, but only if she could catch him first. She decided she needed to adopt a casual approach, not wanting to startle Leo into darting in the opposite direction, down the aisle where the steward would catch him.

Leo stood and rounded the galley's corner. Now he was trapped. Crouched low, Anni followed. She turned the corner and stood up immediately.

In the galley, a stewardess was arranging the drink service cart. Anni spotted the tip of Leo's ginger tail twined around an open lavatory door.

"Gotcha," Anni whispered.

"Sorry?" asked the stewardess. "Did you need something?"

"Bathroom," Anni mumbled. She skirted toward the lavatory door, thinking Leo would be easier to catch now that he was cornered, even though she hated the idea of taking away his freedom.

With the restroom door ajar, she blocked the opening with her foot, just in case Leo backtracked. She inched her way inside and closed the door behind her.

The bathroom's interior surprised her. Compared with the narrow galley, this restroom was impossibly big—almost too big for the allotted space.

She didn't see a toilet, or even a sink, only a long Formica countertop that ran along the wall, which curiously ended next to an ornate wooden doorframe. Beyond that, there was an extra lounge, where Leo sat waiting for her atop a table, purring. She needed to step over a short lip in the wall to get in because the bottom of the strange doorframe wasn't flush with the bathroom's floor.

Anni gave Leo a weak smile. "Sorry, but you're gonna have to come with me."

Leo stood on his hindquarters like a meerkat and said, "I'm afraid not, dear girl. Welcome to the Wood Realm; you have just arrived on Moon Zephyr."

CHAPTER 15

THE HAND

When Lexi opened her eyes, she was in almost total darkness. A hint of light issued along a door's edge that was slightly ajar. As her eyes adjusted, Lexi realized she was inside a closet. She tried to move, she tried to speak, but she couldn't. It was as if she were paralyzed from the nose down. She had no idea how long she had been like this and could only recall running up three flights of the school's stairs before everything went black.

Lexi trained her eyes on the crack of light issuing through the closet door. As her eyes adjusted, she recognized the room beyond. It was where she and Anni had spent years playing games, doing homework, and staring out the vast window onto the school grounds, but the common room had been upturned and ransacked. From her position, she could tell that she was inside the narrow coat closet near the common room's double doors.

Unexpectedly, Anni darted past the door and ran into Lexi's bedroom. Filled with relief, Lexi knew it would be okay; Anni would find her. But Lexi had forgotten she had left a note with the doll, telling Anni to meet her at Mabel's apartment. All she wanted to do was show Anni the velvet tapestry with the Golden Bee and start explaining everything.

Lexi's relief fizzled. If Anni found the note, she would go to Mabel's next. Lexi tried to move again, but it was no use. Her body refused to obey her commands.

Anni raced out of the bedroom, stopped in the middle of the common room, and bent down to pick up something off the ground. Lexi recognized the object as her broken eyeglasses, but they weren't real; Lexi only wore them because Teddy told her that she needed to wear them as part of a disguise. It was just one more thing to add to the list of explanations she would need to share with her best friend.

Come on, Anni. Figure out I'm in here. A small grunt escaped Lexi's lips as Anni stood frozen, holding the broken frames.

The weight of a gloved hand fell on Lexi's shoulder. She tensed. Warm, sticky breath smelling of stale tobacco wheezed in her ear, "Not a sound, girl. Someone wants to meet you, and if you behave, I might let that friend of yours live."

CHAPTER 16

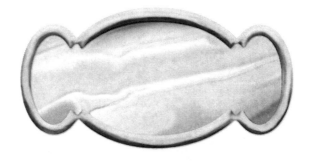

QUEEN'S MIRROR

Anni braced herself against the bathroom's counter where Leo sat staring at her like he was waiting for an answer. The floor beneath her moved and warped. Was her mind playing tricks?

Her shirt pocket shifted. Brat peeked out and muttered, "Moppins! What have you gotten us into?" before he ducked back inside.

It was all she could do to hold onto the counter as gravity pulled her down. Beneath her fingertips, the stiff Formica countertop rematerialized into a round, polished wooden table. The airplane's previous sterile gray lavatory walls disintegrated and were replaced by an enormous circular room saturated in sprightly oaken hues. It was meticulously organized, like a showroom for gardening tools.

Leo jumped down from the table and looked at Anni. "Sorry we tricked you, but it was the only way to get you on the Zephyr without an E-pass." Leo pranced over to the far side of the room, where a great oak door opened. A blinding light poured into the room accompanied by a breeze of overpowering metallic and sugary smells. One whiff made Anni heave and her knees went wobbly. She planted both hands on the table; beads of sweat trickled down her forehead as she attempted to move. The room wasn't swaying, but she was. Head throbbing, her knees gave way and she crumpled to the floor.

"Thanks, Leo," said Oliver, whom Anni hadn't seen standing by the door.

"My pleasure, dear boy," said Leo. "Happy to oblige. We all must do our part. Now, if you'll excuse me, I need to see a man about a dog."

Lying on the floor, Anni watched Leo paw the door open and disappear through it. Briefly, more light filled the room, piercing her retinas, along with overpowering earthy scents. Just as Leo left, two rusty-haired teens walked in.

Of the two, the girl with long, blazing red hair spoke first. "Honestly, what were you thinking…bringing *that thing* here? Didn't you even consider DeFunkifying her first? Ollie, the whole Zephyr knows she's here…"

"Miranda? Eggs!" Anni said with disbelief. "Oh, no. Please get me out of here."

"Ha ha," said the rusty-haired boy who walked in with Miranda. "I…like… her. She's smart, too." He had the same strong jaw as Miranda, and they had the same blue eyes, but his hair was more orange than red, curlier than hers, and windblown. There was a definite strut to his walk as he approached Anni. "Hey, kid. I'm Jay, but seems you already know my evil twin sister, Miranda." Jay laughed at his own joke.

Miranda gasped and her lip curled as she eyed her brother.

"Just ignore her. I do," said Jay, just a few inches away from Anni's face. He inspected her like she was something foreign. Anni tried to move, but the pounding strain in her head prevented her. "Relax, kid. You're not going anywhere with that much Funk. Trust me." Jay winked at Anni, stood and turned to face his sibling. "I can't remember the last time we had a full-on Super-Funked human on the Zephyr."

"Idiot!" hissed Miranda. Her teeth were clenched so tight, they were in danger of cracking. "Don't make friends with her, she's a human!"

"What's the matter? You afraid the little human might find out your full name and take all your Leprechaun gold?" Miranda scowled as Jay turned to Oliver. "When the Funk hit the Zephyr, Mir totally tripped. It was priceless."

"Shut it, Egghead," spat Miranda.

"Not cool." Jay smiled and shook his finger. "I wouldn't use that kind of language in front of the *human*! For one, it's bad for Elemental relations, and

B, you're only two requirements away from your *Continuus Humanus Educatio E-pass*. I know how bad you want it, and I'd hate to see you screw that up."

Miranda pinched her nose. "For Elsakes, is it me, or did *she* bring all the Funk from the human realm onto our Zephyr? It stinks!" She turned her back to her brother and asked Oliver, "Who's wrapping things up?"

"That would be me," said a calm voice behind Anni.

Anni turned her head and discovered that the voice belonged to the relaxed, handsome-looking teenaged boy who had gotten on the airplane just after her. His smile was arresting; however, there was a problem. Where was the rest of his body? His head floated midair through a mirror-like surface that was surrounded by a thick wooden frame. The reflective surface shimmered like water when he glanced down at Anni. "Hiya. I'm Mackenzie. Just collecting your bags." His arm passed through the sparkling glass. "Oye, Ollie, heads up!" He tossed Anni's backpack and Leo's carrier in Oliver's direction.

"Mac!" Jay whistled. "Queen's Mirror, now that's some risky business. Wait a second…you can't travel to a Zephyr by Queen's Mirror unless you're already in the air…wait, no! Tell me you're not on an airplane right now? Aw, man."

Mackenzie laughed, and grinned at Jay. "Hold up. I'll be right out." Mackenzie's head vanished beyond the Queen's Mirror's shimmering surface. Somehow, his presence in the room soothed the general atmosphere, but when he disappeared, Anni felt sick again.

"Ugh, gross!" Miranda moved farther away from Anni and closer to the door. "Jay! Don't bother Mac. Let him finish. Her Funk is getting worse by the second."

Finally, Mackenzie walked through the Queen's Mirror and the rippling surface turned solid and clear like glass. Anni was relieved to see that his body was still attached to his head, which helped make her nausea dissipate. She had heard about Funk enough to understand that, whatever it was, it was most likely what was making her sick and unable to move. She couldn't explain it, but when Mackenzie was present, she felt better: less sick and calmer.

Mackenzie faced the mirror, raised his left hand, closed his eyes, and muttered under his breath. The reflection dulled and the thick wooden frame deflated into a wispy sheet that resembled aluminum foil. Mackenzie peeled it from the wall, gave it a whack, and, like a tape measure, it rolled neatly into a walking stick. He twirled the stick over his knuckles with a flourish before he handed it over to Oliver.

"Thanks, Mac. I need to return this." Oliver grinned and made his way toward the door. "You'll take care of the rest?" Miranda was out the door first. Jay followed and said, "Skurf later, Mac?"

"Naturally," said Mackenzie, pleasantly grinning.

Helpless, Anni lay flat on the floor as Mackenzie approached. He placed his hand on her shoulder. A moment of serenity and total peace washed over her. She wanted that moment to last for an eternity, but her eyes grew heavy.

"No worries," said Mackenzie. "I'm a Water Elemental; I'm sure you'll feel better soon."

The door opened one more time, and four new people walked in. They peered over to get a better look at Anni. Several of the newcomers were speaking all at once, but Anni heard Mackenzie say, "Ms. OggleBoggle, this is Anni Moon."

A spirited little woman, definitely the oldest of the four, was dressed in shades of tangerine. Some of her stray pink and gray strands of hair barely made it into the bun atop her head. "We have much to discuss, my dear," the old woman said to Anni. "I've been waiting to meet you."

"Yugi San, Anni. Anni, Yugi San," said Mackenzie to a short man with more hair in his Van Dyke-styled beard than on his head. Yugi kneeled down on the floor beside Anni. He didn't speak, but his brows furrowed over squared spectacles as he took her hand and checked her pulse.

A preppy-looking girl dressed in shades of lavender, with a curtain of long black hair, inched forward. She had a serious face but blushed when Mackenzie said, "This is Daphne and—"

"And I'm Squirt," said a very excited boy who bobbed into view, unable to wait for an introduction.

Mackenzie leaned in. "The worst part is over, but you'll need to rest."

Anni reached for Mackenzie's arm. "Lexi. I need to find Lexi."

Against her will, her eyes closed and she fell fast asleep.

CHAPTER 17

SQUIRT

POUND. THUD. POUND. THUD.

Anni moaned. An aching unlike anything she'd ever known throbbed inside her skull. Her eyes were still closed, but she sensed a bright light all around.

A breezy current drifted under her nose: heady smells of spices, sugary flowers, woods, metal, and earth. Beneath her body, her fingertips touched a cold marble slab.

"Oh, good! This is so exciting! You're finally awake."

"Oo, my head," said Anni. Her blood vessels were beating like drums, and it sounded like someone was shouting at her down a long tunnel. The deafening sounds made her eyes water as she slowly cracked one eye open.

The fuzzy outline of a boy's head hovered over her, his dark hair swirled upward like a Kewpie doll. He had plump cheeks, bright tawny eyes, and full lips that parted into a great smile, but then he started talking very fast.

"Ssshhhhh. Too loud." Anni raised her hand to her forehead and a white crystalline powder fell from her arm. "What's this crystal stuff on my skin? It looks like salt."

"Sorry." The boy giggled. His sunny eyes and smile invaded his face, making him look younger than the other boys—Mackenzie, Oliver, and Jay. Also, he was a lot shorter, or maybe it was the massive round room that dwarfed him. "Oh that? It's for the Funk. I made it. I call it *Scrubus DeFunkertas*. It's mostly a Sel de Mer, with essences of Verbascum, Taraxacum, Equisetum, and some other stuff. Trust me. You needed it. You smelled. Bad. But that's normal for humans. You know, 'cause Funk is smelly. And since you couldn't bathe, I put it on your arms and legs. The good news is it worked. It's a complicated blend. I've got the recipe somewhere if you want it." He shoved a small jar into her hand. "You'll need to apply it every day until—"

"Wait…I've seen you…before," said Anni.

"Yep, that's me! I'm Squirt." He spoke very fast. "My real name is Sharif Qamar Uma Isra Tau Mukerjee, but it's way too long to remember. Anyway, everyone calls me Squirt. Wow, I've never met a human before. I mean, face to face. I've seen humans tons of times, but never met one up close." He beamed at her. "Welcome to Moon Zephyr. Yugi told me to watch you. This is Yugi's house. How old are you? I'm thirteen."

"Yugi? Is that Zelda's brother?"

"Zelda? Who's that? No, Yugi's Yugi. You saw him before you passed out. You're in the Wood Realm, on a floating island, just over London. The Elofficium don't know you're here. You've been asleep for twelve hours. I've been making and remaking a tonic every hour. Just in case you woke up. Made eleven so far. It's for your Funk." He leaned in and sniffed. "I won't lie; it's bad. But don't worry. You're nice and hidden. The Elofficium won't find you here. Not yet, anyway. The Zephyr's a mad house. Elementals are freaking out because of the Funk. They don't like Funk or humans, but I'm different. I like you, even though you're the first human I've met! Oh, should I close the curtains?"

Anni could barely follow what Squirt said as he raced across the room, pulling a thin rice paper shade across several curved windows. She winced as she raised herself up onto her elbows. Her entire body throbbed. "The Elofficium?" she asked, barely above a whisper.

Squirt dashed to a cluttered worktable and retrieved a thermos. He poured a silvery molten liquid into a teapot and hammered a hardened, puce tinted fruit. Shells flew higgledy-piggledy across the room. His hands moved fast as he added the seeds of the fruit to the teapot, which he poured into another container, and finally, holding the steaming mug in his hand, rushed over to her. "Here. Drink this. It's your tonic."

Anni raised the cup to her nose. It looked like molten puke-colored acid and smelled worse than a thousand rotten eggs. She reared her head back, gagging from the odor. "*Eggs*…It smells like…I can't drink that."

Squirt's face fell. "But you have to. Your Funk—"

"She doesn't understand what Funk is," said Brat, perched on a bookshelf above.

"Brat!" said Anni once she spotted him. "Why were you curled up in a ball? I needed you." She tried to get up. Unsteady, she clutched the table. "Oh, I don't feel well—"

"Course not! You're mopple-toppined," said Brat. "You didn't DeFunkify. You brought Funk with you from the human realm. Take Squirt's tonic if you want to feel better. Funk won't go away by itself, you've got gobs on you. It'll only get worse, and you don't have time to be messing about. You should have eaten that candy bar Egbert gave you."

"Hey, how did you know about that candy bar? I thought you were asleep." The contents of the mug wafted up into Anni's nostrils. She coughed looking at the swirls of green and silver. "Eggs. Seriously, I'm not being rude, but I can't drink this."

"Pinch your nose," said Squirt. "Your Funk makes it smell worse than it is. Please. You have to. I promised Yugi I'd make you better."

"What's Funk?" Her eyes were watering, as pressure surged in her temple while a high-pitched ringing sound started up in her left ear. A second later, it felt like someone was hammering a chisel into her forehead.

"Nasty business, Funk!" Brat frowned. "It floats around in the ether, like a shadow of negativity that sticks to energy fields of living things. It's like gum in your hair unless you learn how to get rid of it. Elementals fight the Funk every day."

Anni frowned at him. "I don't have an energy field."

"Yes you do. All living things have energy fields. It surrounds your physical body. Even thoughts, or ideas, can grow a life force. Humans call it an aura." Anni scowled. Brat shook his finger. "The world is not made up of everything you can or cannot see, Anni Moon. Make no mistake. Moppins, now where was I? Oh, Funk, imagine the tiniest thought or idea drifting about in the air. If it is a negative, hateful, fearful or worrying thought, it's looking to find another one just like it. Evil thoughts are the strongest; they work like magnets, clustering together with other thoughts until they turn into Funk; it breeds, compounds, and spreads across realms, where it infects all manner of things. Humans are oblivious to Funk, which is convenient since they create most of it. How your lot can be so blind is anyone's guess!" Brat threw up his arms and shook his head. "Funk dulls your mind, coats your energy field, like a bubble of grime; it is absolutely disgusting. Elementals have to mind the Funk. It can kill us if we don't. We call it *the slow death*."

"Gross! I look like a bubble of grime? Can anything stop it?"

"Younger humans have stronger energy fields. Adult humans always look grimy to us," said Brat. "Human cities are infested with Funk. And now it's stuck to you."

"Great," said Anni, who pinched her nose and gulped Squirt's tonic down.

"Oh! I almost forgot!" Squirt darted across the room to one of the tallest and dustiest bookshelves. When he found what he needed, he raced back and handed Anni a small book titled *Mind Your Funk and Get Funktastic! Human Edition.*

"This book will help. Brat's right—Funk is serious. We fight the Funk every day here on the Zephyr. That's why we take tonics, elixirs, tinctures, potions, and a healthy number of baths." Looking thrilled, Squirt rolled onto the balls of his feet and said, "So? How'd it taste? Give me every detail. You're my first Funkified human."

"Uh," said Anni, staring back at him, speechless. It was hard to describe, but instantly she felt the pain begin to siphon away like water being sucked from a straw. She didn't know where it was going, but she felt a sensation trickle from the crown of her head, over her face, down her neck and shoulders, torso, legs, and strangely, out the tips of her toes. It took a moment to take stock of how she felt because other than a low-grade headache, she felt a million times better than she had two seconds ago. Lighter than she ever felt before.

"Strange," Anni said. "It was like water washing away dirt." Squirt frowned.

"Like I said, mopple-toppined." Brat shrugged. "Her taste buds are kerfuffled."

A flood of questions surged like new, clean blood pumping through her veins, and she blurted out, "Who's Yugi, and where am I?"

"You don't listen, do you?" Brat folded his arms. "You're in the Wood Realm."

"Is that on a map? It's not like I even know what Elementals are!"

"She doesn't know?" Squirt's face fell as he turned from Anni to Brat. "That is *so* not cool, mate. You need to tell her."

"For Elementals' sake, my job description does *not* include human acclimation." Brat harrumphed. "Oh, very well then." Brat turned to Anni. "Elementals are a race of beings whose souls are connected to the elements: Earth, Water, Wood, Fire, and Metal. We are the oldest living things on this planet, and other E-systems, planets, but never mind that. Some look like humans, and some don't. Some look like animals, or insects, or what humans call aliens, but it's very important to note: Elementals are not born like humans—we aren't born with bellybuttons. Our gestation is a creation of the mind. We are born through the process of intention." Anni frowned. "Moppins! Try wishing then, but that's not the right word. Elemental parents mentally and emotionally create life by will, until an Elemental is born. Okay, moving on. We don't travel as humans do. Some Elkins live in human cities, but the rest live in dimensions that are half a degree lighter than the human realm—where we can see you even if you can't see us, just like where we are now. There, that should suffice."

Brat cleared his throat. "It must be why Egbert sent you here. You're on a Zephyr; a floating island, to be precise. We are about seven rings over the United Kingdom, which, by the way, is impossible to travel to without an E-pass! Moppins, if I knew we'd be traveling here by Queen's Mirror, I wouldn't have stowed away in your pocket, because now we can't leave!"

"What?" Anni felt the blood drain from her face. "Above England? Oh, no! How? Eggs! *Egbert!* He tricked me! And so did you! You've met Lexi before, haven't you?"

"Yes," said Brat. "So what? That's not a crime. I've delivered messages to Teddy, too, but those are confidential, so don't even ask. Never mind. We're both stuck here unless you can find a legal way off the Zephyr. Moppins, there's no use complaining. What's done is done. You need to get a move on! They're expecting you at Moon Manor as we speak."

"No. Wait. Brat, I did you a favor. You have to help me get out of here. Please."

"If I could, I'm not sure I would. You don't listen very well and you don't follow directions. Moppins, you're not the only one in this kerfuffle. I'm stuck here, too!"

"What do you mean? Eggs! Isn't this your home?"

"Tee hee hee. You're funny," said Squirt, giggling.

Anni stopped to look at Squirt. "Er, thanks." She turned back to Brat. "What about Lexi? Is she here? Did they arrive yet?"

Squirt stopped giggling. Brat looked down and said, "Lexi's not here."

"Are you sure? Like, one hundred percent positive? Because she could—"

"I searched the Zephyr while you slept. She's not here, at least not yet." Brat wrung his tiny hands. "Moppins...Elofficials will want to speak with me about that. The Fleet has me on record as the last Elemental who delivered her a message—"

"You didn't. Teddy did. He sent her a package—" The words flew out before she realized it. "*Eggs!* I didn't say that! You didn't hear that."

"Tee hee hee. Ha ha ha ha!"

They both looked at Squirt and said, "What?" in unison.

"You're a human and you said *eggs*," said Squirt, fit to burst.

"So?" said Anni. "I heard someone say that once, and it stuck."

"About that." Brat frowned. "Elementals, not all, use the word *egg* in combination with other choice words, when they refer to humans. It's considered a vile description in certain circles. Funk makes humans smell like rotten eggs to Elementals—that and adult humans' energy fields, which are disconnected and aren't used properly, have withered into egg like bubbles constantly knocking them in the head. Humans don't even notice."

"Right," said Anni. "So you're sure Lexi's not here? It could take hours to fly to England, especially if they left after I did...wait a second. How did I get from the plane to a floating island? It didn't land. I walked into the bathroom and..."

"Oh, let me tell," said Squirt, beaming. "It's an awesome story! All Elemental travel uses some form of wood, and you traveled here by *Queen's Mirror*, which is way beyond cool. Amazing, really. See, it's a mirror with a special wooden frame that you can walk through and then, boom, you're wherever you're meant to be. The best part is that no one knows where you're traveling to or from but you. The Elofficium have no idea. Queen's Mirrors are rare; Elementals can go their whole lives without ever seeing one, but I did!"

"If I got here that way, how do we know Lexi didn't, too?"

"It all comes down to Funk." Brat shook his finger. "If she did, her Funk would've hit the Zephyr. Only I'm not sure the Zephyr could take another hit like the one that followed you. Another blast like that might dislodge it from the sky. It's exactly why the Zephyr's crawling with Elofficials; they are looking for the source of the Funk, which means you. If you don't get to Moon Manor and surrender yourself before the Elofficials find you, they will throw you in the Egghouse. And me next!"

"So you're sure Lexi's not here, then?"

"Moppins, unless she's an Elemental. Then we wouldn't know."

"Yeah. Right. I think I'd know if my best friend in the entire world wasn't human, thanks, and I'm pretty sure she has a belly-button." But, for the first time, Anni wasn't so sure and started to wonder if Lexi knew about this world. After all, Teddy and Mabel did. "Brat, we have to go back and find her. How can we get one of those mirror thingies?"

"Has the Funk damaged your brain?" Brat huffed. "And your hearing? That was a one-way trip. For El'snozzing sakes, traveling through a Queen's Mirror means *there is no record of our travel!* Egbert didn't get you an E-pass to travel here the normal way, which means you and I are here on this Zephyr illegally! And if the Elofficium or the Fleet find out, my First Order Elservice Messengers of Messages Badge will be stripped for life, and for the cherry on top, I'd be tossed into the Bughouse all because of you!" Brat shook his head.

"He's right," said Squirt. "Queen's Mirrors are definitely not Elofficium approved. Don't worry, though. Only a few of us know how you got here, and we won't say a word. The bad news is that the Elofficials are after someone, but no one, and I mean no one, travels to a Zephyr that way, so they won't even suspect that's how you arrived."

"Wait. Were *they* the ones who were after me and Lexi at school?"

"Someone was after you in the human realm?" asked Squirt.

"Yes. At my school. Two people were talking about kidnapping Lexi and me. They had our names and our school pictures. Why is this happening?"

"Hmm, well, I can't pretend that I don't hear things in my line of work, but there were rumors circulating around about the Murdrock takeover," said Brat, looking severe. "Don't hold me to this, but I have reason to believe Teddy knew something was afoot. The only logical reason why someone would want to get to Lexi, or you I suppose, is if they thought you two had information about Teddy, and if that's true, then that's very bad."

"Oh, you think," said Anni, "someone *was* after us. I didn't imagine it. I told Egbert, and he acted like I was being stupid. I think he was covering something up. What about these Elofficials? Could they be the ones after us?"

"That's highly unlikely," said Brat. "All human travel to Elemental realms requires an E-pass and proof of DeFunkification, which takes six months. Squirt's right: you're not in their log, and they don't even know your name." Brat looked between them.

"Your Funk bought us time," said Squirt. "They've been busy rebalancing the Zephyr." Squirt animatedly acted out as he spoke. "It was hilarious. Like a wave hit us. Bam! Electricity—POW! Static blew everyone's hair straight up. Boing! Mine's still up. Then a gust of the rotten eggs hit us. Stinky! Some Elementals nearly passed out." He chortled. "Cleaning crews are everywhere. Even Miranda tripped. Jay said it was priceless."

The corners of Anni's mouth lifted as she tried to imagine it.

"I wouldn't be so pleased," said Brat. "If you actually followed my instructions, we wouldn't be here." He looked like he was feeling sorry for himself. "This is a snozdoddle-sized mess. If the Elofficium arrest us, we won't see Lexi until we get out."

"Yugi's place cloaked your Funk, but our time's up," said Squirt. "We—"

The piercing sound of a strangled bird echoed outside. Squirt raced to the window and pulled the curtains aside. Anni followed him.

Through the branches, in a clear patch of light, a flock of birds flew in a V formation. They dropped eighty feet in a matter of seconds, maneuvering like nothing she'd seen before. "Whoa," said Anni with a gulp. "Is it bad?"

"Oh Moppins! Here we go!"

"No," said Squirt. "It's worse."

CHAPTER 18

DAPHNE

It wasn't birds but a gang of kids who pierced holes through puffy clouds. Their leader disengaged from the pack and headed down to Yugi's deck, with something kicking and screaming over his shoulder.

"Quick! Hide by that door," said Squirt, looking up at the sky. "Trust me. You don't want them to see you. Half of them have Elofficials for parents. I don't know why they're here, but if they land on the deck, open that door and run downstairs. I'll follow."

Anni moved to the door close to the window and peeked through the shade, watching the group of teenagers in the sky overhead. "How are they doing that?"

"Skurfing? It's like skateboarding and surfing the air currents. Can only do that around Zephyrs, not in the Noos—sorry, I mean human cities. Funk destroys the air; it would knock them out of the sky. It looks cool, but it's not. Makes me puke. That's why I'll never be a Wood Elemental. Whispering to the wind and all that stuff, I can't do it."

"Would it get me off the Zephyr?"

"I seriously don't recommend it, but you could try," said Squirt.

"Don't fill her brain with nonsense," huffed Brat. "Skurfing won't get you off the Zephyr. I would know. LimBough is the only way to catch a TreeTransport if you really want to leave. That's how we Elementals travel. The Orb over the Lake will take you straight to LimBough, but you'd still need an E-pass and an Opus Stone to cross the bridge."

"I can't wait to get my Opus Stone," said Squirt.

"Hey. I know that guy," said Anni, looking at the guy hovering over Yugi's deck.

"That's Jay," said Squirt. "He was there when you arrived. He's cool."

"James Bartholomew Xavier, *put me down now!* " yelled a girl at the top of her lungs, her long, dark hair covering her face. "I don't have time for your games."

"Aww, come on, *Floppy*," said Jay to the girl, who bucked and squirmed on his shoulder. "That wasn't nice. You know the rules about name sharing. Hey, Squirt." Jay waved and seamlessly managed the girl onto the deck without messing up his wild red-orange hair. "There you go, Flopster. Delivered as promised!"

"You're a jerk! Stop calling me that!" The girl's curtain of black hair covered her face as she pointed at him. "I told you over the grass, not the sky."

"Where's the fun in that?" Jay smirked. He winked at Anni and said, "You're welcome, *Daphne*. See you later."

Daphne harrumphed and turned her back as Jay soared up into the sky to meet his friends. She bent her head forward to give it a little shake and whipped her long black hair into a high ponytail. Anni noticed Daphne had two long silver strands hidden in her black mane just over her right temple.

Daphne turned to Squirt and said, "Can you get us out of here unseen?"

"No problem. She's ready to go. Right, Anni?"

"Oh," said Daphne, turning red. "I didn't see you there. Sorry you had to see me get so angry. Jay's annoying, but I can say that, he's my third cousin." She thrust her hand. "I'm Daphne Kim, by the way. Nice to meet you. Sorry to rush you, but we need to go. The Elofficials are doing a house-to-house search. How's your Funk?"

"I like her style," said Brat. "Straight to business."

87

Daphne moved in closer, and sniffed. "Headache?" she asked, spritzing the air around Anni with something that smelled of lavender and salt.

Anni waved her hand and coughed. "Yeah. It comes and goes."

"For snozdoddles' sake! You'll never get to the Manor at this rate," said Brat.

Daphne turned to Squirt and handed him a rolled piece of parchment. "Yugi said if she has the slightest headache to follow these instructions exactly. Can you do it quick? We should have left already. Krizia expected us an hour ago."

Squirt chuckled. "Krizia will give anyone a headache."

Daphne shot him a look. "Don't worry, Anni, Krizia's not that bad."

Squirt coughed something under his breath that sounded like "liar" as he raced back to his cluttered worktable and studiously referenced Yugi's list.

"Do you know if my friend Lexi arrived? Is she with Egbert?"

"I'm not sure if she's here," said Daphne. "Actually, I don't know Egbert, but after I read about an early Elemental death date and a stolen artifact, I heard you were coming."

It was the same news story Anni had seen in Headmistress Turnkey's office, the same one that claimed Teddy Waterstone was dead. She wasn't going to start that discussion. Too painful. "Did Yugi speak with Egbert?"

"I was with Yugi," said Daphne, "when Van's sister, Zelda—"

"Zelda? You know Zelda?"

"Actually, no, but I know Van. He's Krizia's husband. She runs Moon Manor, well, Krizia's in charge of Moon Zephyr. Egbert didn't tell you any of this?"

"Egbert never tells me anything. I shouldn't have trusted him."

Squirt rushed over with a new mug, filled with an even darker liquid that truly looked like dirt. "Here," he said to Anni. "You can't meet Krizia until you drink this."

Anni took the new mug and gulped it down. She made a face. "If this Krizia person is Egbert's friend, I'll pass on meeting her." She turned to Daphne. "Please, just tell me how to get off this floating Zephyr island thingy. I have to find Lexi."

Daphne turned pale. Squirt grinned. They said, "*Nofcourse*," a combo of Daphne's "No" and Squirt's "Of course."

Daphne turned to Squirt, red-faced. "You can't help any more than I can. Why would you make a promise like that?" She looked out the window and gasped.

Anni followed her gaze and peeked through the shade. Two extremely tall people wearing long black cloaks, each with big gold badges on their left shoulders, strode across the lawn toward Yugi's place.

"Els! We have to go. Now! They're coming." Daphne turned to Anni. "If they catch you before you get to the Manor, you'll be—"

"Tossed in the bughouse," said Brat.

"Or worse. In the *Egghouse*," said Squirt.

"Language, Squirt. It's not so simple," Daphne said quickly. "A lot was done to get you here, and I can't undo it. Your Funk, well…if they catch you, you will be locked up for a minimum of six months. It's imperative that I take you to the Manor. You'll be safe there. A lot of people could get into trouble if you don't. Besides, your vouchers, the people who will look out for you while you're here, are waiting for you at the Manor. They have E-passes for you and your friend Lexi. We need to leave now; otherwise, I can't help you."

"They're expecting Lexi? They have a pass for the both of us?"

Daphne nodded.

"Fine," said Anni. "Let's get this over with."

"At last!" said Brat. "Don't dawdle. The sooner you get sorted, so will I."

Squirt ushered the girls to Yugi's front door. They stopped when they saw the shadows of the Elofficials darken Yugi's frosted window. Anni stared at the wooden coffered walls. Was this a trap?

"This way," said Squirt. He pushed on a wall panel, and a door opened. They passed through a passage, which led into a magnificent garden shed. "Phew. That was close."

Shed was the wrong word. *Garden museum* or *ballroom* was a better description. Beautiful glass cupboards lined the walls, filled with garden tools and instruments displayed like objects of art. Anni realized this was the room she'd entered into the Elemental world. There was the glossy, round oak table where Leo had sat hours ago, just before she had passed through the Queen's Mirror, but there was no mirror in sight.

"Over here," Squirt said, standing in front of a cabinet in the far corner with a broken door, which bore a sign that said, *Caution—Broken*.

"Can you take us to the hothouse?" said Daphne. "It's the shortest walk."

"No problem." He pulled the sign away. "Anni, take my hand. And don't let go."

Anni took his hand and they were plunged into total darkness. The tunnel was misty and a strange smell of burned hair wafted around her head. When they exited, they were inside yet another shed, which was small and cramped.

"Let me make sure it's clear," said Daphne.

Daphne exited first. Squirt followed. They were in the middle of a large garden next to a massive building that looked strangely familiar. Anni needed to do a double take. Whoa! All that this building was missing was the pink paint. Moon Manor was an exact replica of Mabel's old apartment building, the Edgewater, but how could that be? Things were getting weird. Was this the final proof that Mabel was an Elemental?

"Oh," Daphne gasped, staring at Anni's head. "What did you do, Squirt?"

Squirt looked from Daphne to Anni. His eyes popped wide.

"Oh, no," said Squirt. Daphne stood speechless. "I did it again! What did I do wrong?" Squirt paced, murmuring something that sounded like a list of ingredients.

Anni grabbed a few strands of hair. It took a second to realize what she was seeing. "My hair was brown. Now it's red. I look like Bozo the clown."

"Is that good? Does Bozo have rainbow-colored hair?" asked Squirt.

"Eggs! Squirt, is my hair more than one color?"

"Well, yeah," said Squirt. "Um, but it's pretty. It'll be better when it stops changing colors so fast. Don't be mad, I'm sure it's a side effect from the Funk." Squirt pulled out Yugi's instructions, read, and reread them carefully. "I did all that…what did I miss?"

"Can I see?" asked Daphne, taking the parchment. The very bottom of the scroll was folded and, concealed in the crease, was the last part of Yugi's instructions, which said:

*_**Be sure to add all above first, and then stir with aurum spoon.
Otherwise dissipation will occur through hair follicles._*

Squirt saw the fold and clapped a hand to his forehead. "Oh no! No, no, no, no!"

"That means the Funk," said Daphne, "is trapped in your follicles."

"I'm so sorry, Anni," said Squirt, jumping to his feet. "Why did Yugi trust me? I'm a total failure. I should resign my Earth studies. I'm not fit to be an Elemental. I'll never get my Opus Stone, or be a real Elemental. It's hopeless." He plopped to the ground in despair.

"We don't have time for this," Daphne whispered to Anni. She put her arm around Squirt. "You are an Elemental, and of course you'll get your Opus Stone. Don't be so silly."

"Yeah," said Anni. "Lexi's more important than my hair. It's...whatever."

"Really?" Squirt jumped to his feet. "Really, Anni? I won't let you down again. I'll do whatever it takes to make it up to you. I promise. I'll help you get back to Chicago, and then we can eat Swiss cheese."

"Okay," said Anni, hitching up her backpack, thinking only of Lexi.

They trudged across the lawn toward the Manor. With each step, the grass shriveled under Anni's feet. Once they crossed Moon Manor's threshold, an invisible force field blasted all three of them off their feet and onto their backsides.

Grass started to rot underneath them. She could smell it, but she couldn't move. By the look of it, neither could Daphne or Squirt.

"PURPOSE?" The question bellowed in the air as four blurry, semi-opaque shapes hovered over them.

In a different voice, someone cackled, "Lookie 'ere, mates, I fink we caught ourselves a reekin' little Eggwit and her two accomplices."

CHAPTER 19

MOON MANOR

Anni couldn't move. Her eyes darted everywhere, looking for an escape. She started to feel dizzy and see black spots. There was nowhere to go. These had to be Elofficium guards. She was done for.

"Very funny, Knox," said Daphne. "I know it's you. We really don't have time for this. Krizia knows we're coming."

"Whether I am 'oo you fink I am, that ain't the point. I can't let a stinkin' Eggwit reekin' of Funk in the Manor without an E-pass. Krizia's orders."

"Anni has an E-pass. It's inside. I'm sure Krizia wouldn't mind bringing it down for you. Should I go and get her? I'm sure she's not too busy for that."

"Uh, nah need for that. Fritz, Biancah, eyes on 'em two," said Knox as he physically materialized along with three other guards, all four dressed like traditional Beefeaters. Knox pointed at Daphne and Squirt. "Fort and I'll take the Eggwit in."

Knox nudged Anni. He was as mean as he was ugly, and his hands were clammy, too. She glanced back at Daphne and Squirt, but neither of them looked encouraging.

As Fort and Knox frog-marched Anni into the Manor, she was shocked to see that the building's exterior was a replica of the Edgewater. Even the atrium's lobby interior held similarities to Mabel's apartment building, minus the Elemental flourishes. Real flowers covered every inch of the walls. The honey-chocolate-hued floor spelled something out in golden sparkles under their feet.

"Welcome Minder Knox, Welcome Minder Fort, Welcome Anni Moon."

Knox pushed her onto a floating silver disk. The fluffy, cloud escalator raised three stories, but there were no handrails. Certain she'd fall through and plummet to the ground, she didn't notice when they reached the top.

Fort left them in front of two enormous doors covered in intricate carvings she couldn't read. Knox opened them and shoved Anni inside. The room was so vast, it had at least twelve Persian rugs from one end of the room to the other. A woman sat at a large desk at the farthest end of the room. Anni couldn't make out the woman's face; there was a long queue of people waiting a turn to see her. She assumed the woman was Krizia.

Once Anni entered, there wasn't a welcome reception. Almost all of the queued Elementals turned to look at her, with scowls, and some didn't even look human. Half of the crowd could pass as people, but the rest were animals, standing upright, and a mixture of insects and aliens, dressed in clothes. Nevertheless, nearly all of them glared at her and several pinched their noses, while a few hissed, scoffed, and tittered.

Anni sniffed her arm and started to wonder how bad she actually smelled. Without much consideration, she made her way toward the line.

"Oh no, you don't. Come here," said Knox, pulling her out of the queue and toward a small desk mounted with so much paper, Anni could barely see the person behind. "Ah, Verity, funny seein' you 'ere."

Verity's lips pursed. "What do you want, Knox?"

"Half a mo, Verity, 'cause that's another chinwag entirely." His face split into a broad smile and revealed several silver-capped teeth. "Nah, if you wanna chat about our lil' date, you know the one—the one you asked me fer, the one that we ain't 'ad time ter schedule."

"Knox," said Verity, tapping her fingers. "You're here because?"

"It's wot I've got 'ere that matters." Knox chuckled to himself. "I'm sure you'll find it 'ilaaarious. But I've bin told, by an unreliable source, mind, that you've bin expectin' this lil' Eggwit. I have the right mind to giver 'er to the Elofficials."

Anni flinched when a tall man entered the room behind Knox. This man was dressed in a long gray cloak and top hat; it was the same uniform the Elofficials were wearing when they approached outside Yugi's door. Was she caught? Verity appeared relieved to see this man, but Knox didn't notice and assumed her smile was for him.

Knox winked at the secretary. "Course, if yer interested in a lil' cuppa now, I could bunk off and toss 'er in the Egghouse wif the other nutters—"

"Not necessary," said the tall, well-dressed man. "You may return to your post."

"Leach—Maeleachlainn, oh-uh, I mean, Mr. Spongincork…Sir, 'twas—"

"Take your leave," said Maeleachlainn Spongincork with a look that Anni thought was a sneer until she got a glimpse at his whole face. She shuddered. A scar in the shape of a hook slashed across his left cheek. She wanted to run from the room.

"Maeleachlainn, I should warn you," said Verity, tilting her head toward the desk at the other end of the room as she handed him papers and a tablet. "Krizia's in a mood."

"Indeed," said Spongincork. He followed her gaze and the long line of impatient Elementals waiting until finally, his eyes settled on Anni. "Box the Funk."

With a swish of his cloak, Maeleachlainn Spongincork strode to the other end of the room to join Krizia. Anni looked at the secretary. Verity rolled her eyes and, with an unapologetic shrug, pressed a white button on the side of her desk.

There was no warning. A clear rectangular box rose up from the floor and surrounded Anni. It sealed itself around her with only a few inches to spare above her head and shoulders. She panicked and started breathing harder, afraid she'd suffocate. She grabbed her key necklace with one hand and pounded against the transparent enclosure with the other. Nobody paid her any attention.

"*Relax, Child,*" said Whiffle sleepily. "*Save your strength. They cannot hear you. You're not going to expire. Just. Breathe.*"

"Whiffle?" Anni gasped. "How'd you…did you have something to do with this?"

94

He didn't reply. She slumped to the floor. Cold air was rushing in from the bottom.

To Anni's shock, Finnegan strolled into the room, as cool as can be. She jumped up and screamed his name. No one turned. No one heard her. Finnegan walked past Anni without even a glance in her direction. She couldn't believe it when he jumped the queue. What was going on here? If all these people were Elementals, did that mean that Finnegan was one, too? He sure looked comfortable. It dawned on her that nearly everyone she knew was acquainted with the world of Elementals—everyone but her.

She had no idea how much time passed; it could have been hours. Different Elementals, mostly animals dressed in clothes, came and went; several stared at her like an animal at the zoo. When the queue was down to a handful of Elementals, two new people entered the room: a short, older man and a young woman.

The young woman looked upset while speaking to Verity, pointing in her direction, but Anni couldn't hear what they were saying. The young woman was plainly dressed in a beige sheath, her long, dark hair was neatly braided, and she waved at Anni with a gentle and modest smile, which, apart from Squirt or Daphne, made her the friendliest person on the Zephyr.

Beneath his square cut glasses, the short man wore a patient expression. He looked familiar. Anni remembered that he was Yugi. A large satchel hung over his shoulder. It overflowed with a variety of grasses, sticks, and long tubers, and his boots had spare bits of sod stuck between the spiked tips. His hands were sheathed in strong, fibrous work gloves that held two distinctive tickets with the words *E-pass* written boldly on the paper.

The newcomers waited in chairs next to Verity's desk for Krizia. The young woman was the first of the two to walk toward the other end of the room. Her meeting was brief, and she waved at Anni before she left the room. Yugi's meeting was just as short as the young woman's, but he didn't wave to Anni when he left.

Annoyed, Anni couldn't help but wonder how much longer she had to wait inside the insidious box. At long last, Verity approached and Anni thought she might be able to get out. Verity placed her palm over the box's surface and shrugged again.

The bottom of the box rose two inches off the floor. A surge of air, like a turbo jet revving up its engines, built up pressure beneath the box, making it rattle and creak. It blasted forward. The force slammed Anni backward as the box headed straight for Krizia's desk. It was going too fast. It wasn't going to stop. Anni screamed. It slammed to a halt.

Anni rubbed her nose. All she could think about were bugs on car windshields. As she pushed aside strands of her flashy hair, she felt an unexpected smile spread across her face. At first glance, the woman sitting at the desk looked like Vivian Sugar, then Anni's smile vanished. A plaque on the desk read Ornella Krizia. Upon closer inspection, she knew she wasn't Vivian. Krizia had a pulled face, exaggerated by her severe bun.

But Krizia took no notice of Anni. She reviewed stacks of papers next to the scar-faced man who Verity had called Maeleachlainn, who had ordered Anni to be *boxed*. They acted as if she wasn't there. When Krizia finally glanced up, her lip twitched. Her gaze was penetrating and unpleasant. "You will forgive the box, human. The Manor's Funkometer has reached our daily limit," Krizia raised her hand and said, "You may speak now."

Anni cleared her throat. "Um, is Lexi here?"

Krizia stared at her for a long moment. She pulled the E-pass from her desk and said, "You are Anni Moon, yes? And, Alexa Waterstone is this Lexi you are referring to?" Anni nodded, "You were to arrive together. Can you explain where she is?"

"I...I don't know." Anni's voice cracked. "Egbert said he was bringing her—"

"My sister-in-law, Zelda Scurryfunge, explained that Mabel Moon and Teddy Waterstone were you and your friend's previous guardians?" Anni nodded. Krizia scarcely took a breath before she paused to scrutinize Anni. "I wonder… what do you think has happened to your so-called friend?" Krizia's gaze was paralyzing. "I suppose you don't read *The V.O.I.C.E.*"

A projected newspaper flashed a bluish hue a foot in front of Anni's face. It was exactly the same holographic newspaper Anni had seen when she opened the desk drawer in the Headmistress's office. The news article looked just like the one she had read about Teddy, except this time, there was a school photo of Lexi.

THE VOICE - ELEMENTAL NEWS, WORLD NEWS & OPINION

Editor-in-Chief:
Verbum Smith

THE V.O.I.C.E.

Saturday, June 2
County Fleet

THE VIRTUAL OMNINAVIGATIONAL INCLUSIVE CONNECTING ELEMENTALS

NEWS   OPINION   E2   BUSINESS   ARTS

WATERSTONE KIDNAPPED...

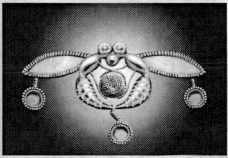

Kidnapping Rumors Surface in the Waterstone's Case

OpEd By: PENELOPE W. POTBOILER

The Elofficium confirmed that Theodore Waterstone's charge, Alexa Waterstone, student at Waterstone Academy for Girls, Chicago IL, was kidnapped Saturday, June 2nd. This report was authenticated just 24 hours after Teddy Waterstone's early death date was announced. The Elofficium have a short list of suspects. Sources suggest that they are looking at *Moon* family members.

Alexa Waterstone, thirteen years old, was last seen at Waterstone Academy (currently under acquisition by the philanthropic Murdrock Family) on the morning of Saturday, June the 2nd. Waterstone Academy, one of a few highly regarded private Elemental/ human educational establishments in North America, was in good standing with the Elofficium until they discovered that there was no record of classification for Alexa Waterstone. Lacking proof as to whether the child was human or Elemental goes directly against Section #3353 of Elofficium Rulings and Regulations. A school spokesman, Vivian Sugar, declined to comment.

Whether the Fectus are responsible for the kidnapping, Elofficials will not issue a statement until a thorough investigation has been completed. If true, then Alexa Waterstone's fate is far worse than her departed uncle's.

If Alexa Waterstone is an Elemental, is she related to the Moon family? If so, who are/were her parents? Does the kidnapping have anything to do with the priceless Elemental artifact? Or is this an extension of a family curse?

The Moon family has had its historical share of great privilege and power as well as tragedy; however, Mabel Moon's role in the devastating events that led up to June 21st, thirteen years ago, known as The Great Catastrophe,* coupled with recent events, have left members of the Elemental community questioning if the Moon family is in fact cursed.

The Great Catastrophe was not only defined by a failed prophecy, compounded by the massive loss of Elemental lives, but as the devastating reminder of the last Elemental birth. Although Elementalkind may well be on its way to extinction, this report should be a reminder to you, my dear readers, that our lives, all our lives, are very precious and that we must be vigilant in the protection of our youth, for they are the very last of our kind.

*A Moon Manor representative issued a statement that a memorial anniversary will take place in August.

CHAPTER 20

DOWN THE CHUTE

A nni didn't want to believe Lexi had been kidnapped. There had to be some mistake. Egbert said Zelda had found her, didn't he? Krizia's voice echoed in the distance, saying something about the *Fectus* being responsible, whatever they were. Anni felt numb all over thinking about the line, "If true, then Alexa Waterstone's fate is far worse than her departed uncle." This meant only one thing: Lexi's life was in danger—or worse. Only, Anni didn't know what could be worse.

"Clearly, you cannot provide further information. I will report our meeting to the Elofficium so that they will not detain you or take you into custody." Krizia scribbled a note. She continued to speak without looking up. "As such, I will grant you temporary clearance to reside on this Zephyr for the duration of six months, by which time other plans will be made for you to travel back to wherever it is that you came from."

"*No!*" Anni found her voice at last. "I need to go home. I need to find Lexi."

Krizia squinted. "She's my family! I have to find her. Egbert is looking for her. He knows where she is. You need to send me back now."

Krizia whisked her index finger in the air. There was something about her manner that strongly reminded Anni of Egbert.

"Miss Moon," Krizia said with a fierce stare. "You have jumped the Elemental residency queue by six months; for humans, this is simply unheard of. Consider yourself fortunate that my sister requested I allow you clearance to stay on Moon Zephyr. I am a very busy woman, and your arrival has completely exasperated my schedule due to the excessive levels of Funk you brought with you. In fact, Elofficials are roaming the village right now looking for you." Krizia paused to look at Anni's hair. "Judging by your appearance—it is clear that your guardian, Egbert, has not seen fit to acquaint you with our ways. Therefore, this tedious task falls upon our already engaged shoulders."

Krizia secured her glasses and scribbled another note. "As such, we are duty bound to maintain your well-being while you are with us. You have been granted three vouchers for the duration of your stay. Mr. Maeleachlainn Spongincork here, is one of them." Anni didn't find him friendly. "He has seen to your lodgings at Spadu Hills; it's the only part of the Zephyr that can withstand your levels of Funk. Mr. Spongincork has seen to your work detail, as well. Yugi San will attend to your Funk and, lastly, Diana will assist with your general acclimation. You may direct all questions to her, but be advised, she's an extremely busy woman, as well, so keep your questions short." Krizia looked down to scribble another note. "You would do well to follow our rules. The alternatives are not agreeable, not even for an Elemental. That's all. You may go."

Anni had no words. Somehow, this Elemental world didn't feel too different from Waterstone Academy, except that Krizia was a whole lot scarier than Egbert.

The air below her feet started to stir again. It sucked at her legs like a vacuum, and a creaking noise rippled inside the box. Earthy smells wafted upward. A billowing gust of steamy air filled the transparent cell, turning it into a muddy gray cloud.

Without warning the floor beneath her vanished. Under her feet, dozens of chutes moved in every direction with colorful items flashing out of view; Anni swore she saw a carrot. Her ankles wobbled as she pinned them against the sides of the box.

Anni looked up. Spongincork stood beside the cell. When he touched the box, a slot opened, large enough for a small business card to pass through. The card winged its way into her shirt pocket. Spongincork's hand hovered over the spot that Verity had touched earlier. Anni shook her head pleadingly. He grinned and returned to the desk beside Krizia.

The transparent cell-box started to crackle. Like a paper bag being squished from the top, it started to collapse in on itself. Anni's eyes darted everywhere looking for help, but none was to be found. Suddenly, at the far side of the room, the double doors to Krizia's office opened. Egbert Frode Moon walked in, alone.

Desperate to talk to him, Anni beat against the box's crackling walls. However, the box crumpled into the office's floor, taking her with it—and poof, she was gone.

Somewhere inside Moon Manor, Crisp, the new cook's apprentice, cradled a large silver bowl over the compost chute. Once he opened the bin's lid, a whooshing cry rattled against the metal slide, and he spotted two huge brown eyes peering back at him. He yelled. The thing in the chute yelled. The boy jerked. His bowl of scraps shot into the air and landed on his head.

Meanwhile, outside and behind Moon Manor, Daphne and Squirt moved toward the compost yard, encircled by a low brick fence.

"Where's Anni?" asked Squirt.

Daphne raised her shoulders and bit her lip. "Yugi said to meet her here."

Squirt peered over the brick wall and lifted a bruised banana peel, trying his hardest to stifle a giggle. "Funk aside, this stinks more than Anni."

Daphne eyed the piled heaps. "You shouldn't make jokes."

POUND. CLANK. THUMP.

POUND. CLANK. THUMP.

POUND. CLANK. THWACK.

The sounds of screeching metal reverberated off the building and trees. Daphne and Squirt both looked up.

"AAAAAHHHHHHH."

Two stories above, a blur of black and neon streaked over their heads. It landed on top of a pile of dried lettuce leaves, instantly disintegrating into brown dust, leaving a pair of black-and-white-striped socks sticking out from under the mire of lifeless vegetation. Anni's backpack tumbled out last and landed by Daphne and Squirt's feet, unsullied.

"Anni?" Squirt called out.

"Not funny now, huh?" asked Daphne and waded into the muck first.

Squirt followed. They managed to uncover Anni's arms and legs and remove most of the scraps clinging to her body. But her hair, ever unlucky, was coated in a greenish slime that neither of them dared to touch.

It took longer to locate her shoes, which had slipped off inside the chute. Anni was not a lot of help, which was why Squirt and Daphne hooked her arms around their necks and dragged her into a clearing.

Speechless, they all sat on a patch of dry grass. Daphne and Squirt pulled bits of carrot, potatoes, and banana away from each other's clothes. Their eyes shifted toward Anni every few seconds, concerned she wasn't moving or speaking.

Anni stared off into the distance like she was in a trance. After a few minutes, she cleared her throat. "I was just…dumped…down the garbage chute!"

Squirt didn't smile or laugh, and his staunch expression looked wholly unnatural.

Anni frowned at them. "Why is all this happening? What is this crazy place? Who are you people? First you turn my hair crazy colors, then you send me into a building where people treat me like…like I'm some kind of…I don't know the word! And dumped me down a garbage chute…"

She took a series of deep breaths. "What's worse, what's terrible, is that my best friend in the whole world has been kidnapped! Lexi's like a sister, the only family I have left, and she's gone! She was in your news! It said her fate was worse than Teddy's because the Fectus have her! I don't even know what that means!"

"*Oh no,*" said Daphne, wide-eyed, making Anni feel sick.

"Egbert's up there, I saw him, but I don't know if he saw me! Now I'm stuck here for six months before I can leave, but I can't stay! I have to go. How am I supposed to find Lexi while I'm trapped here? It's all my fault. My fault. I should have made Lexi tell me what was bothering her. I didn't know. I didn't know. I should have listened to Egbert and stayed with Lexi the entire time, like I said I would. If I did, none of this would have happened."

It took all her strength, but she refused to cry. That never solved anything. Besides, she didn't know Squirt or Daphne well enough. She slowed her breathing and forced her mind to focus. She needed a plan, to come up with something, anything.

Daphne and Squirt stared at her with a combination of concern and sympathy. They sat in silence even though they, too, were covered in the same smelly refuse, until Squirt lowered his nose to his shirt. "I can't take this smell a second longer." He stood up and waved them to follow. "Let's clean up. I've got extra coveralls. Come on, Daph, Anni, you'll feel better after you change."

Anni followed them like she was on autopilot, racking her brain as they took turns hosing off their hands, arms, and legs. Squirt and Daphne held their breath and gritted their teeth as they helped rinse out Anni's hair. Squirt offered her the cleanest towel he could find in the garden shed to wrap up her wet hair. He then handed each of them a one-piece zippered jumpsuit in a bright shade of orange. Anni glanced at the jumpsuit. It reminded her that she was a prisoner on the Zephyr.

"Orange isn't exactly my color," said Daphne.

"No problem. What color, then?" asked Squirt.

"Lavender for me," said Daphne. "Anni?"

"I don't care."

Did it really matter? They were talking about things as if everything was normal. Squirt flipped the tag under the collar. His tongue stuck out as he played with the tag, but nothing happened.

"I'll do Anni's," said Daphne, who took the garment and instantly changed Anni's coveralls from orange to black. "I'm partial to lavender."

"Thanks," Anni mumbled.

After they changed out of their dirty clothes, they put them in a canvas sack.

Squirt offered to carry Anni's backpack. "Your hair should be dry now." He pointed to the towel on her head. "That sucks up loads of water. I should know. I used to spill things a lot in the beginning, but Yugi hasn't given up on me yet. He's still my Earth Studies teacher. Now if only I could get my Opus Stone…"

Anni's hair was the last thing on her mind. She wasn't going to turn down his help, but she wasn't sure she could trust either of them. Finally, she said, "Going back to Chicago is useless now. I need to find out where Lexi is. I don't know how you can help me do that, but that's my plan. If you can help with that, then good."

"I made a promise to Anni and I keep them," said Squirt. "Daphne will, too."

"Squirt! Don't volunteer me for things I can't do. It's not easy to get off the Zephyr. It's almost impossible for underage Elementals to leave, you know that."

"Daph, don't say that. We have to help Anni. This is serious!"

"I don't doubt that," said Daphne. "I don't have a Queen's Mirror or an Opus Stone. Unless you secretly have access to either one."

"What's an Opus Stone?" asked Anni.

"Oh, man," said Squirt, his eyes lit up. "Elementals get their Opus Stone when they come of age, usually at thirteen. Then you find out what kind of Elemental you are. I think I'm Earth. Once you know, you get to travel, study abroad, figure out your Elemental purpose, meet humans, and eat human food! That's what I'm going to do!"

"Humans don't have Opus Stones, and he doesn't, either," said Daphne.

"Low blow, Daph," said Squirt, frowning. "Why are you being so mean?"

"I'm not trying to be; I'm making a point. Even if Anni went through the Orb into LimBough, she couldn't use Tree Transport because she doesn't know where Lexi is. What's your plan, Squirt? I'd love to hear it."

Daphne was certainly clear, and it sounded to Anni like she had thought this through. Anni said, "What you're saying is that I should give up."

"Anni, I am truly sorry about your friend, but leaving the Zephyr is impossible. Believe me. Traveling between our worlds is something Elementals can only do with a guardian or until we come of age and get our Opus Stone. You can't travel in LimBough without one. It's like an I.D.—I guess like a human's driver's license. All LimBough travelers are registered with the Opus Stone Network. You could travel with someone else's Opus Stone, but that's about as easy to get as a Queen's Mirror, so…"

"Lexi wouldn't give up on me," said Anni. "I can't give up on her."

"Geez, Daph. How about some thunder with those rain clouds. Sure, I don't have an exact perfect plan." Squirt squared his shoulders, turned to Anni, and said, "but I'm going to help you, I promise. I don't know how yet, but I will."

"I hope for Lexi's sake you can help her, but for now, I need to get you to your lodgings," said Daphne. "Diana said Spadu Hills. Is that right, Anni?"

"Yeah," said Anni.

"That's not even in the village," said Squirt. "Why there?"

"Hold on, I should double-check," said Daphne and looked at her wristwatch.

"Hey, Egbert and Zelda had that watch. What is it?"

"This? It's an Omninav, not a watch. It's way more powerful than a human smartphone, but it fits on your wrist. It can access your optical nerves, so the wearer sees everything in 3-D. It has GPS too. Actually, it does more than I could possibly explain."

"Show off," said Squirt. Anni noticed that he didn't have one.

"Can it get news reports like the one I read in Krizia's office? Could you tell me if they mention anything about Lexi?"

"Of course," said Daphne before she shot Squirt a look and returned to her Omninav. "I don't understand. Diana advises that we cut through the village and try to not be seen by any Elofficium. Krizia's paperwork probably hasn't been processed, which means we better be extra careful. Seriously, if an Elofficial sees you, they might take you in."

"Fantastic," said Anni.

Only Squirt didn't seem to understand her sarcasm because he smiled at her and said, "Like an adventure. This is going to be so much fun."

Together, they set off from Moon Manor down a long cobblestone drive canopied by giant trees.

"Did Krizia tell you who you'd be meeting at Spadu Hill?"

"No," said Anni. "A man, Sponge-in-a-cork, took care of it."

"Spongincork!" said Squirt. "You mean *Leach*. What'd he do for you?"

"He's my voucher, or something." She pulled out the card from her shirt pocket and showed them.

"No!" said Daphne and Squirt simultaneously.

CHAPTER 21

THE BASEMENT

Lexi stood frozen. She wanted to yell and scream Anni's name, but she couldn't. The stranger's hand gripped her shoulder tighter. Lexi couldn't see her captor's face, and whoever it was waited until the coast was clear before he pushed her out into the upturned common room. Lexi's legs moved against her will and obeyed her captor's steering grip.

Lexi was going to run, but she couldn't. He directed her into the hallway toward the low-lit, creepy service stairs that none of the students used if they could help it. Down they went, five flights of stairs with her captor wheezing behind her.

The damp chill and smell of the stored foods told her that they were in the school's cellar. They shuffled down a long, narrow hall until they were directly below the kitchen. They stopped in front of a massive tarp that covered something set against the wall.

Finally, her captor moved in front of her. Lexi studied him, not sure if the heavy, dark hooded robe concealed a short, round body. She couldn't even make out a face under the hood. He swept aside old paint cans that cluttered the floor and pulled the spattered old tarp from the wall. Behind it was a dirty mirror, framed with rotting wood that oozed a tar-like substance.

"You first," said her captor in a gravelly voice.

She didn't move. She knew what it was even though she had never traveled by Queen's Mirror before, but he didn't wait for her. He used something that felt like a cane and pushed Lexi through the murky glass.

Waterstone was behind her, and she couldn't turn back.

CHAPTER 22

ZELDA SCURRYFUNGE

I can't believe Leach is your voucher. He hates kids, and humans even worse."

"Thanks, Squirt," said Daphne. "What he means is that some Elementals think they are better than humans, more evolved. I disagree. I think we can each learn something from one another."

Anni started to wonder how many of the people at Waterstone Academy were Elementals. Only Lexi would understand how she was feeling now; they were the only two who didn't fit in.

"Yeah, he put me in box," said Anni.

Squirt's eyes widened. "He boxed you? Jerk."

"Oh," said Daphne. "I wondered about the chute."

"So," said Anni. "Putting people in boxes is not normal for you people?"

"No," said Squirt. "But Leach has tossed Elementals into the Egghouse. Anni, stay clear of him. Whatever you do, don't let him know what you're up to."

That was one more thing to be concerned with. She didn't know how she'd keep track of it all. "What's the Egghouse?"

Squirt laughed. "You know, the Nut-house, where you put the nutters. Take your pick; we've got loads of words…the Metal house for Metalheads."

"Squirt! Really, you shouldn't use that kind of language. It sets a bad tone," said Daphne. "What he meant was that it's a place for those who can't get along on their own without help. You know, a little unstable, and they can't think straight."

"Yeah, we have those, too—you know, in the land of humans."

"Right, but here it's a bit different. For Elementals, a part of them is actually missing. Our Opus Stone is our spirit, our life force; it's part of our soul. If it becomes damaged or lost, that part of us gets lost into the ethers like a blade of grass in the wind, never to return. It's the saddest fate we Elementals could ever face. There's a facility on this Zephyr called the Essence House, it's a part of the Murdrock Serene Center." She eyed Squirt. "Some call it the Egghouse. Ours was funded by the Murdrock Institute—"

"Murdrock? They bought my school, Waterstone Academy."

"Really," said Daphne. "The Moons and Waterstones are the oldest Elemental families. They were the first ones who fought to keep up relations with the humans until…Anyway, the Murdrocks are another old Elemental family. They've loads of influence in both the human and Elemental realms."

"That's because they're all a bunch of crazy nutters. All they want to do is make the E2 happen," said Squirt.

"That's total speculation," said Daphne dismissively.

"What's the E2?" asked Anni.

"Some Elementals want to make a new Earth without humans," said Squirt. "But, all the heads of Elemental families from each Element have to agree first. Only half said yes. It's the dumbest idea in the whole universe. If they all agreed, all the Elements would be ripped away, no earth, no wood, no fire, no metal, and no water. All that would be left behind would be a calcified crater of Funk, and Earth would look like Swiss cheese." Squirt paused. "I hear that tastes good, Swiss cheese. I haven't tried it, but I want to try some when I go on my KewS.T. " Anni frowned at the word, which prompted him to say, "Oh, sorry, a KewS.T. is a short trial visit to a human realm, like a quest. Anyway, when I do mine the first thing I'm going to do is eat Swiss cheese," said Squirt dreamily. "Humans are too cool to lay them all to waste. E2's a dumb idea. It'll never happen."

Next to Lexi's disappearance, that was possibly the worst thing Anni had ever heard. The images in her brain left her speechless.

"Thanks for putting it so delicately, Squirt," said Daphne. "Really, this debate has been going on longer than we've been around. Anni, I wouldn't worry about it."

Anni's mind started to drift as they made their way to the end of the road. Dazzling flickers of light dappled a curved sidewalk that led to the town's center. She was nervous thinking about how she might plan her escape. Who would help her? As they rounded the corner, the view blinded her.

Squirt looked at Anni. "Why're your eyes closed?"

Daphne pulled a pair of sunglasses out of her impossibly small hip pack. "Here, put these on. It'll remove the glare." She helped Anni. "Oops, I forgot to tell you, your retinas will need to adjust; it's a Wood element thing. Don't worry, you'll get used to it."

In truth, Anni didn't want to get used to anything, but when the sunglasses were secured, she opened her eyes. It was breathtaking and nauseating all at once. Color and lights refracted from unbelievable surfaces. The largest culprit was an enormous body of water in the center of the village; a floating orb hovered in its middle.

"That Orb takes you to LimBough—Elemental TreeTransports will take you anywhere in the world," said Squirt with a wistful gaze.

Anni stared at the Orb. "How can anyone reach it?"

"There's a bridge that opens up to it," said Squirt nonchalantly.

"It's not that easy," said Daphne. "You need an E-pass and an Opus Stone."

Intrigued, Anni kept her eye on it until she was distracted by the structures and surfaces of the shops and galleries that circled the town. Like the cobblestone path, they were not made of normal materials. Not one store looked alike in shape or size, and each shop seemed determined to outmaneuver its neighbor in some kind of visual competition. All the buildings were decorated in an array of unique formations, harnessing varying materials to create special façades for the store's intended purpose, like unique mascots or billboards that advertised their specific wares.

Anni spotted Oliver up the road watching them when Squirt's hand shot up for a high-five as he said, "Mac!"

Mackenzie, the guy from the plane and Oliver's accomplice, approached them and ushered them to the side of a building. He spoke in a hushed tone. "I know where you're headed, but you should know there are two Elofficials at the end of this block. I'd take a different route or wait until they leave. I'll keep an eye out." He left and walked in the direction of the Elofficials.

"What's the plan, Daph? I don't know of a different route."

Stunned, Anni couldn't believe her eyes. Each storefront manipulated the elements: various colors of fire; water that bubbled, trickled or froze like ice; air in shapes of clouds or mist; all kinds of stones and precious gems; earthy materials like flowers, leaves, vines, and bark; and giant fruits and vegetables decorated the exteriors.

"Um, I don't know. We could take the alleyways, but if they are back there, too, we'll be trapped, unless…" Daphne trailed off, mumbling.

As they stood there trying to figure out a different route, several Elemental townsfolk walked past them and pinched their noses, which began to draw too much attention. Daphne blushed more every time they scowled.

"Hey Anni, look." Squirt pointed across the cobblestone walk to a building covered in different kinds of fabric. "Daph works there. Let's wait inside."

HARRIS TWEED HABERDASHERS CLOTHING EMPORIUM's exterior walls consisted of hundreds of alternating fabrics. The shop looked too crowded to hide inside, but *The V.O.I.C.E.* news article projected in the store's window caught Anni's eye. It flashed the same picture of Lexi, and an image Anni hadn't seen—a huge photo of the missing Elemental Artifact, a golden bee-shaped piece of jewelry. It looked near identical to the image of the gold-stitched bee on velvet cloth she had sewn into her tank top. This was what Lexi was going to tell her about. What did the bee mean? Was it why Lexi was kidnapped?

The article with the bee image was posted in every shop's window as far as she could see. It said, *Missing! If Seen, Contact The Elofficium!* Anni clutched her coveralls where her bee patch was safely hidden. When she looked down, she noticed a golden thread creeping through the zipper. She would need to re-stitch it again, and soon.

"Uh-oh," said Squirt. "Elofficium straight ahead."

"Follow me," said Daphne, taking Anni's arm and pulling her into an alley between two buildings. "We need to hide."

They raced behind several buildings until they came across one that had a square, leaden door that Daphne opened. "Get in."

They bent down and hid in the back of a stock room where hundreds upon hundreds of bolts of fabrics hung from the ceiling, walls, and endless stacks of cubbies. Murmurs of voices filtered into the storeroom from the visibly bustling front part of the store. Anni realized they were inside Haberdashers, where Daphne worked.

"Stay low," whispered Daphne.

In the far corner of the stockroom sat an old woman sorting through different spools of thread. Another two workers sat gossiping, rather than working.

"Ms. Thimble, what have you been eating again? It smells awful in here," said an insect-thin woman with googly eyes.

"Eeehh? Sorry dear, what'd you say?" replied the old woman.

"Never mind her; she's deaf," said a fashionable-looking younger man with a nose that was so pointy, you could put a hanger on it. "Did you read the news in *The V.O.I.C.E.* article? All that talk about the missing artifact, just like three years ago. I vote we rename the Zephyr. Moon is so passé."

"Well," said the googly-eyed woman. "I'll bet anything a Moon family member did it. They're a troubled lot. Cursed, if you ask me."

"Really? You think so?" asked the young man.

"Don't look so surprised. The same thing happened when Mabel Moon disappeared. Another artifact went missing—then poof. She was dead."

Anni didn't like this conversation.

"How do you know this?" asked the young man.

"Everyone knows that the Moons are powerful, but I've heard they had a secret society that got busted up after the *Great Catastrophe*. Then Mabel Moon was banished to the human realm, because she didn't protect the Prince. And let's not forget that the Moons have had more than their fair share of Metalheads in the family."

"Really," the young man gasped.

"Eeehh? Sorry dears," said Ms. Thimble, wrapping ribbon around a spool and humming to herself, oblivious to their conversation.

The googly-eyed woman ignored her and went on. "And you know that bee artifact that's all over the news? Well…" She lowered her voice. "I've seen one sewn on a cloak that came in for a special order last week."

"No," the young man gasped for the third time. "What does it mean?"

"Don't know, but if the Elofficium found out there would be trouble."

"Look," said Ms. Thimble so loudly that she shocked the two whisperers. "Elofficium's come to pay a visit to the shop. Wonder what they want?"

"Let's leave," whispered Squirt, nudging Daphne and Anni.

Daphne's brow furrowed, like she was irritated. She led them out the back door onto the crowded cobblestone walk. With no Elofficials in sight, they tried to blend in.

"Just keep your head down." Daphne grumbled.

A familiar—but faint—sound of tiny bells caused Anni to stop and look around. For some inexplicable reason, Zelda Scurryfunge was scurrying across the cobblestone walkway toward a short queue of Elementals at the water's edge, where a bridge expanded and retracted across the lake to a huge silver Orb in the middle.

Anni took off after her. "*Zelda? Zelda!*" she yelled at the top of her lungs.

There was only one person in front of Zelda when she looked back at Anni. With one hand on her hip, she said, "My goodness, Anni. Is that you? What's wrong with your hair now? It's blue."

"Did you bring Lexi? Egbert said you found her. Was that true? Where is she? The news is wrong, right? Please say it is."

"Afraid not. No idea." Zelda lowered her eyes and shook her head while digging through a small satin pouch and pulled out a small piece of paper. "Last time I saw her, she was with you. Wish I knew more, but fear not. If I know Egbert like I know Egbert, he'll get to the bottom of this. He'll find her. You can be sure of that. Bother, I'm late." Apparently the metal bridge that led to the Orb had retracted while Zelda was talking to Anni, but when Zelda laid her E-pass ticket on a glassy pillared gate, the metal bridge expanded across the water. Zelda didn't waste a moment; she got on and started walking fast.

"But—" Without thinking, Anni followed Zelda onto the bridge that moved like a conveyor belt. "Wait! Tell me more. I saw Egbert in Krizia's office. You must have talked."

For some reason, Zelda was moving two times faster than she was.

"I wish I knew more, dear," Zelda called back over her shoulder, but the distance between them not only doubled, it quadrupled.

Anni ran after Zelda but it did no good. It felt like she was running in the same place. By the time Zelda reached the Orb, a door appeared, she walked in, and it sealed itself behind her. Zelda was gone.

On the cobblestone walk, Daphne and Squirt were jumping up and down, yelling and waving at Anni. Miranda stood by them laughing, as masses of Elementals congregated around them. Oliver was there, too, disapprovingly shaking his head, as he pulled off his jacket and shoes. She didn't understand what they were saying, but she heard funny clicking sounds vibrating beneath her. When she looked ahead, she finally understood. The bridge was no longer connected to the Silver Orb; it was retracting.

"*I see that you've discovered your own folly,*" said Whiffle. "*Beneath you lay ancient waters, which I can assure you won't take pleasure in its embrace. A pity that we haven't yet reached an accord; under proper tutelage you would not find yourself in these vexing situations.*"

Anni spun around and raced back toward the village. "Not now, Whiffle, unless you want to tell me everything, like where's Lexi?"

"*You humans desire information like your fast food.*"

The bridge was catching up. Noise from the village grew in volume. Even more Elementals of all shapes and sizes gathered at the water's edge. Several complained, but the majority cheered—not for Anni, but for the bridge.

"*On the bright side, look at how many you've inspired.*" Anni ignored him. "*Shall I commence with the formalities? Yes, I think I shall. I chose today to present you with a proposal, one that is dually beneficial. It is binding and permanent, provided you agree. However, only three requests will be made; this is the first. What say you?*"

"Either tell me what I need to know, or leave me alone!"

Her legs were pumping hard. She was so close. The bridge port was within her grasp. Just. A. Few. More. Strides. Five. Four. Three. Two…

SPLASH!

The bridge disappeared and released her into the water. Deceptively heavy, the water was unlike anything she'd ever felt before. It gripped her body, making it impossible to stay afloat.

She paddled to the edge of the lake's basin, but there was no ladder. Above, the orange afternoon skies disappeared and filled fast with flinty clouds. The air went crisp, and a chill flooded her bones.

Above the chorus of yells and laughter, Daphne and Squirt yelled, "Hold on! Help's on the way!" But it was too hard. The weight of the water, combined with exhaustion and cold, paralyzed her, and she sank.

"*As you wish.*" Even under water, she couldn't escape Whiffle's strident tones. "*But, while you contemplate your last breath, be aware of your obstinate nature. Upon my third proposal, there shall be no other. I will speak to you again in a few days' time. In the meantime, have a pleasant soak.*"

Her right hand grabbed at the air, then her eyes closed.

CHAPTER 23

PITHY PURPLE PLUME BERRIES

When Anni opened her eyes, she thought she had been having the strangest dream. The pale yellow walls and beautiful upholstered furniture looked remarkably like Vivian's office back at Waterstone Academy. Even the colored sky was pouring rain, but when she looked closer, it wasn't the school grounds she was seeing. The window showed a bird's-eye view of the Zephyr's village circle, and Anni saw that the lake had been half drained.

"You had us worried," said a gentle voice.

Anni hadn't noticed that a woman wearing a beige tunic was sitting next to her, but when she peered into the woman's face, she realized it was the kind young woman who had waved to her earlier in Krizia's office. "And to think," said the young woman, "you almost left us without even saying goodbye." She smiled amusedly and, with a very gentle touch, she tucked a strand of Anni's blue-green hair behind her ear. "Not to worry, we forgive you, even Oliver does. He jumped in after you sank. Do you remember falling into the lake?"

Anni rose from the chaise and turned around. The room was full of people. Daphne and Squirt were carrying trays and setting them down on the coffee table. Two Manor guards stood sentry by a door. Maeleachlainn *the Leach* Spongincork stood close to the two Moon Manor guards; the very sight of him made Anni shiver.

"Speak for yourself, Diana." Spongincork's lip curled up into his scarred cheek, as his angry eyes flashed at Anni, even the guards, Knox and Fort, scowled, too. "Oliver's still DeFunkifying at Soak House Springs, and it'll be raining for weeks until the lake refills itself. We'll have a lot to answer for. Make sure that *she* reports to Spadu Hills before dusk. I will *see* to the other things." He stormed out of the room, and his guards followed.

"Don't mind Maeleachlainn; he's grouchy. We haven't been properly introduced; I'm Diana," said the woman in a warm and welcoming voice as she rose from her seat. "I apologize for your treatment at the Manor."

A short man entered Diana's sitting room carrying another tray. Anni recognized him from Krizia's office. He wore the same glasses, but didn't have his satchel and he was wearing a shamrock-covered apron over his work clothes, bright orange dish gloves, and was holding the largest tray yet.

"Yugi San will be monitoring your Funk levels, kind of like a doctor. He'll prepare some tonics for you to take while you're with us. He'll make sure you feel better."

"Hello," Anni said.

"*Konbanwa*," said Yugi and quietly went back arranging items on a large coffee table with Daphne and Squirt's help.

"How do you feel?" asked Diana delicately. When Anni didn't answer, Diana continued, "Falling into the Lake isn't good for humans or Elementals. It can alter your memory, but it also absorbed some of your Funk." Diana paused. "I'm guessing no one explained what that is to you, but the simplest definition for Funk is a bunch of heavy, unpleasant thought forms that attach to your physical body, weighing it down because they haven't been properly released—kind of like psychic garbage. Yugi and I believe that the saltwater in the Lake absorbed most of it, which is why the lake's being drained, but that's not to say that your Funk is completely gone, and you can't afford to lose too much of it too quickly, which is why we will have to monitor your health."

Images flashed through her consciousness of long metal grates retracting and then Anni splashing into the water below. She looked down and noticed she wasn't wearing the black jumpsuit as before. Instead, she was back in the clothes she had arrived in, but they were clean and dry. "I remember falling in, but how did I get here?"

"Thank goodness your memory is coming back. When they pulled you out, you didn't know your name," said Diana tenderly. "Some skurfers were in the area and pulled you out just in time. They brought you here. Daphne helped me get you into some dry clothes, and you fell asleep an hour ago."

Anni grabbed at her chest, searching for Mabel's key. It was there under her shirt, but something else was missing. She looked down and saw that she was wearing her black tank top, but the metallic thread from the velvet bee patch she had sewn inside it was gone.

"Is something wrong?" asked Diana.

"Um," Anni stalled, starting to panic. "I'm missing my, my backpack."

"It's behind you," said Daphne. She handed Anni her backpack from behind the chaise. "Everything's inside, even that patch on your tank." Anni thought her heart was going to stop right there and then, but Daphne winked at her. "It was hanging by a thread, so I put it inside your bag to keep it safe. If you like, I can sew it back on for you later."

"Daphne, that's a lovely gesture," said Diana. "Anni, Daphne's one of the Zephyr's expert seamstresses." The tips of Daphne's ears went crimson. "Oh, don't be so modest, Daphne. You should take Anni on a tour of Haberdashers later, when she's feeling better."

Anni was glad for Diana's diversion. She felt her cheeks flush just as Daphne's had done. Daphne knew her secret. There would be no way of avoiding that conversation; all the village shop windows had a similar image of the Bee on it with the headline: *Missing Elemental Artifact—contact Elofficium if seen.* She unzipped the backpack and sure enough, there was the velvet cloth along with Lexi's doll. Both were completely dry and safe.

Frowning, Squirt carried a food tray. "Leach isn't coming back, is he?"

Diana grinned at him. "Hungry, Squirt?"

"Starving." He put down the tray and raced to the plushest of chairs. A wonderful whiff of food met Anni's nose and her stomach growled.

"Please start," said Diana to Daphne and Squirt. "Anni, before you begin on this wonderful meal Yugi San prepared, he needs to check your essence levels."

Yugi was at her side already, holding her wrist like he was taking her pulse. This went on for several minutes. She watched her reflection in his glasses as he stared into her eyes. He pulled a couple of purple bean-shaped berries out of his pocket and placed them on a small, empty dish in front of her. He finished by waving his arms around and above her head and went into the kitchen without a word.

"He'll be back shortly. Please go ahead," said Diana.

Anni was famished, but also glad she felt better than when she first arrived. She sat on a small poof next to the large coffee table, which was loaded with a variety of complicated teapots, steaming kettles, and a vast grouping of unusual dishes and foods. Each person had a contraption that held a smoking, small iron pot with a hot liquid inside. She watched Daphne and Squirt take two wide-angled soup bowls and deposit what looked like tiny capsules inside. Over those, they poured the steaming hot liquid from the teapots and covered them. Next, they set about making different drinks with a similar sort of process, this time using long, cylindrical copper vessels that emitted frosty mists.

"Try this," said Diana, who offered her an impossibly thin porcelain teacup filled with a purple liquid, one of Yugi's purple berries. "Yugi's specialty, *Apium Passiflora*."

Anni sipped from the cup. It was delicious but not filling. Squirt uncovered his bowl, which was full of leafy greens and thick noodles that didn't look real, but more like an impression of noodles. Nevertheless, Squirt slurped it up even though it was steaming.

When she finished her drink, Daphne held out a small tray stacked with two dried crisps of lettuce with splats of what looked a lot like ketchup, mustard, and mayonnaise between them. Anni took a crisp and popped it into her mouth, but this elicited surprise and a couple laughs, mostly from Squirt. Her lips puckered and kept on sucking inward. The wafer instantly sucked all the moisture from her mouth.

"Anni, that's…that's not how you…ha ha." Whatever Squirt said after that was lost. He laughed so hard that he bent over and rolled onto the floor. It took him a while to regain composure, but by then, Yugi had returned to the room and settled next to Anni. He demonstrated the proper way to fix the dried lettuce crisp meal, which was the same process as with the noodle bowls and included her remaining berries.

Anni's mouth was so dry, she could barely pucker. Diana whipped up another drink and offered it to her. It was pink, topped with misty lavender foam, and had hundreds of tiny, speckled floating balls inside. It looked too beautiful to drink, but Anni was desperate.

"Essence," Diana answered. "Your taste buds now know the essence of Unda Viola. I'm sure you have many questions, perhaps too many to keep track of at first. But simply put, our diet is a little different from the one you may be used to. The one thing that sets Elementals apart from humans is our extremely developed senses. When it comes to nourishment, many of us can get by on Essences alone."

"Oh," said Anni, starting on her noodles. "So you don't eat food like humans do?"

"It's not so simple. Just as humans from different countries eat differently, so do we. A lot of what we eat depends on where we live and our Element. For example, I am classified as a Wood Elemental, many of us live on Zephyrs, and because of that we require a special diet to maintain our energy. There are other kinds of Elementals who live here, too, and they also require a slightly different diet to fulfill their energy needs."

"Tell her how many Elementals there are," said Squirt.

"We are just over 1 billion." Diana laughed. "We've been around since the planet formed, and we live longer than humans. It might interest you to know that many Wood Elementals have permanent residences in the human cities— like your hometown, Chicago. There are five classifications of Elementals: Earth, Wood, Water, Fire, and Metal—"

"The Wood Elementals made LimBough," said Squirt, unable to hold back his excitement. "They're the most human-like of all the Elementals; experts at travel, philosophy, and creativity. Fire Elementals are usually leaders. Some people think Water Elementals are the most powerful because they can influence feelings. Earth Elementals are very strong; they're master producers and planners, and Metals were architects but—"

"Thank you, Squirt," said Diana, smiling. "And while they are all different, no one is greater than the others in terms of value or importance. Each provides a significant contribution to the whole." Diana took a generous pause. "I cannot pretend Elementals are very different from humans, especially when it comes to addressing inequalities and certain biases. We Elementals have many of our own political issues and problems. Elementals and humans have a long history, but it's my job to make sure things are easy for you, Anni."

Anni couldn't shake the feeling that there was more to what Diana was saying, but a triangle pot started to steam and hiss. The aromas made her mouth water, and all she could focus on was eating whatever was inside.

"Dessert! Oh Anni, you are gonna love this!" said Squirt. "Bet you never tasted anything like the Pithy-Purple-Plume-Bean-Berries."

Daphne started preparing several tiny mugs and saucers, just like the kind Anni had seen espresso served in, but only a bit smaller. Yugi carefully held the pyramid-shaped pot and poured lumpy, mud like liquid into each cup.

Anni felt a little out of place being served. After all, that's what she had done at Waterstone for so long, so she had forgotten how nice it was to be the recipient. Everyone settled back into their seats with their cups to their lips and sipped. Anni raised her cup under her nose and smelled a combination: something like fresh-cut grass, lilacs, chocolate, and almonds. She watched Squirt's face turn bright red as he drank.

She brought the cup to her lips and sipped. Surprised that it tasted nothing like mud or freshly cut grass, her mouth tingled with a complex combination of all her favorite things wrapped up into a tiny drop of nectar.

Another sip, this time breathing in all the aromas, made it taste different. Good, but somehow different. And so it went on until the last drop. The aromas and tastes satisfied all her cravings, leaving her nourished, while her taste buds sang with delight. She enjoyed the meal so much, she didn't notice the table was cleared and that Yugi had left.

The Omninav on Diana's wrist blinked, and a faint silver image about the size of an index card appeared. For a second, a touch of displeasure tightened around Diana's face. It was then that Miranda entered the room, acting as if she didn't see Anni, Daphne, or Squirt. She marched up to Diana and whispered something in her ear.

"Forgive me, Anni, this is Miranda. She's training with me."

"We already know one another," said Miranda politely. "From Waterstone Academy." It was one of her two tones: the one she used for authority figures, while the other, which she used for Anni, was that of pure loathing. Anni wondered if Miranda's distaste for her ran deeper because she was a human, or because of Mabel.

"Well, we have covered very important issues today, food and culture, but unfortunately, we need to cut our visit short. Anni, Daphne and Squirt will take you to Spadu Hills, where Fortensia is expecting you. Tomorrow afternoon, I'd like you to meet me here to discuss your stay." Diana smiled. "Oh, and try not to fall into the Lake before then."

Anni slung her backpack over her shoulders and followed Squirt and Daphne down a set of stairs and out onto the deserted cobblestone walkway of the village. The lake was fully drained now, and the dark skies were pouring rain. She didn't know what to say to Daphne about the velvet bee patch, but she knew it had to be on her mind because all the village shops flashed pictures of it from *The V.O.I.C.E.* article.

Daphne pulled out a three-person-sized umbrella. They made it to the end of the village circle without speaking until, just before a dirt road, Brat flapped under the umbrella and perched on Anni's shoulder.

"Either I'm going snozdoolally or you were going to leave the Zephyr without me!"

"Hi, Brat," said Anni. "No, I wasn't leaving you. I was following Zelda. I didn't know that bridge would drop me into the water."

"Moppins, you're lucky. You could've lost all your memories." Brat made a sniffing noise. "Have you been drinking *ApiumPassiflora*? I could use a cup of that right about now. Anyway, did you see the news?"

"What news?" asked Anni, Daphne, and Squirt.

"Elofficials made a public statement in the case of Teddy Waterstone's death, Lexi's kidnapping, and the missing Golden Bee Artifact. They have charged someone who they believe is guilty."

"Who?" asked Anni.

"I absolutely disagree, mind you, but they have charged Egbert Frode Moon."

CHAPTER 24

FECTUS UNDERGROUND

L exi emerged through the mirror and doubled over. Her eyes watered as her stomach and head seared with pain. It took several minutes before the feeling subsided to a dull ache. She wiped her eyes and turned around to see if her captor followed. He didn't. All that remained was a giant old mirror propped up against a wall. She raised her hand to touch it, but it wouldn't pass through; it had sealed itself.

She was trapped.

Lexi inched down a gray stone hall that led to a vast room filled with a dozen teens, all about her age or older. Four of the most repulsive-looking creatures were herding them into a line. A girl with long, brown hair stood at the end of the line until Lexi joined.

"I'm Kat," said the brown-haired girl to Lexi and a sandy-haired boy in front of her, but the boy looked too proud to respond. Lexi noted that this girl didn't look nervous at all.

"Whatever you do," whispered Kat, "Say you're a human."

"I will not," said the sandy-haired boy.

"Fine," said Kat as she turned to Lexi and added, "It's your funeral."

"Greetings. I'm Mortimer Spence," said a slug the size of a water buffalo. He wore spectacles and a bright purple vest. In one hand he held a list and in the other a glowing sphere, which he found far more deserving of his attention than the group in front of him. Although articulate, he sounded as if he had said the same thing a thousand times before. "The Fectus welcomes you. May you never leave….State your name and age."

By the time it was Lexi's turn, she opened her mouth but no words came out. Terrified she said, "Lexi…Wwwaterstone… twelve."

"Human or Elemental?" asked Mortimer, tapping at his sphere.

She paused and said, "Huuuman."

Mortimer looked deep into her eyes. "We'll see about that." He looked back at his sphere and tapped something into it. "Go to the left. Collect your uniform."

Lexi walked to the left, where eleven teens were handed dirty, rag-like bundles. On the right stood the proud-looking boy, all alone with no bundle. Kat nudged Lexi when the guard forced a drink down the boy's throat.

"Why did they do that to him?" asked Lexi.

"It's not safe to be an Elemental in here," said Kat.

Two more guards, even more monstrous than the first four, clapped both of the boy's arms in chains and took him away through a steel door just as another person entered.

"What do we have today, Mortimer?" asked a young man dressed in a red leather and steel-spiked suit, taking pleasure in the fear reflected in the teens' eyes.

"Huuumans, meet Spike," said Mortimer with a laugh that Lexi thought was directed at her. "At least, they claim to be human. Where do you want them?"

"Ha ha, better hope that's all they are," said the boy named Spike. "Take seven for service. Put the rest in the Brouwen."

Lexi was more annoyed than afraid. Whatever the reason, she was reminded of Anni—who'd be tough if faced with a boy like this. What she wouldn't give to be with her best friend right now, but she only had Anni's spirit to console her.

"You," said Spike, sneering at Lexi. "You got something you want to say?"
Lexi didn't realize she was scowling when she said, "No."

"I don't like her. Put her in the Brouwen," said Spike.

"As you wish," said Mortimer. Spike and the guards took the first seven kids, leaving behind Lexi and the remaining three. Mortimer slithered away in the opposite direction, leaving a trail of slime in his wake. "Follow me."

CHAPTER 25

SPADU HILLS

A fire burned inside Anni's gut that no amount of Yugi's *ApiumPassiflora* could fix. In two days' time, her life had been altered in ways she could never imagine. But to have Egbert, whom she didn't even like that much, be accused of such terrible things bothered and confused her. She knew Egbert had great respect for Teddy and Mabel. After all, Teddy helped him through something sad from his past—"tragic" was the word Mabel used when she defended Egbert's terse nature. Mabel once said, "Egbert is a fine man, but deeply wounded. Try to look past his ways and see him as if he were a small child."

Anni didn't know what to think of that then, or now. "Show me the news article."

Daphne quickly scrolled through her Omninav. Anni could tell by her furrowed brow that it wasn't good, and she would have wagered that Diana must have seen the same article when they were together.

They huddled under the awning of a closed flower shop and read *The V.O.I.C.E.* article in silence.

THE VOICE - ELEMENTAL NEWS, WORLD NEWS & OPINION

| Editor-in-Chief:
Verbum Smith | *THE V.O.I.C.E.* | Sunday, June 3
County Fleet |

THE VIRTUAL OMNINAVIGATIONAL INCLUSIVE CONNECTING ELEMENTALS

NEWS   OPINION   E2   BUSINESS   ARTS

MOON NAMED IN WATERSTONE CASE

Elofficial Suspect Moon in Waterstone's Case

OpEd By: PENELOPE W. POTBOILER

Elemental Egbert Frode Moon, a longtime associate of Teddy and Alexa Waterstone, partner at Waterstone Academy and Mabel Moon's heir, is the prime suspect named in the Waterstone case.

As of yet, Elofficials have not been able to contact Mr. Moon for questioning. Elofficials brought Mr. Moon's assistant, Rufous Finnegan,

in for questioning, but determined his cognitive functioning had been significantly altered and is currently undergoing tests and treatment at the *Murdrock Serene Center*. Elofficials gained access to Mabel Moon's residence, where Mr. Moon is thought to reside. Within said residence, Elofficials found soil samples that matched the grounds of the Brazilian Museum where the Elemental Golden Bee Artifact was stolen. Since Egbert Frode Moon has turned off his Omninavigational device and cannot be contacted,

126

Elofficials have issued a warrant for his arrest and request that all individuals who know his whereabouts report it immediately. He is wanted for theft of the Golden Bee Artifact, the kidnapping of Alexa Waterstone, and the murder of Teddy Waterstone.

In related news, Mr. Orge Murdrock, who recently acquired Waterstone Academy for Girls, made an announcement. *"Although saddened by the loss of Theodore Waterstone, I vow that no other innocent life will be placed in jeopardy. As such, Waterstone Academy will remain closed until the culprit is caught."* His statement was issued just hours before the North American polls closed naming Mr. Orge Murdrock the *Chief Elofficialis of the United States of America*, the highest Elofficial office an Elemental can obtain within each country.

"You don't think he did it, do you, Anni?" asked Squirt with a worried look.

Egbert irritated her to no end, but in her heart, Anni didn't think he could be guilty of these things. Then again, nothing was as it seemed. "I don't know," she said. "But I know he was very close to both Teddy and Mabel."

"You can't seriously consider this piffling-pseudo-news-narrative-bunk," said Brat. "I've delivered messages to Egbert, and for him. He's not the warmest of Elkin, and sure, perhaps he's a bit detached from his emotional receptors, but if anything, he is an honest man. I think he was set up."

"Up until two days ago, I didn't know about Elementals," Anni said. "What if he hid other things? He was in charge of Mabel's half of Waterstone, which, by the way, he just handed over to the Murdrocks as if it was a piece of paper. What if he got rid of her and Teddy, too?" She didn't really believe that, but said it out of anger.

"You can't mean that," said Brat. "Waterstone was struggling, if you must know. Teddy had plans to close the school, but I didn't tell you that. I could lose my badge for revealing confidential information."

"If it means saving Lexi's life, don't you think you should?" asked Anni.

Daphne and Squirt didn't say a word.

"Moppins," said Brat, exhausted. "Don't we need to go?"

They started walking again. They cut down a dirt road and the rain stopped.

"Tell her, Daph," said Squirt. "Tell her what you told me."

"I'm really sorry about what happened to you in the village, at the lake," said Daphne. "Not all Elementals are like that. It was terrible how some cheered....I changed my mind; I'm going to help you and Brat get off the Zephyr and find Lexi."

"See, Anni. I told you she'd come around," said Squirt, bouncing.

Anni turned to face her. "Even if it means breaking the rules?"

"Actually, I think you know I can." Daphne pulled Anni aside, away from Squirt and Brat. "You know I saw your *golden bee* patch. Diana didn't, and that was because of me. You'd get into a realm of trouble if the Elofficials saw it—interrogated, for a start. It's your secret, and I'll keep it that way, but it's the other reason why I want to help you."

It was more proof that the old velvet cloth that she and Lexi had found was important and linked to the stolen Golden Bee Artifact. "Okay," Anni agreed.

They walked back to join the others.

"Are we cool now?" asked Squirt, beaming. "Told you Daph would help."

"For Elemental's sake, why are we on this road?" asked Brat with a mix of concern and panic. "This must be a mistake."

"No mistake," said Daphne. "She's staying with Fortensia at Spadu Hills."

"What? Why?" Brat halted midair. "I can't stay, I mean, she can't stay there—"

"Why not?" asked Squirt.

Brat's eyes bulged in horror. "Why not? Moppins! Don't you know? Unscrupulous Elkins, Scandaroons, and that sort hang out there."

"Actually, Brat," said Daphne. "Anni doesn't have a choice. She has to stay here. This *is* the only part of the Zephyr that can support her levels of Funk for more than six hours. Diana would never let Leach send her here if it wasn't safe."

"Leach? I should have known." Brat harrumphed.

They reached the end of the dirt road. Spadu Mountains would have been a better title for the place, as two massive slabs of jagged rock braced each other, forming a huge, haunting chasm beneath.

A weather-beaten sign hung over a spindly, two-story dilapidated shack barely attached to the hillside except for a few metal bolts keeping the building in place. Further down, there was a dark cave nestled within a fissure of the hillside, ornamented by rust-covered lamps, remnants of old tracks, and abandoned mining carts lying in ruined heaps.

A lopsided, weathered post stuck out from the ground between the cave and building with a sign that read:

WELCOME TO SPADU HILLS
HOME OF THE FINEST BLACK GOLD

Dust-caked windows revealed little more than the smudges of their fingertips and noses. It was too difficult to see inside, but the door's rusty sign said OFFICE.

Squirt tried the door. It was unlocked. He stepped inside first, and the girls followed. The floors creaked and moaned under their weight. No surprise, but the interior was no tidier than the exterior. A desk, pinned against the wall, lay scattered with papers, hand-sized shovels, and odd-shaped lumps of dirt.

Mounds of dirt stood everywhere—on the counters, shelves, and windowsills, even inside test tubes. Squirt was most interested in the dirt in the tubes, while Daphne and Anni stared at an enormous, two-foot platter that hung against the wall. A yellowed index card taped to the wall said *Ring gong for service!*

"I don't know about that," said Daphne as she peered past another doorway into an empty sitting room furnished with chairs and a fire. "Hello?"

Anni decided that the instructions were simple enough, but where was the instrument used to ring the gong? She looked under papers, under the desk, behind the cabinet, and inside drawers.

Squirt squished the dirt samples between his fingers, smelled it, and continued inspecting the other piles.

"Why are you touching that?" Brat asked Squirt. "Don't you know what that is?"

Anni spotted a soft drumstick lying under a small piece of fallen plaster. Deciding it must go with the gong, she positioned herself in front of it and pulled her arm back.

At the same moment, Brat, Daphne, and Squirt looked up. "*No!*" escaped their lips a second too late.

Anni drove the drumstick into the metal plate. The impact returned with an unexpected force.

The room and everything in it shook like a massive earthquake. All of them raced outside, but even there, the hillside shook. Deep within the bowels of the mountain, a fierce and terrifying noise echoed forth, roaring like a black bear waking up after a long hibernation.

A screeching cloud of gray, black, and brown flying objects swarmed the air, surrounding them in a dense, impenetrable fog. Instantly, Brat dove straight into Anni's shirt pocket, curled into a ball, and shivered.

Anni covered her eyes and ears. Nothing could be heard over the din. Her whole body tensed as she waited for the maelstrom to pass, Daphne and Squirt at her side.

Just when the screeching died down, a booming sound broke free. It bellowed off the cave's walls.

"WHO…RANG…THE…BELL?"

CHAPTER 26

FORTENSIA SPADU

A symphony of shrieks filled the air as a massive shroud of winged creatures encircled the woods. Hemmed in on all sides, Anni, Daphne, and Squirt couldn't run, and Brat burrowed into the smallest recess of Anni's pocket. The only clear path was the one in front of them, but that was the direction of the creepy voice.

A large, formidable shape emerged from the mouth of the cave. It trudged over a set of deteriorated railway tracks that led from the cave's entrance and moved in their direction. The trio froze as something moved toward them. It wasn't a man or a beast, but a woman, who pulled a bandana from her neck and dabbed her dirty face. Covered in muck from head to toe, the original color of her overalls, boots, gloves, and hat was impossible to distinguish. Muddied cracks lined her face as she squinted to examine the three standing before her.

The woman leaned against her spade and asked, "Which of you three rang the bell?"

The minute she spoke, the winged creatures vanished into the woods and the remaining dust in the air settled. Anni cleared her throat, glanced at Daphne and Squirt, and walked toward her. "I did."

The woman thrust her hand forward, and Anni trembled in response. The woman's body shook with laughter as she jumped off a wooden platform she was standing on, decreasing her size by half.

"Gets 'em every time!" she said, still laughing. "Didn't mean to frighten you, even though I did. I'm Fortensia Spadu." Fortensia grabbed Anni's hand in a vice-like grip before shaking it. "Knew you were coming. I like to have a bit of fun when I can. Scared your friends. Look at them—still shaking."

Anni smiled. She pretended to act calm, ignoring the tremors in her hand when she waved Squirt and Daphne over. The color was gone from their faces. Daphne offered a quiet hello as Fortensia clapped her and Squirt on the back, still chuckling.

"So you need a place to bunk. Gotta tell you the truth, I'm not one much for the lah-dee-dah rules, but I've got a small room, only nobody's been up there in…well, don't know the last time anyone's been up there. I'll need help loading guano tomorrow. After that, it's just bagging the stuff, but that's only if you can handle it. Most Elementals can't do the work—too dense for them—but you're human, so you should be just fine. Mind you, it's not the same thing as guano from the Noos—meaning, this stuff won't kill you if you breathe it in."

She paused and wiped her brow. "Anyhow, I'm managing five different Zephyrs, so I'm not here all the time. That Spongincork fellow signed you up for the work already. He didn't bat an eye when I said guano."

"Guano?" asked Anni.

"Don't know what guano is?" asked Fortensia with a chuckle. "Right, you must be a city slicker. Guano's black gold, that's what it is. A farmer or gardener wouldn't be caught dead without some. Family tradition in these hills, harvesting guano for Elementals and humans alike, for centuries."

"So, it's like dirt?" asked Anni.

"Hah! You're a regular comedian. Naw, it's better than dirt, girlie. It's the finest fertilizer this side of all the Zephyrs. I have over a thousand species producing the stuff. It's so pure, you can't even use it straight. Nope, too powerful that way. Nah, you gotta mix a cup to every ten bags of dirt. Course, then I suppose you can't call it dirt anymore, 'cause my guano changes the molecular structure, makin' it super dirt."

"Hmm, scooping dirt, that's not too bad," said Anni.

"It's not dirt," said Squirt, smiling. "Guano is bat poop."

One look at Squirt and Anni knew he was serious. She turned to Daphne, but her cheeks flushed pink and she didn't make eye contact. "Wait," Anni said. "For as long as I'm here, my job is to scoop up bat poo?"

"Yep, but only in the morning." Fortensia clapped Anni's shoulder and almost made her knees buckle. "Gotta play to stay. Them's the rules here: everyone works. And seems that Spongincork fella has some other jobs lined up for you."

"Fantastic," said Anni with a heavy dose of sarcasm.

"Aww, I envy you. Wish I could get in there and do it myself. Salt of the earth kinda work. You'll see. It's dark now; we'll have to wait until morning to start. All right then, I'll build a fire inside and show you to your room when you finish up out here. Nice to meet you two," said Fortensia, waving Daphne and Squirt goodbye.

The sky over Spadu Hills was clear and had turned to dusk in a blink. Stars peeked out behind white fluffy clouds. A chill filled the air, but there was no rain here. Daphne and Squirt said goodnight and reminded her that they would get her the next afternoon. Anni watched them leave, thinking that things could only get worse.

Forgetting to shut the door, Anni stood in the hallway of the cluttered office. She watched Fortensia stroke the glowing embers in the sitting room's fire pit. Without her new friends, sadness filled Anni. Even from the inside, Fortensia's ramshackle house didn't look safe. Anni silently prayed that it wouldn't collapse during her stay. She looked down and found her arms shaking. How did it get so cold all of a sudden?

"Come in or you'll catch your death," said Fortensia. "Weather here's not like where you're from. In these parts, nights reach freezing. You should remember that."

Once Anni passed the threshold of the sitting room, a blast of heat bathed her face and body. The orange glow of the fire cast a warm and cozy mood. Fortensia set a huge cast-iron kettle over the flames to boil water. The small sitting room had only a few wooden chairs and the threadbare rug in the center.

"Grab a seat; you're not a guest," said Fortensia as she pulled a large metal basin to the foot of the nearest rocking chair and poured the steaming water into it. She walked over to a wooden bureau precariously leaning against the wall and pulled handfuls of dried odds and ends from glass jars lined atop it. Then she tossed them into the steaming liquid.

Fortensia put her hand into the water to test it. Clearly satisfied, she plopped down into the rocker and put her bare feet into the steaming mixture. She melted into the chair, closed her eyes, and moaned with relief.

Anni sat there in silence and studied her surroundings. Though meager at first sight, the cozy room looked perfectly suited to the likes of someone as rugged as Fortensia.

"Still here? Must have dozed off. Suppose you're wondering where your room is. Last room at the top of the stairs over there. Just pull the hook." Fortensia smiled and pointed across the room. At the far end, against the mountainside wall, stood a narrow doorway with a rickety stairwell leading to the upper floors.

"By the way, Jay delivers food from the Noos from time to time. If you want something, write a note and stick it on the pitchfork outside the front door." Fortensia closed her eyes and resettled into her chair.

Anni walked through the doorway and up the staircase. It creaked under her weight. On the second-floor landing, she saw Fortensia's bedroom, the only room on the floor. The stairs ended on the third-floor landing, but there was no door or room in sight, only a square hook resting in the ceiling. Anni gave the hook a tug and, without warning, a wooden staircase shot down and pinned her to the floor. At first, she thought she was trapped, but after a little nudge, the stairs easily pushed back into place.

She righted the stairs and climbed up. Submerged in darkness, only a mere crack of light fluttered against the attic wall. Anni tiptoed her way toward the light as plumes of dust wafted up her nostrils. She pulled back a ratty curtain. Starlight revealed a small room with a sleeping bag propped in the corner.

"You can come out now," Anni whispered to Brat. "No one's here."

Brat shuffled in her pocket. "I'm fine right here, thanks."

"Suit yourself, but you're going to have to come out sometime."

Anni unrolled the sleeping bag and got inside. She used her backpack as a pillow.

"I hope Lexi's okay," she muttered into the darkness. "And not scared…"

Brat shifted himself out of her pocket and laid down on the backpack beside her head and said, "She might be stronger than you know, but I'll do whatever I can to help you find her."

"Brat, what do you know about Mabel and why she was banished from here?"

"Moppins, that was a sad story. For centuries, Elkins put their faith in an old legend of an Elemental prince who would come along and save our people, our planet, and allow us to live in harmony with the humans—teaching them our ways so they could evolve and take ownership of their choices. So it happens, an Elemental boy was born on Mineralstone Isle, a special kind of birthing Zephyr, and he matched the description of the legend. He was born to two old families, Murdrock and Moon. A great celebration was to take place in the human realm in honor of his birth. Mabel was head of the protection detail, along with dozens of the finest Elementals at her command. Only, things went very wrong, and for some unexplained reason, she was absent from the ceremony. I'll save you the gory details, but later, the Fectus claimed responsibility. The Prince, Eleck, was kidnapped along with his mother, a sweet woman named Isobella, and his father was killed on the spot. Thousands of Elementals lost their lives that day; it's the *Great Catastrophe* of our time. Mabel took full responsibility for her absence. Her name was tarnished and she was asked to leave Moon Zephyr. It also marked the last day Elementals were born. Mineralstone and a couple others like it went defunct—Elemental teens like Daphne and Squirt are the last of our kind."

Anni didn't say anything else. They both drifted off to sleep.

The next morning, nutty smells of hickory wafted up through the cracks in the floorboards. Anni peeled herself away from the army-green sleeping bag. In the daylight, the attic was actually bigger than she thought, but soot covered every surface.

"Morning, sleepy head." Brat was perched on her head. "You slept an entire day."

"What? No!" Anni shot straight up. "I lost a whole day? This can't be happening!" This was the worst way to wake up: furious with herself. "Why didn't you wake me up?"

"Couldn't. Maybe it was the lake, or too much Funk," he said. "Daphne and Squirt couldn't wake you up, either. Yugi looked at your eyeballs, then gave Fortensia some tonics. By the way, I'm not sure, but I'm a little worried she saw me when she poked her head in."

"That's another thing to worry about."

"She's downstairs. And if it's all the same to you, I'd like to hide out up here today."

"No way. You go where I go. Come on. In." Anni pointed at her pocket.

She made her way downstairs. Brat grumbled a few choice words at her but stopped once he heard Fortensia whistling.

Fortensia was hunched over a pot facing the fire. "Mornin'. Glad to see you finally came around. Have a seat…" She handed Anni a bowl of what looked like gruel. "For your strength. You'll need it today."

Anni warily eyed the food.

"Go on. It's porridge. You know, human food. We don't all eat twigs and puffs of air to survive, you know. I'm an Earth Elemental. I need more substance than most of the lot here does. I travel to the human realms every week."

Anni took the bowl and wondered where Fortensia went in the human world. She was ravenous, but it tasted delicious. When she finished, bits of porridge were still stuck to the side of her cheeks.

"Healthy appetite. I like that." Fortensia offered Anni another bowl.

Immersed in her bowl of buttery oats, Anni was grateful. When she finished, she spotted a decorative wooden perch sitting on Fortensia's coffee table that hadn't been there the night before; it was big enough for a parrot.

"Suppose you're full now? All right, we'll get started soon enough." Fortensia stuck two fingers into her mouth and whistled, but Anni didn't hear a sound. Fortensia smiled. "Can't give you the tour without Jasper."

A large, glowing orb, about the girth of a volleyball, whisked into the cabin. Anni pressed against her chair as the buzzing object flitted around her, sniffing like an excited puppy until it finally sat on the wooden perch. Brat shivered in her pocket.

"Anni, Jasper. Jasper, Anni. Jasper helps me in the caves."

Squat, with long feathery wings, Jasper was 100 times the size of a regular insect and resembled a dragonfly. Fortensia placed a small umbrella over the birdhouse and cooed, "But he hates guano droppings, don't you, Jasper?"

Jasper buzzed brightly in reply.

Fortensia filled her belt, grabbed Jasper's perch, turned to Anni, and said, "Let's go."

Disintegrated rail tracks at the mouth of the cave trailed deep into a long, dark tunnel. Huge boulders lined the cave's entrance. Inside, creatures like Jasper flitted about, lighting their way. As they walked deeper, Jasper's light shone the brightest.

Ahead, Anni noticed that the tracks had crumbled into the ground, and two lonely mine carts sat like decaying antiques, barely held together by bits of wood. Anni breathed a sigh of relief that the tracks ended because the carts looked positively dangerous.

"Hop in," said Fortensia, pointing to the farther of the two carts.

Anni gaped at Fortensia like she was insane.

"Safer than it looks. Trust me."

Not in the mood to question Fortensia's sanity, Anni climbed gingerly into the front seat and buckled two small straps over her lap. It was all she could do to humor Fortensia because there was no way they could move without tracks.

Fortensia squeezed in next to her, holding Jasper in her lap. The cart's wood creaked and moaned as if about to explode into a shower of tiny toothpicks.

"Down," the woman said with a robust force.

The cart took off like a bullet—not down, but straight ahead.

"Hold on."

Anni gripped the sides of the cart as it barreled forward. She liked the feel of the musty wind as it rushed past, suddenly thrilled by the speed at which they throttled forward without more than a foot's worth of light ahead of them. Jasper glowed and buzzed happily in his dropping-proofed perch.

Fortensia's face broke into a broad grin. Wanting to see more, Anni leaned over to inspect the view to the left of the cart. Despite Jasper's glow, all was dark below.

Without warning, the cart hurtled forward. Anni screamed and Fortensia laughed as the cart shot straight down, not on an angle, but on a ninety-degree free fall without any tracks beneath them. Something glimmered below; it was the ground, and it was coming up fast. They were going to crash. Every muscle in her body tensed. She clenched her eyes, jaw, and fists, bracing for the collision. But no collision came.

A luminous glow, brighter than Jasper's light, surrounded them. Anni peeked through one eye. The cart floated over a sparkling riverbed, the light almost ethereal, and slowed to a stop.

Fortensia clapped her hard on the shoulder. "Good girl. Kept your marbles on the way down."

Anni was only able to steady her breath because she was shaking all over. She wasn't the only one; Brat was shivering inside her pocket.

"Come on. Hop out. Take a look around." Fortensia pointed to a mountain-sized pile of slimy guano. "This is it!" She smiled like a mother hen.

Anni climbed out of the cart. She looked up at the dark shapes that flitted above. "What are those?"

Fortensia laughed. "What, the Raterons? Why, they make the guano. I provide room and board for their service; that's our agreement."

"Funny, they look like Fleet messengers."

"Shhh," said Brat, who trembled when the Raterons rustled and shrieked above.

"Well, don't you tell them that," whispered Fortensia. "In fact, I wouldn't mention that word in here. They're all part of the Raterons species, but that lot over there," Fortensia pointed, lowering her voice further. "Calls 'emselves *Pirats*. Don't know the particulars, but they don't get on with them Fleet Raterons. And I don't get mixed up in any of their business, other than packing up the guano. Neither should you." She gestured to the largest mound, next to a radiant riverbed. "All right, down to business. This pile of guano here needs to be bagged, sealed, and shuttled to the top. First, I need you to help load up the hover-flats. See those bags? All of them gotta go." She pointed to a wall of prefilled guano bags and two long, empty pallets. "All right, you can suit up over there."

Next to some spades and lanterns were extra coveralls and rubber boots, about Anni's size. She dressed and wrapped a scarf around her mouth and nose. First, Fortensia showed her how to scoop, bag, and seal the guano. Then they filled up one long hover-flat and half of another before Fortensia got ready to leave.

"Gotta take this lot to the loading dock. Jay will come back for the second hover-flat. Fill it up and leave it up top. I won't see you 'til tomorrow morning. Oh, and before I forget, there's another cart over there. Only two directions. Hook it to this hover-flat and say 'Up' to get to the top and 'Down' to get down here. Cart'll do the rest. Much as I'd like to chat, these bags won't sell themselves. You're a tough nut; you'll be fine."

Anni watched Fortensia hook her carts up; it seemed easy enough. She climbed back into the cart, leaving Jasper behind for Anni, bellowed "Up," and shot into the air like a rocket. As Anni watched, she felt something trickle down her head and shoulders.

"Gross," said Anni when she realized it was guano droppings. "What am I doing in here? This is crazy. I need to leave, not scoop up this stuff."

"Glad you think so," whispered Brat. "What's your plan?"

"You know, I think I got a good one. Why are you whispering?"

"Avoiding..." His tiny arm pointed upward. "*Them.*"

"Hmm," she said, looking at how many more bags of guano she needed to load, when suddenly she figured it out. Anni grinned broadly.

"What?" Brat gave her a sideways look. "Why are you smiling like a three-headed *Snaca-doodtod?*"

"Because it won't be much longer now, Brat. I just figured out exactly how to get us off this Zephyr. We'll be home before you know it."

CHAPTER 27

THE BROUWEN

L exi squinted as she and the other prisoners followed Mortimer through a cloud of steam issuing from a car-sized copper cauldron in the middle of a massive quartz quarry.

"Welcome to the Brouwen. You will be peeling, chopping, slicing, stirring, boxing, and jarring," said Mortimer. He left a trail of slime behind him that was promptly swept up by a crew of small mutant creatures, half armadillo—half porcupine.

The vast crystalline crater looked out of place after walking down from the dank brown tunnels above. This room looked like a massive kitchen for cooking something, although Lexi didn't know what it was for just yet. A steaming cauldron the size of a house sat in its center; the vapors escaping from it tickled Lexi's nose and made her feel sick.

"This is where you will work and live. Unless, of course, anyone here would prefer a dark, dirty cell on the prison block." Mortimer paused as if this was his attempt at a joke, or perhaps he was giving the four of them a chance to pick that option.

There were more slugs like Mortimer, but smaller, working around the cauldron. Human teenagers ran up and down ladders, others worked at tables, but all of them had heavy bags under their eyes. Lexi thought the private, dark cell sounded preferable.

Mortimer moved his small group through the crater and up to the mouth of an endless tunnel. "This is Bee Hall," he said, waving absently at what looked like a subway tunnel lined with millions of small glass jars. Each one had tiny little creatures similar to lightning bugs trapped inside. They glowed a bright, electric blue color with a touch of gold.

"Oh," said the girl Kat, who reached out and touched the glass of one of the small jars. Lexi watched as the wisp of light inside glowed even brighter, which then created a chain reaction to all the jars next to the first.

"Do not touch the ingredients!" said Mortimer in a frightening tone.

Lexi jumped back, trembling. This was the first time he made eye contact with them, and she didn't like it, because his eyeballs were blood red.

"Only Brouwen Masters add the final ingredients to the Plantanana Juice," he said, leaning over Kat and Lexi. "If you so much as lay another finger on those jars, you'll get an audience with our Queen, the Naga Yaga herself. Trust me: most die of fright just from gazing into her lidless eyes."

"Your lodgings are in the room behind here." Mortimer showed them with a tiresome wave. "The first patch of dirt you see is your bed. Change into your uniforms and hurry back."

Kat shrank back and raced into the room. Lexi followed her inside. One person lay asleep on the dirt floor, a bedraggled stick of a girl with matted hair.

Quickly, they changed into their rag uniforms and piled their human clothes in the cleanest dirt corner they could find. When Kat's back was turned, Lexi hid her pearl necklace inside one of the folds of her clothes before she followed Kat back out.

"This way," said Mortimer once they exited their dirt caves and headed back into the Brouwen.

Lexi took one more glance at the mysterious lights inside the jars. She had never seen anything like it before. The shelves looked like little beehives.

"You know what they are, don't you?" asked Kat in a whisper.

"No. I don't," said Lexi. "Do you?"

"It's why you don't want to be an Elemental, not in here, anyway. Those lights, in the jars, come from *cracked* Opus Stones." Lexi frowned at her. "Oh, I forgot. You're human…uh, like me. The Naga Yaga does the *cracking*. She rips out the soul from the body while it's still alive, puts them into these jars, and then they sell the *cracked* Stones."

"What do they do with the lights in the jars?"

Kat pointed at the cauldron. "We're the slave labor that gets to cook them."

Lexi gulped. She couldn't help but think that the lights had grown dimmer once Kat said that.

"Follow. Follow," said Mortimer, stopping at a busy chopping table loaded with boxes of fruit that looked a lot like bananas. "You'll be paired off with a sous-chef. You will do exactly what they say. Understand—"

At first, Lexi was so caught up and horrified by what Kat said that she didn't notice the bedraggled girl who had been asleep in the cave when Lexi and Kat changed. Now this girl was fully awake and interrupting Mortimer. Lexi did, however, recognize what the bedraggled girl handed over to Mortimer.

"Happens every time," said Mortimer dryly. "Which of you brought this pearl?"

CHAPTER 28

MOONSTONES

"This is absolutely disgusting," said Brat, sandwiched beside Anni. "I don't know what I was thinking when you suggested this. Why in snoz' sakes did I listen to you?"

"Shush! Do you want to leave the Zephyr or not? Now, be quiet and don't move," said Anni, peering through the small holes of the bag. "I think I can hear Jay coming. And whatever you do, don't move a muscle."

The soft crunch of footfalls surrounded them. Anni held her breath until the hover-flat rose off the ground and started moving. It wasn't exactly comfortable with her and Brat stuffed inside the burlap sack surrounded by other bags of guano, but at least it would get them off the Zephyr, and through LimBough, where Anni and Brat could escape to the human world.

Brat made a face at her and crossed his arms in protest. It wasn't like they were sitting in the guano; they had themselves sewn inside an empty sack, which was positioned on the middle of the hover-flat and surrounded and barricaded in by other bags on all sides so that no one would be the wiser.

Anni assumed her plan worked because Jay didn't check the sacks and the hover-flat rose off the ground, business as usual. Jay whistled as if everything was normal. Anni and Brat sat in silence as the hover-flat made its long procession to the village. When they overheard Elementals talking, Anni smiled. They had reached the loading bridge.

They overheard Jay talking to someone. Anni smiled at Brat. They were finally on their way off the Zephyr, right under everyone's noses. It was so simple; she couldn't believe it. Everything went just as planned…until the top of their bag split open.

Jay's wild red hair blew in the wind and he was smiling. "Nice try, and major props, kid, but I don't miss a trick. If you must know, it was your Funk."

"Then pretend you didn't see me," said Anni. "Please, just let me go."

"Can't. It's more trouble than it's worth." He fluffed his hair back and said, "If I let you cross that bridge, you'd be at the bottom of that near-empty lake. Come on, sweetheart. Out." He reached out a hand.

Anni sighed loudly, covering up Brat's harrumph, and took Jay's hand. A few Elementals in the vicinity watched her and scowled. It was still raining over the Lake, and it wasn't even half full. Mad, sad, and completely resigned, she brushed herself off, jumped off the hover-flat, and walked back to the dirt road. "Don't say it, Brat."

Jay strolled over to her. "Look, kid, I might be able to help you out."

Wet guano dripped down her face, but she didn't wipe it away.

"Tell me where you need to go," said Jay. "And I'll see what I can do. You do know where you're going, right?"

That was the question, wasn't it? She didn't know where Lexi was. That was another problem entirely, but if he could help her get there, her problem was solved.

"I'm not sure yet."

"Well, you gotta figure that out. *Capisce?*"

"Yeah, I get it," said Anni, wondering why up until now, no one else had been willing to help her. Here he was, giving her a chance. "Why do you want to help?" She wanted to kick herself for asking, but he was Miranda's brother. She couldn't be too careful.

Jay laughed. "Straight to the point. I like it. I also like to do favors. You never know when you're going to need one. And that's all you need to know for now."

"So if I gave you a location how long would it take you to help me get there?"

Jay scratched his chin. "A day, two on the long side. Not to worry, kid." He winked. "Oh, and try not to attract too much attention." Jay headed back to the loading bridge.

Elementals had stopped to stare at her, but she didn't care. This was her first big break. "See," she said to Brat, who flew out from his hiding place in Anni's pocket and landed on her shoulder. "Wasn't such a bad idea, was it? That's our best offer yet."

"Hmm, we'll see." Brat pointed up at the sky. "Why are those Fleet messengers zooming around over the—"

"Anni?" Squirt ran toward her, flanked by Daphne. "Whoa, your hair's green. Why are you covered in…is that guano? Tell me you didn't hide—"

"That's right," said Brat, scowling at Anni. "We got caught hiding *in* the guano."

Squirt started to giggle and had to hold his side to stop from laughing harder.

"Stop it, Squirt," said Daphne. "Anni, I wouldn't make any deals with Jay, you can't trust him….Come on, let's go back to Fortensia's. Brat…keep a low profile."

Anni didn't want this one piece of hope taken away, so she didn't tell them.

"Diana had to cancel today," said Daphne. "But we also came to warn you. Spongincork ordered an escort to take you to all your work duties starting tomorrow."

"What? Why? I don't need an escort."

"It's because of the Lake," said Squirt, still grinning. "If they found out that you tried to escape this morning, you'd get a twenty-four-hour guard. That's not all. Brat—"

"Not out loud," said Daphne and whispered to Brat, "Keep your head down."

"Why do I need to keep my head down?" asked Brat.

"Fleet are patrolling the sky," said Squirt. "Elofficials hired them."

"Impossible," said Brat. "The Fleet works *with* them, not *for* them. It's in our by-laws. I've been gone a couple days and our whole world's upside down."

"All Fleet on this Zephyr have been ordered off message duty and are on patrol duty. Sorry, Brat," said Daphne. "There's a warrant out for your arrest."

"What? Me?" asked Brat. "I told you." He poked Anni's chest. "I told you I would get into trouble. Here it is. Moppins, where can I go?"

"Shush. You don't want them to hear you," said Squirt, pointing up above at two Fleets flying overhead. "Get back in Anni's pocket."

"We can't talk out here," said Anni, seeing Fortensia's house in view. "Let's get inside, and we can figure it out there."

"That's not all," said Daphne as they made their way inside. "Strange stuff is going on at the Manor and the village. Shops are shutting down regular service for the next couple days. I've only got a half-day today at Haberdashers. They said they were doing inventory, but we already did that a month ago."

"Yeah," said Squirt. "Since when does Moon Manor have guards around the clock?"

They made their way inside Fortensia's, and once Anni was sure they were alone, Brat flew out of her pocket.

"Moppins, I'm done for. First chance, you're going to leave without me," said Brat, who flopped down on Fortensia's bench and covered his head with a droopy wing. "Go on, turn me in. Throw me into the Egghouse."

"Calm down, Brat. I won't leave without you," Anni said, even though she had no idea how she was both going to find Lexi and clear Brat's name at the same time. "I promise I'll get you out of trouble. I don't know how yet, but I will help you."

"I have an idea," said Squirt. "You won't like this, Brat, but this might help you both. Fleet service is restricted in only one place on this Zephyr. Spadu Hills! I know this because I tried to send a message here but couldn't. Something to do with the Raterons having issues with Elofficials. Anyway, Brat, you can hide safely there and you'll be able to get underground news. You know, rub some elbows."

"I didn't think of that. Good idea," said Daphne.

"No. No. No. Not a good idea," said Brat, wringing his tiny fists. "I swore an oath. If I even so much as 'rub elbows,' as you so eloquently put it, with *Pirats*, my Fleet status will be revoked." He snapped his fingers. "Just like that, and I'll get the bunk."

"Haven't they already done that?" said Squirt. "But they'd never suspect that you'd hide out with the *Pirats*—"

"Really? You think it's that easy?" Brat crossed his arms. "Okay, I'll just stroll into the largest congregation of villainous and corrupt denizens north of the Mediterranean and say, 'What's up, Pirats? I'm gonna hang out with you for a few days. If that's cool.' Mopple-toppined nonsense! What makes you think they'll even trust me or let me stick around?"

"But you told me, back when Anni arrived, that you had a cousin on this Zephyr," said Squirt. "Didn't you say he could get you underground information?"

"One-eyed-Nimmy is thirteen crackers short of a dozen. Information, yes, he can do that, but keep me safe? I'm not so sure. *Pirats* aren't friendly. If they so much as find out I'm Fleet...Nope, the Egghouse sounds better already."

"Diana might be able to help," said Daphne. "She consults Fleet on behalf of Moon Manor and deals with their advisory board."

"Brat, I know this is a lot to ask," said Anni, trying not sound too desperate. "Think of Lexi. If you hang out with One-eyed Nimmy, you might help her."

"Oh, I see how it is." Brat snorted. "And, what exactly are you going to do for me?"

"I'll ask Diana to get you cleared with Fleet," Anni said. "I'll beg if I have to."

Brat paced. "Fine. I'll do it for Lexi, but I want Squirt to take me to the cave."

Anni knew they still had a long way to go, but she felt better knowing she had help.

"Good. They're gone," said Daphne as she pulled a small velvet pouch out of her hip pack. The exact emblem of the bee from Anni's patch matched the one on this bag. "I could get into enormous trouble for this, and the less people who know, the better. I told you I would keep your secret, and now you know one of mine. By the way, if you want me to sew that velvet Bee patch back on your tank, I will."

Anni nodded, but didn't interrupt.

"Moonstones are not commonly used anymore. It's a long story, but in short the Elofficium has banned anything that has to do with prophesying. All right, now think about finding Lexi and carefully pull out five stones, one by one, and set them down in a circle. These won't say where she is, but they'll help us understand what's involved."

Anni focused on finding Lexi and pulled out exactly five stones. They were long, flat, and oval and had an opalescent shimmer. Daphne noted each one as they were pulled. Each one glowed a different color with a single word on its surface: DRAGON, WOOD, PORCUPINE, JAGUAR, and BEE.

As the words appeared, Daphne gasped. "Oh my Els, wow, I…uh, I've never seen *Dragon* come up before, or *Bee* at the end. Hmm, Dragons are considered an unfavorable dangerous sign, I'm being polite when I say that…Actually, this is way more advanced than I can read right now. I need to do some research. Memorize those words."

"But Dragons don't exist. How can that be bad?" Anni wondered what the big deal was. "It's just a bunch of animal names. It's not like it's telling us the future."

Daphne swiftly collected the stones and carefully placed them back in the pouch with a certain amount of reverence. "Anni, you don't understand. That's exactly what these stones do. Auguriums, sort of like Elemental fortunetellers, were masters at reading the Moonstones; they used them to record prophecies for every single Elemental child that has ever been born. The Moonstone readings have been documented for centuries, all of them have been true, all except one…. And you're wrong: dragons exist, or they did. They have a reputation for being vile, dangerous creatures, and you can never trust them. One dragon shared sacred Elemental secrets with a dangerous human, who used that information to bring about Funk and destruction and other horrors that started a whole chain of events pitting Elementals against humans."

A knock at Fortensia's door surprised them both, but when Anni turned around, she couldn't believe who was standing in the doorway.

CHAPTER 29

BASIL BOGGLE TEA SHOPPE

Anni rose, blinking several times just to be sure she wasn't dreaming. Vivian Sugar stood in Fortensia's doorway.

Daphne stood and said "Hello" first.

"Sorry," said Anni, still stunned. "Miss Sugar, this is Daphne. Come in."

"I'm not interrupting, am I?" asked Vivian. "I can come back if you like."

"No," said Daphne. "Actually, I need to be going anyway. Anni, I'll see you later. Nice to meet you, Miss Sugar." And she left them.

"I expect you are surprised to see me here," said Vivian. "Here, on the Zephyr."

Anni nodded, speechless.

"Oh, dear," said Vivian, looking nervous. "Where to start? With the truth, I suppose...Anni...I'm an Elemental. Moon Manor is my family home. Mabel was my aunt, and Teddy my uncle. I came to Waterstone Academy after Mabel—well, you know, to help Teddy out. Teddy and Egbert made it plain to me that I could not share my family associations without discussing or explaining the Elemental world to you. I'm very sorry about that, especially if I have lost your trust and your friendship; that would grieve me greatly. Honestly, I have been beside myself once I was told about Lexi's disappearance, and you gone as well. I've tried in vain to find Lexi. Egbert would not allow me to help him—to put it mildly, he and I do not get along. You might like to know Headmistress Turnkey is on the mend. Al-though I didn't know it at the time, she and Egbert used the expulsion as an excuse to get you and Lexi away from school and somewhere safe. Anni, I would have come sooner, had I known you were here. But on the off chance that you arrived here, I asked—begged—my sister Krizia to allow you to stay."

"She's your sister?" Anni wondered when people would stop keeping so much from her, but she directed her irritation at Egbert and could barely contain her frustration with him. "I told Egbert that Finnegan was responsible. Finnegan was working with someone, I don't know who; they planned to kidnap Lexi and me. Egbert tricked me into coming here. I have to leave and find her. I don't know where she is. I'm so worried. Can you help me leave? I could come with you. We could look for her together."

"Oh, Anni," said Vivian with a pitiful gaze. "I'm afraid my influence here is not strong enough to get you off the Zephyr. If someone was after you as well as Lexi, I can understand now why Egbert sent you here." Vivian paused. "I can see that I have let you down. Will you allow me to do something to make it up to you? I am just as much your relation as Egbert is, and with your permission, of course, I can petition the Elofficium to become one of your vouchers while you stay here. Would you like that?"

"Yes, yes." Anni nodded, starting to feel calmer. She loved this idea. If only it applied to the human world as well! Vivian would speak frankly to her, not treat her like a child like Egbert had, and she wouldn't keep any secrets. Anni knew Vivian would help her in any way that she could, just as she had at Waterstone Academy.

"Excellent; I am so pleased. I'll go straight to the Elofficium office. It could take up to two weeks to approve the paperwork."

"Two weeks? Lexi can't wait two weeks. It has been four days already!"

"I know, Anni. I know. I...I don't know what else I can do." Vivian's brows furrowed as she placed her hand on Anni's shoulder. "But I promise I will search for her in the meantime. I will do all I can to find out where Lexi is. Okay?"

Even though she didn't like the idea of waiting, Anni cleared her throat. "Yes, okay." It was the best offer she had yet, and with Vivian on her side, hope buoyed. She felt better.

Once Vivian left, Anni felt the pressing weight of her loneliness. It was unbearable. She decided to shovel a few bags of guano, and visit with Brat, but he was nowhere to be seen. After she filled two dozen guano bags, she left the caves to wash up and eat some cold porridge. She went up to her room early for bed and wrote in her journal.

Next morning, Anni got up early. Too anxious to sit around, she did her chores in the caves with the hope of seeing Brat, but there was still no sight of him. By midday, Squirt arrived minutes before her guarded escort to Moon Manor. Grateful for Squirt's company, she told him she was concerned about Brat. Squirt promised he would check the caves later and told her Daphne was filling in at Haberdashers. Anni wondered if Daphne decoded the Moonstones, and if the stones could really tell her future.

Fort ushered Anni to the compost heap where, days ago, she had been unceremoniously jettisoned into the largest mound of rotten scraps. He handed her a rake and a shovel. "Have fun," he said and laughed as he walked inside the Manor.

"What am I supposed to do?"

Squirt had left to get his orders from the Manor, so he wasn't there to help, either. A note on one of the shovels said, "Flip the compost and rake it over. Repeat until you've done the whole pile. Guards will be watching. If you don't, we can arrange something with the Elofficium instead. –M. Spongincork."

She looked up and saw Fort grinning at her from the Manor's second-floor balcony. The compost heap was half the size of a tennis court. Unbelievable. She gritted her teeth and slowly made her way over the low brick wall and into the shallowest pile.

The sun was on her the whole time as she dug, flipped, and raked. Blisters were starting to form on her thumbs, and just when she thought she was making headway, a massive pile of freshly chopped vegetables and other slimy things flew through the overhead chute, landing partly on her and her newly shoveled rows.

That was it. She threw her shovel, which landed hard on a huge brown crate in the far corner. She grumbled as she waded back to the brick wall.

Across the lawn, Squirt was running toward her. He waved his hands and yelled, "*Get out!*" She had no idea what he was screaming about. She turned around and saw what can only be described as an oversized worm with an enormous mouth and rotating razor-sharp teeth burrowing through the composted layers. It was moving as fast as a lawnmower over tall grass and it was heading right at her. She screamed. Squirt was too far away and her left foot was stuck in a melon rind.

An arm yanked her over the wall. It was Oliver. "You're making my job hard to keep you alive." He grinned. "Oh, and try not to pet the worms while they're eating." He sauntered back inside the Manor. Anni had the strong desire to chuck the melon rind at his big, smug head, but she couldn't. He had saved her life twice now.

Squirt jogged over. "Phew…" He panted. "Who let the Royal Worms out? They only come out at night. They'll need some tea leaves or they'll get sick."

Stunned, Anni watched the creature zip back and forth, fast as lightning, eating up the mounds of compost until there was nothing left but dust. Altogether, it took less than three minutes before the worm inched passively back into its crate.

She must have looked like she was still in shock because Squirt led her to the large glass greenhouse, sat her down, put some goopy ointment on her blisters, and gave her a glass of water. In no time, her hands were as good as new and she watched him flit around, filling empty vials with colorful waters. He took a single flower, whispered something to it and placed it into what looked like a test tube, which he attached to a glass wall panel. Within a millisecond, the entire side of the greenhouse was filled with thousands of the same flower. She went to touch one, thinking it might be an illusion or a hologram of a flower, but she was surprised to find that they were all real.

"Cool, huh?" said Squirt. "I've got something even better." He leaned his left ear up to her face. "Do you see it? Bet you don't. It's in my ear."

At first she didn't see it, but inside, barely visible, was a thin tendril connected to a tiny pea. "What is—is it moving?"

"Only slightly," he said. "And this is just the baby bud, small enough to put in your ear, but over here—," he pointed to something that resembled a tiny snapdragon with dusty, pale pink petals— "this little beauty is called *Antirrhinum Gemin*. I call it Eaves-Dropus. It's extremely unusual and it isn't cataloged in *Acceptable Elofficial Plant Guides*. The thing about this plant is that when you place it next to a different flower species, it mimics what the other flowers look like, but that's not all. It has another use, which is why it camouflages itself. It's a listening device."

"Really? Could I use it find out more about Lexi?"

"Yes! And that's only one of my brilliant ideas," he said, brushing off one of his shoulders. "But don't tell Daph, not yet. She won't approve. Anyway, it'll be ready in a couple days."

"I want to help," said Anni. If she could just overhear where someone thought Lexi was taken, then she could to tell Jay. "Fort's coming for me. See you tomorrow."

She couldn't imagine what new twisted job Spongincork's brain had come up with and arranged for her after shoveling bat poop, compost, and encountering flesh-eating worms. Fort escorted her through the village—it was still raining over the Lake—and finally back to Spadu Hills. The next day was the same as before; she shoveled guano and more compost, even though she couldn't believe there was the same amount as the previous day. She was left thinking that maybe these would be her only chores, but instead of heading back to Spadu Hills after her second day of compost duties, they stopped in the village.

Before they turned right by Haberdashers Clothing Emporium, Fort turned left up the cobblestone walk. It was crowded with Elementals under umbrellas that hovered over their heads like the one Daphne had used a few days ago. The narrow walk was a jumble of Elementals coming and going out of a building called Mooncakes Café. Fort stopped in front of another building, Basil Boggle Tea Shoppe, which, from the outside window, looked completely deserted inside.

A small bell rang when Anni opened the door. The storefront windows provided an excellent view of the bustling village, which stood in contrast to the deserted shop. It was empty except for one person behind a long bar: Mackenzie. He looked just as happy and mellow as when she had seen him the first time, and she secretly admired his repose. If she even had an ounce of his ability to be calm and not worry so much about Lexi, her fingernails wouldn't be the tiny nubs she had whittled them down to.

"Hiya," Mackenzie smiled. "Diana will be down in a few minutes. Thirsty?"

Remembering that Mackenzie was a Water Elemental, Anni wondered if that was why she felt so calm and agreeable around him. "Okay." Anni sat down at the bar as Mackenzie went into the back, and didn't see Miranda.

"Listen up, Egghead," said Miranda, forcing her already strong jawline to jut out even more severely. "I don't know why you're here, but I don't trust you. There's nothing you can do or get away with on this Zephyr that I won't find out about. So when you do try something, know this: Leach is the first person I'm telling. Just a friendly warning." She sashayed to the other side of the bar just as Mackenzie reentered from the back room.

The bell on the door tinkled as someone entered the Tea Shoppe. "Anni," said Diana. "Let's take a seat by the window." They sat at a four-top table next to a huge, sweeping window with a prime view of the village, which was mostly deserted on account of the rain. Diana grinned, "So I hear you had quite the morning the other day."

Mackenzie brought over two drinks, and Diana said, "Mac, can you please let Effie know we're here?" Miranda shot Anni a nasty look that no one else saw. Diana continued. "Anni, I know this is hard, but I have to ask you to try not to escape the Zephyr."

Anni focused on her drink: orange-tinted water with a glowing blue petal on top. It was delicious, but she wasn't going to waste time talking about Elemental drinks or food. "Lexi's my family, my only family left in the whole entire world. I can't just hang out here and be happy doing weird chores. I have to find her. I can't just be okay and leave her all alone. She needs me. We look out for each other. I have to find her."

Diana peered deeply into Anni's eyes and very seriously said, "I understand more than you might know. I know it's asking a lot of you to try to be patient and not get into trouble, but consider that although your chores are unappealing, they are a far better alternative than what Spongincork originally submitted to the Elofficium." Her voice softened. "Regardless, first and foremost, I'm concerned with your safety and well-being. Your levels of Funk are too high for you to leave, and we cannot cure it all at once. Simply put, your body cannot withstand Elemental travel until your Funk fades."

"How long will that take? It's not like I asked to come here."

"A couple weeks, maybe more, maybe less." Diana sighed. "It's hard to say. This wouldn't be an easy adjustment for any human, withstanding Funk or falling into lakes. Anni, all I ask is that you have a little bit of patience and trust."

The mention of the word *trust* made the small hairs on Anni's neck bristle, and *patience* was not in her vocabulary. She hoped Vivian would hurry along her voucher paperwork as soon as possible. Sure, Diana was nice enough, but talking to her about Lexi seemed pointless. Still, there was one thing she needed. "Can you at least help my friend? He's a Fleet messenger." She leaned in and whispered. "His name is Brat. He accidentally traveled here with me, and now he's in big trouble."

"Ah, yes, the one with the warrant. I'll see what I can do. I might be able to pull some strings," Diana said. "But Anni, hold this thought: Elementals are looking for Lexi as we speak." She hesitated. "I know what that feels like...to lose a best friend, and even family. If I hear anything about Lexi, I will let you know."

Anni could almost see her own hope and fear reflected in Diana's eyes and believed her, but she couldn't help but feel that things didn't end well for the friend Diana was referring to, which made her feel worse.

"Oh, she's here at last," said a little old woman with a bubbly voice. She didn't move with the same enthusiasm her voice held: she shuffled, and finally embraced Anni. The old woman was slightly hunched, she wore a patchwork dress under a honeycomb shawl, and all the remaining wispy hairs on her head were pulled into a bun by two chopsticks.

"Uh, hi," said Anni, not knowing exactly how to respond.

"Anni, this is my Elmother, Ephegenia OggleBoggle, and this is her Tea Shoppe."

"Call me Effie, my dear sweet, sweet girl," corrected Ephegenia OggleBoggle. "And welcome to our little family's Tea Shoppe. Diana's a part owner, you know." She winked. "Oh my, it's been so long, too long. Diana darling, I'm just going to spirit this one away for a few minutes, all right?" Old Effie might have been old, but age didn't touch the youth of her happiness, which lived in every crack and crinkle on her joyously lined face. "We have much to catch up on. Haven't seen you since you were a baby. Imagine that!"

"Yes, of course, Effie. I'll leave you two in peace," said Diana with a smile.

"And Anni, I arranged with Maeleachlainn Spongincork to have you help out here in the afternoons, wash a few dishes, et cetera. Mac will explain. You can eat all your meals here, and Yugi will schedule daily checkups to help your Funk. Now, I'm going to see what I can do about that thing we discussed. Okay?"

"Secrets?" said Effie, beaming. "Oh, how I delight in the worlds of the unknown!"

"You can always contact me through Daphne, or Miranda if she's around," said Diana. "Miranda, be sure to show her how things work."

Anni didn't dare glance in Miranda's direction and gladly followed Effie to the back room where they passed through doors and down a short hallway.

"My husband Basil was batty about tea," said Effie. "As you see, we're not very busy. Mooncakes Café is newer, a novelty, but I will say, we still have the best customers, and sometimes in life, you will learn: this is this because that is that."

Anni didn't quite know what to say to that.

Effie opened a small door, and Anni followed her into a comfortable little hut that was full of windows. Happy shades of lemon yellow and apple green greeted them at every turn, with a merry crackling fireplace in the center of it all. Treasures of all kinds covered every inch of the walls: trinkets, patchwork designs, statues, cards, letters, books, gemstones, beaded necklaces, maps, charts, candles, easels, antique china, rag rugs, plants…the list was endless. It was not the utility room Anni had expected.

"This looks like someone's house," said Anni.

"It is. It's my house. Don't tell anyone, but I've got Incantare doors here and there."

"Incantare?" asked Anni.

"It's a lot like magic!" Effie's eyes sparkled. "Incantare is enchanted wood, and in the shape of a door, it will whisk you off to a different place, so long as both the doors are made of the same wood. It's a great help for an old gal like me, takes me where I need to go, but just a bit quicker." She beamed, looking around her house. "How do you like it? It's decorated with all my travels so I can see my friends and family every day. I'm a big believer in connecting the dots, because, after all, our lives are made up of little dots. Don't you agree? You look like the sort that would."

Anni nervously smiled. It was true; the place was packed full of stuff, but it didn't feel cluttered. Everything was exactly in its right place. Effie's life was literally living on her walls. "It's nice," she said, looking at the hand-sewn linen maps. "Do you travel a lot?"

"Elementals do have that advantage, don't they? I adore adventures. Do you like treasure maps? I do. I find that life is full of adventures, and many dots to follow."

Anni didn't quite understand what that meant.

"Yes," Effie said as if responding to Anni's own thoughts. "Life is full of dots. There's always change, rush, and worry—you can count on that—but the dots are there. They are everywhere, waiting for you to connect them."

"Dots?" asked Anni. "I don't see any dots."

"Oh, but my darling girl, you will, you will." Effie's eyes grew wide. "They pop up when you least expect it, they tug ever so gently at your heart strings, and of course your heart always knows where you can call home. Yes, yes, just listen and look. The dots are everywhere, and then you know, you know it's time."

Anni wondered if Ms. OggleBoggle was a little confused. "You said you knew me when I was little?"

"Yes, yes." Effie pulled out photos of various babies she named off. All of the pictures had the same glowing background. "Here's my Mabel. You remind me of her, and my Diana, I've seen them all make their way into this world. It was like yesterday when I met you and Lexi, another special girl. Don't worry about her, dear. She'll be just fine. The thing is, in life, sometimes things happen that we cannot explain, but you must know that. We might not always like it, and the passion of youth is hard to match, but really, it's all just an adventure, only you don't know it until it's nearly over. "

Hearing Effie say Lexi was fine gave Anni a small spark of hope. "What do you know about Lexi and Mabel?"

"Lexi is very special. I feel her life force even if she is thousands of miles away. You must believe in her right now. That is very, very important. You have no idea how powerful intention can be. Your strength will give her great strength, and my dear, Lexi will need it."

Anni blinked back a tear. Effie patted her arm and said, "Mabel loved you very much. I know that she is with you, even though you do not see her. When you get as old as I do, you often see things that others don't. Oh, my sweet girl, don't mind me or the ramblings of an old woman. Before you know it, you'll be hearing voices in your head, too." She smiled at Anni and gave her a knowing look that pierced right through her act of senility. "But if you do," she said seriously, "you should at the very least listen."

Was Effie completely befuddled? Did she know about Whiffle?

"Oh my, oh my, look at the time. You've got to get back to the shop. Your friend Daphne has arrived. Thank you for bringing sunshine into an old woman's home. I'm having a little party in a couple days, and I'd love it if you'd be my guest of honor." Effie ushered her through the doors that led back into Basil Boggle's Tea Shoppe. "Remember the dots. Don't forget the dots."

Inside the Tea Shoppe, a few tables had been taken. Mackenzie looked relaxed, chatting up the customers at the bar. When he spotted Anni, he said, "Tomorrow, I'll fill you in on what to do. It's easy. Diana said to give you tonight off, but feel free to hang out. Daphne's over there. Oh, here are your tea leaves; Effie said you'd ask for them."

Anni gasped. Mackenzie laughed and said, "You'll get used to it."

She made a beeline for Daphne's booth and started feeling hopeful. Whether or not Effie OggleBoggle had all her mental faculties well sorted was questionable, but for Lexi, she'd do just about anything.

"I've got it," Daphne whispered. "Sorry it took me so long to decipher this, but the *Scriptorium* has been closed for two days on account of the rain and humidity. Apparently, it's bad for paper. I had to beg the owner's son to let me sneak in to do research because the Manor's library had nothing on the *D-word*." Daphne secretly handed Anni a list. "Normally, I would say that the first one," she pointed to the word *Dragon*, "spells out danger in a major way, or is a really bad omen, but you simply can't read the stones that way. There's an art to understanding them. And then there's the order in which you pulled them from the bag to consider, too. Everything in the Elemental world is interconnected."

Anni read the list.

Dragon – protection, caution, an invitation, insight, life, and power.
Wood – an Elemental classification, travel or journey, understanding.
Porcupine – signals faith, innocence, and trust.v

Jaguar – strength, vision, must embrace the gifts, and transformation.
Bee – circle of life, dedication, positive outcome, goals, and sacrifice.
Key words are based on the order you chose the cards: PROTECTION, TRAVEL, TRUST, TRANSFORMATION, and SACRIFICE.

"They don't say where Lexi is, though."

"I told you before they're not that specific, but if you look only at the key words from the order you pulled the stones, you're going on a journey," Daphne whispered. "Anni, this is a big deal. Like I said before, the *D-word* doesn't commonly come up. I read about that, and when it does, it's super important to pay attention to all of the words listed on the line after it, especially because it's followed by Wood, but because it ended with—" she whispered even softer— "*Bee*. That's a huge, big deal. You're going on an adventure, and I absolutely want to come with you. You're going to need my help; I've been to LimBough."

"You didn't speak with Effie OggleBoggle earlier today, did you?"

"Effie, as in Ms. OggleBoggle, the oldest Elemental alive? No. I wish. Why?"

"I was just with her," said Anni.

"Really? I've only seen her once in a crowd."

"Yeah, well, she was telling me about dots, connecting them, and adventure. She also told me to give Lexi strength with my thoughts."

"Of course she did. Intentions are the most potent force. Elementals know that better than anyone. We are given a list of words at Haberdashers, and we're required to use them for every single stitch." Daphne gasped and grabbed Anni's hand. "You should do what she says. I've heard that she's attuned to the higher planes and unbelievably wise. I know for a fact that the oldest Elemental family heads come here just to consult her on important issues."

"But how do I do that for Lexi?"

"Every night, or when you're alone, close your eyes, breathe, and see her in your imagination the way that will help her best. If Ms. OggleBoggle says give her strength, see her being strong somehow." Daphne paused; patches on her cheeks and the tips of her ears were red. "You didn't answer my question. Can I come with you?"

"Okay, but first, we have to find out where Lexi is." The truth was, Anni hadn't thought that far ahead, and she didn't know if Jay could even get both of them off the Zephyr. "Why do you want to go? Do you have a way for us to leave?"

"I might have a way, but trust me, you'll need help. Everything that's happened up until now—the news reports, you coming here, the patch, the Moonstones—they've been like little signs I've been waiting for. It's like what Effie said. I'm connecting dots, too."

The door of the tea shoppe jingled. Miranda walked inside, followed by Oliver. Both of them scanned the crowd. When their eyes landed on Anni, she huffed.

"What?" Daphne glanced over her shoulder. "Miranda, yeah, I know. We usually avoid each other, but ever since you arrived, I've been finding that hard to do. Oliver pulled you out of the Lake, and he's looking at you right now."

"I know. Everywhere I go, there he is. He saved me from becoming compost today, you know, Royal Worm food, but I don't need a babysitter! What's his deal?"

"The Mondays used to be a famous family." Daphne leaned in. "They've lived up to every prophecy made about them; I read about a few of them at the *Scriptorium*, which is amazing they still have those records in print, especially considering all the Elofficium rules about banning anything to do with Auguriums and prophesizing. Anyway, Oliver's parents helped build the Elofficium decades ago, but they went missing after the *Great Catastrophe*, and that's when the Elofficium changed. I don't know if there ever was a prophecy made about Oliver, but I've heard he despises them, and it's why he's an Elofficium apprentice."

"What! He's one of *them*? But he brought me to the Zephyr. I don't get it!"

"Yes. Actually, I thought it was strange, too. Whatever you do, don't let anyone know about the Moonstones, especially him or Miranda. We'd be in huge trouble."

Anni laughed with sarcasm. "Yeah, I think I'll skip that conversation."

"If I was you, I'd be extra careful they don't know what you're up to, and when they're around just act normal and try to ignore them."

"Ignore who?" said Squirt, louder than the girls would have preferred.

Daphne jumped. "Where did you come from?"

"Come on, we've got to go." He winked three times. "News is waiting for us."

CHAPTER 30

THE PEARL PENDANT

L exi was escorted out of the Brouwen before she even had been assigned a job. Another slug, like Mortimer, but smaller, led her through a maze of underground tunnels. He also had creepy red eyes, but what grossed her out was the way he gripped her pearl necklace in his slimy hand.

They walked for some time. On the way, they passed gruesome creatures that stared and grunted at her as a sort of intimidation; she was thankful that none of them touched her.

Her guide stopped before a long purple carpet. Guards like the ones she had seen earlier stood sentry in the hall. The slug handed the necklace to the nearest one. The guard wiped off the goo and nudged Lexi onto the carpet. She followed her new minder toward a lavish set of double iron doors. The guard holding her necklace gestured for her to stay and went inside.

Lexi couldn't stop the tremors in her arms or legs. She waited next to two other sentries, both of whom looked like a mix between a human and a boar. They had long tusks that poked up from their lower jaws and snouts like pigs.

Once the doors opened, the guard nudged her inside a palatial room, which frightened her in a different way than the guards had. It was designed for human comforts, decorated in rich reds and browns, with leathered furniture, huge polished tables, and a few massive Queen's Mirrors that didn't ooze with Funk-goo like the one she passed through.

Lexi walked toward a table at the end of the room, quickening her stride when she saw the hideous gaze of the wall-mounted animal heads staring back at her.

A man sat with his back to her in an egg-shaped chair. He was talking to someone, but Lexi didn't see a phone. Behind his chair was a huge glass window that overlooked a colossal underground cavern. It gave him a prime view inside a massive stadium that was filled with rows and rows of grotesque monsters of all shapes and sizes.

She noticed her pearl necklace resting on the table close to the man in the chair.

A servant entered the room and placed a tray with a steaming cast-iron pot and different-sized cups on the table. She watched the servant's hands as he mixed and poured different things into each cup, his hands moving fast but not dropping a single bit. When it struck her that she had seen those hands before, she looked up at the servant's face. The shock alone might have knocked her down on the spot, but her eyes did not deceive her. The servant looked exactly like her Uncle Teddy, except for his nose, which was purple and extremely bulbous.

CHAPTER 31

THE S.E.C.

A nni, Daphne, and Squirt raced through the rain-drenched village, splashing water on protesting Elementals in their wake. The girls dashed inside Fortensia's house to make sure the coast was clear while Squirt went and collected Brat from the cave.

When it was safe, Brat flew out of Squirt's shirt pocket. His clean uniform was replaced with a dirty, ragged blue-and-white-striped vest; he wore a tiny bandana, a patch over his left eye, a fake mustache and tattoo. He removed his eye patch. "Moppins, that's better. Don't think I don't see your smiles. One-eyed Nimmy insisted I dress the part. This isn't fun for me, you know, and while we're on the subject, before I tell you what—"

Anni interrupted him. "Diana said she'd help you. She's working on it right now."

"Fine. Good. Fine. Fine. Now that I've been reduced to a common scandaroon, which I'll add has been very hard on my sleep schedule, not to mention my digestion, which is completely on the fritz; you simply wouldn't believe what constitutes as food for that lot, and then they go and hang upside down. Heathens."

Done complaining, Brat sang a rhyming tune.

The secret twelve are to delve under a sacred lune
A circle binds gathering minds opened by a rune
Don't forget never fret or it'll be to Sune
The time Esright to understand
To follow the absent moon
A circle binds gathering minds
Betwixt and between noon

"Whoa," said Squirt. "That's unexpected. Daph, is it—"

"An S.E.C. meeting." Daphne nodded and paced. "That has to be why things have been so strange lately."

"Huh?" said Anni.

"Yes, that's good news," said Brat. "But only if you can find out where the meeting's being held. I have no idea!"

"Right," said Daphne, tapping her chin. "We know it starts at twelve noon, but we need to figure out the place, and which day—"

"That's the easy part," said Squirt with a giggle. "Yugi makes me keep track of the moon cycles for new seedlings in the greenhouse. An absent moon is another word for a new moon. The next one's in nine days."

"Hello. Hi." Anni waved at them. "I don't speak Elemental, remember? What's S.E.C.? Why is this good?"

"Secret Elemental Council. They're having a meeting," said Brat.

"So?" asked Anni. "Why is that important?"

"Because," said Daphne, "the S.E.C. will know exactly where Lexi is."

"Exactly," said Brat. "It's no coincidence that they are meeting now."

"If these members know where Lexi is, then why haven't they rescued her yet?"

"Actually, I've been wondering what's taken them so long, especially since that Golden Bee Artifact was stolen. I mean, even if they have a general location, it's not easy to infiltrate the Fectus lair, and Lexi could be anywhere; the Fectus has an underground network system that crosses countries and even a few continents. I bet they're setting up a meeting to go in and find her." Daphne looked directly at Anni in a knowing way. "The bee symbol—you know, the one in all the village shop windows—is the S.E.C.'s logo."

"Eggs! I didn't know that," said Anni.

"Yes," said Brat. "More precisely, the bee represents our Body Elemental."

"Even humans have one," said Squirt, nudging Anni's arm. "But ours live in our Opus Stones. I don't know where humans have theirs."

"The bee is our essence," said Brat. "Our being. It's the very first part of us to be formed. It starts out like a wisp, or a tiny vapor of essence."

"Right," said Squirt, touching his stomach. "It grows and grows inside of us, and then, when we come of age, it reveals itself. I've heard it even tells us our Death Date."

"The Elofficium put an end to all S.E.C. gatherings," said Daphne. "They ruled the S.E.C. as dangerous to the Elemental communities because they believe it's unhealthy propagating myths, legends, and anything that sounds like fortunetelling. All bee symbols and artifacts, or anything associated with it, like Auguriums and Moonstones, were promptly removed from Elemental society, and those who use them or break these rules face consequences."

"But that bee image is all over town, in your news. I see it every day when I walk through the village," said Anni, noting Daphne's face had flushed.

"Freedom of speech. The Elofficium can't control the news," said Brat.

"Not yet, anyway," said Daphne.

"And what are Auguriums?" asked Anni.

"Hm," said Brat. "Auguriums are special Elementals; they have two jobs in our world. A select few *were* chosen to nurture and assist in the Elemental birthing process because all Elementals are born on special Mineralstone Zephyrs, where all of us start out as infinitely small wisps of light. As I told you before, we are not like you humans, who are born by a mother and a father alone; we are all created by intention. The other Auguriums are seers, who *used* Moonstones to read different Elemental prophecies, but most of time, they can just look at an Elemental's Opus Stone to figure out what they'll become or do. But they *were* bound by their own codes and laws of recording, and used the Moonstones as confirmation for their work," said Brat.

"Why did you say *were*?" Anni noticed Daphne and Squirt didn't meet her eyes, and an uncomfortable restlessness permeated the room.

Brat cleared his throat. "Do you remember the prophecy I mentioned about that Elemental boy who was supposed to cure all malcontent between humans and Elementals?" Anni vaguely nodded and he went on. "After *the Great Catastrophe*, everything in our world went from bad to worse. Not only did thousands die that day, but after that summer solstice, Elemental children stopped being born. The Auguriums warned us that this was tied to the prophecy about the boy, but after so much loss, the Elofficials put their foot down and declared that they had had enough with this prophecy. The Elofficials managed, supported, and changed Elemental society at a time when our kind was grieving the most."

"But what does that have to do with Lexi?" asked Anni.

"We don't know, Anni," said Daphne. "But that's what we need to figure out. Actually, I don't think that any of this is a coincidence. As far as I know, the S.E.C.'s main purpose was to support the belief in the prophecy and help it come to fruition. The Golden Bee Artifact didn't appear and disappear by accident. I think it's tied to Lexi somehow, and I know you don't think she's an Elemental, but did you consider if someone else thinks she is? What if they're after the artifact because they think she has it? Teddy Waterstone was her guardian. He is a part of the Moon family, and even though it might be speculation, I've heard that they're the original founding members of the S.E.C."

There was no denying it now. Anni had to accept it; Teddy and Mabel were Elementals. Lexi said the velvet cloth was part of a tapestry Mabel owned. Daphne might be right; if someone thought Lexi had the Golden Bee Artifact, it could be the reason why she was kidnapped.

"The day before Lexi disappeared, she got a doll in the mail. She thought it was from Teddy. It had a clue with it. We followed it, and we found this." Anni showed them the golden-threaded bee on the velvet patch.

Brat and Squirt gasped.

"After Anni fell in the lake, I saw it," said Daphne. "So now we all know. We need to make a plan, and like Squirt said, we have nine days before the new moon."

"Why does it have to be on a new moon? If they know where Lexi is, they should just go," Anni huffed. "I just don't understand these Elemental rules."

"New Moons are auspicious," said Brat. "Great things can be achieved when started correctly. Farmers plant seeds on new moons because they grow best at that time. Great wisdom and intentions can also be attained on a new moon."

"We just need to figure out where the meeting's being held," said Daphne.

"What place do Elementals refer to as the circle of fellowship?" asked Brat.

"Moon Manor," said Squirt.

"Right. But which room? There's like a hundred," said Daphne.

"That's the right question," said Anni.

Brat flitted back and forth between several of Fortensia's office windows. "Moppins, we have company."

"What? Who is it?" asked Squirt beside him.

Anni and Daphne ran to the window, too. Knox and Miranda were walking down the road and heading straight for Fortensia's house.

"Moppins! Moppins!"

"Brat, hide in Squirt's pocket," said Daphne. "Squirt, here, take this shovel."

Once Brat was hidden, the three friends walked outside.

"Stay calm," whispered Daphne.

Anni walked straight at Miranda and Knox before they could reach Fortensia's door. "Why are you two here?"

"Mind your manners, girl. Seein' as Fortensia ain't here tonight, I'm on guard 'til morning to watch you, little Eggwit. Her office will suit me just fine," said Knox, who then turned to Daphne and Squirt. "You two are expected back at the Manor." He smiled. "And Miranda here has offered to escort you back, and be sure you don't stop along the way."

"Early curfew," said Miranda, grinning at Anni and the other two. "I'm just here following Spongincork's orders."

"What? We've never had that," said Squirt, looking at Daphne for confirmation.

Anni couldn't believe it. "Well, you can't stop me from walking my friends out." The three of them pushed past Knox and Miranda and headed for the cave.

"Where does he think he's going?" asked Knox.

"Squirt's putting back the shovel he borrowed," said Daphne, who whispered to Squirt, "Go ahead. I'll stay with Anni."

"Say hi to the *Braterons*," said Miranda, sneering at Anni and Daphne.

"Wot?" said Knox.

"My mistake," said Miranda smugly, even though Anni knew it wasn't a mistake. "I meant to say *Raterons*."

When Squirt didn't react, Anni guessed he hadn't heard her. She glared at

Miranda for him—and for herself and Brat. How Miranda found out about their smallest friend, she didn't know. She assumed either Miranda guessed about Brat or discovered something while working for Diana. Anni would put her money on the latter.

The tips of Daphne's ears were burning red, and Anni knew her well enough to know she was furious with Miranda, even though Daphne didn't say a word. When Squirt made his way back out of the cave, Daphne casually said, "See you later, Anni. Have a good night."

"Bye," said Squirt with a cheery smile, as if the *Braterons* comment went over his head.

Miranda followed behind them, but turned to wave at Anni with a big glowing smile. She was on to them, and that worried Anni even more.

"Inside, green hair," said Knox, thumbing Anni at the door.

Green hair? Clearly, it was the best he could come up with; proof that not all Elementals were quick-witted. She didn't give him the satisfaction of a response, walked inside, and ran up to the attic.

The next morning when she woke, she went downstairs to eat before heading to the caves where she could speak to Brat, hopefully in private. Knox had been replaced by Fort sometime in the early morning. He followed her into the cave and watched her work in silence. Brat was nowhere to be seen. The only good thing that came out of it was several Raterons seemed to have expert precision and dropped what amounted to the shape of a crown of guano on top of Fort's head. This put him in a bad mood, enough to say, "Your other chores are canceled today. There's a Funk leak on the Zephyr, and you're staying put. You're not to leave Spadu Hills, and no visitors allowed."

Anni was fuming by the time she made it back outside the cave. When Fort was cleaning off his head, she heard, "*Psst!*" She turned around and spied something hiding in a crevice of the cave's outside wall. "Brat? Is that you?"

"Not so loud, missy!" It was a creature like Brat, but with matted fur that probably hadn't seen soap in ten years, half a dozen scars, and an eye patch. Anni wondered if this was One-eye Nimmy. "Listen, girlie, I can't talk long and your friend can't talk to you in the caves with the others watchin' him, still being tested. He's gotta look the part, and that means no fraternizin', get me drift?"

Anni nodded. "Is he okay? How's his stomach? Are you Nimmy?"

"Yep, that's me. He's fine, and so is his dainty constitution. Just tellin' you the deal cause he's been frettin' about everything. Real stand-up guy. Okay, I gotta go."

It wasn't a comforting chat, but at least she knew Brat was okay.

It turned out that Fort was as good as his word. Anni couldn't leave Spadu Hills, no one came to visit, not even Jay for guano pickup. When Anni counted the number of days she had been on the Zephyr she realized Lexi's birthday, June tenth, and her own birthday, June eleventh, had come and gone. She tried to read the book Squirt gave her, *Mind Your Funk and Get Funktastic! Human Edition*, a dozen times, but aside from the book's advice to spin every day, she had no access to tonics. Only Ms. OggleBoggle's advice helped pass the time: imagine Lexi being strong.

In the early hours on the fifth morning of her isolation, the tenth day on the Zephyr, Anni lay wide awake, plotting a way to escape her guards and find Daphne and Squirt. She rolled over in her sleeping bag, contemplating climbing out the attic's small porthole window. The sun was streaming in through it in an odd way, like something was blocking it. She got up and pulled back the flimsy curtain, only to find a pair of wild, crazy-looking eyes staring back at her.

She screamed.

CHAPTER 32

EAVES-DROPUS

E ggs!" Anni screamed.

She raced down the rickety stairs. Knox was half-asleep when she bolted past him, saying, "Someone. Outside."

He followed, and they just caught sight of someone running down the road.

Knox flipped on his Omninav and shouted, "Village Circle—Spadu Hill Road, Assist," and took off after the perpetrator.

There was no way Anni was going to stick around in case whoever that was peering in the attic window decided to come back. Quickly, she raced upstairs, grabbed Lexi's backpack, and ran down the road after Knox.

Those wild, ghostly blue eyes flashed through her mind over and over until she reached the end of the road. The village was relatively empty. After all, it was still drizzling, but not as much as it had been four days ago. The lake wasn't full yet, but it was getting close. It was early still and several shops were still closed, but on the bright side, there was no sign of Knox. She pressed on until she made it to the other side of the lake, past Haberdashers, and outside Basil Boggle Tea Shoppe.

It was a relief to see that the Tea Shoppe was open, and her relief grew when she spotted Jay through the shop's window, sitting at the bar and talking to Mackenzie. She also noticed her own reflection; her hair, a deep cast of orange, was wet from the rain and she wrung it out before entering.

"Morning, Anni." Mackenzie beamed. "You've good timing. I just baked a loaf of my famous pelta bread, which is excellent toasted. Would you like some?" Anni nodded. "Keep her company, Jay. I'll just pop in the back to get some more."

Jay waited until Mackenzie went into the kitchen. Then, in a low voice, he said, "Haven't seen you around, kid. Did you find out where you're going yet?"

"I'll know in a couple days," said Anni determinedly. "Why haven't I seen you picking up guano at Fortensia's?"

"I thought you'd know about the Funk leak. They shut down the road to Spadu Hills. Haven't been able to contact Fortensia, so I've no idea if that was true."

"Or if Spongincork made it up," added Anni.

"Exactly. Anything's possible when it come to Leach."

"How can I contact you?"

"There's a pitchfork outside Fortensia's office. Leave a note."

"Yeah, but Fortensia's not in town."

"No worries, kid. I'll find you."

"Here we go," said Mackenzie, carrying a large plate of steaming toast that looked a lot like cinnamon bread, and a small tray of condiments. "Jay, you know where the extra plates and silverware are. Anni, try some Chadulcis tea. It's outstanding."

"He's not kidding," said Jay.

Mackenzie poured a luscious, foamy, caramel tea that looked so good it made Anni's mouth water. A symphony of aromas wafted under her nose, but when it touched her lips, the tea tasted so creamy and decadent, she thought she might fall off her chair. It was by far the most delicious thing she had eaten on the Zephyr.

Famished, Anni was careful this time to mimic how they prepared their toast, not wanting a repeat of what had happened at Diana's place. She watched as Jay and Mac put the different spreads on their toast. One looked like sweet buttercream honey nectar, and the other, a bluish jam with huge, round, gummy-like seeds. After one bite, she thought that this breakfast was better than anything she had ever tasted at Waterstone Academy. Ever.

"Anni! I haven't seen you in days! Stupid Leach wouldn't let me leave the Manor," said Squirt, bursting into the room and thumping down next to Anni at the bar. "Chadulcis tea and pelta toast! Mac, you read my mind. This is a great morning!"

She couldn't help but smile. Even with the gloomy rain and her worries mounting, Squirt was a ray of sunshine. Still, Anni had dozens of questions. "I haven't seen you or Daphne for days," she whispered to Squirt so Mackenzie and Jay didn't hear. "Did you guys find out anything about the...*thing*?" She knew she couldn't risk saying it aloud, and she also wanted to know about his Eaves-Dropus, which had to be ready by now. "Why did Miranda take you back to the Manor?"

Between large mouthfuls, he said, "We've been locked up at the Manor and forced to clean it top to bottom to get ready for some fancy Elofficium party Krizia's hosting before the..." he winked, "*new moon*. Daph and I have to wait tables and stuff, and wear these ridiculous uniforms that make my neck itch." He chewed. "Daphne's at Haberdashers; they're crazy busy and she's been slammed with orders."

The bell on the door jingled. Before Anni turned to look, Jay waved and Mackenzie said, "Hey Oliver, want some pelta toast?" There was no way Anni could express her concern to Squirt about needing time to work on their plan.

Squirt waved at Oliver as he swallowed. Then he whispered, "We've been pulling all-nighters working on, *you know...stuff.* Yesterday was the first day we were able to leave the Manor, I slept all day, but Daphne found something. She wrote something up this morning, and told me to head over to Spadu Hills and show you." He pulled out part of what looked like Daphne's Omninav from his shorts pocket so she could see, then slipped it back inside. He shoved one last piece of pelta toast into his mouth and said, "Ready to go?"

"Yes, please," Anni said, relieved to be doing something. "Thanks for breakfast."

"Sure," said Mackenzie. "And I'll see you this afternoon? Diana told me that if I didn't see you today, I should walk over to Spadu Hills and get you myself."

"Yup, see you then." Anni nodded. Anything was better than being stuck alone at Spadu Hills with only Fort or Knox as her company.

Bubbling with excitement Squirt dashed out of Basil Boggle Tea Shoppe, but in his rush he plowed into Miranda, who was on her way in. She dropped her umbrella and cursed.

"Oops! Sorry. Didn't mean to make you mad, Mir. How about a little fairy jig to cheer you up?" Squirt started singing as he did a funny little dance, which involved a lot of twirling around Miranda, who stood there tapping her foot with folded arms. Jay and Mackenzie caught sight from the bar, both pointing and laughing, and if it was possible, Miranda looked even more annoyed than before. To spare herself more shame, she pushed past Squirt and headed to Mooncakes Café instead of Basil Boggle's Tea.

Anni didn't know what it all meant, but it was one of those great life moments that she wouldn't forget, and she'd bet all the money in the world that Lexi would have enjoyed it, too. She waited until she and Squirt both stopped laughing and said, "Fairy jig?"

"You know, human folklore? Those stories about how we dance humans into the fairy world," he said, still giggling. "Yeah, I got moves, I know. Elementals don't normally do stuff like that, but that silliness was just for her. Fire Elementals loathe those stories and get really mad when they hear anything to do with a *fairy jig*; it drives them nuts, mostly because they're a bunch of hotheads, that and most of their kind live in the human realm. She totally deserved it. I heard that *Braterons* comment. So, so, so not cool. And, I might be wrong, but I think she's following you."

"Great. I'll add her to the list along with Oliver, and the window peeper."

On the way to the Manor, Anni explained what had happened that morning.

"That's creepy! We shouldn't talk out here, but my special plant is ready to go; only I haven't been able to do any of my usual deliveries until today, and you can help, but first let's go to Yugi's." Squirt took her to the smallest greenhouse, the same one they had used the day she arrived. Inside, there was a *bump, bump, bump*ing sound on the ceiling that came from above the secret passageway to Yugi's place.

"Wonky hover cart has a mind of its own. Just duck underneath; it won't bite." He led her through the dark, damp tunnel into Yugi's immaculate workshop. He pulled two chairs over to the biggest table and they flipped on Daphne's Omninav.

Several documents opened and spilled out in the form of a projection onto the table. At the very top of each one were yellow Post-its with scribbled notes, and beneath the documents was a huge blueprint of Moon Manor.

The first note from Daphne said, "Anni, we *really* need to fix your Funk. Early this morning, I saw Yugi and told him that you needed more tonics."

Squirt searched the room until he spotted them. "Did you read *Mind Your Funk and Get Funktastic*? It'll help you get ready for LimBough."

"I've been spinning clockwise, twenty times, three times a day."

"Good. Here, take this now," said Squirt. He handed one of Yugi's tonics to Anni. "Daph's like a mad genius or something. Look at this…"

Daphne's note said, "It's so obvious, I don't know how I missed it before in Brat's song. *A circle binds gathering minds opening with a rune.* That means only one thing. The room we are looking for will have some kind of portal with a rune inscribed on it. And *The time Esright to understand*, Esright confirms this because he was the first Elemental on record that studied Runes and their meanings. Hopefully, we can narrow it down to a few rooms in the Manor, but we don't have a lot of time."

Daphne's third note said, "We should use the air ducts to listen in on the meeting. They travel along all rooms, plus the Metal will mask most of Anni's Funk. It'll be easy to sneak you inside, Squirt, but with you, Anni, there is one problem: Moon Manor's Funkometers. It's like a huge vacuum that turns on every night after 7 p.m. It sucks out any form of Funk from all the nooks and crannies of the Manor."

Squirt snorted. "Did she forget that the meeting is in the afternoon?"

Anni shrugged. He had a point. They continued reading.

"I know the S.E.C. meeting is at noon and you're probably saying, 'what's the big deal?' But ever since you arrived, Anni, the Funkometers have been going on and off all week at different times. Anyway, see what you come up with. I may have another idea, but we can only use it as a last resort."

Squirt and Anni poured over the plans. Even though it was a projection, the blueprints were the hue of old parchment. The Manor was dated as built in 1545. Anni realized she'd never seen anything five hundred years old.

It took a while for them to figure out the drawings and that, with the flick of a finger, they could see a 3-D model of the building and dissect and bisect it to get a bird's-eye view of the inside. Squirt tossed out several ideas, but Anni nixed them all because every entry point had alarms attached to them.

It took Anni less than a minute to figure out *the* solution, even though it was the absolute last idea she wanted to pitch, purely because of her pride, but there was no time to waste. After she was sure it would work, she had to concede and tell Squirt.

Carefully, Anni showed him by tracing her finger over the air ducts, so that Squirt could see how they all intersected with each maintenance room on every single floor. The maintenance room was her best entry point.

"I get it, but how do we get you into the maintenance room?" asked Squirt.

Anni moved her finger down the blueprint to the third-floor level. There was only one other metal contraption that fed directly from the maintenance room and directly to the outside of the building. "Oh, yeah, yeah, that'll work," he said. "That's genius, but wait, no. Anni, that means…"

"That I'll have to climb in through the garbage chute? I know, but it's our only option," she said. "I never thought I'd agree to this, but this is the only way in and the metal will protect my Funk. I just don't know how to get up there; it's three stories high."

Squirt jumped up and said, "I know! We'll use the wonky hover cart; all it does is go up anyway. It'd float into outer space if I didn't tie it down. You're a genius, Anni."

There was one last note left under the final blueprint. "I was extremely lucky to get hold of these blueprints from *Brittle Books Archiva & Scriptorium* without signing them out publicly for all the Elemental world to see. Squirt, Betty Brittle will be waiting at table eleven to have tea and dessert at 6 p.m. tonight at Mooncakes Café with you."

"No, no, she didn't! Not that, not her," said Squirt, pulling at his hair and looking desperately at Anni. "She likes to smell hair, my hair. She's so weird. She said she wanted some as part of her collection. Her brother Alton's not much better. He collects fingernails. For Elsakes, Daph, you did this on purpose."

"Can I see the Omninav?" Anni took it and found that it was almost as easy as using a computer. She scrolled through its search engine, looking for news—especially *The V.O.I.C.E.*—and clicked on Penelope Potboiler's articles. She reread the first one about Lexi, and then the others again. It was as she remembered. Questions bubbled up in her mind, but none more than one specifically. What was the Fectus? She searched it on the Omninav. Hundreds of terrible images popped up one after another, but they didn't explain anything until she came across one definition.

"Fectus—an unspeakable evil force plaguing humans and Elementals alike. The Fectus have headquarters in every country known to man. They burrow into the recesses of the Earth, where they are better situated to divide and conquer human thoughts, emotions, and ultimately the essence of all living things. Their primary goal is to create chaos and destruction. Responsible for and fully associated with the Vile Trade, the trading of *cracked* Opus Stones is solely directed by their feared Queen, the Naga Yaga, whose growing militia has a strong adult contingency, largely grown from the abduction of human children and wayward teenagers, who are manipulated and turned into denizens. They are used to ferret out and target Elemental children living in disguise in the human world. The Fectus harvest Opus Stones from Elemental children, who later are rumored to turn into grotesque monsters* with detachable souls that spread chaos and Funk across the land.

"*It has been reported that in rare cases, the Fectus have been able to force some human children into producing an Opus Stone, age being a huge factor. Most die in the process, but the living bear a worse fate, as they are forever enslaved by the Fectus army."

Anni couldn't read any more; it was better not knowing. Lexi wouldn't meet that fate because Anni would find her before then. She didn't notice Squirt had stopped complaining about Betty Brittle and agonizing over his tea date.

"You shouldn't read about that; we don't know if it's true," said Squirt. "Whoa, we better hurry. I'm supposed to be in the Manor. It's Eaves-Dropus time. Remember?" He smiled. "Let's get ready." He grabbed the tonics Yugi had made. "Almost forgot these."

It was then that Anni realized they looked suspiciously like the phosphorescent greenish medicine Lexi used to take, which made her wonder if Lexi was in fact an Elemental after all.

Together, they loaded up Squirt's hover cart. It was laden with individual varieties of flowers, each one sticking out of a glass test tube filled with glowing water. The Eaves-Dropus had its own separate glass case. Anni disguised herself as best she could with overalls and a garden hat to tuck in her ever-changing colored hair. Squirt checked that his ear bud was secured and then gave Anni hers. When she put it in her ear, tendrils sprang to life and wrapped around her earlobe. It was an odd sensation, but once it settled, it was easy to forget it was there.

They reached the Solarium, but before they crossed the threshold, she said, "What if the Funkometers are on?"

"There's only one way to find out," he said with a twisted grin.

This was definitely beyond the category of staying out of trouble that Diana would approve of. They passed the threshold without incident and made their way to the second floor outside Krizia's office. Anni was still nervous. There were no Manor guards and everything was a bit too quiet.

"Okay. I'll go inside," said Squirt. "Pretend to work on those." He pointed to a floral arrangement on a nearby table and opened the door to the office, holding a small tray of four tubes filled with three flowers and one Eaves-Dropus. "Hi Verity…" And the door closed behind him.

Anni kept her head down, even though there was no one in the hall, until Krizia's office doors burst open and someone yelled, "GET OOOOUUTT!"

CHAPTER 33

UNCLE TEDDY?

Lexi locked eyes with the servant who looked exactly like her Uncle Teddy.
"Ha ha, that thing is not your dear departed uncle, girl. It's just my little party joke. Slug, take off your ring. Leave it on the table," said the man sitting in the chair, his back to Lexi, as he still faced his window.

The servant pulled a silver ring with a glowing stone off his finger, and just like that, his body transformed into a slimy slug creature like Mortimer, the Fectus ambassador, with the same blood red eyes. Lexi shivered. She was so disgusted it left her speechless, but this day of tricks wouldn't end. The man behind the desk turned his chair around.

"Alexa Waterstone, isn't it? Hm, judging by your reaction, I'm sure I need no real introduction, but I would still prefer for you to call me Mr. Murdrock." He turned to his servant and said, "You may go." He turned back to face Lexi. "I like my monsters to look a touch human, especially when they handle my food. You understand, I'm sure."

Lexi opened and closed her mouth a few times, but no words formed. This didn't appear to surprise Mr. Murdrock.

"I'm sure you're wondering why you're here. That's what I would want to know if I were you." He lifted her necklace off the table and examined the pearl pendant. "But you see, the main question I'd like to ask you, and feel free to lie if you wish because the truth always comes out…" He was staring intently at the pearl between his thumb and forefinger. "Is this your Opus Stone? Were you spirited away as an infant to live in secret, concealed within the human world, but all the while an Elemental living as a human in disguise?"

Lexi felt a fresh wave of panic overwhelm her; her legs started to quake and her knees knocked. "No," she lied. "I don't know what Elementals are."

Mr. Murdrock watched her. His eyes smiled as if he expected her answer, and his charismatic charm never left his face when he said, "Of course, whatever you say, but I'm going to keep this," he motioned to her pearl, "to be sure this isn't someone else's Opus Stone. You understand." The double doors opened behind her and two sentries waited. "Back to the Brouwen now. The Plantanana juice doesn't make itself, and it seems we can add some new ingredients."

Lexi was ushered out of Murdrock's room, but on her way out, she saw the proud, pale-faced Elemental boy walking in—but he didn't look as proud as he had before. Spike escorted him in by one of his chained wrists. Lexi gasped when she saw that his other wrist had broken free of the chain, his right hand had transformed in to a bear's paw.

Then it dawned on her. What would she turn into? She didn't have long to ponder that question. A terrifying man that was half bear—half gorilla stopped right in front of her and roared at her escort, "I'm in charge of taking her back. Go back to your post." The creature-man watched the guard leave, and he said to Lexi, "Move!"

Terrified, Lexi followed along in silence. She had no idea where they were headed, and none of it looked like the way she had come. Her legs felt like jelly as they descended farther into the bowels of the underground until they reached the prison block.

The half bear—half gorilla man opened a cell door. "Get in."

Lexi did as she was told. Inside the cell stood a young man with a kind expression. "I will not hurt you," he said. "I'm here to help you, and in turn, perhaps you can help me. It's what Teddy would have wanted."

CHAPTER 34

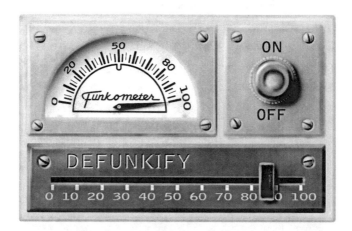

THE FUNKOMETER

Anni froze on the landing when a rotund little man dressed in a fine silk tunic and flashy shoes stumbled out of Krizia's office. He was muttering something under his breath. Anni pulled her garden hat down and pretended to fluff the flowers on a nearby table. Krizia followed the man out into the hall and she said, "Van, you're underfoot. I need you to go and leave me to my business."

Anni had never met Van, but she knew he was Zelda Scurryfunge's brother. When his face broke into a grievous expression, he reminded her of a frog, but looked nothing like his sister. Anni felt a little sorry for him being married to Krizia, until she heard his simpering voice. "But Ornellipoo, you need rest. You're not well. I'll do your—"

The steely glint in Krizia's eyes made her look like a bull in front of a red flag. "You will do no such thing. I'll finish my own work. Leave now." Anni thought she might drag Van away by his ear when she hissed, "Never call me that in public, and turn on the Funkometer." She went back into her office and slammed the door.

Squirt giggled as he exited Krizia's office a second later. His eyes were round and excited as he said, "It's done."

"Really? That was fast," Anni whispered as she started pushing the hover cart back in the direction they had come. "Krizia told Van to turn on the Funkometers. We should go."

"Leave the cart," said Squirt. "I'll get it later. Quick, follow me."

They left the cart in the hall by the table. Squirt took Anni's hand and raced down the Manor's main staircase as fast as their feet could carry them. Anni was worried they might look suspicious, even though Squirt could barely hold back giggles. They zipped past Van, who was still mumbling to himself in the foyer. Squirt was fit to burst with laughter when they noticed that Van's hand loomed over a small wooden box inset in the wall; Anni guessed it must have been a Funkometer switch.

The floor of the Manor's foyer lit up with a message that said, "Goodbye Squirt, Goodbye Anni," as they darted out the front door, almost running right into Oliver, who was walking up the Manor's front steps. A ringing sound pinged their ears. They ran until they reached the nearest greenhouse.

"Did you hear that?" asked Squirt, followed with copious laughter he could no longer hold back. "Ha ha, that was the Funkometer." Anni could have guessed it herself, and although she was more nervous than humored, Squirt's laughter was contagious. "That…was…the most fun…I've ever had. Ha ha!"

Once they crossed the Manor's lawn, they laughed together. It was the most exciting thing Anni had done on the Zephyr, yet it reminded her of the times when she and Lexi used to sneak off to the clock tower when they were supposed to be inside the school.

"We did it," said Squirt, catching his breath.

"You're right, it—" she said.

They fell silent and stared at one another, wide-eyed. Krizia was talking to her secretary through the Eaves-Dropus ear buds. Krizia said, "One more thing, see to it that the eastern conference rooms on the seventeenth and nineteenth floors are cleaned and the woodwork polished, and be sure to put in a daily order for flowers."

"You heard that, right?" asked Anni. "Could one of those be the meeting room?"

"Not sure," said Squirt. "I'll check when I fill the flower orders, but I hope so."

Anni had to leave Squirt to his duties, because she was due to meet Mackenzie at Basil Boggle Tea Shoppe. When she arrived, he showed her how to wash the dishes, stack them, and how to organize the tea tins. Under Mackenzie's tutelage Anni was able to whip up several customers' orders whether it was a Fruet-frizzwizzbee, a Sprakanberie, or even a Cocopanakos. Mostly, she worked in the back room, which she liked because there was a one-way mirror she could look through to watch the patrons. It was terrific for avoiding Miranda and Oliver, both of whom came in more than once.

Before Anni headed back to Spadu Hills, Daphne came in looking frazzled; her normally sleek hair was a tangled mess, and she didn't even blush when she passed Mackenzie. Anni took her to the back room, where Daphne whipped out her tape measure and said, "Don't even ask. I don't have a lot of time to explain." Daphne took Anni's measurements, including her head. "I can't believe Spongincork lied about the Funk breach. Diana's furious with him. She even sent Miranda a strong message, once I told Diana what she said about Brat. I'm only sorry it took so long. I've got to get back to Haberdashers in five minutes, but I had to tell you, Diana said Brat might be cleared with the Fleet in a week, but only on the condition that he keeps a low profile and doesn't get caught." Anni was relieved to hear this. "The Manor's hosting some kind of InterElemental Elofficium party the night before," she whispered, "*the S.E.C. meeting*, that's why I've been sewing at Haberdashers all day."

"Ouch," said Anni as Daphne pinched her skin.

"Whoops, sorry...." Daphne's eyes looked heavy. "I haven't slept much these past few days...Squirt told me about the chute and I think it'll work, but he's still mad at me for arranging his date with Betty. I told him that everyone has to do their part, but I'm not sure we can shift your Funk with tonics alone. I have another idea, a backup, but it's not foolproof....Okay. Done. Now I've got to go, but I'll see you tomorrow."

"Uh, okay. Bye." Anni watched Daphne bump into three tables and the door on her way out of the Tea Shoppe.

Anni walked through the village on her way back to Spadu Hills alone, but relieved her escorts Fort and Knox had abandoned her. About 300 yards from Fortensia's house she spotted two Elementals standing in the middle of the woods with their backs to her, talking animatedly with their hands. One of them briefly turned around.

"Zelda?" Anni yelled and ran toward her. A large crack echoed in the trees. When Anni got to the spot where she had seen them, the Elementals were gone. The whole thing gave her a weird feeling. She raced back to Fortensia's, opened the office door, and locked it behind her. When she turned around, she jumped. Someone was already inside.

"Ah, it's you," said Fortensia, dropping herself into her chair in front of the fire. "Don't know about you, but I've had a rotten week."

"Why?" asked Anni, calming down.

"Elofficium seized all my bags of guano in LimBough. No explanation. And to add fat to the frying pan, all my orders were mysteriously canceled. It's that Spongincork fella; he's up to no good. Now I know why them kids call him Leach. Parasite. He left me a note that they're gonna inspect my caves, and all the Raterons, you name it."

Anni felt guilty for her attempted escape in the guano bags. Then she thought about Brat and the fact that she hadn't seen him for days. Miranda must have said something about him to someone at the Elofficium.

"I see your mind turning. And no, I knew about your escape plan—well," she chuckled, "everyone at the dock saw you. Gave me a laugh more than anything; don't worry, you're not the reason for the canceled orders. And while we're on the subject of secrets, I know about your little friend Brat. Met him down in the cave this afternoon."

Anni's forehead beaded. "You did, I mean, you do?"

"Nice little fella, proper as all get out, but a nervous chap; turns out he has good reason, too. Spongincork wants to inspect my caves, calling it quality control; he wants a working inventory of all the legally registered Raterons. I told the Pirats about the inspection and they're taking off as we speak, but your friend stayed behind, that's how I met him, and it turns out the Pirats think your friend Brat is a brave little fellow, too, go figure. If I was you, I'd get him somewhere safe where he can lay low for the next couple days."

Anni nodded. She had no idea what to do with Brat and prayed that between Daphne, Squirt, and even One-eyed Nimmy—if he stayed behind, too—they might figure something out.

"Oh, and another thing. You're not workin' in the caves anymore. Generally,

I like to work alone; it helps me think. You'll be livin' here, and that's that. Spongincork can sit on my pitchfork before I follow any more of his orders. Are we square?"

Anni laughed. "Yeah, okay." She genuinely liked Fortensia.

For dinner, Fortensia made a kind of stew over the hearth. As they ate, Anni asked questions about LimBough and what it was like to travel to different countries through TreeTransport with huge loads of guano.

Fortensia gave her the brief version. "You need to check your E-pass and Opus Stone to cross the bridge, then you enter the Orb. You gotta move quick and make sure your guano flats are on the right platform. You need to know your Rootways, which TreeTransport you're taking, too."

It was enough to boggle the mind. Anni realized then that she really did need Daphne's help after all. First thing in the morning, she decided she would find Jay and tell him he'd need two E-passes.

It was a long and exciting day, and she had no trouble falling asleep. However, the next morning, when she woke, a face hovered a few inches over her head with two ghostly, whitish-blue eyes.

She screamed.

It couldn't be! But it was. Rufous Finnegan was in the attic! He leaped away, flipped open the attic door, and made to run, but not before he grabbed Lexi's backpack.

A combination of shock and fatigue overwhelmed her. She couldn't let Finnegan steal Lexi's backpack after she vowed to protect it; she couldn't let him get away.

Before she gave chase, she realized there was no need. Rolled up inside the pair of clean overalls she had used as a pillow the night before was Lexi's patchwork doll. She scrambled to check her tank top. The bee patch Daphne had reattached for her was still in place, and Mabel's key was still hanging from the chain around her neck. Everything was fine, but was it? Anni realized too late that her journal was still inside the backpack and now in Finnegan's possession.

Did Finnegan know about Lexi's doll? Was that what he was after? What did he want with it? Finnegan had to be the one at her window the day before, but was he the one with Zelda in the woods, too?

Anni raced outside. Fortensia had just caught sight of Finnegan running out of her house and was on her Omninav reporting it; however, she refused to let Anni chase after him. Fortensia said it was too dangerous to chase him alone and gave Anni her Omninav instead. In no time, Daphne and Squirt were at Spadu Hills.

The trio walked into the village, but Anni was dejected. She explained what happened that morning, but the loss of her journal gripped her in way she couldn't hide. It was like losing Mabel all over again and only highlighted the fact that Lexi was gone, too. What Daphne seemed most interested in was the color of Finnegan's eyes. She kept asking, "Are you sure they looked whitish blue? What color are his eyes?"

"I don't know. Why does that matter?"

"Whitish-blue eyes indicate an addled brain, and a loss of mental control."

They had a late breakfast at Basil Boggle Tea Shoppe in a booth to themselves. Anni had wrapped up Lexi's doll and slung it under her arm the whole time; she wouldn't let it out of her sight. Daphne and Squirt agreed that it was best if they spent the next four nights with Anni at Spadu Hills. They told her it would give them time to go over their plans, reviewing the air ducts on the 3-D map, but Anni knew they wanted to cheer her up.

As sure as their word, that evening, Daphne and Squirt arrived at Fortensia's with their pillows, sleeping bags and clothes in hand. Anni couldn't shake the loss of her journal, but she appreciated their company all the same.

The next morning when Anni awoke, Daphne, Squirt and Brat were waiting downstairs with Fortensia around the hearth. Sitting on the table was a huge pot of Chadulcis tea, a freshly baked oat loaf, and a present wrapped with a blue bow.

"Someone told me," said Fortensia, "that we missed your birthday."

Before Anni could ask how they knew, Squirt jumped up and shoved the present into her hands. "Open it. Open it! I can't wait. We've been working on it all night!"

Anni smiled and unwrapped the gift. It was a beautiful new journal. In truth, she knew it couldn't replace the one Mabel gave her, or the last three years of her life that she had recorded in its pages, but it was a very kind gesture.

"Actually, it's not a replacement," said Daphne, her ears pink. "It's a fresh start."

Anni opened the journal and laughed aloud. On the title page it said: *Anni Moon's Compendium To The Elemental World, with love from Daphne, Squirt,*

Fortensia, and Brat. The pages were filled with Elemental words and their written meanings, each one written by hand and initialed by the author, and all of Brat's included hand-drawn pictures.

"Look." Squirt flipped some pages. "There're blank pages for you to write stuff too!"

Brat flew onto her shoulder. He wrung his hands. "Do you like it?"

"I love it." Anni grinned. "I never knew you were an artist." Brat blushed.

Anni hugged each one of them in turn. Daphne poured the tea while Brat passed out napkins. Squirt's cheeks were stuffed with cake before Fortensia divided up the rest of the loaf. Anni sipped her tea, watching them, feeling so happy and lucky to have such a wonderful group of friends in her life, and even though Lexi wasn't there, she was in her heart.

The next three days passed like clockwork; they ate breakfast in the village, Daphne headed to Haberdashers, while Anni and Squirt worked at the Manor; late afternoon they met up at Basil Boggle Tea Shoppe and walked back to Spadu Hills for dinner with Fortensia. Even Brat joined them, and didn't mention his digestion once. However, on the fourth night, Daphne and Squirt slept at Moon Manor since they were expected to work late into the evening for Krizia's hosted InterElemental Elofficium Social Extravaganza.

The next morning, Anni went to the Tea Shoppe for breakfast, but it was closed. Anxious, she went to the Manor and did her chores early. When she came back to the village it was deserted; many of the shops along the cobblestone walk had closed signs in their windows, too. She couldn't believe her luck when she spotted Jay, but all excitement faded a second later when Miranda walked out of Mooncakes Café with a woman Anni assumed was their mother, as they all had the same fiery red hair. They were headed in her direction.

She dashed inside Haberdashers, and for once, it wasn't crowded. Ms. Thimble, the old lady from the back storeroom, was sitting at the register, smiling at her. Anni thought she must have been blind because Elementals never smiled at her.

"Picking up an order, honey?" asked the lady. "Daphne, this lady has an order."

Daphne looked exhausted. Her sleek, straight hair was a mess and her clothes were wrinkled. She mumbled, "Order number? Anni!"

Daphne pulled her into the back of the shop. "I'm glad to see you. I was going to come find you, look…" She pulled out a long, shimmering length of cloth. "It's a *somasuit*, it's like a glove for your body that fits over your clothes. It should mask your Funk."

Anni pulled the somasuit over her clothes. It fit like a second skin. Even the hood covered her head perfectly, and once on, it was weightless. "How does it work?"

"The secret is in the threads, a Dwarrow secret, I guess. I've been working on this suit for ages, but I haven't had anyone to try it out on until now. We need to test it at Yugi's. Dwarrow hair works like metal, but it's flexible so you can move in it. Basically, it should hold in your Funk. It also does something else, but I'll show you that part later. It should work in LimBough, too. And speaking of that—" she pointed to two small backpacks sitting on the floor. "There are enough supplies, tinctures, food, sleeping bags, and a tent in those two bags to keep ten people happy for a week."

Grateful, Anni flung her arms around Daphne but ended up knocking her to the ground; Daphne was so tired, she fell over. They laughed and Anni offered to help Daphne finish up with her duties. Together, they organized the last five wrapped packages ordered for pickup that morning.

Anni carried the packages to the front where Ms. Thimble said, "Thank you, Daphne," just as the woman who looked like Miranda and Jay's mother came into the shop. Anni ducked behind a giant pillar of spooled threads. The woman came in alone and collected her order, which was, strangely, under the name "Sune," then she left the shop.

Anni went into the back where Daphne had finished tidying up.

"What's Miranda and Jay's mother's name? It isn't Sune, is it?"

"It's Firestone, just like theirs," said Daphne. "Why do you ask?"

"I must have been wrong. This woman just picked up the last packages, and I thought she was their mother."

"If the packages are gone, I can go," said Daphne. "Let's get over to Yugi's."

Daphne handed Anni her brand-new backpack, which she stuffed Lexi's doll into, along with the somasuit. They got to Yugi's before Squirt arrived, so Daphne decided to surprise him with Anni wearing the somasuit. They waited in Yugi's garden shed downstairs. When they heard him whistling at the door, Daphne said, "Slip your thumb into the cuff and squeeze. Don't move."

The fabric shimmered like liquid mercury, and maybe it was her imagination, but she thought it grew tighter, too. The somasuit reflected just like a Queen's Mirror.

"Hi, Daph!" said Squirt, smiling as usual. "Where's Anni?"

Brat flew out from his inside pocket and said, "But she's here. I can smell her."

"No, you can't," said Anni, pulling the fabric off her head.

"Moppins!" yelled Brat, and he flew into Squirt's chest.

Daphne giggled.

"Y-y-you…" Brat stuttered. "You almost scared me to my Death Date. How long have you been sitting there?" He flew over to the table and touched the cloth. "Is that Dwarrow hair? It is. Where'd you get this?"

"We should be asking Daphne that question," said Squirt. He folded his arms and narrowed his eyes.

Daphne looked at them both and twisted her hair. "If Anni gets into a tight spot, she can use it to sort of blend into a background without being noticed, so long as she doesn't move. It's not a big deal. Fort and Knox wear it, too; it isn't as uncommon as you think. Actually, you're missing the point; the reason why she's wearing it is the fibers are impenetrable. It will hold in and mask her Funk."

"But if she gets caught in this," said Squirt, "she'd get into major trouble."

"Daphne's right. What's the big deal?" asked Anni.

"The big deal is that Dwarrow hair comes from Metal Elementals," said Brat.

"Yeah, that's right," said Squirt. "They've been pushed off into the human realms because they sold secrets to the Fectus."

"Don't tell her that; it's total discrimination. You heard what Diana said. All the Elementals need one another to survive, and they can't without the Metals," said Daphne.

"Yeah, but it's true. Anyway, regular Elementals aren't supposed to hang out with Metals," said Squirt. "They've metal fingernails, too."

Anni remembered the hand with golden fingernails reaching through Mabel's trunk.

"How do you know you haven't already made friends with one? Huh? Anyway, there are exceptions to that rule," said Daphne in a huffy tone that bordered on disappointment. "And you should talk, Mr. Eaves-Dropus. That illegal hybrid could get you in more trouble than Anni and me combined."

"What hybrid?" asked Brat. "I'm gone for two days, and now you two will be arrested before me." He sighed. "At least I'll have company in the Egghouse."

"We should talk about tomorrow," said Anni.

"She's right," said Daphne. "We can find a way to use Squirt's plant. There are four rooms where the meeting might take place." Daphne used her Omninav to pull up the blueprints of the seventeenth and nineteenth floors, including the specs for the air ducts. "Anni, you and Squirt will be here and here on the seventeenth floor. Brat, since you can fly, I thought you could monitor these two rooms on the nineteenth. Does that work?" Everyone nodded. "My guess is that S.E.C. members will be traveling old-school, *Imago*. Anni, that's traveling *through* paintings."

"Didn't the Elofficium decommission most of them ages ago?" asked Squirt.

Anni said, "I think I saw Zelda do that in Mabel's apartment."

"Well, it makes sense," said Brat. "If you were from an old Elemental family and still had one, wouldn't you still use it?"

"Good point," said Daphne. "Okay, back to the plan. I'll find a safe place to hide on the eighteenth. From there, I can use my Omninav to direct you through the air ducts. Squirt, can you have four Eaves-Dropus ready by tomorrow?"

"They already are, Daph."

"Tomorrow, Operation Air Ducts meets here at ten a.m.," said Daphne.

"Yeah," said Anni. "And let's just hope we don't get caught."

CHAPTER 35

OPERATION AIR DUCTS

That night, Anni bolted the attic door shut and Brat stayed with her. She had a restless night, tossing and turning until six in the morning, when she finally gave up on sleeping. Brat, on the other hand, slept like a log.

Anni triple-checked her new backpack, making sure the doll was still inside. Her hair had turned pale pink, which was Lexi's favorite color; Anni only hoped it was a good omen. She joined Fortensia for breakfast, realizing that it was the last one they'd share together. Anni had a hard time keeping her jitters at bay, and although Fortensia gave her funny looks, she didn't say a word. Once Fortensia left, Anni and Brat made their way to the Manor.

Squirt was outside the greenhouse at nine. He had two heavy bricks holding down the wonky hover cart. "Good timing," he said. "I wanted to get this in place under the chute, but first, I'll need to clear a path through the compost. Want to help?"

"Sure," said Anni, grinning. "And it's the last time I need to shovel that stuff."

They walked over to the compost heap with shovels in hand, excited and nervous about the afternoon. They had reached the low brick wall when they heard Knox say, "Aw lookie 'ere, I got me an Eggwit first thing in the mornin'."

Squirt puffed out his chest. "She's helping me."

"Not today, she don't. And neither do you if you gets me drift. Manor's shut up. Village, too." Knox pointed at the solarium doors. They were chained shut.

Anni's mouth fell. This wasn't happening.

Squirt grabbed her hand. "Come on." He waited until Knox was far enough away. "Let's go to Yugi's. Daphne will find a way around these goons."

Brat flew ahead of them through the shed passageway. When they entered Yugi's lower garden room, they found Daphne pacing and talking to herself.

"What's going on?" asked Anni.

"I left the Manor this morning to go to Haberdashers to work on a few final things, but my key didn't work. When I got back to the Manor, they had already ushered all staff out. They refused to let me in, and every exit is sealed until five p.m. tonight."

"What?" asked Anni.

"No," said Brat and Squirt simultaneously.

"But we'll miss it! This can't be happening," said Anni.

"Daph, is there another way in?" asked Squirt.

"No, not that I know of."

Anni walked past Daphne and threw herself onto a wooden bench, her hands over her eyes. She felt like crying, but no tears came. Squirt sat close to her, and Daphne joined him. This was the worst news possible.

Eleven a.m. came and went.

"Brat," said Daphne, "could you sing the song again?"

"Salt in wounds, Daph," said Squirt, gesturing at Anni. "Come on."

Anni didn't say a word, but she nodded to Brat as if she was saying, "Go ahead."

Brat sang the song one more time and Daphne screamed, "It's not over! We still have a chance. How could I have been so stupid? I mean, all the other hints were right in front of my eyes. How could I be so literal?"

Daphne started to laugh hysterically. Squirt and Brat looked really concerned when she started flapping her arms wildly around the room like a goose.

"Daph," said Squirt in a calm voice, "maybe you should sit down."

"No. I can't. This is important and unbelievably simple."

"Moppins, get on with it already and tell us."

"Okay," she said. "Do you remember the last line of the song? '*Betwixt and between noon*'...I can't believe I fell for it."

"Fell for what?" asked Anni, starting to hope.

"*Noon* isn't referring to the afternoon like we thought, but to the number twelve. *Betwixt and between* refers to midnight, when the veils between worlds and dimensions are the lightest. Don't you see? We still have another chance. Tonight at midnight!"

"Excellent!" said Squirt. "Operation Air Ducts is back in business!"

A chill of foreboding arrived long before midnight.

Anni didn't take any chances once the doors opened at five p.m. Although relieved to have the protection of Daphne's somasuit to block out her Funk, Anni didn't like leaving behind the backpack with Lexi's doll. Squirt promised to hide it safely at Yugi's place before he, Brat, Daphne, and Anni made sure their Eaves-Dropus ear buds were working and they could all hear one another.

The second the Elementals were allowed back inside Moon Manor, Anni turned her somasuit to its reflective mode. Brat hid inside her hood, concealed and on the lookout, while she and Squirt wrangled the wonky hover cart out of the tool shed with a thick, heavy rope and pulled it through the compost heap into the ready position before she got on it. The smells of rotting fruit wafted into the air as Squirt struggled to hoist the hover cart up inch by inch until Anni was able to climb into the rubbish chute.

Daphne hid inside a closet on the eighteenth floor. Everyone had trackers, so it was easy for her to follow them on her Omninavigational device and give directions through the air ducts. Anni wanted to tell Daphne not to talk so much as she scaled the dark, stinky, slimy metal rubbish chute; she had to concentrate and move slowly in order not to slip. One loud bang would reverberate into the kitchen, and the last thing they needed was a chef's assistant to poke his or her head inside the chute and see Anni's face looking back.

It took thirty minutes before she reached the third-floor maintenance room. It turned out that Daphne's instructions were perfectly timed because as soon as Anni emerged from the chute into the maintenance room, the service lift opened, and Squirt was on it. From there, they went up several flights. Anni got off on the seventeenth; Squirt took Brat up to the nineteenth, and then he went back down to the seventeenth.

Ten minutes to midnight, all three of them were on their respective floors and in position. Anni inched her way closer to the ventilation grate. From there, she had a good view of a dark mahogany room, walls decorated with different paintings of what looked like the same man, and a vast oval conference table in the center.

"Anni, when the meeting starts, get as close to the grate as possible," said Daphne. "The air ducts act like a microphone; they'll pick up everything, even your breathing, Squirt."

Squirt and Daphne argued about ambient noises until Brat told them to shut up. It reminded Anni how serious it was; getting caught was not an option. Sweat dripped from her brow; either it was the somasuit or her nerves. She didn't know which.

"I'm picking up commotion on nineteen," said Daphne. "Brat, be ready."

"Oh, thanks for giving me the non-action floor," whispered Squirt.

It was then that Anni noticed a small extra room through a second vent that wasn't on Daphne's blueprint. This antechamber wasn't joined to the conference room by a door or a hallway. The antechamber appeared accessible only by a life-sized portrait of the same man in all the other paintings. The inscribed nameplate on the frame read: *Alejandro Sune*.

Sune was the same name used at Haberdashers. Anni whispered this to Daphne.

"Alejandro Sune! 'Don't forget never fret or it'll be to Sune.' That's it," said Daphne. "Squirt, find Brat, come meet me. Anni, I'm going silent until the meeting's over."

Anni didn't expect Elementals to arrive through the room's actual door, but the first person who did gave her a shock. Wearing a long brown cloak, Oliver Monday set down a tray with a pitcher of water and empty glasses. He pulled up his hood just before more Elementals arrived through the different paintings.

Anni watched as they gathered in small clusters, possibly greeting one another before sitting around the table. It was then that she noticed someone move inside the small antechamber room. A broad, stocky-looking Elemental, possibly a man, also cloaked from head to toe, stood silently like he was watching the S.E.C. members. He flipped something shiny in his hand as he observed the arrival of the Secret Elemental Council members, and when the members took their seats, he walked through the Sune portrait. Anni thought that maybe he could have been the leader, because as soon as he entered the room, everyone went silent. He took the seat closest to the vent and rested his hands on the table.

Anni gasped. He was the man with the golden fingernails!

CHAPTER 36

WHIFFLE STRIKES AGAIN

Anni's heart pounded, full of fear and wonder. She wanted nothing more than to interrupt the meeting and demand that the man with the creepy golden fingernails give her Mabel's locket. Despite her anger, she noticed the back of his cloak sported a giant golden image of the Bee. It was an exact replica of the golden-threaded patch she had sewn onto her tank top, and identical to that stolen Elemental Artifact, the Golden Bee, the same Elofficium banned image in the Elemental newspaper that was plastered all over town in every window shop. Daphne was right; the Golden Bee *was* the S.E.C.'s symbol, which meant that all of the cloaked members had to be S.E.C. members.

Who was this man? Why did he take Mabel's locket? She wondered what Lexi knew about this. She had known the Bee was important enough to want to take her to Mabel's and show her. Was this the final proof that Lexi was an Elemental? Anni wasn't going to believe anything until someone told her face to face. She needed to hear it from her first before she would believe that. Even though most of the clues pointed to yes, there was still so much she didn't understand. At least she knew one thing: she was a human—that was an unmistakable fact that everyone here was quick to remind her of.

The Council had starting talking. Anni's mind was racing. She was keeping an ear out for Lexi's name, but mostly they discussed Elofficium leads and protocol. Not once did they mention Teddy, Mabel, or the fact that the Golden Bee Artifact had been stolen from the Brazilian Museum. It wasn't until just before everyone got up to leave that two Elementals confirmed a latitude and longitude of the place where "the girl" was last seen.

Anni hoped that "the girl" they referred to was Lexi, but she couldn't be sure because the meeting adjourned much faster than she expected. She prayed that Daphne got the numbers as Elemental after Elemental passed through the wood panels, one by one. Only the man with the golden fingernails waited until everyone else left the room before he placed a small, oval object on the table. Then he, too, went through the portrait and into the antechamber. From there, he vanished into another wooden wall and was gone.

Anni's breathing got heavy and she could feel her whole body start to shake when the realization hit: the oval disk on the conference table was Mabel's locket. Did the man with the golden fingernails leave it behind on purpose?

Without hesitation, she pried open the ventilation grate and lowered herself onto a low cabinet just below. She jumped down, grabbed the locket, and held it in her hand to be sure it was the real thing. It was.

Happy memories of Mabel flooded her mind before alarms blasted all around her. Just over the din, she heard shouts and footsteps pounding down the halls.

Locket in hand, she scrambled back up into the air duct. She closed the grate just in time, before the door to the room burst open. Krizia charged inside, followed by Maeleachlainn *Leach* Spongincork, and Van.

The alarms echoed off the air ducts, making it impossibly loud for Anni to hear anything else. Sweating like mad, she didn't dare move a muscle. The idea of getting caught was not an option.

"A human set off that alarm," said Krizia to Maeleachlainn. "Find her."

"As you wish," said Leach, and he dashed out of the room.

"Ornella, my love," said Van in a simpering tone, as if Krizia were five years old. "You really mustn't…"

"Hush. Make yourself useful."

"But honeykins, how do you know…"

Anni had to escape, but she couldn't turn around inside the air duct without making noise. Her hands were drenched in sweat, which made it hard to get a grip on the metal ducts. She shifted backward and kept moving without knowing where she was going. Disoriented, she inched along for what felt like an hour. Worst yet, she had lost all contact with Daphne and Squirt and had no idea how to find them.

Sweat pouring down her back, the somasuit constricted around her ribcage as if her perspiration had shrunk the fabric. Up ahead, she spotted a vent that curved down just like the one she had entered through the maintenance room. It probably wasn't the same one, but she didn't care. She wanted to get out of the air ducts before someone found her.

Anni inched past a vent that overlooked a hallway below, but when she spotted Krizia, she froze. Krizia had a grin on her face, and it appeared that Van had caught someone. He pushed a reluctant pair toward Krizia. Anni swallowed hard. It was Daphne and Squirt. They must have gotten caught when the alarms went off.

"Having a late night party?" Krizia asked. "There's only one person on this Zephyr that could set off those alarms, and I believe you two can answer that question."

"Uhh, I uhh," Squirt stammered.

"Actually, it's just me and Squirt. We lost track of time. Nobody else is with us. I swear," said Daphne, pink-faced.

Anni felt terrible. The only thing she could do to save them from getting into more trouble was to escape without being seen. The question was how.

"Van, take them to my office. I'll deal with Anni myself."

Anni waited for them to leave. She slid out of the air duct and ran blindly down the first deserted hallway she saw. The seventeenth floor was a maze of halls, with few doors and dozens of dead ends.

There were no windows, so she couldn't orient herself to where she was. When she saw two double doors, she ran, hoping that once inside, she could find a window, but they were locked. She spun around, making sure there weren't any other doors. Only a huge painting hung at the end of the hall. Underneath stood a low table with a vase of flowers on it. There was no place to hide.

"Stop!"

The sound echoed through the halls. Anni went cold; it was Krizia. She was close—too close—and Anni heard Van's mumbling voice somewhere close by.

Panicking, Anni pressed her sweaty thumb to the somasuit's sleeve to turn on the reflective mode. A crackling noise rippled through. It short-circuited. With nowhere to go, Anni was stuck. Krizia would turn the corner any second. She was going to get caught. All Anni could think about was letting everyone down, especially Lexi.

"*Jump into the painting,*" commanded Whiffle.

Anni spun around. A wide painting hung over a small table at the end of the hall.

"Ornellipoo," simpered Van. "There's no one else here. You need your rest."

Anni watched as Krizia's foot stopped around the corner of the wall and waved her arm as she said, "I'll rest after my Death Date. Go turn off the alarms!"

Anni stared at the painting of a country garden, then looked back at Krizia's foot.

"Let go of my wrist," yelled Krizia. Half of her body came into view. Anni stopped breathing. Krizia yanked her arm back and almost lost her balance. In seconds, they would be face to face.

"*Run,*" cried Whiffle.

Anni ran. She didn't know if she trusted him, but her legs were pumping hard.

"*JUMP!*"

With a flying leap, Anni closed her eyes and threw herself at the picture. She braced herself for a crash into the solid wall. Her foot kicked the vase of flowers off the table and Anni hit the ground at the same time the vase shattered.

Krizia barreled down the hall like a freight train.

Anni's lungs emptied. Her throat constricted. Krizia thrust her hand out, ready to seize Anni up off the floor, but Krizia's hand only grabbed air.

"*She can't see you,*" said Whiffle dully. "*She has not what you have in your possession and so cannot pass.*"

The alarms stopped. No matter how many times Krizia touched the painting with her hand, she couldn't pass through it. Anni understood; she was on the other side of the painting, in a kind of a chamber that Krizia could not enter.

Able to breathe again, Anni lifted herself off the cold stone floor. She watched to see if Krizia's eyes tracked her movements; Anni was invisible to her, but she still felt the threat of Krizia's stern gaze piercing through the canvas.

Slowly, Anni backed away and followed a dim flickering light down a narrow cold cement corridor. Her somasuit grew so tight she had to pull it off. Her clothes underneath were drenched in sweat, and the chill in this hall made her teeth chatter. She sneezed.

"*Gesundheit.*"

"All right, Whiffle, enough with the secrecy. Come out and show yourself."

Whiffle didn't answer her.

She followed the light and discovered a candle resting on a small table in the center of a two-story room. Books enveloped one huge wall, interrupted only by three small wooden doors. A long, dusty communal table rested in the far corner next to a sizeable object covered by a thick canvas. In the center of the room sat a small cot made up with crisp linen sheets, a woolen blanket, and a nightgown.

A note was propped up on the pillow. Anni picked it up and read:

> *Anni-*
> *It is not safe to roam the Manor tonight.*
> *Sleep here. You'll be safe.*
> *-A friend*

She dropped the note, spun around, and searched the room for this so-called *friend*. She ran to the doors and jiggled each handle, but they, too, were locked. Then she saw something familiar.

"*A friend?* I know it's you, Whiffle."

In the far, shadowy corner of the room, there was a staircase, the kind you see in very old libraries; the kind that runs on a wheeled track above. Each step closer brought a wave of goose bumps. Could it be?

She climbed the ladder. When she reached the top, all the little hairs on her neck stood on end. In the ceiling, there was a smooth wooden panel. Oak. Exactly like Mabel's trunk.

This was it: the last piece of proof Mabel was an Elemental, and the ladder, which led to Mabel's bedroom in Chicago. It also meant she could go back home. Right now!

Excited and scared, with trembling hands, she fished out Mabel's key. She tried to find a latch or a lock, but there wasn't one. The wood panel was completely flat. That didn't stop her from tracing every inch of the wooden panel, but each time, she came up empty. There was no way to open it from where she stood.

She stepped down one rung at a time, running it all over in her head. Was she imagining things because she wanted everything to fit into a happy little fairy tale? Or was she so desperate that she couldn't come to grips with the truth that Mabel was truly gone, and Teddy, and now maybe even Lexi, too?

"I beg you. Spare me from the melodrama inside your mind. More agents are at play than your capacity to comprehend."

A red-hot poker flared in her gut. "Are you reading my mind? Stay out. Stay out! Stay out of it!" she yelled at him. "Tell me everything right now! Why am I here? Where's Lexi?"

"Must we continue to have this irksome exchange? Listen to me, Child, and listen well. Direct all your queries regarding Mabel Moon to a better recipient, for I shall not ease your mind with the technicalities of her plans, which in my fine opinion are well beyond your comprehension at this juncture. However, after some duration, I will impart all my knowledge. Translation: you will know everything, but not until I deem so, and definitely not until after we strike an accord, which eventually you will agree to. Therefore, I ask you, please do us both a service and refrain from asking insipid questions! "

Anni conceded to silence. Fatigue had taken its toll. Her hands and legs trembled with each step down the ladder. She went to the cot, pulled the dry nightgown over her head, and wiggled off anything damp. She pulled the woolen covers over her legs and sat there holding Mabel's locket when she noticed a small hook on the back side. She snapped Mabel's key onto the hook, and the locket clicked open.

Inside were two small slots: one was empty and the other held a tiny rock, rough and porous like lava stone. With the tip of her finger, she barely touched the stone's edge when a searing flash of light blazed behind her eyeballs.

At a speed faster than light, a part of her—she didn't know which—soared over darkness as images of a dreary underground world zipped by until she landed in a large room. Inside the room was a young blond boy standing in front of a mirror, clutching at his stomach as he yelled in pain. The door behind the boy burst open and armored guards rushed in and surrounded him. One in particular laid his armored hand on the boy's shoulder. The boy snarled as his face grew red. He looked up into the mirror, and a chill overtook Anni. She was sure he was staring directly into her eyes.

She blinked and she was back in the room, sitting on the cot. She clamped the locket shut and pulled the covers the rest of the way up. Her body melted into the sheets, and the second her head hit the pillow, she was asleep.

CHAPTER 37

OGGLEBOGGLE'S MAPS

A patch of bright sunlight peeked through a high window in a far corner of the room. The sun was too high in the sky to be morning. Was it afternoon already? The day before seemed like a blurred memory and, for some reason, last night's sleep was the soundest she had gotten since she had arrived on the Zephyr.

Right away, she saw that her hair was back to its original dark brown. Her clothes—strewn on the floor the previous night—were laundered, even the Dwarrow-haired somasuit, and folded neatly in a little stack.

She dressed in a rush and wrapped the somasuit around her waist, under her shirt, to keep it hidden. The light made the room look very different. She raced up the ladder, but the wooden flat was still sealed. Then she tried the three doors again, but they were locked. She walked down the corridor toward the painting she had entered through the night before. Knox still stood guard, looking bored as his finger worked hard on something inside his nose.

"*You won't be leaving that way,*" said Whiffle.

"Really? So, how am I going to leave?"

"*First, I have but one request.*"

"Why should I agree to do anything when you won't answer my questions?"

"*Always with this minutiae and the vexations of a human mind—incapable of perception outside the corporeal form. Bother someone else with your queries.*"

"Why couldn't Krizia follow me?"

"*Details, details…your presence here is no accident. I share a hand in this encounter.*"

"Why? What do you want?"

"*This is not the moment to explore all the rudimentary particulars, however; I would like to submit my offer of assistance, providing you accept.*"

"I just want to find Lexi and bring her back."

"*At last a convergence of wills, where we may assist one another.*"

Anni wouldn't get her hopes up, but she would listen. "Go on, but speak normal."

"*According to my observations, you do not possess any other language skills other than a haphazard understanding of English. Therefore, I shall continue in your native tongue. I submit an offer, a binding contract, if you will. In this process, you shall recover something lost, more plainly, your associate.*"

"You mean my friend Lexi, right?"

"*Once you acquiesce I will bind the contract with a sacrifice. Before you recover your associate you will be required to fulfill your part, which will cure a longstanding anguish within the Elemental world.*"

"You have the wrong person. I just want to find Lexi. That's all."

"*You are free to do as you wish, but the totality of your learned independence is influenced largely by your humanity. As I explained before, I shall present this offer to you three times. This is the first…*"

It started to feel like a game, like Whiffle was toying with her. She walked over to the wall with the doors, focused on getting out of this room.

"*…I can feel your denial, and that is your answer. This knowledge would greatly pain your Guardians, if they were here to bear witness to your obstinate nature.*"

"Egbert put you up to this?"

"*That is not of whom I speak. For the gift of knowledge must be earned. The ending of a material form does not retire the entity's presence in your life.*"

"Er, right." Anni didn't understand what Whiffle was getting at, although the insult made itself crystal clear. "Can you please tell me how I'm supposed to get out of here? Knox is blocking the painting and these three doors are locked."

"*Of course. You may choose a door. The choice must be made by pure instinct and instinct alone. Only one exit is offered for each day. Choose wisely…*"

She had three choices: try to sneak past Knox and find her way out of the Manor, pick the correct door and go through it to who knows where, or pick the wrong one and hang out with Whiffle for another day. There was no contest. She inspected each of the three doors, hoping for some differentiation. Glints of light reflected off the metal doorknobs, but they all looked the same.

Instinctively, she took Mabel's locket and key and held it in her hand as she closed her eyes. She stood still and said to herself, "I need a door to take me out of here so I won't get caught by Krizia, Leach, or the Manor guards."

Anni opened her eyes and zeroed in on the door to the far right. She strode over and turned the handle. It opened. A surge of strength washed over her. The corner of her mouth lifted. She couldn't help these good feelings. She felt empowered for the first time in her life, and she knew she could trust herself.

Without hesitation, she walked inside. The door slammed shut behind her. It was similar to the tunnels between Yugi's shed and the Manor gardens—it was dark, damp, and musty. She walked for some time until she finally saw items lining the wall, items that accumulated as she moved forward.

The passageway grew tightly crammed with rakes, brooms, ladders, rolled canvas rugs, dusters, buckets, and cupboards filled with colorful bundles of yarn that budged up against her as she made her way toward a pint-sized door. She shuffled sideways, knocking spools of yarn from their perch. They tangled around her arms and legs. She tripped and fell through the door, along with all manner of items that heaped on top of her.

"Right on time," said Ms. OggleBoggle with a smile and a twinkle of her eyes.

"Effie? What's all that clatter?" asked a prune-faced woman who pushed her way into the pantry. This woman eyed Anni and said, "Is that a human?"

"Agatha, meet Anni. She's my honored guest," said Ms. OggleBoggle.

Agatha stared severely at Anni with a mixture of surprise and disgust. "None of your other guests came in with such a mess."

"Everyone in the world comes with messes," said Ms. OggleBoggle, still smiling.

Anni stood. She was inside Ms. OggleBoggle's house. She remembered she had been invited to a party, which had to be today. It was strange that the door she chose brought her there. Diana appeared around the corner and said, "That's all right. I will clean it up."

Busted. Diana's expression made Anni think that she knew all about what happened last night in the Manor. Quickly, Anni said, "Ms. OggleBoggle, I can clean it up."

"Effie to you, dearest. Now, I'll hear none of that. I've neglected my guests long enough and I want to show you off." And with that, Effie OggleBoggle snatched Anni's hand with a tight grip for someone her age and whisked her off into the next room.

It was a boisterous gathering. Effie OggleBoggle sat down at the table and gingerly patted an empty seat next to her, showing Anni where to sit as she started pouring her tea and offering wafer-thin biscuits.

Diana sat in the chair next to Anni and quietly said, "You didn't have anything to do with the Manor issue last night?" Anni stalled, sipping her tea, searching the room for the best exit and noticed Manor guards walking around Ms. OggleBoggle's property. She couldn't go that way. Diana smiled. "Never mind. I have a feeling I don't want to know."

The long oval table was packed with at least fifteen guests. Several conversations were going, but one intense discussion lorded over the rest. Next to the loudest man sat someone she recognized: Oliver. He was seated next to a loud, burly man with a heavy South American accent who proudly kept clapping Oliver on his shoulder and saying, "Next to the lost Prince, the Auguriums gave my nephew the most outstanding prophecy, but he doesn't live his life by it. He serves the Elofficium; no prophecies will decide his fate. Tell them, Oliver! Tell them how you've shunned tradition, unlike your parents. Tell them!"

When Anni caught Oliver's eye, she shifted in her chair, not wanting to look like she was eavesdropping on his conversation. She was reminded of what Daphne had said about Oliver disliking prophecies. She couldn't help but notice that Oliver hesitated before he nodded in agreement with his uncle, and wondered if he was being honest.

Avoiding his gaze, Anni scanned the group. What caught her eye was something she had heard about over and over, but had never actually seen up close: Opus Stones.

Several Elementals seated at the table were wearing their Opus Stones prominently displayed; each stone was inset in beautiful, ornate metal fittings fashioned as rings, belts, necklaces, bracelets, broaches, tiaras, and one sat atop the head of a cane. They all appeared to be distinctly different in color and size, but Anni found one correlation, the older the Elemental, the larger the stone. When it occurred to Anni that Effie OggleBoggle was the oldest one there, she turned to see what Effie's Opus Stone looked like, but didn't see one on her. In fact, she couldn't recall seeing them on any of the other Elementals she had met like Leach, Krizia, Yugi, Diana, or Fortensia. She would have remembered, because the most striking thing about them was the way they glowed, like they were alive.

Throughout the tea brunch, Anni couldn't help but catch glimpses of Effie smiling at her, and at one point, the old woman said, "I'm so happy you could be here today."

Anni smiled back, but for the life of her, she couldn't figure out why she was there. Agatha scowled at her from time to time, but no one else noticed her. Truth be told, she was antsy and desperately wanted to leave and find Daphne, Squirt, and Brat. Her mind raced with questions she'd ask them: about the coordinates, where Lexi was and how they would get there, and when they could leave.

Her train of thought was derailed when Oliver's uncle pounded his fist against the table, stood, and said, "A menace! How can you abhor my view? Those humans willingly find ways to destroy the planet daily. Their accountability is laughable. They murder our brethren, and continue to multiply like a plague. Humans are vermin; they are the enemy. Their nature is fueled by their egos and greed-driven vanities. Generation after generation, they continue to worsen, and all for what, I ask you? I'll tell you: it's their longing for total domination over the other, man against man, country against country, it does not matter. I vote we should strip the Elements from them and make a new world without them."

Oliver's uncle harbored a weighty presence as he roared for attention. Everyone felt it, stunned into silence, but Anni swore she saw the ghostly image of a giant bear linger behind him, which prompted her to think that if this man were an animal, he'd be a bear.

"Ignacio, really," piped up a woman sitting across from Oliver. "All this has been said before and will be said again."

"Father, control yourself," said a young man sitting on the other side of Ignacio, whom Anni assumed must be Oliver's cousin. "There's no need to draw your bile here. Ms. OggleBoggle, please excuse him."

Effie, it appeared, had been following the conversation. First she smiled at Anni before she said, "Your feelings run deep, Ignacio." Her eyes were glossy. Everyone was silent. "True, everyone must be heard. After all, isn't life about discovery? Aren't we *all* here to learn and make choices? The truth lies somewhere in between."

Anni understood what Daphne had said about Elementals coming to Ms. OggleBoggle for advice because the guest sat in silent contemplation for some time.

"Ignacio has a point," said a man across from Oliver. "We are not blind, and we do see the atrocities they commit daily. And though these humans have proven capable of change within each century, the change is too small and our needs are too great."

"Yes, Marcus, but there are many humans that work in our aid. The Fectus has engineered the Funk to blind the fields of their minds, bodies, and emotions; the humans have little course to guide them under such duress," said a woman next to the man Marcus.

"Speak nothing of the blindness, for my ears shall leave," said Ignacio.

"Father, surely you must consider that humans are no less experienced than underage Elemental children. They lack understanding and need proper educating, not—"

"Children, yes, but children with deadly weapons, and idiocy for brains—"

Ms. OggleBoggle cleared her throat, smiled, and looked right at Anni. "Lovely banter, wouldn't you say, my dear?" Everyone in the room turned with interest and observed her, and at the moment Anni wanted nothing more than to slip under the table. "Ah, I see you all have noticed my honored guest, Anni Moon." She smiled proudly. "Did I mention that this little human is also my relation?" Nearly every jaw fell, including Anni's. "Oh, dear I must have forgotten that. Well, I do like surprises." Effie stood. "Dear ones, my spark is fading and I require the sustenance of a quiet respite, so please continue the lively conversation as I depart for my afternoon nap. Anni, would you join me?"

Anni knew her face was red, but she was happy to get out of there. Effie's sitting room was decorated very much like the rest of the house, except the walls were filled with framed embroidered images, all of which looked a lot like old pirate maps, but for some reason they looked familiar, and Anni couldn't quite figure out why.

"I see that you like my decorations? Ooofff." Ms. OggleBoggle sat down. Her knees made a little popping sound, and she rubbed them. "Sometimes, my bones like to be a part of the conversation, too."

"Effie," Anni said, wondering. "Exactly how am I related to you?"

The little old woman said, "Well, dearest, that's simple. You were Mabel's family, and that makes you my family. Now, tell me, what do you think about my collection?" She pointed at one specific framed map. "Have you ever seen one like it before?"

Anni patiently glanced up again. Within that brief moment, she knew she had come to the right place after all. She had picked the right door that would help her find Lexi, because it led her here. Everything had fallen into place. She found the last clue that had been staring at her since before Lexi was kidnapped.

"The doll...Effie, I have to go. I have to go now."

"Connecting dots, I see." Effie grinned. "Go on then, go ahead, but if I were you, I'd use my Incantare doors to the Tea Shoppe, it'll be faster. And my dear, do remember this: you must always listen to your heart, for it will always lead you *home*."

"Thank you," said Anni. She hugged Ms. OggleBoggle and dashed out.

CHAPTER 38

THE CRACKED PEARL

A nni inched her way through Ms. OggleBoggle's house, trying hard not to attract attention. She felt terrible for not saying goodbye to Diana, especially after she had helped Brat and been so nice to her, but there was no time to waste.

She opened Effie's Incantare door to the secret hallway that led to Basil Boggle Tea Shoppe without anyone seeing her and went in. Absentmindedly she gripped Mabel's key, wondering what she'd face once she left the Zephyr.

She turned the doorknob to the Tea Shoppe's door…

"*You summoned,*" said Whiffle. "*Did I give you a fright?*"

"Eggs!" Anni jumped. "Do you always wait to bother me until I'm alone?"

"*Child, I am not tethered to that suit, which you believe to live within. I can bother you anywhere.*"

"Are you a ghost? 'Cause if you are, go haunt someone else!"

"*I am no mere specter. If you must know, I found myself pondering our last conversation when you called out. Therefore, here I am. Quite willing to receive and give credence to our binding agreement.*"

"Binding agreement? I didn't call out or summon you or whatever." She opened the door to the Tea Shoppe. "I'm not agreeing to anything you say, so leave me *alone!*"

Anni walked into the Tea Shoppe; it was full of customers—and every eye was on her. Before she could make a beeline for the door that led to the village, Oliver stepped out in front of her. Anni jumped back. "Oliver? But how did you—?"

"I know about the Incantare doors," said Oliver. "Listen, I'd appreciate it if you didn't mention what my Uncle Ignacio said back in Ms. OggleBoggle's house." He pointed at a far booth by the windows where Daphne and Squirt sat staring at them both. "You know, to your friends." He paused. "Because…I don't really think like him."

"Fine, okay," said Anni annoyed and antsy. "Sure, whatever."

Anni rushed over to the booth where Squirt stood, but Daphne remained seated. Neither of them looked happy to see her.

"We need the doll," Anni, whispered. "Where is it? Did you find Lexi's location?"

"Hold on," said Daphne, guardedly. "Where have you been? Last night, we were tracking you on the Omninav. One second you were in the Manor, the next, you completely disappeared off the Zephyr. Where did you go?"

"That can't be," said Anni. "I was in the Manor all night. I fell asleep in this strange room, woke up this morning and stumbled into Ms. OggleBoggle's tea party, where, strangely, I was the guest of honor—trust me, it's been a weird night and morning."

"We thought you left by Queen's Mirror," said Squirt, sounding hurt. "Without even saying goodbye to us first."

"Sounds like her style," said Brat, poking his head out of Squirt's shirt pocket. "Leaving, not telling anyone. Making plans, having tea with others, not inviting us—"

"Eggs!" Anni blurted, calling far more attention to herself than she intended, which prompted her to lower her voice. "Brat, I promise you, it really wasn't like that—"

"Did you make a secret deal with Jay?" asked Daphne, scowling.

By the looks on everyone's faces, she knew Brat had told them about her chat with Jay regarding getting E-passes. "I'll tell you everything. First, let's get out of here," said Anni, feeling way too many eyes on them.

They exited Basil Boggle Tea Shoppe and found the village extremely crowded. The weather was sunny and bright without a single rain cloud above. The Lake had finally refilled itself to the level it had been before she had fallen in.

Anni waited until they were out of the village, then she told them what happened to her after the S.E.C. meeting right up to the point where she burst out into the crowded Basil Boggle Tea Shoppe. She skipped the part about Whiffle because her lips locked each time she tried, and finally ended by explaining that after Jay caught her in the guano bags, he offered to get E-passes into LimBough so long as she gave him a definite location.

Daphne scowled, "So you were never taking me with you?"

"No, it's not like that. I keep my promises," said Anni. "I can't travel through LimBough without you. I know that. I was going to ask Jay for more E-passes."

"You guys were going without me?" asked Squirt, looking left out.

"Told you," said Brat. "Always thinking about herself."

"No. Brat. Stop. I want you all to come. I'll need all the help I can get."

"Moppins, no, I'm not coming. Had enough adventures already. Diana's sorting things out with Fleet, and I've got to stay right here until that happens."

"Look," said Anni. She could tell they were still upset. "I feel bad about Jay, but that was weeks ago. I wasn't trying to be selfish. Lexi's my only family left. I was thinking about her first. I'm sorry. I've never had friends like any of you until I came here. I didn't mean to hurt your feelings. I'm really sorry if I did. And I want you all to come."

Daphne twisted her lips. "I'll agree to your deal with Jay, so long as he only gets us open-ended E-passes."

Squirt hugged Anni around the middle and said, "This has been the most fun I've ever had in my life. I love you, Anni. Come on; the doll's hidden at Yugi's."

Daphne, Squirt, and Brat explained how they escaped Van and left the Manor through an open door on the first floor with keys conveniently hanging in the lock, and how they slept at Yugi's, taking turns watching the Omninav in case Anni showed up on the radar. Before they had a chance to tell her more, a group of skurfers soared above. Anni spotted Jay's red hair and knew it was him before he landed in front of them. Daphne harrumphed.

"You're a tough one to find," said Jay. "Fortensia told me to give this to you."
He handed Anni a letter.

> *Anni Moon:*
> *Your presence is requested at Moon Manor.*
> *3 p.m. sharp.*
> *-Maeleachlainn Spongincork*

"That's in ten minutes," said Squirt, peeking over her shoulder.

"Eggs!" Anni looked at her friends. "I'm not going."

"Look, kid," said Jay. Leach is totally wiggin' out. Don't know why, but he
was at Spadu Hills last night and this morning. You don't want that kind of heat
on your tail, especially when you've got *special* plans." He winked. "Now, tell me
the good news."

Anni looked at Daphne. "First, we'll need open-ended E-passes for all of
us."

Jay whistled long and low. "This is turning into something bigger than a
simple favor." He ruffled his hair, eyeing her and her friends. "Hmm…let's say
I can do that. I'll only agree on one condition, but before I tell you, what's the
location?"

Anni looked expectantly at Daphne.

Daphne looked side to side with a pained expression until she finally said,
"Peru, in the middle of the Amazon jungle."

"Peru? Huh." Jay chuckled. "Well, it just so happens that'll work out fine.
All right, I'll get you the E-passes, but here's the deal: I'm coming with you."

Daphne gasped. "No, nope. No way. He's not coming."

Anni gave Daphne a look that said, *what other option do we have?*

Anni turned to Jay. "Can you get the E-passes for today?"

Daphne eye's narrowed. "Just the E-passes."

"But, Daph—" said Squirt.

"I'll get the Opus Stones," said Daphne, shooting Jay a disgusted look.

"Hilarious." Jay smirked. "I can't wait to see how Floppy here pulls off her
part of the bargain. But, I'll meet you at Fortensia's in two hours." And he left.

Daphne's cheeks flushed. She refused to make a comment about how she
would get the Opus Stones but said, "Squirt, take Anni to the Manor. You and

Brat get the doll. I'll meet you both at Fortensia's place." Without another word, Daphne left them on the road and headed back to the Village.

There were no guards when Anni arrived at the Manor, and the alarms didn't go off when she passed the threshold. She made it all the way to Krizia's office uninterrupted, which was empty aside from Krizia and Maeleachlainn at the far end of the room. Automatically, her muscles tensed, remembering what she had been subjected to the last time. Mentally, she was ready for anything but, emotionally, a low-grade panic set in.

Krizia was at her desk, and though she didn't look up, her puffy eyes betrayed a deep exhaustion. Leach, on the other hand, sat beside her, looking perfectly rested, drumming his fingers on a highly polished wooden box on his lap.

"Can you explain your actions last night?" asked Krizia.

"I don't know what you mean," said Anni, trying to stay calm.

"I see," said Krizia. "Maeleachlainn, you were right; she spurns authority. I have no time for these games. Therefore, Maeleachlainn will monitor all your activities on the Zephyr from here on out, but first I have some news to share with you."

Anni's jaw slackened.

"Are you catching flies, girl? Close your mouth," said Krizia. "My sister-in-law Zelda Scurryfunge has been reported missing; she was last seen with Egbert. The Elofficium have named your dear uncle as their prime suspect, and yet he's conveniently missing, too."

Was it Zelda Anni had seen in the woods five days ago, or did she imagine it? What about Finnegan? Wasn't he responsible? Before she responded, Krizia continued. "In light of the events that occurred in the Manor last night, I have decided to restrict you to Spadu Hills forthwith. One more thing." She pulled out a small pendant hanging on a necklace. "Do you recognize this?"

The second she saw it, Anni's insides collapsed. She nodded and mumbled, "That's Lexi's." It was a gift from Teddy, the same pearl pendant Lexi used to wrap around her finger when she was nervous, only now, there was a massive crack straight across its surface. Was this the final proof Lexi was an Elemental? If this was Lexi's Opus Stone, did the crack in the pearl mean what she thought it did?

Krizia's demeanor grew weary as she stood clutching Lexi's pendant in her hand. "Maeleachlainn, please finish. I must personally report this to the

Elofficium, immediately."

Speechless, Anni watched her leave the room.

Maeleachlainn Spongincork walked around Krizia's desk and rested the polished box on the edge. He opened it, and removed a thin vine that was swaying in his hand. "Lift your ankle."

Weary with confusion, Anni didn't hear him. Her mind was filled with worried thoughts about what the crack in the pearl meant. If Lexi's Opus Stone was *cracked*, she shuddered, how much longer could Lexi survive?

"Have it your way." Leach bent low and held the vine against Anni's ankle.

Anni looked down as the vine clamped around her leg. It pinched her flesh, and solidified into a dark, dead wood. It hurt.

"Ouch," she said, pulling at it, but it wouldn't move.

"You may go now," said Maeleachlainn with an evil grin. "I'd advise you to return to Spadu Hills no later than four o'clock."

An overwhelming combination of anger and sadness coursed through her. She tore out of the Manor and ran to the greenhouse where Squirt was waiting for her outside with Brat. He had her backpack in his hand.

"Is the doll inside?" Anni asked.

"Yeah," said Squirt with a frown, then pointed at her ankle. "Where'd you get that?"

"Moppins, no!" said Brat.

"Anni," Squirt slowly said, "who put that on you?"

She was about to say Leach when her leg started to jiggle. The anklet was controlling her leg; it was lifting it up off the ground. She couldn't stop it. The anklet leg jerked at forty-five-degree angles, pulling her leg from side to side like the anklet had a mind of its own and was looking for a way around the glass greenhouse.

Suddenly her leg shot her forward like an arrow. Anni screamed. At an amazing speed, it launched right down the Moon Manor's road.

"Help!" she shouted over her shoulder.

"I'm right behind you," said Squirt, running after her, Brat in his pocket.

Anni grabbed handfuls of grass and bushes, but she couldn't slow it down it was gaining speed. The leg with the anklet was now traveling several feet off the ground. With her other leg flailing about in the air, her backside was bouncing painfully off the ground. Anni tried to grip her leg, but the velocity at which she was traveling made it impossible.

Before she knew it, the village was in front of her. The cobblestone streets were packed with Elementals. The speed at which the anklet had been moving was forced to slow down. Evidently it didn't possess the power to propel Anni's entire body over the throngs of people. Instead, the anklet had turned Anni into a spectacle where she was forced to endure the Elementals' points, stares, and laughs as she bounced along the cobblestone walk. Mortification truly set in once the anklet got impatient and started using Anni's foot to tap, tap, tap on the backs of passersby in order to get them to move out of the way.

Her face burned hot by the time she reached a group of teenagers, which turned out to be Oliver, Mackenzie, Miranda, Jay and a gaggle of his skurfer buddies. Seeing their faces made her sick. At least Oliver was quick to make his group move aside. However, when Anni caught the mirrored look of revulsion on his face, it made her feel worse.

As the crowds cleared ahead, the anklet sped up faster. Anni's eyes started to well. She didn't know if it was from bumps and bruises or her pride being dragged through the mud. Once she was out of the village and onto Spadu Lane, she zipped past Daphne, whose face went pale and slack. Mud splashed up Anni's neck and slopped down her back. Even a couple of juicy worms hitched a ride.

Not too far in the distance, smoke clouds puffed from Fortensia's chimney, which meant she was home. Anni wasn't sure if she wanted Fortensia to see her this way. But finally, at long last, her leg sputtered to a stop and plopped her down in front of Fortensia's house, right next to a long stick that was poking out of the ground.

Flat on her back, Anni's trembling legs could barely move. Fortensia, speechless and scowling, swiftly lifted Anni onto a rusty old wheelbarrow and wheeled her to the water pump, where a bucket full of water sat glistening. "You'll thank me for this later." Fortensia dumped the entire contents over Anni's head, washing away the mud. She threw a wool blanket over Anni and slung the girl over her shoulders.

A blast of heat hit her shivering body when they entered the sitting room. Fortensia propped Anni up on her chair next to the fire. "Don't move that leg. I'll fix you up." She adjusted the blanket and handed Anni a steaming mug. "Drink."

Crumpled and defeated in the chair, Anni did as she was told. She tugged at her tattered clothes. Her shirt and shorts were ripped, and her favorite striped socks, a gift from Lexi, had holes. She winced when she heard a sound near the doorway. It was Daphne.

"No sulking. It's bad luck," Fortensia boomed. "Did you know about this, Daphne?" She pointed at Anni's anklet. "Who did this?"

Squirt came in next, panting. Brat flew in at his side. They couldn't hide the horrified looks on their faces.

Anni finally said, "Leach did it."

"Here," said Fortensia as she shoved another warm mug into Anni's hand. "Drink." She paced the room. "I have a right mind to wring that idiot's neck. You're a child. Human or not, he had no right to…She's got cuts, bruises, and that blasted thing on her leg won't come off. Nothing a little salve can't clean up, but that's not the point, is it?" Fortensia roared. "That's it. I'm going to bang down the door at the Elofficium until they let me in. Ointment is in that cupboard. You two fix her up, all right?"

"Yes," chirruped Daphne and Squirt in unison, which seemed to appease Fortensia.

Daphne took out the first-aid kit. Squirt helped apply salve to Anni's face while Daphne worked on the cuts and bruises on Anni's leg. Brat tended to scrapes on Anni's arms and hands. Squirt whipped up a cooling tonic that he put on her bruises, which made them heal in minutes.

Anni's physical pain started to recede with their help, but she didn't care about that. Nor did she care that they had witnessed another fresh barrage of shame brought on by Leach. None of it mattered. All she could think about now was Lexi and that *cracked* Opus Stone. The question that loomed in her head most of all: *was Lexi still alive?*

CHAPTER 39

OPUS STONES

It took Anni some time to gather her thoughts before she could share what she had learned in Krizia's office. Once she did, Daphne stiffened and gasped while Squirt's mouth fell open, and they didn't speak for several minutes until Daphne finally broke the silence.

"There's no mention about Lexi in our news. Zelda, yes, but nothing about Lexi," said Daphne in a high-pitched voice. "The Elofficium always reports *cracked* Opus Stones. They have to. It's their job."

"It's likely that whatever you saw wasn't her Opus Stone," said Brat.

This made Anni feel better, but it was hard to know if it was true. After all, Krizia left the meeting with Lexi's necklace; she said she was heading to the Elofficium with a confirmed report of who the necklace belonged to. Other than that Anni didn't know how Leach and Krizia got it in the first place, or who else knew about Lexi's necklace.

Jay knocked on Fortensia's door, but walked in anyway. "I had to see this for myself," he said, scratching his chin. "You know what this means, right?"

"This is not a good time, Jay," said Daphne, getting up and hiding Brat from his view. "Don't you need to be doing stuff, getting stuff? You know, for the trip?"

"Listen, I'm good, but I'm no magician," said Jay. "Look at her. She can barely get past the office door." Jay turned to Anni. "Look, kid, call me when you get that thing off. I can't help you until then."

"I'm not giving up. We're going," said Anni defiantly. "We have to."

Jay smirked. Squirt turned to him and said, "Give us another hour."

Jay checked his wrist. "An hour?" he turned to Daphne. "And you'll have the Opus Stones by then? I don't want to keep making trips back and forth. I do have a life."

"I'm just wondering," Daphne said, her nostrils flared, "where exactly do you get your Stones from? Obviously, they aren't easy to come by. Unless, of course, you have connections with, say, a certain underground trade? I hope they're not *warmed over* or anything like that."

Jay's playful grin turned sour. "Look, there's no need for that kind of talk. If you can't get your hands on real Opus Stones, there's no reason to get all needle-nosy with me. Listen, Floppy, all you need to do is say the magic words, and I'll get you the Stones, but only if you play nice. Otherwise, I'm thinking that you're gonna need to sit this one out."

Daphne remained calm. "Oh, you mean these?" She pulled out three large Opus Stones from her hip pack. "We'll just need the E-passes, and there's no need to come back here in an hour. We'll meet you at the end of Spadu Hills Lane at dusk."

Jay's face turned a slight shade of pink. He left them without another word. Anni pursed her lips. She wasn't sure Daphne should have annoyed him like that. How would they get the anklet off in an hour? But she couldn't say what she was thinking because Fortensia entered the room.

"You want something done and the Elofficium throws paperwork at you. Human or Elemental, it's all the same," said Fortensia, waving a fist full of forms. "You know, if you keep staring at that thing, you'll all go blind." She chuckled, but no one else did. "Squirt, seein' that anklet reminds me of something... something that looks an awful lot like a rock, but not a rock exactly, more like petrified wood." Anni watched Fortensia tilt her head from side to the side as she stared directly at Squirt. "That is, if you know how to grow something that's not supposed to grow in these parts....Oh, well, what do I know? Guess I'll go fill out this paperwork unless anyone wants to come help me with something outside."

Fortensia left the room. Brat harrumphed, and Daphne looked confused, but Squirt jumped up and punched the air. "I've got it," he said and ran after Fortensia.

"That's Squirt for you. Here one minute, gone the next. Yugi tells him that he's got grasshoppers in his brain," said Daphne.

Anni saw through her attempt to lighten the mood. "What if I'm stuck like this? What if I never find—"

"You can't think like that," said Daphne.

"Exactly," said Brat. "Better to spend your time preparing for LimBough."

"Good point," said Daphne. "When we *debark* from Tree-Transport, the TreePort won't take us to the exact coordinates. We could be in the jungle for a couple days."

"Really?" Anni said. "I thought it would be different, faster."

"Moppins, it's complicated," said Brat. "There are millions of trees. It's not that easy. The same tree can take you to China, or Italy, or Norway. You need to know your trees, know where you're going, and what trees are where. An Arborist usually plans trips for Elkins who aren't used to traveling outside the normal routes. Should we hire one?"

"That'll draw too much attention." Daphne frowned. "We'll play it by ear."

"If you're worried and don't want to risk it, you can just drop me off in LimBough," said Anni. "I'm sure Jay can figure out the way."

"Uh, no," said Daphne. "First of all, I'm not leaving you alone with him. Second, forget about trying to convince Squirt otherwise; he won't leave your side. Besides, do you actually think I'd pass up the opportunity to see how well my travel kits do? I've made kits for Mac and Oliver in the past, but I've never tried it out myself firsthand."

"I almost forgot." Anni handed the somasuit to Daphne. "It almost strangled me in the Manor. I think it's broken. Hopefully you can repair it."

Daphne bit her lip as she inspected the somasuit before laying it aside. "It's a good thing your Funk has cleared up. I only hope it's clear enough for LimBough."

Anni pulled Lexi's doll from her backpack next and showed it to Daphne. "I'm almost positive that the doll's dress is a map. I saw one in Ms. OggleBoggle's house this afternoon. Can you check on your Omninav to see if it matches the area with the coordinates? Maybe it will help narrow things down to the right tree."

"I'll try." Daphne scanned the doll's entire skirt until her Omninav beeped. "You should rest; it might take a while for it to calculate the information and find a match. I'm going to check on Squirt. I'll be back in a few. Brat, will you stay with her?"

Brat nodded and settled on Anni's shoulder. She rested her eyes.

Anni awoke to the sweet smoky scents of licorice, chicory, and star jasmine. Something was slithering across her leg. She almost jerked, but Squirt put a steady hand on her shoulder and whispered, "Don't move, but you might want to keep your eyes closed."

Anni didn't follow his suggestion. Her eyes were focused on her leg, which was propped up over a small cast-iron smoker. The anklet was no longer solid, which not only made her skin crawl, but it was almost impossible to remain still, because its hard, stony surface had turned olive green and was slinking over her leg like a snake.

The smoker made the room warm, and her eyes watered. Repulsed as the vine slithered over her flesh, Anni gripped the chair and ground her teeth in an effort to keep from moving. The vine was dazed and drawn toward the aroma of the smoker, but when she jerked ever so slightly, it rushed toward her knee. It started circling like it was going to wrap around and harden right there, as it had done on her ankle. Her breath quickened and her body became stiff.

Daphne said, "Close your eyes and take a deep breath. Think about seeing Lexi's face when you find her and how happy you'll be."

Brat sniffed upon hearing Lexi's name.

Anni shot Brat a look before closing her eyes. Thinking happy thoughts as the vine slithered over her skin took concentration. She felt it move down her leg again. This, she decided, was the time to have faith, and she managed to control her breath and relax her body.

Anni opened her eyes. Squirt's Eaves-Dropus plant sat on a small hoverdisk about two feet off the floor. Brat nudged the hoverdisk under Anni's leg. The vine lifted the part that most resembled its head, sniffing the air around the plant. Hesitant, the vine uncurled itself from Anni's ankle, inch by inch, slowly reaching out for it. In a single bound, the vine sprang off Anni's leg and onto the Eaves-Dropus. In a flash, the vine looped around Squirt's Eaves-Dropus plant; instantly both plants solidified into petrified rock. Squirt raced the smoker outside and opened all of Fortensia's windows. Brat pushed the hoverdisk out

Fortensia's door with the help of One-eyed Nimmy.

"Brat and One-eyed Nimmy are going to hide that hoverdisk up on Fortensia's roof. If Leach is tracking you, he'll just think you're up in the attic," said Daphne as she hustled Anni into a private room, and handed her some clean clothes along with her new backpack, which held Lexi's doll and her new journal.

When Anni came out, Daphne applied the last bit of ointment to her ankle. "Thank you," said Anni. "Squirt, how'd you—"

"He was extremely lucky. Solved two problems at once," said Daphne. "You totally owe Fortensia for that save."

"It's true. I do owe her. That thing on your ankle was an Eaves-Cavea, a cousin to my Eaves-Dropus," said Squirt. "I never would have figured it out until Fortensia showed me her dad's old book on plant charming. We tricked it into thinking it was reattaching to its mother plant, but now that they are both petrified, the Eaves-Dropus will never change back—so I can't get in trouble. Hee hee. Clever, huh?"

"Moppins, that was easy," said Brat. "It's getting late. Shouldn't you guys get going?"

"Brat," said Anni, standing up. "Are you sure you don't want to come with us?"

"Moppins, you know I can't," said a glossy-eyed Brat. "Suppose this is goodbye."

"Thanks for helping." Anni hugged him, wishing he would come with them. She had gotten so used to having him around, but the more she thought about it, she didn't want to get him into any more trouble. She put on her best fake smile. "I'll tell Lexi you said hi."

"Okay then," said Brat. "Get going."

They had just gotten outside when Anni could have sworn she heard a little sniff. She looked back, but Brat was out of view. She turned and faced the road ahead, joining Daphne and Squirt walking down Spadu Road. Fortensia, too, was nowhere in sight, and Anni started to feel like a heel, leaving without saying goodbye. She had no idea leaving her new friends behind for her old one would hurt this much, but it did.

Squirt put his arm over Anni's shoulder as if sensing her sadness. His gentle reassuring touch made her feel a little bit better, and reminded her of what was ahead.

"Wait," Daphne said, stopping at the side of the road. She pulled items out of her pack and handed them to Anni and Squirt. "I almost forgot. Put these on. It's our disguises. People won't recognize us unless we look them straight in the eye. So whatever you do—"

"Don't look anyone straight in the eye," Squirt repeated. "Unless they've got some Swiss cheese, then you know—"

"Be serious," said Daphne. She helped Anni by adjusting a black baseball cap on her head, which covered half her face.

"Whoa," said Anni, as her hair grew five inches longer, and turned a deep amber color. She then buckled a thin belt around her waist and a green peasant skirt fell to her feet. "Do I look different?"

Daphne took a step back and smiled. "Yes, you do."

"I like this!" said Squirt. His navy windbreaker lengthened his torso and made him a head taller than both of the girls, which for him was a lot.

Daphne put on a headband that turned her hair white and a belt that changed all her preferred purple-hued clothes into shades of red. "It should do," she said. "But Squirt, remember to put on your hood when we reach the village and, whatever you do, don't make eye contact with anyone except for each other." She handed each of them a highly polished stone that looked like it was lit from within. "There are small pockets in your clothes where you can keep them safe. You only need to take it out at the bridge. I think."

With wrinkled brows, Anni and Squirt cautiously took them.

"What?" said Daphne. "They're not mine. They're Diana's. I'm not sure how she got so many, but my guess is that she inherited them. Plus, using other Elementals' Opus Stones is a great way to travel incognito."

"Daph, don't you think that's sort of like leaving a trail?" asked Squirt.

"No. She has another five carefully tucked away, and that's only what I know about. Trust me, Diana won't miss them."

"If it's traceable, maybe it would be better to use one of Jay's," said Anni.

Daphne sighed. "No. It's too late." She frowned. "That might seem like the logical solution, but we don't even know where he gets his Opus Stones, or if they're from a certain underground trade." Her eyebrows lifted in a discerning manner. "There's only one place to get *warmed-over* stones, and I assure you, it's not a pretty story. The Fectus created the *Vile Trade*; it's where *cracked* Opus Stones are bought and sold. We can't support that. It means you are buying and trading something that cost an Elemental their life."

"*Cracked*," said Squirt. "But that's just a story they tell kids to scare them."

"No. It's real," said Daphne. "I know you both think that Jay is being helpful, but we also need to be careful, too. I asked him where he got his stones because I don't want him to think we're stupid. If we used a *cracked* Opus Stone, we might not get past LimBough, and I don't want to take any chances."

Anni remembered what she read about the Fectus on Daphne's Omninav, and that first news article about Teddy. It said his Opus Stone was *cracked*; the thought made her sick, and this wasn't the time to think about it.

"Okay, back to the plan," said Daphne. "Anni? Ready?"

"Yeah." Anni nodded. "Let's go."

They walked through the low-filtered light of the forest to the edge of the town. The sun had just started to set on the village walk. Jay was waiting on a nearby bench.

"Impressive," he said, walking over. "Right on time, but let's make a quick detour back to the woods, if you don't mind."

Jay handed Anni two clear rubberized foot coverings. "You'll need to put these on your feet, kid. That bridge holds the memory of everything that crosses it. You don't want another dip in that Lake, and these should buffer that memory."

Anni looked at Daphne. "Is that true?"

Daphne blinked in surprise. "I...I can't believe I forgot that." She turned to Jay. "Thank you. If you didn't remind us, our trip would have ended right here."

Jay's lopsided grin returned. "Don't mention it. I'll walk over with Squirt. Then you two follow me. I'll pause at the bridge. Squirt will go first, then Anni, then you, Daphne. I'll take up the rear. Pass through the Orb, take an immediate right, and walk slowly. Once you're inside, I'll pass you and take the lead. Okay?"

All three of them nodded.

"Hold these in your left hand." Jay gave each of them their open-ended E-passes. "Have your Stones ready in your right."

Squirt and Jay took off, Anni followed behind. Elementals crowded the walk. The shops were busier than she'd ever seen them. Grateful for her disguise, her heart pounded nonetheless. She weaved through the crowd, avoided eye contact, which was a good thing because she briefly spotted Miranda talking to a woman two shops down from the bridge.

Jay bent down next to the bridge, pretending to adjust his left shoe as he mouthed instructions. Without a hitch, the bridge extended for Squirt. Anni was next. Her legs felt like jittery springs, twanging with each step. She placed the E-pass on the glass surface just as Squirt had done.

"Now the Stone," said Jay under his breath.

"Oh," she breathed, a little less confident. She hadn't seen Squirt do this part.

She placed the stone on the glass, and a subtle blue light pulsed underneath. Daphne was behind her, but Anni just stood there. She didn't know what the blue light meant. She turned to look at Jay. He rolled his eyes and mouthed, "*Go*," but the nudge from Daphne was the thing that snapped her out of it.

As if on autopilot, her legs took over and Anni stepped onto the bridge. Squirt was more than halfway to the Orb. She didn't dare look behind her to see where the others were but focused ahead, making sure that the bridge was still connected to the Orb, unlike last time. If it was going to disconnect, it might occur after Squirt passed through. Her stride widened as she got closer and closer.

The Orb opened before Squirt and swallowed him whole. In a few more paces, it would be her turn. The bridge was still connected; Anni watched it anxiously and pressed on. In a matter of seconds, she would be there, leaving the Zephyr at last.

When she got closer, she saw her reflection and realized the Orb was a giant mirror. She held her breath and counted down. Five. Four. Three. Two. One. As if she was a regular Elemental, the Orb opened for her and she passed through.

Before the Orb closed behind her, something whooshed past her face.

"Moppins, you'll never find Lexi without me," said Brat. He settled on her shoulder, hidden in her hair.

CHAPTER 40

LIMBOUGH

Once inside the Orb, earthy scents of roots, leaves, and bark wafted up into Anni's nose. She paused beneath a cathedral-sized arch that was only one of thousands lined up in circular rings above and below her like the interior of a giant beehive. To her left and right, Elementals of all shapes and sizes exited other arches, walking with purpose onto a massive bough-braided avenue ahead.

"Now, *this* is the way to travel!" Brat sighed. "Moppins! Don't just stand here; you'll get trampled. Keep moving."

"This place is amazing," said Anni, not paying attention to where she was going.

"Right, right, go right," said Brat.

Anni turned right onto a wooden bough. Tiny lights beneath her feet glowed with a message that said, "*Welcome to Espalier Way. Please move forward. Mind the branches.*"

"Thanks," she said to Brat. "I'm glad you're here."

Espalier Way had two paths: one to enter and the other to exit. Turning left would have spit her back through another arch, and probably not the one she had entered.

Anni moved into the growing throngs of Elementals, all of them walking faster than she did. It didn't take long to estimate that, with the continual influx, she could easily get separated from Daphne, Squirt, and Jay in no time. Being shorter than most of the commuters, Anni started to worry. "Brat, do you see Squirt? I can't find him."

Moisture collected on her face; LimBough was very humid and she hoped her disguise wouldn't be affected. She scanned every direction, drinking in the sights—including the different kinds of Elementals that walked like humans but were actually half or mostly animal. The expanse below looked like a trailing network of ants going to and fro. She shook her head in wonder when it dawned on her that she had to be over a thousand stories up. She wondered how Daphne managed it all by herself until she spotted Squirt's windbreaker.

She raced ahead and tapped his shoulder. "Right behind you."

Squirt had a mile-wide grin on his face. "It's amazing!" He spoke so loudly that several Elementals turned and stared.

"Yes, yes," said Brat. "Moppins, don't draw attention."

"Oops." Squirt giggled. "Hey Brat, you came…where's Daph?"

"Here," said Daphne, who cut around them and whispered, "I heard you, by the way. Squirt, you might want to try keeping your voice down. Jay passed you two a while ago. Follow me. Don't stop, and don't draw attention." Her long white ponytail swished past them as she whipped around a tall man with a thin, insect-like body and an oblong head.

Espalier Way ended at an epicenter, where queues formed around dozens of round wooden platforms, a lot like elevators except without cables, doors, or anything holding them up, and only a clear partition to prevent anyone from falling off.

Each queue was labeled differently, and once each platform filled to capacity, it made its descent. Anni had no idea which one to use; some stopped on every floor, some on every other floor, some on every odd-numbered floor, and some on every even-numbered floor.

Daphne expertly moved past all the queues and headed straight for a platform labeled "For Rest Express." This was by far the largest platform of all, which carried thirty travelers at once. Jay was already waiting in the middle of the line. Anni and Squirt hurried after Daphne, making it just in time, as passengers twenty-nine and thirty.

Even after a hundred rides, Anni would never be able to take it all in. The steady descent barely gave her a view of the different levels, but she spied several bustling floors aptly named Break Branch Upper, Break Branch Middle, and Break Branch Lower. On these floors, commuters rested in Treetop Cafés, and Log Lounges advertising rest and relaxation. Alongside the cafés, there were hundreds of shops with signs that read:

Last minute wares!
SALE—SHIELD FIELD PROTECTORS…
<u>Fit in in style!</u>
Banish Squatters & Fake Your Friends
Don't leave El without it - **Unimaginable Elixirs**
Tickets to TreePorts Across the Globe
El-Necessities Here FUNKTASTIC ON SALE!!!
E-passes Organized.

The For Rest Express moved too quickly to see more, but it made Anni think how much fun exploring all of it would be if Lexi was with her.

Anni looked down. Masses and masses of trees, in all shapes and sizes, like ancient sentinels, populated the never-ending ground level. There were multiple vast areas that were scorched and charred, with only burned stumps where trees once stood; one word came to Anni's mind when she spotted it: humans.

"Don't turn around," said Daphne in a hushed voice. "Stay still. Keep looking straight ahead." Daphne took a breath. "Diana's on the platform behind us."

Anni swallowed the gasp that almost escaped. She even felt Brat curl his tiny claws against her shirt as he, too, went rigid.

"After we get off," Daphne whispered, "I'll pass you. Stay back and linger for a minute; tie your shoe or something. Make sure to leave enough room between us so that we don't look like we are traveling together. I'll stop in the first shop I see. You stop in the next one. I'll meet you there."

Anni hadn't thought about running into any Elementals she knew. If Diana caught them, it could ruin everything. She had to act like she had been to

LimBough so many times that it all looked mundane. She felt a small pang at the thought that this was probably the first and last time she'd ever get to see it.

The landing was quiet and quick. Elementals hustled off the platform in single file lines. Anni followed them, glancing in every direction, looking for a place to slow down so Daphne could pass them, but there was no place to stop.

She spotted Jay. He stood next to a giant information center. She veered toward it and waited there. Jay was on the other side of the booth, but he didn't walk toward her or speak. When she knelt down to tie her shoe, he rushed over to a store called *Blend*, which sold an array of T-shirts, jeans, and tennis shoes.

Anni stood up too fast and didn't see the duffle bag, about the size of a small carpet. It knocked her against the kiosk, causing a great commotion. The small man who carried the bundle apologized profusely, trying to explain that it was his fault that he didn't see her.

"It's okay. I'm—"Anni said, but the rest of the words got stuck in her throat. Diana was walking their way. The man pleaded for forgiveness even louder than before. She tried to use his body as a visual shield, but he was shorter than she was. Diana would be sure to see her face in a matter of seconds, and then the little man looked at her very oddly.

There was no time for this. Anni crouched down. "I forgot to tie my other shoe. Could you make sure no one else bumps into me while I tie it?"

The little man's face split into a smile as he proudly stood by her.

Brat, meanwhile camouflaged in Anni's hair, kept a close eye on Diana. He whispered to her where Diana was until she was out of sight.

"Thank you," Anni stood. "You're a lifesaver."

The short little man looked satisfied to have helped. He had two antennae on his head and tiny little wings on his back. He handed her a vial of gold dust, bowed, and left.

"That was a Papillion!" said Brat, astonished. "Why did he give you aurum dust?"

She shrugged and held out the vial for a better look. "What is this?"

"Moppins, hide it, hide it. Put it in your bag. It's very precious."

She spotted Daphne's white ponytail bobbing in the crowd and took off after her. Anni passed beneath a red and blue sign that said Root Way One walking at a steady pace until finally she caught a glimpse of Daphne's red-and-white tartan skirt.

Phew. Everything would be okay. All she needed to do was find the next shop. She walked ahead and looked around, but there wasn't another shop in sight. Instead, Root Way One split into three forks: Root Way Two, Root Way Three, and Root Way Four. She slowed, clenching her fists, glancing left, then right. Should she take a chance on Root Way Two? This was so stupid. Just as she was about to turn around, she decided to stop, close her eyes, and breathe deeply.

When she opened them, she looked down Root Way Three and saw Jay up ahead. She traced his steps for some time, all the while passing other Root Ways that branched off into different sections. One section was completely sectioned off, burned to a crisp for miles in one direction, just as she had seen from above.

There was a smattering of shops here and there, but they were smaller and stocked only with basic Elemental wares. She noticed signs mapping out trees by origin and continent. To her left, she was looking at one Root Way that was completely blocked off due to flooding when someone yanked her off the main path.

"Where are the others?" asked Jay.

Anni peered around, but there was no sign of either Squirt or Daphne. "I don't know," she said. "Are we in the right place?"

"Yeah, we are," said Jay. "I'm glad Daphne warned you about Diana. I couldn't, she was watching me. All right, kid, you stay here. Don't move; I'll turn back to see if I can find either of them. I'm supposed to meet a friend anyway. Daphne should be fine. She knows the port better than she led us to believe, but do me a favor: keep an eye out for Squirt."

Jay walked off in the direction that they came from.

Anni stayed right where he left her, nervously looking around. "I bet you'd feel better if you were up there with them," Anni said to Brat, pointing at all the Fleet messengers zooming overhead.

"I'm fine where I am, thanks. I don't need to be spotted, especially now."

A huge projection screen floated above them. *Elemental Omninavigational Network - Bringing the News to You When You Need It* ran across the bottom of the screen like a ticker. Anni couldn't be sure, but it mostly appeared to be stories, running headlines, and a few video clips. Her eyes grew heavy as the pictures rapidly changed.

With a shaky finger, Anni pointed up toward a collection of tree branches. Hundreds of eyeballs were blinking down at her and everything below. "What... is that?"

"Humans. Human children, to be precise, and yes, they can see you and me and everyone else here," said Brat. "You've heard the children's tale about looking into tree stumps filled with water so you can see the little fairy people, and in that scenario, we're the little fairy people."

"How can they see us," she said. "Won't they tell?"

"Of course they will. Children are gifted with sight, but who'd believe them?"

"Good point," said Anni. "It's amazing, but you're right."

"Moppins, look up at the Haloscreen."

A photo flashed on the vast projection screen of the *Elemental Omninavigational Network* news page. Finnegan's picture flashed first, followed in succession by images of Egbert, Teddy, Lexi, and Zelda, then they were gone. It bothered her, seeing all their faces so large like that, like they were a news story.

Anni went back to looking for Daphne and Squirt. She noticed a woman standing next to an information desk, haggling with a computerized halo attendant, trying to get some last-minute E-passes. This woman pointed at someone to Anni's left and yelled, "Stay there, I'm coming." She looked familiar somehow, but it wasn't until the woman entered a TreeTransport waiting area that Anni recognized her.

Her stomach did a flip. She had just met that lady at Ms. OggleBoggle's house. Anni straightened her cap, adjusting its brim lower on her head.

"Agatha," said another familiar voice; it was Diana.

Diana and Agatha stood in front of a TreeTransport *embark* line, which Anni assumed meant that they were leaving. She prayed they wouldn't recognize her. Agatha walked up to the attendant, handed her an E-pass, and went through the Tree-Portal first. Diana was next. As if in slow motion, Diana handed over her E-pass, smiled at the lady, and moved forward. She briefly looked back over her left shoulder and locked eyes on Anni.

Paralyzed with fear, Anni froze. Diana's vague gaze felt like it lasted a century. At long last, Diana walked through the TreePort.

"Moppins, did that just happen? I need a tonic bath and a straw, stat," said Brat, hyperventilating. "My heart can't take this kind of pressure."

Anni finally exhaled. Hands trembling, she sighed. They had made eye contact. But what did that mean? Did it even matter? Apparently not, since Diana left anyway.

Squirt raced over. "Hi, guys. How's it going? This place is unbelievable. I—"

"Quiet," hissed Brat as several heads turned in their direction at once.

Squirt pointed at Daphne, who was heading toward them.

"Where's Jay?" she asked, a little out of breath. "We need to get in line, otherwise we'll miss our TreePort. I know why you're freaking out."

"How much would you like to bet you don't know?" asked Brat.

"I think Diana saw me," said Anni.

"If she didn't stop, she didn't recognize you. Besides, this is what Elementals do. They travel all the time. Most of them know the ins and outs of this place better than you know the back of your own hand. We were bound to see someone. I would have been shocked if we didn't. Anyway, we've gotten this far, haven't we?"

As the waited for Jay, Anni glanced back up again at the branches. Eyeballs were still there, blinking down at the whole of LimBough, only there were more than before, and for some reason, several settled around the area where they were.

"Squirt," said Brat. "Who's that guy Jay's talking to?"

"No idea," said Squirt.

A lanky young man bobbed irritably in front of Jay. The jerky young man even raised his voice, causing several Elemental travelers to turn in their direction.

"*No…*" Anni hissed. She gripped Squirt's arm harder than she meant to.

"Ouch," cried Squirt.

"It's Egbert's Minion," she said, "*Rufous Finnegan…*"

Out of nowhere, border patrol guards wearing Elofficium badges surrounded Jay and Finnegan. They cuffed Finnegan's wrists. The commotion did not go unnoticed by the Elementals passing through. The tension broke when the Elofficium guards took Finnegan away, and Jay was urged to follow without a public display.

The quartet watched in suspense as Jay glanced back at them with a quick shrug as his way of saying, "Kid, you're on your own."

"Was Finnegan the friend Jay was supposed to meet?" asked Brat.

"I warned you about Jay," said Daphne. "He has some unsavory connections."

"At least they got Finnegan," said Anni. "That's all I care about."

"For snozdoddles' sake, we better get a move on," said Brat. "Just seeing those Elofficials is kerfuffling my hair."

There were only two travelers queued for the TreePort titled Mangrove Peru. "This is the trickiest part, so listen carefully," Daphne said. "I'll *embark* first. Anni, you and Brat go second, Squirt, you last. I'll wait just past the portal door. I'll hold out my hand to grab yours, Anni. Then you and I will do the same for Squirt. Inside, we will find the right *debark* TreePort. Okay?" It sounded confusing, but they had made it this far.

"Get your E-passes ready," said Daphne.

An attendant with a bark nametag that said *Peggy* smiled at Daphne first. Anni nervously watched their interaction.

"Hello, Miss," said Peggy. "Where are we traveling today?"

"Ucayali Region, Peru," said Daphne, handing over her E-pass.

"Beautiful this time of year. Have a lovely time," said Peggy.

Daphne disappeared behind the TreePort. Anni was next. She stepped forward and handed her E-pass to Peggy, who only smiled, which threw her off. She had prepared to say she was going the Cusco Region, just to make it look like they weren't all traveling together.

With nothing left to do, Anni walked up to the *embark* TreePort, which shimmered a grayish-green. It wasn't transparent like the Queen's Mirror or the Orb. She finally walked through; Daphne was right where she said she would be, standing in a long, vast oaken hall that swirled with mist up into its starry ceiling.

Squirt came through the gray-green sheath. They held hands as Daphne led them through the paneled corridor. Several arched portals were marked *Debarking Gateway Ucayali Region,* but there was one problem. Each one had different kinds of trees listed for each unique TreePort; it was imperative that they find the right one.

"We are looking for Cinchona."

"How about these?" said Squirt, pointing to three portals positioned side by side.

Brat flew over to each one to check them out. Anni looked through the portals, too, and could have sworn she saw a Swedish farm, a Japanese countryside, and an arboretum.

"Maybe," said Daphne. "It could be any of them. One will bring us closer while another might take us farther. We're looking for a portal next to the

Ucayali River. We only get one shot at this. Once we've *debarked*, we can't come back through the TreePort."

"*Straight ahead, second TreePort to the left,*" said Whiffle, but only Anni could hear him.

Anni had no clue which one it was, but the idea that they might exit the wrong one was not a mistake she wanted to make. Perhaps it was a rash decision, but she decided to trust Whiffle. "This one," she said, pointing to the portal he suggested.

Brat, Daphne, and Squirt stood before the TreePort. A faint trickling sound of water came through, and Daphne *debarked* first. Squirt went next, and finally Brat, then Anni.

It was close to three a.m. in Brazil, something Daphne told them she had considered before leaving the Zephyr, which was evening in the U.K. They found a spot close to the river but far enough away from the TreePort to set up camp. Daphne's stellar camping gear was so well made, it took minutes to get the tent, sleeping bags, and campfire set up. Squirt started a hearty legumen stew, and toasted pelta bread, while mixing elixirs.

Daphne pulled up a plotted projection on her Omninav. She sat with Anni and showed her the path they would take along the river in the morning.

"I synced the map on the doll's dress to the landscape of this area, but the only part that matched perfectly was the blue stitching at the bottom. It's the river. Nothing else makes sense on the doll's dress except for this X. This area is described as *The Sleeping Tree*, but I have no idea what that means."

"That looks close," said Anni. "How far away are we?"

"Maybe a half-day's walk. Only, there's no paved path. We'll have to move through a lot of brush. I'll try to plot the easiest route. We should rest until dawn."

Anni got up and moved next to Squirt, who busied himself by the fire. "Here, take this," he said, shoving a small purple bottle into her hand while he placed a cork in the top. "It should be good by tomorrow."

"What's this for?" asked Anni.

"All living things have energy *fields* around their bodies. That's why they call humans Eggheads, because they don't take care of theirs. Fields should surround their body from head to toe, but I've heard that humans have basketball-sized egg-bubbles that bump against their heads. It's why I laugh whenever you say *Eggs*."

"Oookay…"

"This is a *Shield Field* tonic," said Squirt. "It pushes Funk away."

"I'll take mine now, thank you," said Brat, downing it.

Anni decided to take hers in the morning. She got settled in the tent, amazed at how something so big packed so neatly into Daphne's satchel. The silvery-hued structure revealed small skylights where sleepers could stargaze before drifting off. She had finally gotten off the Zephyr; she deserved one good rest, even if it was only for a couple hours.

As dawn was breaking, Anni awoke to find the tent empty. Outside, she saw Daphne tending to Squirt's stew as he sat huddled in a blanket, looking ill.

"You needed proper light," Daphne chastised. "You should've waited until morning. What were you thinking? Half a week's supply is wasted."

"Ugh, please stop talking," said Squirt, shivering under the blankets.

"What's going on?" asked Anni.

"Ohhhh, not so loud, not so loud," said Brat, huddled next to Squirt. Brat, too, had turned a deep shade of green.

"Did the Funk get them?" asked Anni, worried.

"Hardly," said Daphne. "Squirt mixed the tonics all wrong, and before checking them, he and Brat drank it. Now they're both sick, and I have to neutralize the bad batch."

"Mopple-me-toppined," said Brat, cross-eyed. "My brain's kerfuffled."

"Here." Daphne handed Anni two different-sized mugs. "Can you give these to Brat and Squirt? It's a *fixer-upper tummy tamer tonic*."

Anni handed Squirt his mug first, seeing as Brat looked the worst and he might need help. Even his tiny whiskers were green. She held the smaller mug for him as he gingerly took sips. Squirt, on the other hand, took one whiff from his mug, turned a shade of blue, and said, "I'm gonna be sick…"

Anni pulled the steaming mug away just in time as Squirt yakked all over his boots. It was disgusting. There were tufts of dark hair mixed into his vomit. She turned away before she got sick, too. At least Brat managed not to throw up and continued to sip from his mug without complaint.

"You better drink that, Squirt!" Daphne scolded. "Your goof has left us with only a quarter of elixirs. We'll be lucky if it's enough. Aside from this *fixer-upper tummy tamer*, nobody's taking tonics unless it's absolutely necessary."

"I was only trying to help," said Squirt, feebly.

They were so close to finding Lexi, Anni didn't want them to fight. She helped Squirt drink his tonic so Daphne didn't get annoyed.

"Anni, throw some dirt over that gunk," said Daphne. "I need my nose to concentrate, and that smell is interfering. How're you doing, Brat?"

"Still mopple-toppined," said Brat, looking a little less green.

Anni grabbed piles of fresh dirt and plopped them on top of the offending blob. When she went back to grab some more dirt to dump on Squirt's boots, she could have sworn she saw four to five leaves rustling right next to him, but she put it down to the wind.

CHAPTER 41

THE TREE OF DEATH

Anni packed up the camp while Daphne finished up with the tonics. Brat started to return to his normal coloring. Squirt didn't fair as well; he needed double the dose of the *fixer-upper tummy tamer* tonic before he could walk.

Over the course of four hours, the girls took turns shouldering Squirt through the rainforest. It slowed them down and was complicated by the intermittent tropical showers.

When it was Anni's turn to lead the group using Daphne's Omninav, an hour had passed until she stopped. "If we keep following the Omninav's directions, we'll be moving away from the river. That doesn't seem right."

"I agree," said Brat. "There's nothing ahead. This map doesn't make sense."

"But we can't pass over the river," said Daphne. "We need to trust the Omninav and follow the suggested path around it."

"I call time out. I need to rest," said Squirt, his legs wobbling as sat down on a tree stump. "Daph, let's just triple-check the map."

"Fine." Daphne took the Omninav and started punching buttons.

Anni sat beside Brat and Squirt as they drank the last of their tonics. She pulled out a water flask and whispered to them, "I think we're lost." They sat there and watched Daphne twirl a few strands of her hair around her finger, which she only did when she was nervous.

It was hard to be optimistic when they weren't moving. Anni pulled Lexi's doll out of her bag and handed it to Squirt. He absentmindedly grabbed the legs and held it upside down with the skirt hanging over the doll's head while Anni rearranged her bag. When Anni looked up she noticed something. The stitching on the reverse side of the skirt looked exactly like some of the symbols of trees and rocks she had just seen on the Omninav.

"The map's reversed. Look, there's *the Sleeping Tree*." Anni pointed at the doll's skirt.

Brat clapped his hand to his head. "For snoz' sakes, it's been with us the whole time."

"What? Where?" Daphne took the doll.

Sure enough, the underside layer of the skirt was an exact topographical map of the jungle. The doll's dark brown stockings perfectly resembled a tree, and its green shoes made a perfect impression of the treetop canopy.

"That's the forked tree back there," said Squirt, pointing, too.

"Here." Daphne handed the doll to Anni in the exact same way Squirt held it. "Hold it steady, just like that." She positioned her Omninav and re-scanned the doll.

With the mapping program complete, the four of them huddled together and watched as a projected image canvassed the jungle's undergrowth. A blinking dot pointed the way with a *You are here* sign. The Omninav revealed that they were less than two miles away.

They surged forward into the woods. The excitement must have invigorated Squirt because he was able to walk on his own, and led them to the edge of a precipice. The ground sloped a long way down, into a forest of skinny trees, but there wasn't a huge tree in sight.

"It's not here," said Daphne. "The *Tree* should be right here."

"The map's obviously wrong," said Squirt. "Let's keep walking."

"No, Daphne's right," said Brat. "The *Sleeping Tree* should be right in front of us."

Anni agreed with Daphne and Brat. It didn't make sense to walk ahead.

Anni heard a snap. Her back was facing the edge of the gradient, but when she turned to her friends there was nothing behind them.

Brat landed on her shoulder and whispered, "Did you hear that?"

Snap. Squirt looked up, too.

Anni trained her eyes on the forest's floor. Leaves rustled next to Daphne's side. Someone was there with them, someone who couldn't be seen.

"I just don't get it," said Daphne, staring at her Omninav as she turned around making quick glances in all directions away from the precipice where Anni and Squirt stood.

"Daphne." Squirt said slowly, staring at the moving ground by Daphne's feet. "Can you come over here?"

"What?" Daphne sounded annoyed. She turned abruptly toward them, but her foot made contact with something invisible and she stumbled.

"Oooouuuuuuccccchhhhh," cried an unseen voice.

Daphne ran toward Anni and Squirt. Something rustled a foot away. Squirt leaped at it but caught air. Daphne locked her arm in Anni's. Squirt spun around to intercept.

"Ahhhhhhhhh!" something screamed.

CRASH!

A ball of tangled limbs tumbled over and down the foothill, through vines and wet mossy debris. As the ground flattened, they rolled apart and separated. Squirt was the first on his feet and helped the girls to stand. Daphne looked the worst of the three. She had a long scrape on her arm and one of her leg warmers was torn.

Anni took a deep breath, checked her friends, and gasped.

Lying in a heap of fresh earth and leaves, wearing something that looked like an abominable snowman costume, was Miranda Firestone. It looked like she was wearing an old-fashioned version of Daphne's somasuit, but this one was so ripped and torn from the fall that it had stopped working.

"Have you been following us?" demanded Anni.

"Congratulations, you have a brain after all," said Miranda. "All of you are in so much trouble. One hit on my Omninav and I can tell the Elemental world where you are."

"Moppins, we're done for," said Brat to himself.

"You can't do that," said Daphne, nudging Anni and eyeing Miranda's wrist.

"Oh really?" Miranda stood up. "I can do whatever I want."

It took Anni a second before she caught on to what Daphne meant. Anni narrowed her eyes. "Go ahead. Make the call. Tell everyone where we are."

"*No*," said Brat and Squirt.

Ready to call their bluff, Miranda raised her arm. Her smug expression vanished. A twig was jammed into her Omninav; it was broken.

Daphne laughed. "Actually, I'd like to know your plan now."

Anni squared her shoulders. "We don't have time for your games. If you ever want to get back to a TreePort, you better tell us what you're doing here."

"Oh, so you're in charge? I'm supposed to follow the human's rules?"

"Yes!" chorused Daphne, Brat and Squirt. Anni smiled.

Miranda rolled her eyes and huffed; her cheeks grew redder by the second. She flipped her hair back, but her movements were irritable and jerky, which made it all the more interesting to watch. "You want the truth? The truth is that I've been watching over you imbeciles from the moment Anni arrived on the Zephyr! Two people told me to watch out for you and make sure you didn't get into trouble: Diana and Oliver."

"Oliver has no idea what I've been doing," said Anni.

Miranda grinned broadly. "See what I mean? Clueless. Oliver knows more than you think. I've been helping him; we've been listening in to your pathetic conversations, and your grand plans to escape the Zephyr." Anni felt Daphne and Squirt shift uncomfortably beside her. "Granted, I've had to stifle my laughter every time you fools made mistakes. I never thought you'd get off the Zephyr, but once I saw your determination to break into the Secret Elemental Counsel meeting, I changed my mind. You got me into a heap of trouble that night. Van caught me when he was supposed to be catching one of you. I set off the alarms. Just wanted to see you scramble, I guess, especially after you got what you came for."

"So *you* left the keys in the door near the conservatory," said Squirt.

"Yes, and I was questioned by that idiot Knox for over an hour."

"If you're working with Oliver then where is he?" asked Daphne. "Jay got arrested in LimBough. Did you know that, or did you plan that?"

"Coincidence and genius. My brother's a moron. I'm not sure how I knew about your travel plans initially—that was the coincidence part—but once I did, I sent him five open-ended universal E-passes. He didn't even suspect they were from me."

"That still doesn't explain why you are here," said Anni.

"You don't actually think I'd let two Elemental children and a human take the credit for finding and rescuing a vital object on the Elofficium's task list? I'm here because I'm going to find that stolen Golden Bee Artifact and get the credit for returning it to the Elofficials. Besides, you don't even know what it stands for, do you?" Miranda paused. "Let me enlighten you. That artifact single-handedly reminds all Elementals to disobey Elofficium rule so that a bunch of Eggheads can pretend some silly old legend is real. Do you really think that Elemental boy who was born from two great families can really save us all? Do you really think he's still alive after the Fectus took him? It's ridiculous!" She narrowed her eyes at Anni. "Humans and Elementals living together is a huge mistake, and no Elemental will ever change that. You can blame the Metalheads for that."

Daphne's face flushed red. "Don't talk to Anni like you know her!"

"Did you forget that I am the most experienced one here? Not to mention the only one of us here with an authentic Opus Stone. And by the way, if you were informed, which you clearly aren't, you'd know that the tree you're looking for is called the *Tree of Death*, because those who enter the wrong way don't come back alive."

"We're not here to find the artifact. We're here to find Lexi," said Daphne.

"That's right," said Squirt. "We just want to find her."

"Strange," said Brat, perched on Daphne's shoulder and looking at her Omninav. "*The Sleeping Tree* should be right over here. We should be right next to it."

All that stood before them was a bunch of stringy vines.

"You mean the *spooky Tree of Death*," said Squirt with a chuckle.

"Ridiculous!" said Miranda. "You can't even find it…"

SNAP!

They all jumped.

CRACK!

As if on command, a colossal trunk, as wide as a building, appeared out of thin air. Hundreds of vines fell from above. Carved stones that looked like little fat people sprouted up across the jungle floor and forced them to move. Dozens of huge black-and-white feathers rose from behind woodland objects.

Daphne grabbed Anni's hand. Brat quivered on Daphne's shoulder. It was impossible to determine what the feathers belonged to; some were singular while others rose in multiples. They inched their way back against the massive trunk while Squirt stood protectively in front of Brat and the girls.

Miranda wouldn't have it. She walked into the center of a clearing and said, "I demand you show yourself, creatures!"

"No," said Squirt as he tried to pull her back, but she resisted.

A young man, clad only in a loincloth and a feathered headdress, deftly landed a foot away from Miranda, making her flinch. As he landed he repeated, "*Creature?*" The young man with a shaved head growled, "I have a name, it is Kuar, and these are my people. You are the creature here. I give you fair warning to leave now."

Miranda scowled at him. "I'm not taking orders from someone dressed like you! I am superior to you in every way. Get out of my way, savage. I'm on Elofficium business, and you cannot interfere."

"No," said Squirt.

The young man smiled at her. "We don't recognize your laws here. We eat your kind for breakfast."

Miranda's jaw slackened, but she caught herself and stiffened up. "Nice try. Now get out of our way. I am going to the *Tree of Death*!"

A global catcall echoed around them, and hundreds of natives appeared from behind trees and rocks and seamlessly slid down vines.

"You have one second to turn back," said the young man as he crouched low.

As if time had slowed, Anni sensed everything around her; Daphne trembled beside her; Brat's breath rattled; Miranda defiantly narrowed her eyes. When Anni looked down, silver hairs lifted on Daphne's arm and, for a split second, it almost looked like tiny feathers had sprouted. Just then, Squirt loped in front of Miranda. The young native sprang up at them from his low crouch, kicking up earth.

Squirt pushed Miranda aside as he yelled. "No! *She's my sister!*"

Shock registered on Miranda's face, and everyone else's. The young native spiraled in the air aimed at Squirt, but his body, from his hind legs up, transformed in the process. Before they could blink, the young native morphed into a hulking jaguar with massive claws and fangs. Anni fell to her knees, terrified that her funny, lovable friend Squirt was about to be ripped to shreds.

Squirt clutched his throat. A roar erupted from his mouth, echoing off the forest floor like the boom of a sonic pulse. A wave of electricity crackled the air, and just like that Anni witnessed Daphne, Miranda, and Brat crumple to the ground. Squirt transformed; he morphed into an even larger jaguar than Kuar.

A tangle of brown and black fur clashed head on. They moved so fast that all Anni could see were teeth and claws rippling across the ground. And then, they stopped. Teeth bared, the jaguars growled. Slowly, they backed away from one another, heads low. One bowed lower than the other, and when it transformed back, it was the young native, Kuar.

Anni looked down at the striking black-brown jaguar crouched protectively in front of her. Hissing sounds escaped behind his clenched jaws and massive fangs. She couldn't move from the shock.

The young native bowed and bent low before Squirt. His people did the same.

Slowly, Squirt switched back from beast to boy. Shoes and shorts came first, then his torso reappeared, but it took a few seconds before his head took its original form. The sweet smell of the ocean lingered in the air. An aura of tranquility took over, as a soothing hum emanated from a luminous emerald stone, which hovered by Squirt's feet. Anni turned to Daphne, but she, Miranda, and Brat were still lying unconscious.

Squirt jumped. "Anni I finally got my Opus Stone! Can you believe it? Wahoo!"

"Yeah. Um," said Anni staring at their friends. "Are they going to be okay?"

"Uh-oh. I think so. Opus Stones can create shock waves. Remember when you got to the Zephyr? Elemental forces can have dramatic effects when mixed with Funk. They should be fine." Squirt beamed his usual happy-go-lucky smile as he picked up the emerald stone, about the size of an acorn. When it touched his skin, the humming stopped. "I'm a full-fledged Water Elemental, just like Mackenzie."

"Now I know why you're always calm. You're also a *cat*, in case you didn't notice."

"Did we forget to tell you about that?" Squirt giggled.

"Um, yeah, you left that bit out....Can all of you turn into animals?"

"Yeah, a lot can. You should see your face!" Squirt laughed. "I never expected to be Water. My mother's a Fire Elemental, males don't often take after their mother's Element. My dad was an Earth Elemental. That's why I've been practicing and tutoring under Yugi."

"Umm, right, but the cat thing?" Anni pointed at Kuar and the other natives.

Squirt laughed. "I can't explain that, but…" He crouched to whisper to her, "I think this tribe believes I'm related to them." He giggled. "Weird, huh?"

"How do you know that?"

Squirt giggled. "Cat communication?"

"Hmmm, what about the Miranda thing?"

"I didn't say anything, because I was waiting for the right moment to tell her. She can be kinda prickly sometimes, especially when it comes to her half siblings."

"I can think of a better word."

"We have the same mother, but different fathers. She gets touchy about our mum but that's another story."

"I'm happy for you. It's a beautiful Opus Stone." She smiled. "Wait until Daphne sees it." She couldn't help but think how this separated her from them, and most of all, Lexi.

The young leader of the clan raised his head with reverence. "I am Kuar Naheul, Prince of the Jaguar and Cat people. You may call me Kuar."

"Hi, Kuar. I'm Squirt." He turned to Anni. "What should we do?"

Anni said to Kuar, "Can you show us the way to the *Sleeping Tree?*"

Kuar whistled. Two women picked up Daphne and Miranda as if they weighed nothing, threw them over their shoulders, and raced up the middle of the biggest tree as though they had invisible suction pads on their feet. A young boy scooped up Brat and did the same. Then Kuar motioned for Anni and Squirt to follow him.

"This way," said Kuar, who showed them the notches built into the tree, a spiral of teeny stairs. "Please follow."

Anni frowned at Squirt. "We're supposed to climb up that?"

"Or I carry you," said Kuar.

She watched the nimble Jaguar people deftly whisk Daphne and Miranda up the side of the tree. It looked like they walked on air. Then she saw how they used the vines to help their ascent. She turned to face Kuar. "And if we fall?"

"I will catch you, but you won't. I can see you already have the skill."

Holding a vine in each hand, she placed one foot on a small peg in the tree. The vines cradled her, sometimes wrapping around her waist to offer more support. The repetitive movement reassured her. Before she knew it, she had climbed thirty feet.

A hundred feet up, a treetop city greeted them. It expanded as far as the eye could see. Everything was interconnected, either by petrified branches, vine slides, or boughs that lifted like seesaws from one level to the next.

They followed Kuar toward the center of the village. There, they had to cover their mouths and noses because of the sulfurous smells that emanated from rotten wood that surrounded a charred tree trunk. The closer Anni got, the more her eyes watered. She wasn't the only one. The Jaguar people appeared frailer, too. It was as if the tree's illness affected them on a deeper level.

"I will take you to Chief Vidar," said Kuar. "He may help you in your request."

As they ascended another level, the scorch marks in the tree grew bigger, and the sulfur stench that invaded their nostrils intensified. The remnants of what once had been a palatial balcony were crowded with sick natives. Anni had never expected to witness such intimate and private moments, as Jaguar families surrounded the sick who were preparing to leave their bodily forms for good. This platform, full of dozens of wood and stone sculptures fashioned in the shape of animals, struck Anni as being a sacred place. The statues were mostly carved like cats, but there were at least two statues of a strange winged creature she didn't recognize. Many were festooned with wreaths of flowers and grass. All of them had little wisps of twinkling lights that hovered around the effigies.

In the center stood a massive round altar of stone. It shimmered brightly even though it was completely shaded by the trees. It was close to this object, where the Jaguar people laid out cots and deposited Daphne, Brat, and Miranda.

"Your friends rest in care. They should wake soon," said Kuar and indicated they should move on.

At the highest point in the village, the view was breathtaking. Concealed behind large palms, a royal throne room was visible on a private platform. Two guardians assisted a weary medicine man as he carried out decayed bowls filled with noxious oils. The medicine man reported to an even older man who gazed across the sea of treetops. His attire suggested he was the chief. They hung back as Kuar reported to him.

The chief turned to Squirt and Anni. "I am Chief Vidar. Welcome. It is our highest pleasure to receive and attend to you and your friends, Squirt. I knew your father. He was a great man and a king among his people in the East."

"Thank you," said Squirt. "This is Anni. We need your help."

She cleared her throat and said, "We need to enter the *Sleeping Tree*."

The old chief laughed. "I apologize, but passage is impossible."

Squirt's face fell.

Chief Vidar missed nothing. "It is not I who prevents your passage. Once the Opus Stone commences, your body cannot withstand another transformation. It is far too weak." Vidar's eyes were kind, but weary. "The Tree no longer sleeps. It embodies death and the weak cannot enter. Otherwise, it would consume their life force. Only the strong may pass through." He sat back and studied them.

Anni stepped forward. "Can I go?"

"You can't go alone!" said Squirt.

The chief looked at Anni in size and stature. "You are human, yes?"

She faced Vidar. "Yes, I am."

"Humans cannot return. It's not been done," said Vidar.

"I don't care. I don't have another choice…"

Vidar raised an appraising eyebrow. "We all have the freedom to choose," he said. "If you were to enter, a part you must leave behind, a part that cannot absorb what is to be seen inside. To enter without doing so would leave an indelible mark on your being, a scar so deep, it could tear you in two."

"I don't care. I have to go," said Anni.

"Ah, the stubbornness of youth. I see I can't persuade you." Vidar raised a hand to his lips, tapping them. "Human you are, but you are also still a child. There is power in that, and as such, your chance for survival is greater. I cannot spare any of my people to join you. My best men are weak and in great need of conciliation. But if you wait, we can offer the assistance in a day's time."

Anni didn't want to hear any more. She was so close. Every fiber of her being was ready to go. "I can't wait. Lexi needs me. She's been in there too long already." She glimpsed Squirt's concern and said to him, "I have to go, even if it's alone."

The chief said, "Although there are many entrances into the Fectus world, at present, this tree is the only one in this area. If you must go, then you must follow me."

He led them into a chamber. Perhaps once it had been an opulent throne room, but now, a dying creature lay on the floor, partially covered with a woven tarp. Its flesh was scarred and the wounds oozed a tar-like mucus that seared holes into the wood flooring.

Five shamans chanted over the figure, but it didn't seem to do any good. Deterioration progressed just until death was imminent and then, inexplicably, the creature's body revived itself, disallowing the completeness of death and welcoming the rebirth of pain anew. The idea that this creature was trapped in a vicious cycle of agony made Anni retch.

Chief Vidar's body swayed as if he'd lost strength upon entering the chamber. The guardians helped him stay upright as he placed his hand over his heart. "My people and this creature share a union," he said in a slow, soft tone. "He is our guardian and our soul. We share in its cursed pain." He paused. "It is neither alive nor dead, as its twin exists in permanent torture. The two can never recover so long as they are separated."

Under the burlap, Anni saw two giant charred wings that mirrored the exact shape and size of the burned tree trunk. However, it was difficult to see what kind of creature lay beneath. Bandages covered most appendages, preventing the hemorrhaging viscous fluids from spreading over the floor.

"Who did this?"

Vidar looked even older in that moment and lowered his head.

"Where you travel, you will see many evils. Perhaps you may encounter those at fault." His lip curled. "The *Fectus*, of course, are responsible, but their queen, the Naga Yaga, is directly responsible for this Ancient's pain. She wields the *Umbos,* an abomination that divides the essence from the corporeal form. Naga Yaga has many pawns at her disposal, and this Ancient is not the first of her victims. My wish is that you do not happen upon her true minions, for they are a formidable group who won't hesitate to harm you. We have great knowledge of their inner workings because my people enter into her world in disguise, always searching for information to help heal our beloved Ancient. As you have witnessed—" he pointed toward the memorial statues— "not all of my people return in one piece."

The true horror of the story chilled Anni to her core.

Squirt moved to her side. "You can't go. I won't let you go in there alone. Not without help. You have to wait for us to go with you."

She was terrified, but she couldn't let him see it. "You've already sacrificed enough for me. Lexi can't wait. I have to go while I can."

The chief took a vial from a medicine man and held it out to Anni.

"Promise me one thing, Anni," Squirt said. "Please come back. Promise me that. That tonic's no joke. At best, you could have neon-colored hair for months. At its worst..." He stopped. His watery eyes said the rest.

She understood his meaning, looked him in the eyes, and said, "I'll be back, okay? You're a great friend, Squirt. You and Daphne have done so much for me, but now, I've got to do this for Lexi. She's my family, and she's in there." She hugged him, took off her backpack, and once again left the doll in his care.

The only thing of value she had was Mabel's locket and key. They were sentimental only to her, and she felt safe going in with them. She turned to Vidar and said, "I'm ready."

"Drink this to protect the most important part of your being which you cannot live without, your essence. This will ensure your success, but know it will alter your physical form. The Ancient trapped below is tortured because he has been separated from his, but his fate is not yours. Do not take fear with you on your journey, for you will find much of that below. Set your intention before you drink, set all fears aside, and all will be well."

Anni took the vial and repeated his last words, "all will be well," then swallowed it. The liquid tasted like acid and scorched her throat all the way to the pit of her stomach. A faint vapor traveled from her body, out the tent, and settled on the altar outside.

Chief Vidar pointed to a curtain behind the beast. Two guardians pulled the silk back, revealing a rotted fissure large enough for a small car within the charred trunk.

"You are brave, young human. Kuar will show you the way down. He will escort you to the bottom, but from there, you must travel alone."

She followed Kuar into the tree. She wanted to look back, but her task was hard enough without seeing Squirt's worried face. Humid air filled the dark expanse below. Kuar's barely dressed body was near invisible except for the faint glow of two circles that appeared to be tattooed on his back and shaved head. She held on to vines as she trailed after him, down thin wooden steps that spiraled down the inside of the trunk. She concentrated on the circles the entire way. All her other thoughts escaped her consciousness until finally, her guide stopped at the bottom. She couldn't believe how quickly they reached it.

Kuar stood before a tunnel. He smelled the air and watched the passage carefully until it was safe to speak. "I apologize. I cannot take you farther. I leave you here, brave friend." He touched the spot between Anni's eyebrows and chanted something that sounded like a prayer. His finger was cold to the touch, but when he removed it, Anni felt a swirling sensation behind her eyes that radiated up her spine.

"I must go now."

"Thank you, Kuar. You can call me Anni, Anni Moon."

Kuar bowed. "Anni, daughter of the Moon, may the Ancients protect you and fortify your soul. May the warrior within come forth and bring great power to your journey."

CHAPTER 42

WHIFFLE'S SACRIFICE

She watched Kuar disappear into the darkness and thought about what he said. Did she have a warrior within her? She hoped so.

Slowly, she walked down the tunnel. The walls were damp and her throat tightened, fit to gag from a dank smell that lingered in the airless passage. A fresh wave of panic hit her when she realized she couldn't keep her hands from trembling.

Steeling her nerves, she pushed ahead. As long as she moved one foot in front of the other, it seemed manageable, even though there was no end to the tunnel in sight.

Refracted light bounced off greenish tubular objects stuck inside the walls. Tangled roots made the ground uneven, and forced her to boulder climb over crevices.

The tunnel dead-ended into a steep cliff. Far below, she caught sight of a flat mesa, visible only by distant flickering lights, and cacophonous cheers that echoed off the underground walls. Though she couldn't see what created the noise, she felt deep in her bones that the mesa was where she needed to go. The longer she stood there, the more the raucous sounds made her feel sick and weak.

Something was coming up the path behind her. Alarmed, Anni dove behind the nearest rock before two burly creatures approached. She inched around a boulder that sat precariously on the edge of the cliff overlooking the mesa, hundreds of feet from the ground. The creatures tromped past her and stopped on the other side of the boulder, speaking in husky tones.

The one that spoke first was picking at his tusk-like teeth with a bone. "Willin' a wager 'oo can spread ta most Funk tonight? Bet ya, come on. I've got me some good uns picked out. They light up the Squatters fast and sucks all the joy out. I like ta hopper and work quick, see. No lingerin', not me. Nah, I spin 'em. Humans never see it comin' when they're doin' chores. I gets me Squatters planted in every room. Best way to generate long-termers, that's stayin' power."

Anni thought she would squeal with fear when the other creature's snake-like tail slithered over her foot. "Naw, 'tis not for me. I work slow—more powerful like. I pick at 'em. Make 'em afraid of 'emselves. Rub out self-trust, then 'em only listen to me, and then they beg. Naw, I take pride in me work, 'tis an art. Me numbers might be low, but me Squatters can power the Fectus cross one small country."

"Ha! We'll see 'oo 'as the stayin power," said the beast with tusk teeth.

The very sight of these unnatural monsters made her sick. Whatever they were discussing, it didn't sound good, like they were taking something from humans, making them sick. Were they responsible for spreading Funk? Was that their job? She shouldered herself against the rock to keep her balance, and a cry nearly escaped her lips.

"*Don't utter a single word, Child,* " said Whiffle, who for once Anni found welcoming. "*Steady your breath, Child. Do it now. You don't want them to sense you.* "

Anni did her best to breathe in and out as slowly as she could.

"*Now, with care, gaze upon your arm,*" he said kindly.

She couldn't understand, and looked at her arms and hands as instructed. They were covered in long, dark hair. Her body was covered in fur, too. Her hands sprung to her face. Her blood pounded in her ears as her fingers traced the outline of a monkey's face.

"*Uncontrolled emotions will make you ill,*" said Whiffle. "*Breathe now to leash them, otherwise your disguise will fail you. You must settle them for the potion to work.*"

A part of her wanted to scream, another wanted to cry. She panted until the panic ebbed away bit by bit. She whispered, "The vial from Vidar did this to me?"

"*Indeed, but do not use your human voice, speak only with your thoughts. I can hear them if you want me to. You cannot walk around in your human suit in this realm. Vidar did you a service. You have transformed like many before you who have infiltrated the underground searching for answers. This is necessary to achieve your goal.*"

"Whiffle, what do I do?"

"*Have you considered my proposal?*"

She hesitated. The truth was she hadn't. She thought she could do this on her own. "Can you promise you'll help me find Lexi and get us both out of here safely?"

"*Alas, do you not recall our last exchange? I believe I stated quite clearly that if an accord was reached, I would be of assistance in the locating of your friend.*"

"Yes, I remember that part. But you didn't say you would help us escape. If you agree to that…then I will agree to whatever it is that you need."

"*At last, we have an accord. I will assist in your departure; yet it is imperative that you appreciate how much depends upon you. I cannot force your hand but only create a confluence of opportunity. You must be the one to act. Should I provide instruction, you must be precise and swift in action. Upon mutual agreement, I, too, shall relinquish something of value. A binding Elemental custom.*"

"I guess that sounds okay….So then, you're an Elemental, too?"

"*Of course, but let us not waste precious time on etymological technicalities.*"

"It's not like I can see you."

"*You will see me when the time is right. I cannot risk it, if perchance a Squatter is afoot. Rest assured I will be near you at all times. You will not be alone.*"

"Great. It's not like I even know what a Squatter is."

"*Alas, and such is my point entirely. However, it does you no service to be ignorant. Squatters cower in corners, like spiders, only ten times their girth but nearly invisible to the adult human eye, but small human children usually see them, which is often why they dislike the dark. Squatters absorb and read emotions, primarily powered*" *by fear. They relay this back to the Fectus so they can target areas and build Funk. Now you are armed with knowledge, so mind your emotions. Are we in agreement?"*

"Yes. Will you at least tell me where to go?"

"Follow after those two abominations."

She had no desire to go anywhere near them, and it felt unnatural to move along in a monkey's body. She trailed after the hulking creatures. With each step, her new body felt more agile than before and moved faster than she expected down the sloping crevice.

Before long, they reached a bridge that led directly toward the mesa. Up ahead, the abominations split off and moved away from the bridge.

"Cross the bridge."

Narrow and raised, her passage was shadowed by a massive, stadium-sized enclosure that surrounded the inner part of the mesa. One glance backward, and she realized she was in the belly of the underground. After the bridge, there were several paths around the stadium, but she didn't know which to take.

"You must reach the nucleus. Within the auditorium is where the Fectus congregate. You must blend in with the masses of creatures below."

She walked up to a gated entrance and was trying to peer through the cracks in the wall when an arm reached out and pulled her shoulder. A thin girl, dressed in rags, took on a ridged defensive stance before Anni. She spoke with a hoarse, raspy voice. "You're not supposed to be here today." She had a dirty bandana over her face, her skin was caked in filth, her hair was a wild mass of muddy curls, and she squinted when she spoke. "If the border patrol found you, you'd be flayed alive. Follow me. Come on."

Anni hesitated. The girl was so filthy, it made her uncomfortable.

"Follow her," said Whiffle.

They wove their way through a maze of passages until they were one floor above the auditorium, where the din made it almost impossible to hear.

"You're in luck," said the girl in a hoarse voice. "I've finally found what your people have been looking for. But you'll have to wait for my sign after the first service. Remember, when you're seated at the table, only pretend to drink the juice. After everyone is served, wait for my signal. I'll take you to where it is. Now, go. Find a seat and don't look obvious."

Anni had no idea what this girl was talking about. What service? The girl ushered her into the center of the mesa. Larger than five football field stadiums, it was packed with endless rows of tables crowded with the most unnatural beasts Anni had ever seen. Several seemed to resemble that of the primate persuasion, but most were hideous hybrids from mythology books, with the odd addition of horns, hooves, talons, claws, tusks, and snake-like appendages. Anni stumbled against the wall as a sickness surged inside her. She scanned the rows of tables filled with creatures. There wasn't one free seat in the auditorium.

The girl who led her inside was standing at a bar covered with hundreds of tankards filled with an ocher liquid. Anni spotted a gap on a bench close to the bar and was glad to see that it was next to an exit.

"*Go,*" said Whiffle.

Anni raced toward the seat, jostling between and around slow-moving creatures. She didn't see the armored leg that kicked out in front of her. She tripped and fell over. A roar of laughter erupted.

"That'll teach you to mind your manners, you filthy animal."

Anni didn't know if monkeys could scowl, but if they could, she was doing it. An ironclad foot was an inch from her face. Her eyes trailed up the armored suit. It was embellished with tiny spikes, and she traced the spikes until her gaze landed on the bully's face, a pale blond boy about her age, or possibly a year or two older. His tight jaw smirked, as he squinted down at her like she was prey. He uncrossed his arms, thrusting out his chest as he brandished a red leather whip in his right hand, like he was about to beat her with it.

"Get out of my way, Spike," said the savage girl Anni had followed inside. "I have a job to do. I suggest you step aside so our customer can grab a seat." The girl pushed her way around the ironclad bully. It was clear he didn't intimidate her. She held two jugs in her hands, and by Anni's view, purposely spilled the liquid over one of his legs.

"Thirty-three! You did that on purpose," Spike whined.

Anni brushed dirt from her face, got up carefully, and inched away once Spike dropped his whip and removed a visor over his eyes. She saw that he was just a boy, but not just any boy! This was the exact same boy she had seen when she touched that tiny lava stone inside Mabel's locket, the same boy who looked like he was being tortured. Her hand flew to her chest, but the locket and the key weren't there.

"*Do not think on that now, Child. Take the seat.*"

She put it out of her mind and ran to the bench. The empty spot was right between two hulking apes who pounded their empty flagons against the table singing a chant. Along the row, others boasted about how many humans they would oppress that night, while others reminisced over the ethereal experience the Plantanana juice gave them.

Not to look out of place, she grabbed an empty jug and pounded it in unison with her tablemates. With each thud, the mug left ringed indentations on the table. Her arms were stronger than she realized. She searched the crowds for the girl who had helped her twice now, who Spike referred to as Thirty-three.

The singing and the pounding grew louder as the creatures waited for their empty tankards to be filled. She couldn't make out the words of the song, except that every line ended with the word *Funk*. Anni's row was the last to be served, but the girl, Thirty-three, was nowhere in sight. Losing patience, her gaze darted all around until she spotted movement up above. A large disk hovered over different parts of the stadium, but on the disk there was a strange looking chair that hopped around precariously to the edge.

Anni bristled. It wasn't so much a chair but a throne made of bones that bounced on a massive, vile-looking bird's leg. In the throne sat a cloaked figure that held a wooden staff with long, bony fingers and wore a crowned kabuki mask. Anni wasn't sure, but she'd be willing to bet it was the dreaded Fectus Queen, Naga Yaga: the one Chief Vidar had described, the one responsible for all the *cracked* Opus Stones, and possibly, the one who ordered Lexi's kidnapping.

Anni trembled when the Naga Yaga looking directly at her table. She averted her eyes, not wanting to draw attention, but it was hard not to notice the creepy chicken-legged throne leaping about as it encircled the upper parts of the auditorium like a death vulture.

Behind the bar, Spike fumed. He complained loudly that his leg sloshed every time he moved. Nearby creatures laughed. Spike lashed his whip against the walls.

"*Enough!* No more singing!" he yelled. "Barmaids, finish the first service. Fill the flagons. We have a schedule to meet."

Human-looking teenage girls and boys raced around the tables filling mugs with lightning speed. Thirty-three, however, was the fastest of them all and finished her section first, ending with Anni's table. The beasts sitting beside her guzzled their drinks, the golden liquid slobbering down the sides of their mouths. Anni didn't know how to fake drink and empty her flagon at the same time, so she followed her neighbors' lead. She closed her lips and let the drink fall down the sides of her mouth—and was soaked in the process.

By the time the creatures drained the last dregs from their flagons, something strange started to happen. Gray shadows started to pulse and writhe over their hulking torsos, which one by one started snapping away from their bodies. Anni couldn't take her eyes off the ghostly forms as they soared upward past the Naga Yaga toward the cavern's roof.

The gray shadows slithered and coiled like ghouls on Halloween, twisting and turning around long fang like stalactites that glowed an inky, reflective coppery hue.

Anni gaped. It wasn't an ordinary stalactite; it was a *Queen's Mirror*. This was how the monsters left the Fectus lair. She shuddered, and dropped her mug on the table. It was the juice, the vile juice that turned the creatures into these pulsing shadows. She felt sick when she looked up at the thousands of apparitions vying their way into the Queen's Mirrors, ready to spread Funk and the Naga Yaga's evil bidding.

"Faster, Thirty-three! Ready the second round. No sluggishness," said Spike.

"You're the only slug here, Spike," said Thirty-three.

Spike frowned and his eyes narrowed. Creatures that still had their shadows still attached broke into guffaws. The ones that didn't looked like they were stuck in some kind of trance. Anni's skin crawled when she noticed their eyeballs turned a whitish blue.

"And my name isn't Thirty-three," said the girl. "Get it right. It's Lexi."

Anni stared at the girl. Surely, it couldn't be Lexi. Anni scanned the girl from head to toe; those dirty tattered clothes, the wild hair covering most her face, no glasses, that rag covering her nose and mouth. This girl looked taller, and thinner, but perhaps without her baggy school sweater it was possible. Where was the meek Lexi she knew and loved? This girl was feisty and tough. But then she saw Thirty-three roll her eyes just as Lexi had done a million times before, and Anni knew it was her.

"Take caution, Child...mind your breathing," said Whiffle. *"Blink back those tears; they will be your undoing."*

Fleshy human fingertips emerged through the fur on her right hand. Anni gulped. If she transformed into a human right there, the consequences would be dire.

"*Child, breathe. Surrender not.*"

She tried not to hyperventilate, and bit down on her bottom lip, focusing her breath. Underestimating her strength, the metallic tang of blood told her she broke skin.

"What's this?" Lexi charged toward Anni. "Spike! Get over here. This one's gone and busted his lip. It can't transform now. Take him out of here."

Anni tensed. What was Lexi doing?

"I'm the boss, Thirty-three! You take the orders! Remove the beast yourself."

Swiftly, Anni rose and followed Lexi out of the coliseum. Intimidating creatures jostled and shoved past her through the main interior corridor. A group of humans was being herded past her into the coliseum. She couldn't shake the feeling that one of them looked an awful lot like Oliver, but that was impossible, or was it?

Lexi led them past throngs of monsters, each one more gruesome than the next. When they finally reached a vacant tunnel Lexi spoke. "I think you fooled him."

Anni stopped walking. Clutching her throat, only soft gurgling sounds escaped.

"You're new to your form," said Lexi. "Your vocal cords aren't working yet. Don't worry. You can trust me. I'm on your side."

Lexi was helping her. Wasn't it supposed to be the other way around? The sight of her friend so transformed, so brave, overwhelmed her.

"*Mind your feelings…*"

But Anni couldn't. Her legs gave way and she dropped to the ground. Voices echoed, heading their way.

"Uh-oh." Lexi pulled Anni behind a small boulder. "Stay here. Don't move."

"Barmaid! What are you doing down here?" demanded a guard. "You're supposed to be in the coliseum."

Anni didn't hear Lexi's reply because at that moment, a piercing sound rang in her left ear. Her stomach cramped and her body started to burn with fever. Her hands and feet started to switch back and forth between human and primate.

"Phew," said Lexi. "I got rid of him…oh no, you're starting to change. Quick, lean on me. I've got to get you out of here. I can't promise we won't run into anyone else, but if you switch back, at least you can talk and tell me who sent you."

It took all her strength, but Anni managed to hook her long hairy arm over Lexi's shoulder and hobble deeper and deeper into the tunnels. Anni thought they were lost when the last tunnel ended with a stone wall guarded by three stacks of cairns. Lexi lifted the top flat stone resting on the middle cairn, and the wall behind it shuddered and lifted.

"Hopefully, no one heard that," said Lexi.

It was dark, but Lexi definitely knew the way. Together they shifted around tight corners of an underground maze. Anni felt her human hair hanging down over half of her face. The ground sloped downward as they walked in near pitch dark. Bit by bit, her body returned to its original form. She felt stronger with each step, which was good because Lexi couldn't support her as the walls narrowed. They walked single file, then sideways around vast boulders, with Lexi in the lead. Anni couldn't believe how strong Lexi had become.

"We're almost there," said Lexi. "You're doing great."

At last, they stopped at a dead end. Anni couldn't see her body, but when she touched her face and neck, they were hair free.

"There's a torch around here," said Lexi, palming the walls. "We've been lucky so far, but once I open this door, we have to move very fast. I'll take you to the cell. It's not a pretty sight. Stay clear of its talons; it's not in its right mind."

With her back to Anni, Lexi struck a match. She found and pulled the wall lever. As the narrow door in the wall lifted, a dank stench flooded their nostrils: a combination of sulfur, rot, and waste.

"This way," said Lexi, sprinting into the chamber.

Up ahead, lamplights flashed on the cellblock. Voices of chamber guards forced Lexi to turn backward, but when she came face to face with Anni, Lexi stood there, frozen, gaping at her friend in disbelief. The guards grew closer. Anni grabbed Lexi's hand and pulled her back inside the tunnel. Anni fumbled with the wall's lever and barely managed to get it shut. She blew out the light. They stood in silence as the guard's footsteps stopped.

No matter what, the girls knew they couldn't risk speaking in case the guards were within earshot of the tunnel's wall. In the darkness, they waited and listened. Anni squeezed Lexi's hand, and Lexi gripped hers in return. They heard the guards grunt between catcalls as they heckled the prisoners. Anni prayed that they would pass, and after what felt like an age, their voices finally trailed away. Lexi lit the torch again. No amount of dirt could cover the pale shock that registered on her face.

"Anni?" Without waiting for a response, Lexi threw her arms around Anni and started sobbing. Anni hugged her back. Both their cheeks were wet with tears before they pulled apart. "I don't understand," said Lexi. "How'd you find—"

"You wouldn't believe me, or maybe you would," said Anni, thinking about the fact that Lexi was an Elemental. "I know…" She took a breath. "I know you're an Elemental. I wish you told me, though, but when I saw your pearl necklace *cracked*, I thought they destroyed your Opus Stone and—"

"Oh, no," said Lexi, bursting into tears again. "I'm so sorry. I wanted to tell you…so many times. There are so many things I don't even know…but that necklace was only a gift from Teddy. I don't have an Opus Stone."

"Really? I was so worried. I've been trying so hard to find you, to rescue you…but you don't seem to need my help. You're so, um, different…"

"I'm not. Anni, really." Lexi sniffled. "It was strange. I don't know how many days passed. One day I saw you in my mind, telling me to be tough. So I pretended I was you, and it worked. It made me stronger than I've ever had to be in my life."

"Hmm." Anni wondered if Ms. OggleBoggle's advice helped. "Well, you're not staying a second longer. We've got to leave now. Where were you taking me anyway?"

"To the creature the Jaguar people are looking for. I met Kuar shortly after I got here. I've been helping them find it. It's been trapped down here, and I only found it yesterday.…Shhh, someone's coming!"

"On the cellblock?"

"No," Lexi hissed. "Behind us. Down the tunnel! We have to go, now." She flipped the lever, and they raced out of the cellblock. It was empty. Lexi searched the wall for the soft spot that closed the tunnel from the other side. "It's here somewhere…"

Watching Lexi panic, Anni searched the wall, too. Finally her hand passed over a soft stone lever. The tunnel's door shut with a thud.

"Follow me," said Lexi, looking more like the anxious Lexi Anni was used to.

They raced past several rusted iron doors until they reached the largest one. It had bolts the size of tree trunks. Lexi tugged on the small lock that kept the food door closed. It was just big enough for the girls to slip under—but it was locked.

Lexi grabbed a clip of keys from her belt. They slipped from her fingers and fell into a pile of rotten food. Her hands shook as she sorted through the muck for the key.

Anni heard the thud of the wall panel. "Someone's coming!"

Lexi retrieved the keys and tried the lock. "Almost there…just…one… sec…" She found the right key and opened the little door.

"Get in," said Lexi. "Whatever you do, be quiet. We don't want to wake it."

They slipped inside. A vague glow barely illuminated the far corner of the room.

"The Fectus chained it to the wall. It won't attack. At least, I don't think it will."

Anni looked closer. "This looks like the creature I saw in Chief Vidar's village."

"You know Chief Vidar?"

"Kuar led me through the tree so I could find you."

Lexi pulled Anni toward a stone recess. Someone stood just outside the cell door. The latch on the door moved and a shadowy figure entered the room. Anni held her breath and squeezed Lexi's hand. They stood still for several seconds.

Spike walked right in front of them. "Introduce me to your friend."

A burst of light erupted from a huge orb resting upon a pedestal next to the creature, which previously had only a faint glow. The chained Ancient awakened. With the head of a bird and vast wings hinged on its back, it had the stout body and hindquarters of a lion, talons for claws, and plumage for a tail. Anni blinked. It was a griffin.

A thunderous roar pierced the room. The Ancient thrashed in its chains. Huge gashes and scars bubbled over its wrists, legs, and waist.

Spike cracked his whip against the wall in a lame attempt to silence it, but he only made it worse. The Ancient thrashed around more vigorously than before. "Shut up, you stupid beast," Spike said as he made to snap the whip again, but it caught on something behind him. Spike stumbled backward.

Oliver stepped on the end of the tassels. "I wouldn't do that if I were you."

Spike's pale skin flared. He dropped the whip. "I'll teach you to mess with me."

"*Child, I will not hurt you,*" said the Ancient, locking eyes on Anni. But that voice!

Anni moved toward the magnificent chained beast and said, "Whiffle?"

"Anni, who are you talking to? Don't get close," said Lexi, who followed behind.

"*Yes and no,*" said Whiffle, even though the Ancient creature's lips weren't moving, Whiffle's voice was coming from it. "*Your friends cannot hear me.*"

Anni turned back and looked at Lexi's puzzled expression. She was distracted by Spike, who was rushing at Oliver. Just in the nick of time, Oliver dodged him. Spike was now careening toward Lexi, ready to push her into the Ancient or, even worse, right into one of the Griffin's barbed chains.

Anni dove in front of Lexi with her arms thrust out. Spike's cheek grazed her arm.

THUD. BOOM.

Time froze. Face to face, Anni saw a realization in Spike's eyes; he knew she was the one who had touched the lava stone two days ago. A yellow current engulfed the cell. Lexi, Oliver, and Spike collapsed at the Ancient creature's feet. Anni stood there, dumbstruck.

"*Your friends are well. Make haste and pull the thorn from the beast's brow,*" said Whiffle.

"But…you're—"

"*No! You mustn't tarry. Remember our contract. You must pull the thorn.*"

Anni rushed over, taking no heed to her own safety. "I don't see it." She scanned the Ancient's face, a ghostly blue shade mangled in pain. "There's nothing here!"

"*Wait for it…Calm your mind. You must.*"

Anni took a deep breath, close her eyes and opened them. A transparent net made of the finest threads appeared over every inch of the Ancient's flesh. A thorn, the size of a mallet's head, materialized, wedged between the creature's brows.

Repulsed by the oozing liquid dripping from the barb, Anni gulped. "Oh, no."

"*You must do it, now…*"

Militant footsteps echoed outside the cellblock. She edged closer to the beast.

"*Child, pull it now…*"

Anni gripped the thorn and pulled. Her right hand slipped, but her left found purchase. Her muscles felt weak. At last, she freed the thorn. It fell to the ground with a thud and vanished.

The glowing orb on the pedestal surged blasting light onto the creature. The Griffin looked as if two different entities were separating out of it. A second shape emerged from behind. It was even larger: with a long, serpent-like neck, a massive body with wings too huge to unfurl, and rings of sharp, gleaming white teeth that were accompanied by two phosphorescent golden eyes the size of basketballs. Anni shivered when she saw smoke pour from its long snout.

Anni backed away in fright. "Whiffle?"

Meanwhile, the Ancient Griffin's body started to grow transparent, less physical. The orb's light was a reparative; the Griffin's wounds healed as the orb's light coursed down the creature's body, melting the iron shackles, which one by one turned to dust.

"*There is no time for that. Mind your feelings. I am exactly what you think. Now, Child, before the bindings dissolve, you must join your companion's hands. Departure is imminent. Quickly, grab the Griffin's Opus Stone. Grab it to complete your escape.*"

"What Opus Stone? Where is it?"

"*On the pedestal, but do not touch the orb with your own hands. Use the scarf from the red boy's neck. Do this now before the leg chains incinerate!*"

Spike lay alongside Lexi and Oliver. She pulled the red scarf away from his neck and there she saw it: the Golden Bee Elemental Artifact that had been stolen from the Brazilian Museum. She grabbed it and shoved it into her pocket.

There wasn't enough time. The Ancient's chest and wrist chains had vanished. As the Griffin started to heal, a light pulsed over its heart center, amplifying and quickening the rate at which the light spread across its body, only its waist and leg shackles to go. Anni covered her hand with Spike's red scarf. Her fingertips hovered over the sphere's surface. A powerful energy radiated from it, dulling her mind and calming her senses.

"*Don't dawdle, Child! Take it now. Place it in the boy's hand. He alone shall receive the accolades. You shall not draw unnecessary attention to yourself.*"

The cell doors blasted open behind her.

"*Stop! Stop her!*" Spike's guards bellowed as they charged inside.

Anni connected Lexi's and Oliver's hands with hers, and she released the sphere into Oliver's open palm. His eyes blazed open on contact. The look of recognition that flashed across his face made the tiny hairs on Anni's neck bristle.

A rumbling, buzzing sound shook the ground beneath them. The cell's floor, walls and ceiling started to crack. A blast of millions of tiny electric blue lights surged through the prison doors, walls, and floors, knocking all of Spike's guards aside. As more and more buzzing blue lights entered the room, they started to swirl around the Griffin, Anni, and her friends. A vortex started to open and form above the cell's ceiling. The Griffin started to dematerialize with the lights, followed by Oliver and Lexi. All Anni could see now were Whiffle's huge shimmering eyes, mere inches from her own.

"Whiffle, you're a Dragon."

"*Yes, Child, that is exactly what I am, but you knew that somewhere in the recesses of your mind. I am the last of my kind, and my soul is tied to every Ancient creature left on this planet. Their pain is mine, by creation and punishment, and one by one, I must free them all before I can rest and join my kin. Now, do as I say, and allow the boy to take the credit for saving the Ancient; that is part of our agreement.*"

"I don't understand. Why Oliver?"

"*Because Child, I have knowledge you do not. A prophecy, made long ago foretold by the Auguriums, stated that he would have a hand in aiding and restoring Elementalkind's greatest dream. You may interpret that as you please, but I've read your memory, and Mabel told you something similar a long time ago. There are no coincidences in life or death, Anni Moon; everything is interconnected within the tapestry of all that is.*" Anni could barely hold her tongue; she had a million questions, but Whiffle's voice grew fainter and she could scarcely hear what he said next. "*Now, I have bestowed upon you a gift, one you will learn to use in time, but know this: your guardian Mabel would be proud, and you honor her. Remember: Our work has only just begun.*"

Whiffle's glittering eyes faded into the void.

CHAPTER 43

HOME

A cold, swirling vortex whipped her hair and face. Anni caught glimpses of Oliver and Lexi's lulled bodies, floating unaware in the fog. Bright rays of sunlight dissolved the mist, and the fresh smell of crisp wood materialized beneath her body, glowing, renewed with life. Anni lifted her head. They were back in the treetop village.

Oliver and Lexi lay next to her. Oliver rose as Lexi stirred.

"Lexi," said Anni. "We're safe."

Lexi opened her eyes and smiled. "How did we get here?"

"*Anni! Anni!*" yelled Squirt as he raced toward her and pulled her into a giant hug.

"Moppins, you're alive," said Brat, fluttering over Squirt's head until he landed and kissed Anni on both cheeks. "I'm so relieved. Lexi!" Brat flew to Lexi, wiping his eyes before landing beside her, where they had a brief, private conversation.

Daphne's face was streaming with tears as she hugged Anni next. "I'm sorry I wasn't there to help. Thank goodness you're alive. I have a million questions." Then she turned to Lexi and said, "I'm Daphne," and offered her hand as her way of introduction.

Jaguar people crowded the platform. Excitement grew thick and contagious as adulations and cheers were directed at Oliver. Anni couldn't help but enjoy the look of shock on Oliver's face when he realized he was holding the Griffin's Opus Stone and what it meant; that he alone saved their Ancient. However, truthfully, Anni was briefly annoyed that she wasn't receiving any thanks or praise—after all she did most of the work—but when she saw the crowd of Jaguar people surrounding Oliver she was glad she wasn't in his shoes. Finding Lexi was reward enough, even if Oliver got the credit. Unfortunately, she smiled a little too broadly at Oliver's confusion and he noticed her amusement, but she was saved from explaining as more Elementals surrounded him, hoping to congratulate him.

"Squirt, Brat," said Daphne. "Help me get Lexi to a cot. She'll be trampled here."

The sea of bodies divided. Before Anni could blink, Squirt, Daphne, and Lexi were caught up in the crowd. The Jaguar people cleared a path for the shamans to approach, followed by Chief Vidar and Kuar. Hemmed in, Anni ended up beside Oliver.

"My people, today is a glorious day, indeed," declared Chief Vidar. "The freeing of the Ancient was not the only life that was saved. Millions of *Beings* were set free after imprisonment for so many years." He looked up at the stream of lights zipping through the sky, which looked exactly like the tiny electric blue lights from the Griffin's cell. "Rejoice, our loved ones suffer no more, and pass freely into the void that we all must join. As the warriors among us strengthen with vitality, we will free others from their shackles below!"

The crowd erupted into cheers. Oliver appeared relieved to hand over the Opus Stone to Vidar. Then Chief Vidar removed a brooch from his cloak and pinned it to Oliver's jacket. "Oh, no, I can't Great—," said Oliver, his face reddening.

"Please, son, you must," said Vidar kindly. "Your actions have saved us. The Auguriums were correct, and you honor them, regardless of what others believe."

This, Anni supposed, was what Whiffle said about Oliver and his prophecy. She couldn't believe the massive gathering, as more and more Jaguar people clamored up to the top levels of the decks. They chanted Oliver's name while others sang sacred hymns and threw flower petals at his feet. She had to admit that the look on Oliver's face was priceless, especially after all the smirks and smug expressions she had previously endured. He was certainly drawing attention, and clearly more than he liked. Anni thought of Oliver's uncle, Ignacio, and how angry he would be once he discovered his nephew had fallen into the trappings of fate; made a hero, by prophecy. For a brief moment, she felt sorry for him.

Above, Anni spotted the ghostly form of the Griffin she had freed; it circled the air before its semi-translucent body gracefully lowered itself to the deck. The crowd grew silent as Chief Vidar bowed before the Ancient; his hand reverently extended, holding the Griffin's Opus Stone. With gentle precision, the Ancient used its talons and placed the mighty Stone upon its brow. It slid beautifully into place like a jewel in a crown, exactly in the spot where Anni had removed the thorn.

The silence was broken as medicine men rejoiced inside Chief Vidar's throne room; they pulled back the silken curtains as the physical Griffin emerged; all its burned scars and oozing vicious marks were repaired and healed. The deck heaved under its mighty weight as it moved slowly across the platform to meet its ether-like twin beside Vidar. A muted cry escaped the weighty one's lips as luminescent tears rolled from its eyes; flowers bloomed from its salty waters.

The two Ancients advanced toward one another until their foreheads met, the Stone connecting them. Together they levitated off the deck. Ruby red rose petals showered the crowd as they spiraled up, higher and higher until, finally, they merged, making the two one.

Like a shooting star, the Ancient soared across the sky and vanished.

The villagers applauded, wept, and cheered. Rainbows of vermillion, saffron, and gold saturated the firmament. The ether buzzed with electricity. Silence reigned as a cerulean orb gently descended from above. A gift from the Ancients, the crystalline globe floated down toward Chief Vidar and landed in his palm.

Upon impact, the charred Tree of Death pulsed with verdant hues and the scarred bark healed. Sickbeds emptied as the injured were cured. New life sprouted up all around the jungle. Again, Jaguar people chanted Oliver's name in praise.

Anni finally spotted Daphne, Squirt, and Lexi. She moved toward them when Oliver took her hand and said through a gritted smile, "Anni… can you help me…" This was the first time he had ever said her name. "I'm being congratulated for something I don't remember," whispered Oliver. "But I saw your face... what happened?"

"Uh..." Anni mumbled. For a second, she forgot she was bound by contract, making it physically impossible for her to utter one true word about what had happened inside the cave without discussing Whiffle. "I have no idea." The lie rolled off her tongue like honey. "How did you find us?"

"Jay. He told me where you were headed. I tracked Miranda through the Opus Stone Network. Chief Vidar is my grandfather thrice removed; he explained everything when I arrived....I've been inside the Fectus underground many times before....it was brave of you to go down there all alone."

"I don't leave my friends behind," Anni said defiantly. "Are you going to tell me why you've been following me? Or who told you to do that?"

Oliver smiled. "You're a really good friend. But I'm afraid that you'll have to wait a little while longer to get that answer. You, Brat, Lexi, and I have some business to attend to after this. Oh, and make sure you bring the doll."

Taken aback, Anni wondered how he knew about Lexi's doll. Straining her neck over the crowds, she spotted Lexi, Brat, Daphne, and Squirt making their way over. She caught a glimpse of Miranda, who looked excessively twitchy like she couldn't leave the Jaguar village fast enough, standing beside Mackenzie in front of an open Treeport. Miranda's pale white skin flushed beet red, which Anni took as an admission of guilt for the way she spoke to Kuar, and the fact that she didn't procure the Golden Bee Artifact.

"Diana sent a message with Mac," said Daphne, tugging her collar up and giggling. "He's escorting us to LimBough. Yugi and Diana are waiting for Miranda, Squirt, and me. I guess I'll see the rest of you back on the Zephyr, okay?"

"You mean Lexi and I are going back there?" asked Anni.

"Of course," said Daphne. "Even—"

"Moppins, what about me?" Brat wrung his paws. "The Elofficium won't arrest me the second I cross TreeTransport, will they?"

"Yes, Brat. Diana got you a full pardon," said Daphne. "Your Fleet badge is safe."

"You're not getting rid of us that easy," said Squirt, who then handed Anni her backpack she'd left behind. His eyes sparkled as he gave Brat a mini high-five. Squirt then pulled a surprised Lexi into a hug, and finally squeezed Anni, which he didn't pull away from until Daphne tugged on his arm.

"Actually," Daphne giggled, "Diana's message said that Squirt and I are going be *very* busy when we get back. We've been assigned to some of your old jobs." Daphne smiled and shrugged. "But you know what…it was worth it! See you soon."

Daphne hugged Anni again, then Lexi, nuzzled Brat, and walked over to Mackenzie and followed him through the portal. Squirt shook hands with Kuar one last time before he *embarked* with Miranda, who remained uncommonly quiet.

Anni waved goodbye, missing them already.

"Don't fret," said Brat, flying loops overhead as if the weight of the world was finally off his wings. "We'll see them soon. Moppins, smile for snoz' sakes. We're in the clear!"

Anni turned to him and smiled.

"I like your friends," said Lexi, squeezing Anni's hand. "They're nice…"

After the girls bathed and changed into fresh clothes, they joined Brat in a resting area as the sounds of adulations continued into the early evening. When Chief Vidar, followed by Kuar and Oliver, approached, he asked them to join him for dinner. A vast feast awaited them inside the now-cleaned throne room, where Vidar ushered them to sit and eat. Everything they consumed was served on banana leaf plates, platters, and wooden box cups; the crisp scents of wood tickled Anni's nose and a sensation of lightness tingled up from her toes and out the crown of her head. Once they had finished dinner, he requested they stay the night before traveling through LimBough, so the restorative powers of the trees would draw out the impurities and toxins from the poisonous Funk they had absorbed inside the Fectus's lair. Anni hadn't thought about that until she glanced at Lexi and realized she had been exposed to nearly twenty days of Funk, which was probably why many of Vidar's assistants had been administering a constant supply of healing elixirs from the moment they sat down in the resting area.

"Lexi," said Vidar. "Although I can vouch for Oliver and my son Kuar, what I have to say is very important. May I proceed in your friend's presence?"

Lexi looked at Anni, Brat, and Oliver. "Yes, I trust them with my life."

"I assumed as much. Anni, please remove the patchwork doll from your carry bag and hand it to me." At Lexi's nod, Anni did as he said. Vidar placed the doll facedown and used a blade to unstitch a seam hidden under the doll's hair. Within the stuffing rested a small, green gem. "Please," said Vidar, offering it to Lexi.

The moment Lexi's skin touched the green crystal an undulating pulse filled the room, followed by the sweet aroma of spring flowers and ocean air. Anni swore she saw a hundred lights sparkle around Lexi's body, and the energy within the room became electric, as everyone sat straighter, less relaxed, and more focused.

"Your Opus Stone, Alexa dear," said Vidar with a kind smile.

"But..." said Lexi, her brow knitted. "How? Shouldn't I remember getting it?"

"No, my dear, because you were born with it, which is why you are so special. Your stone is not marked by a single Element as of yet; perhaps it will take time for you to discover which Element you are, and again, this is part of what makes you such a unique Elemental. Now, it's time for me to tell you the parts of your life story that only I know....Teddy Waterstone, my great friend, had trusted me with certain secrets about you and your life as a kind of failsafe, just as he had many years ago when you were only an infant. Teddy's intention was to hand you your Opus Stone on your thirteenth birthday, but alas, I am the one to deliver it. This may come as a shock, but Teddy is neither alive nor dead. He is trapped between the two; he has joined legions of Elementals stolen from us too soon." Vidar turned to look at Anni when he said, "He is with Mabel." Lexi and Anni stared at one another. "They are in a place you cannot travel to or save them from, but rest assured they are watching you, and they are with you."

Vidar paused. Anni was glad; she needed a moment. "Lexi, when is your birthday?"

"June tenth," said Lexi. "A day before Anni's."

"That is incorrect," said Vidar. "You were born on the twenty-first of June. Teddy entrusted me with a secret you do not know, one of your parentage. Have you ever heard about the story of the two great Elemental families? Those who would bear a child that would change and heal the overlap between the human and Elemental realms?"

"Yes," said Lexi. "Teddy told me when I was little. It's a kind of fairy story, isn't it?"

Anni realized she knew something Lexi didn't: it wasn't a fairy story, it was part of the prophecy Brat had told her about. Only, Lexi's comment ignited something from Anni's own memory, one from her early childhood, when Mabel used to pull out a beautifully illustrated picture book, which Anni especially loved to look at; all the pages had gold leaf designs depicting the story about a legend of a lost prince in long need of saving and rescuing. Mabel used to joke, and tickle Anni as she said, "What if you save the prince?" and then they would laugh. Anni grew up and completely forgot about it, until now. Was that what Whiffle meant? Was she supposed to save this Prince?

"Alas, it is not a fairy story," Vidar continued. "It is believed that the prince still lives, stolen and hidden among the Fectus. We do not know where he is. The prince was given the name Eleck when he was born." He grew serious. "A great gathering was to take place in honor of Eleck's birth, a year after he was born on the Summer Solstice, in a location where all Elemental forces converged. Mabel Moon was the head of security for the Secret Elemental Council. She had a battalion of elite Elemental service guards on command. Even though she was expected to be present on the day of the ceremony celebrating Prince Eleck's first birthday, Mabel had another mission: she sacrificed her honor to protect another child—you, Lexi. To all Elementalkind, that day was known as the *Great Catastrophe,* one of bloodshed and grief; thousands of lives were lost and all Elementalkind's hope vanished along with Prince Eleck. In the end, Mabel was blamed for the breakdown of security, the loss of lives—Elemental and some human—and ultimately for Eleck's kidnapping. Mabel spirited you, Lexi, away to Teddy, where you would grow up safely, as if you were a simple human. He raised you as an orphan with your friend Anni. Neither Teddy nor Mabel regretted their decisions, only, perhaps, with the exception of the isolation your secret caused you, and that they required you to keep your secret from everyone."

"Mabel did this because Lexi's an Elemental?" asked Anni.

"I don't understand," said Lexi. "Why would Mabel leave Prince Eleck to keep me safe? I'm not special or better than him."

Vidar looked at Lexi with compassionate eyes and said, "She did it because you are his equal, Lexi. Eleck is your twin brother."

A collective gasp punctuated Vidar's words. Everyone stared at Lexi. Anni and Brat looked at one another with wide eyes, then at Vidar, Oliver, and Kuar. However, Lexi didn't look at anyone except Anni, and only briefly.

Judging by Lexi's expression, Anni knew she needed time to digest this information.

"Oliver, you were born a few years before Eleck and Lexi," said Vidar. "The Auguriums had given you a vague prophecy that one day you might restore something to Elementalkind. Aside from returning the Ancient to us, I believe returning Lexi to the Elementals is a part of that." Anni noted that Oliver's cheeks flushed pink. "Do not be ashamed, boy, to claim ownership over your fate. Your parents are proud of you; you must see past your Uncle Ignacio's pride."

Vidar's last comment grabbed Anni as strange when he said *your parents are proud*; she thought Oliver's parents died in the *Great Catastrophe.*

"There is one more thing," said Vidar, jolting Anni away from her thoughts. "By all accounts and definitions, Anni, you are a human. I can read it clearly in your energy fields, and yet there is one piece that puzzles me; a secret, a question that has gone unanswered by both Mabel and Teddy regarding you. I have kept their secret and I will share it now, as you have earned the right to know. However, I do not think it wise to share this with others outside these walls, with good reason."

Lexi glanced at Anni and said, "What is it?"

"Anni, you were born on the same day as Eleck and Lexi, but as to your parentage, I know nothing. Only Mabel knew that answer, but she wouldn't say, and Teddy did not know. What is puzzling is that you were born in the same manner and fashion as an Elemental, on Mineralstone Isle, but you were born a human. I have little else to share, and I would honor the fact that Mabel and Teddy did not share your true birth date with anyone else. I suggest you keep this a secret."

Now everyone was staring at Anni. She didn't know what to make of it, except she understood how Lexi felt. Even though it left her with even more questions, Anni liked the idea that it made her and Lexi closer. Chief Vidar's silence indicated he had little left to share, and before he retired, Anni privately asked him to step aside.

Thinking about what Whiffle had said to her earlier, she said, "Maybe you will know what to do with this." Anni pulled out the stolen Golden Elemental Bee Artifact from her pocket and handed it over to Vidar. "I found it—"

"Ah, I see," said Vidar, looking at Anni with more interest than before. "You've surprised me again, Miss Moon. Rest assured, I can see that it will be returned to its rightful place. I imagine you have questions. Do you know what it means? What it represents?"

"The prophecy." Anni shrugged. "And it's a symbol for the body Elemental."

"Yes, that is true." Vidar chuckled. "The Bee is our greatest symbol, one of transformation, wisdom, mystery and secrets." He pointed to the artifact. "These two bees represent community, working together for the greater good, but also it signifies a call to action. After the *Great Catastrophe,* Elementals forgot to hope, to dream, or to forge a different future where they can evolve. There is a group of Elementals who guard these secrets, and I believe they wanted to remind the Elemental community of its importance again. Even you must have seen this image in the Elemental world more than once?"

"It was plastered all over news articles in shops on the Zephyr, and in Lim-Bough. Why does that matter?"

"It matters because imagery is a powerful device. It's a reminder of change, and that change is inevitable. The Bee means something more, something that cannot be forgotten, no matter how many times it is banned. The act of burying truths only urges others to uncover it, like the lotus seed, which always finds the light even in the darkest of murky waters. The Bee is the center of our collective soul, too potent and powerful to forget." Vidar paused and looked at Anni kindly. "You found this artifact, which means that in some way, your life, your journey is woven into the fabric of the Elemental fate."

It was well past midnight before Anni and Lexi reached their beds, high atop the trees where the air was surprisingly warm and where their quarters were the most guarded. They fell asleep the moment their heads hit the pillows. It was a restful sleep for a change, and Anni was glad for it.

The next day was the Summer Solstice, June twenty-first. Before they left, Vidar presented Anni, Lexi, Brat and Oliver each a fresh green leaf from the *Sleeping Tree* and told them that keeping it on them would grant them safe passage, and if ever in the future they were ever lost, the leaf would help them find their way. He opened a very special portal for them inside the throne room, and all four of them *embarked* at once. It was a very short trip. They exited directly through a huge round hedge in the middle of an enormous garden. Oliver walked out first. He checked the perfectly manicured rows of robust circular hedges. Humans were milling about on the neat, white, graveled walkways.

"Where are we now?" asked Lexi.

"Moppins, this is Kensington Park," said Brat. "We're in London."

Oliver didn't stop. He walked toward a grand brick building with long paned windows at the end of the path. They followed him.

"*We* have a meeting inside. Wait here." Oliver disappeared inside for a few minutes and then returned a moment later. "He's waiting for you three. Last table at the end."

"Who's waiting for us?" asked Anni.

Oliver didn't answer. He ushered them inside past several tables—some empty, some full—until they reached the last one at the end next to a potted citrus tree, where a man sat alone with his back to them. Oliver left them there, which Anni supposed was for privacy, but she didn't need to guess who the man was once she caught sight of his khaki pants that were too short for his long legs.

Lexi ran to Egbert and hugged him tightly. Anni stood speechless. A small part of her assumed maybe he was guilty of kidnapping Lexi, but now, that didn't seem right.

Brat nudged Anni. "Told you he wasn't guilty."

"Lexi," said Egbert, brow furrowed. "I failed you, and Teddy and Mabel by not keeping you safe. I will endeavor to make it up to you in time."

"I'm fine Egbert, really," said Lexi. "Anni found me. I'm safe now."

Anni coughed.

"Please sit down, all of you. Our time will be short…." Egbert turned to Anni and sighed. "I suppose I should congratulate you. You've accomplished, in record time, what many could not. You found Lexi before any serious harm came to her…And now, both of you know about our world. I would have preferred if you learned the details a different way, but that was my fault. I trusted the wrong person."

"I told you about Finnegan," said Anni, finding her voice. "They arrested him."

"Still rash to judge?" Egbert raised his brow. "I can see why you thought so." He exhaled. "But I'm afraid you have it wrong again. Finnegan was taken into custody for Lexi's kidnapping, and although he appeared guilty, it wasn't him. I trusted someone else…the wrong person, it seems." Egbert paused. His gaze drifted out the lead windowpanes. Anni risked looking into his weary eyes. She noticed an egg-shaped bubble around his body; the field around his body was heavily protected like a shield of armor, guarding him in the same way she always sensed but had never seen before.

Anni finally understood what Whiffle had sacrificed: the ability to see what humans do not. Vision was a gift of the Wood Element: however, this didn't make her an Elemental, and just as soon as she realized she could do it, the power disappeared.

Egbert cleared his throat. "Even so, Anni, your reckless behavior…You forget that you are only a child, and I feel justified in asking Oliver to keep an eye on you. What you faced could have easily brought your short life to an end. Here, I thought I placed you far enough away from trouble. Clearly, I underestimated you."

"Egbert," said Lexi. "If it wasn't Finnegan, who was it?"

"Zelda," Egbert said flatly. Anni gasped; she couldn't believe it. "Zelda Scurryfunge, right under my nose, the whole time disguised as a flibbertigibbet. She's a terrific actress, I'll give her that, but someone else had to be working with her. I don't know who. They addled Finnegan's mind; that's no small thing. He'll be spending some time in treatment at a high-security Elofficial facility."

"Orge Murdrock," said Lexi. "He's part of the Fectus. I saw him there."

Anni and Brat both gasped.

"Was he the one on that creepy, jumping throne of bones?" asked Anni.

"No." Lexi shuddered. "That was the Naga Yaga."

Egbert folded his arms and leaned back in his chair like he was thinking; he raised his hand to his head. "I'm not surprised to hear this. Mabel and Teddy did not trust him, even though they ordered me to sell Waterstone Academy to the Murdrocks."

"They did?" asked Anni as Lexi made a small noise.

"Don't ask me why, but now you know what we're up against. In fact, never, ever discuss this publicly, and use every ounce of caution, understood?" The girls nodded. "What happened to you both has changed everything. You cannot return to your previous life in Chicago, especially now that the Fectus knows about Lexi. Waterstone Academy is closed and unsafe at this time. You will return with Oliver. Moon Zephyr is your new home."

Anni felt a rush of conflicted emotions. "Aren't you coming, too?"

Egbert looked apathetic. "I sincerely doubt you will be disappointed once you return. Maeleachlainn's under Elofficium review, and Vivian Sugar will become your new voucher, Anni, but I don't like her, as you well know. Nevertheless, I would advise the both of you to be careful in whom you choose to trust." Egbert looked directly at Anni when he added, "No matter how you feel about them. We need to cut this short. I need to be going."

"Just like that? How about *I'm glad you're alive*? Or *thanks for saving Lexi*?"

Egbert stared at Anni. "Half of the time, I don't even think you listen at all....There is very little I can do at this point to change the course of events."

He turned to Lexi and said, "Now that you are safe, I must inform those who need to know you exist, just one of my last promises to Mabel that I must fulfill. First, I need to gather proof of your lineage, which is why you won't see me for some time. I must do this before I submit myself for review with the Elofficials; they still believe I am guilty."

A rare gentleness washed over Egbert's face that eased his habitually stiff posture. "Sometimes, we need to allow others to think of us as they will." He looked up at Anni with fresh eyes. "Moons are protectors, guardians of things and of people, but our purpose is ours alone to discover. Remember, if Elementals are unkind to you, Anni, it's probably more your association to me and Mabel more than it is you." He looked at his Omninav. "Now, it's time for you both to leave. Elofficials are on their way. Brat, just a quick word."

Lexi stood and hooked her arm through Anni's. It was time to go, but Anni felt like there was so much left unsaid. Brat carefully listened to Egbert's whispered instructions as they turned to leave. Oliver eyed them from the hostess stand, looking serious.

When Anni reached the front door, she glanced back one last time before they exited the Orangery. Brat swooped overhead, making customers shriek with fright. Egbert stood next to a potted citrus tree. In that brief glimpse, she thought his face looked caring, loving—if that was even possible.

"Last stop, Moon Zephyr," said Oliver.

They hurried to a gap in the round hedge. It led straight to LimBough. Anni didn't fully understand the bit about Moons being protectors, but perhaps one day someone would explain. She had to get used to Lexi being an Elemental, but for now, all she cared about was having her best friend back. Anni enjoyed all of Lexi's varied reactions as they traveled through LimBough. Her only regret was that they couldn't spend more time delighting their senses, oohing and awing at everything LimBough had to offer.

A lemon-yellow sky welcomed them as they exited the Orb. It wasn't Waterstone Academy. It wasn't the Edgewater. But the Moon Zephyr felt familiar all the same.

As they walked across the long bridge, massive crowds gathered along the Lake's borders. A grin crept across Anni's face once she realized that the Elementals were yelling Oliver's name and waving banners.

"*He's their hero,*" she said to Lexi in her funniest voice.

"I heard that," said Oliver. "And thank you for pointing that out. I'm glad that at least one of us can find the humor in this situation."

"Well, you are," said Anni, refusing to hide the joy she felt.

"You should know that when we get to the bridge's end, I have strict orders to keep a closer eye on you, and I plan on getting to the bottom of what I can't remember."

"Great. Like I didn't know that already." She rolled her eyes and shrugged it off.

As they made it closer to the bridge's end, Anni took Lexi's hand and held it up. The crowd roared and the girls laughed. Brat did a few loops in the air, and said to them, "Look! One-eyed Nimmy is out and about, too. Moppins, what a gathering."

Daphne and Squirt were jumping up and down and yelling their names. Anni pointed out her new friends to Lexi, starting with Fortensia and One-eyed Nimmy sitting on her shoulder, Jay, several skurfers, Mackenzie, Diana, Yugi, and Ms. OggleBoggle, but she was delighted when she saw the next person in line.

"Is that?" asked Lexi, surprised. "It is."

Vivian Sugar smiled and waved alongside everyone else. Anni instantly felt lighter.

Even though the vast majority of Elementals were there for Oliver, just seeing all the Elementals who were there to see Lexi made her heart soar. Anni raised her hands to her cheeks, which hurt from so much smiling; she found that they were wet with tears. Lexi put her arm around her and squeezed her tight. Whatever Egbert said about Moons being protectors, there was one thing she knew: Lexi had saved her, too, and she couldn't wait to introduce Lexi to everyone.

Perhaps for now they couldn't go back to their old life at Waterstone Academy, but maybe they were exactly where they were supposed to be. Reunited with Lexi, and her new friends, Anni couldn't remember being as happy as she was in that moment. It was just like what Effie OggleBoggle had said about connecting the dots; Anni followed them and now she was home.

Lexi leaned in and whispered to Anni, "Happy birthday."

Anni smiled back. "Happy birthday, Lexi."

Acknowledgments

Work on Anni Moon started and stopped many times over the course of a decade and, because of that, I have a lot people I would like to thank.

To my team of editors, and a special wink to those who taught me how to love an Oxford comma, I would like to thank: Ramona DeFelice Long, Susan Helene Gottfried, Mary Sutton, Melanie Zimmerman, Chase Heiland, Linda M. Au, and Lorin Oberweger. Without your help, eagle eyes, and encouragement Anni Moon might not have seen daylight.

Thanks to: Joel Friedlander for his consultation on cover design; the Book Designers, Tracy and Treana Atkins, Emily Tippetts, and Linda M. Au for interior design and formatting. A special thanks in memory of Harlin Tim Harris for his consultation on graphic design, who was unable to see the final product.

A sincere thanks to my friends Shelley, David, Nick and Tom Dechant, who have been hearing about Anni Moon for years. A mega-watt thanks to my friends, advisors, and early readers Raffy and Rosie Dolbakian, Kate Abed, Emma Abed, Nutschell Anne Windsor, Lissa Price, Anne Van, Elle Jauffret, Larissa Reyes, Kristen Kittscher, Jessica Fry, Sarah Benson, Tim Johnson, Victoria James, Nicole Fearahn, Lindsey Lippincott, Farah Oomerbhoy, Debbie Goelz, Pamela DuMonde, MaryAnne Locher, Drae, Bianca, Darienne Hazel, Clara Dowgialo, Roshelle, Reece McFarlane, Darly, Sunhra, Rosamiee, Ken Magee, Wuckster, LadyShipNull, and Teresa Soto.

Finally, all my gratitude and love to my brilliant husband, Hisham Abed. His spectacular cover art and illustrations make Anni's world come to life, and they allow my imagination to swim even deeper into the Elemental realms.

About the Author

Melanie Abed and her husband live in Los Angeles where they have a tree in their backyard that's a direct portal to LimBough.

If you are interested in finding out when Melanie's next book is being released, please sign up at the link below:

www.melanieabed.com/contact

We will only send out an email for future release dates, your email will never be shared, and you are welcome to unsubscribe at any time. Please feel free to visit www.melanieabed.com for updates and news about Anni Moon and new books by Melanie Abed.

I do love to hear from readers and do my best to reply to all e-mails. Please feel free to send me a message at: melanie@melanieabed.com